Beyond

the

Horizon

JUDITH ROOK

Printed in Australia

Cover artwork by Judith Rook

Cover and internal design by Book Burrow

www.bookburrow.com.au

First printing: May 2025

Paperback ISBN 978-1-7640-2092-3

eBook ISBN 978-1-7640-2093-0

Hardback ISBN 978-1-7640-2094-7

Distributed by Lightning Source Global

NATIONAL LIBRARY OF AUSTRALIA

A catalogue record for this work is available from the National Library of Australia

Also by Judith Rook

RAVENS HOLLOW

Dedications

For my children
Troy Stephenson and Georgia Hempel

The Horizon

Reaching Out to Lost Souls

The rhythmic waves meet the shore,
mystifying the turmoil of the unwanted,
wondering why life can be undone,
threads hanging, disconnected
to the intended.
Sparkling crystals spring from the waves
penetrating the mind,
facing the darkening sky,
waiting for sunrise to illuminate the sky.
A circle of burning splendour radiating,
kissing a saddened brow,
hypnotizing searching eyes,
to escape into the watery womb
from which one came,
born into a life beyond the horizon.

JUDITH ROOK ©

Introduction

Evil Comes in Many Forms, Attacking the Pure and Innocent.
'Suffer the Little Children'

THEY WATCHED THE CLOUDS roll past, floating like three dimensional sculptures. The bright cerulean, blue-sky backdrop, lit by the sun, turning their world to magic for the shortest time. The warmth touched their pale skin.

'That one looks like a giant angel with her tongue poking out at us.'

'I think she has a wand, casting an evil spell.'

'Would an angel do that?'

'Someone has done this cruel thing.'

'Or is it a mermaid that could carry us on her back and escape to another land?'

'That one looks like a chook with a dick,' Joe said. They tried to laugh.

'It does not. I don't think a chook has a dick. Maybe a rooster. Anyway, I think it is an elephant with a trunk.' They both managed a slight giggle.

As the nurse wheeled them out for their time in the sun, she always said the same thing – 'The sun heals,' in her cheery voice. They already realised that wasn't going to be true.

Joe and Elizabeth's beds were next to each other in the polio ward at the Melbourne Fairfield Infectious Diseases Hospital.

Joe Pike had been there two weeks when he watched as the nurse made up the bed next to him for a new patient. The boy who had occupied it had just gone somewhere. He had seen kids come and go during that time, not sure whether they were going home or into the ward where a respirator was needed. He listened to the nurses talking, straining his ears to find out what was going on, why he couldn't move, and why he was strapped to this bed. He was over feeling sorry for himself. He was lying there, asking a million questions about this disease that had invaded his body. He was not getting many answers.

His mother, holding back tears, told him not to ask any more. His father had seemed to age from the day he carried him into the emergency department. Joe realised he wasn't the only one that was affected by this epidemic sweeping through Victoria. The only thing that was working was his mind, and that was running in overdrive. A hidden strength kicked in with the realisation that protecting his mother and father would become his goal.

He smiled at Elizabeth. She was so pale, so frail. His heart went out to her. She tried to smile back but it was too hard. Her mother and father were standing by her bedside. Joe recognised that look, the same as his parents. Did all parents have a look of bewilderment, hurt and fear at having to bring their children to this place of horror?

'My name is Elizabeth Kasper. I am ten years old. I have an older brother and a younger sister. My parents are schoolteachers.' She struggled to get the rehearsed words out. Joe knew the feeling when the breath wouldn't come.

'My name is Joe Pike. I am an only child. My parents are farmers. We milk eighty cows, morning and night. I used to help. I suppose they will manage without me.' Joe had to turn his head away. He thought he was going to cry, not in front of a girl, he just couldn't. That was the start of the battle that would bring them together, while their beds became their homes, and the nurses would become their crutch until the day they would be lucky enough to be able to walk with wooden ones.

Elizabeth did cry. She was a girl. It was expected. She hated her new surroundings; the bright lights that seemed to shine in her face all day and the darkness of the night scared her so much, along with the noises of kids crying and screaming when they had the strength. Seeing a nurse approaching, in her mind she was trembling, but felt nothing in her paralysed body. Being looked after like babies took a lot of getting used to. There was nothing they could do.

It only took a short time for Elizabeth to like the nurses, when she realised how kind they were, except for the matron. She was a wicked witch. The floor shook when she appeared at 10 o'clock on the dot every morning. The whole ward was so quiet. The kids held back tears at that time in fear of being ridiculed for being sooks. They all secretly wished that she was lying in their place on a plank, in pain, unable to move, without her family, with her reality vanishing.

Elizabeth's parents lived in St Kilda, and both taught at the primary school on Fitzroy Street, the same school that she and her siblings attended. They walked to school together every school day, their parents chanting their spelling or times tables along with them, making sure they were prepared for the day.

Those days were gone. She wouldn't be skipping along with her brother and sister. Waves of sadness washed over her, remembering the fun she had with them. Every day that visiting was allowed she watched and waited for them to come, to sit by her bed and tell her what was happening outside the walls that most days felt like they were closing in on her.

The ward had seemed so big the day she had been brought to this world. It now was becoming the smallest, suffocating space. Her parents came to visit when they could. But there was always a reason that they never made it. Occasionally they asked if she was getting better. Sometimes they said it was hard to find the time to get away from her brother and sister. They didn't want them to catch what she had. They said it was because she wasn't as clean as the others, always forgetting to wear the camphor bag around her neck that would have protected her.

At first, she couldn't wait to see them, but as time passed, she realised that she felt bad and guilty. She didn't want to put them through this awful thing she had inflicted on herself – that she deserved. She began not caring if they never came again.

Werner Kasper had met Ingrid at school when they were teenagers, and he had pursued her for a year before she would go out with him. His father owned the merry-go-round at Luna Park. Free rides were enticing. Girls were easy to get.

Ingrid wasn't that interested in riding around on wooden horses going nowhere. Werner wasn't that interesting to her at the time either. She had bigger ambitions than his goals.

Werner couldn't understand why she wasn't interested. It was a blow to his colossal ego, making him keener to make this girl surrender. Eventually it happened. She agreed to go out with him but would only go to one of the nice cafés on the esplanade, or a walk on the pier to let him buy her an ice cream. They became closer by the end of school, both deciding to become teachers.

They began their adult life together. It seemed it was meant to be. Ingrid's parents liked Werner and were very happy that they had decided to marry as soon as they had teaching positions. They were both lucky to get placements close to both families. Ingrid only tolerated Werner's parents. She couldn't communicate with them. They blocked her out. They didn't want her in their family and made it evident with their coolness towards her.

Gerda and Otto had come to Australia from Austria after the first World War. They never told anyone why they had made the big decision to leave their homeland at that time. Werner had been born a short time before they arrived. He grew up as an Australian and was never told much about his parents' life in Austria.

Ingrid had her suspicions that they had escape from something or someone. When the children started to arrive, Jonas, Elizabeth, and Emma, the visits to Werner's parents became less frequent, even though they were in walking distance. Ingrid suspected that Werner sneaked the children down to Luna Park to see his father when she was busy elsewhere.

Elizabeth, like Joe, had no idea what was going to become of her. Tears would run down her cheeks many nights as she laid scared in the dark. Her legs and arms were wrapped in plaster. She found it hard to breathe sometimes, as if there was a heavy weight on her chest. Like Joe, she watched as beds became empty and more children arrived. The only thing that kept her from wanting to die was her favourite nurse, and Doctor Daisy, and Joe, of course.

Elisabeth didn't know what she would do without Joe. He was the twenty-four-hour friend that never left her side. She laughed to herself. He didn't have a lot of choice, not being able to get up and walk away. She was so glad that he never had to go to a different ward or die like the ones that mysteriously disappeared. It was Doctor Daisy and Sister Shirley O'Sullivan that let Joe have a rest from her neediness most days. They watched the door vigilantly for Doctor Daisy.

He sometimes came with the Matron. They were dark days when the doctor was unable to stop and talk when that witch was around. They were the days that she hoped Sister O'Sullivan would come by. She joked with all the kids and insisted that they call her SOS. They were her initials. She said that it meant that she was there in an emergency. 'Just call S.O.S. Remember I'll be there,' and she was, most of the time. It always made Elizabeth feel special, even though she knew she did the same for all the kids.

Elizabeth's dead emotions only came alive when she saw him coming towards her. Joe would always say, 'I don't know why you are in love with old Daisy. He has a face like a cauliflower. He certainly isn't pretty like a daisy.' Elizabeth would blush when Joe made fun of her for loving an old man.

Doctor Daisy wasn't pretty, that was for sure. He had more lines on his face than a road map, with deep crevasses that could have hidden many secrets. The loose skin drooped down, as did his kind blue eyes, but smiling at Elizabeth, his face was surrounded with an aura that maybe only she could see.

His touch gave her the strength she needed to face the next day. Apart from his rugged, ruddy face, he looked so smart with his dark, pinstriped suit and his colourful bow tie, and of course a fresh daisy in his lapel, usually the same colour as his tie. He seemed so tall and strong to Elizabeth, lying staring up at her Doctor Daisy. Elizabeth loved her doctor, only seeing a gentle kindness. He asked this frail child what her favourite colour was one day. Her shy reply was pink. From that day on he wore a pink bow tie and pink daisy. Elizabeth hoped that if she ever got out of this bed and grew taller, she could marry him.

The day came that Ingrid and Werner told Elizabeth that they were moving to the country to find a safer place for Jonas and Emma. They had secured jobs in a school in the area. Her grandmother was going to be looking after her from now on. Elizabeth stared at them in disbelief. Why were they doing this to her? What had she done? Why was she the one being hurt? She knew her mother never liked Grandmother Gerda and she was going to leave her in charge of their middle child? She didn't understand.

If only her mother's parents hadn't died. They would have been so much better than old Gerda.

Elizabeth never spoke. She was finding it hard to breathe. Joe watched as she went pale. The blood drained from her face.

'S.O.S' Joe called, and SOS came running. She asked Elizabeth's parents to wait outside, and she would come and get them when she had settled down. Joe told SOS what had happened, and she consoled Elizabeth as best she could, sitting with her until she fell asleep. The next day Doctor Daisy gave Elizabeth more of his time than usual, convincing her that her friends in the ward were her new family.

They had been there six months, lying, looking at the ceiling, except for the days they were wheeled out into the sun to watch the clouds roll by. They wished they could float away, ride on those clouds and escape the place that had become their home. Elizabeth relied more on Joe than ever now the days were so long. Joe tried to make her laugh as much as she could or was able. Joe relied on his friend too, but tried not to let anyone notice. And that's how it was.

Doctor Daisy was all smiles the day he announced that the plasters were coming off, and they would be using Sister Elizabeth Kenny's method of treating poliomyelitis. He sat down next to Elizabeth and told her Sister Kenny was known around the world for the success she had with her treatment.

'She was an Australian and has your name too, so I think it is worth a try.' His blue, droopy eyes were tear-filled. He explained that they would be putting hot compresses on the affected limbs, then using passive movement to get the limbs stimulated to remember how to work. They would also strengthen the muscles and lengthen the tendons back to working order.

Elizabeth listened, staring into her darling doctor's wrinkled, drooping face. She did not understand what it was all about but, if he said it would work, she believed him. The nurses would spend hours massaging every leg and arm in the ward. A cheer went up when there was the slightest movement from any of the little skinny arms or legs that had become useless. There was always pain, but they all tried to feel grateful. The nurses worked so hard for such little reward. The kids, as young as they were, realised that.

Elizabeth said to Joe every day, 'When I get out of here, I am going to buy SOS a present.'

'Me too,' Joe would echo.

Gerda came occasionally with a long, morbid face, bringing a bag of boiled lollies and two clean nighties, as if that was going to be enough until the next time she came. She took away the ones that were in Elizabeth's bedside drawer to launder for her next visit. Elizabeth wondered why she bothered, as her visits weren't very often.

'The lollies will probably rot your teeth, but I don't know what else you want. It seems you have everything you need here. I don't know what I come for,' her harsh voice spat out the words.

'I am sorry, Granny Gerda, that you have to come. I don't know why they left when I need them so much.' Elizabeth held back tears.

'I didn't want to be left either. I miss my son, and to have to look after you as well!' She did not care if her harsh words hurt the child.

Elizabeth wished she would never come again so she would never have to look at her ugly face. Joe's parents lived on their farm at Little River and the trip to Melbourne took a long two-hour drive, but they came every weekend. Joe told her how the neighbours helped, taking it in turns to do the evening milk so they didn't miss their visits to Joe.

Elizabeth wondered why she was born into a family that didn't care about her, although she'd never felt rejection before the polio. She'd had a mother who kissed her every night before she went to bed and had always cuddled her just as much as Jonas and Emma. Would they have left her brother and sister too, if they were like her?

She tried to put them out of her mind as much as possible. Her mind was strong, and she had nothing else to work with. She and Joe decided to exercise their minds the way the nurses were exercising their limbs. They would recite poems they had learnt at school and tell each other stories that they made up, go over their times tables and spelling. Elizabeth was better than Joe at Spelling, so she became his teacher at those times. They were a team, working to one goal – to get better, get out of the hospital and go back to a normal life. Elizabeth wondered what was going to be normal when she was able to go home. But what home was it going to be with Grandmother Gerda? The thought frightened her so much.

Doctor Daisy came in so cheery, introducing the ward to a very important lady, to see the work he was doing and how Sister Kenny's method of treatment was helping so much. A doctor and scientist from the Children's Hospital, Dame A.J McNamara was working hard on research that was helping to find a vaccination that would stop the virus spreading. The kids were all impressed to meet a Dame, almost like meeting a queen. Their young minds were ignorant of the work she was doing, or how her research would help the world. Elizabeth had no understanding of the ramifications of her work, but it was making Doctor Daisy happy, so she was happy too.

'None of this is relieving our pain now, is it? They just keep saying, 'You must be brave, soon you will be able to walk.' What the hell, I want to get out of here.' Joe showed anger for the first time. Elizabeth thought he was going to cry – a boy worn out from trying, always so strong for her and his parents.

'We are getting little bits of feeling here and there. We will make it.' Elizabeth did her best to reassure Joe. 'Remember we have a date. You are going to take me dancing and teach me the Tango.'

'That's right. I'd better keep trying to get those legs moving.' They both laughed.

Soon they could put their legs over the side of the bed and wiggle their toes a little; Joe's right leg was working better than the left. It was the left one for Elizabeth. They joked that if they tied their bad legs together, they might be able to win a three-legged race with their two good legs.

'I might get back to the milking shed yet. I miss my cows so much – Jessie and Dot, they're my favourites.'

'You have mentioned them a few times, Joe, like every day.' Elizabeth wished she had something to miss.

She had to look forward to going to live with the old bat of a grandmother that she didn't like, and she knew Grandmother Gerda felt the same. Her mother had sent her a few letters and a birthday card. They were always the same words: *Hope you will be at grandmother's place soon and you can make it your home.* Her parents had dispensed with her like an unwanted, diseased dog. They must have been so ashamed that one of their children had spoiled their perfect family.

The day the callipers were fitted they wondered if the torture would ever be over. The weight of a shoe was enough without a ball and chain to tug around. They had to learn to walk with the crutches and the weight dangling off the withered leg. Gerda had to come into the ward to learn how to massage Elizabeth's body the way the nurses had been doing. That added to the torture. There would be no gentle, loving hands when she left SOS and her team.

Their time in the hospital was nearly over. There was talk of them going home. Elizabeth couldn't imagine life without Joe. He would get home and have his cows and his loving Mum and Dad, and Elizabeth wondered if he would ever think about her.

'I will miss you, Joe. We have been together so long I feel we belong to each other,' she whispered.

'I will miss you too.'

'You will have Jessie and Dot to cuddle.'

'I was thinking we should pray for each other every day so we will never forget.'

'That is a lovely idea Joe, but you don't believe. You told me all that God stuff was rubbish.'

'I know, but we had better, just in case there might be something in it. So many people think it will save them, I'm not sure from what, but it's worth a try anyway. It will be a way of connecting, like a message when the sun goes down. We will know that we are thinking of each other.'

'I will, Joe. Every night when the sun goes down, I will pray for you.'

SOS came to her bedside. Her face was grey, and Elizabeth knew she had been crying. 'We have just had some very bad news.'

So early in the morning, Elizabeth thought. Maybe Gerda wouldn't take her home, that must be it.

'Doctor Daisy is dead.' SOS had trouble getting the words out through her trembling lips.

Elizabeth stared at her as if she was paralysed again.

Finally, she managed, 'How could that happen to such a good man?' Tears were running down her face like a flood that covered her pillow. SOS sat with her, holding her hand. Elizabeth looked down, only seeing Doctor Daisy's large hand, so smooth and soft. She was sure his fingerprints had been worn away with hard work. She had wondered how she was going to get by without seeing him when she had to leave the ward and go home. In her mind, the plan had been to get the tram every now and then to the hospital and visit her darling doctor.

Now she would never again see that ruddy face with the kindest blue eyes. She would never forget what he had done for her and the love she felt for him. Elizabeth's grief took her to a place she hoped she would never have to go again. She built an iron cage around her heart and made a vow that it was the last time she would love anyone that way for the rest of her life.

Joe couldn't get her over this sorrow. He felt the anguish himself, but he wasn't attached to old Daisy the way Elizabeth was. He heard the rumours that were drifting around the ward and hoped that Elizabeth wouldn't hear the denigrating stories about her beloved Daisy.

Elizabeth had seen the nurses and the kids whispering. 'What is everyone trying to hide from me, Joe? I know something is going on.'

'It's about Doctor Daisy, about how he died.'

'I thought it must have been old age. He was old and he worked so hard. Why is it a secret? Why shouldn't I know about it?'

'He wasn't what you thought he was, not as good, that is. He had some problems, poor old Daisy.'

'Tell me. I couldn't feel any sadder than I do now.'

'Old Daisy was found dead in the gutter in Grey Street at St Kilda. That's near where you live, isn't it?'

'I don't know what all that means.'

Joe was reluctant to fill in the details.

'Well… men go down to Grey Street to meet women for their comfort. The main thing was that he had been drinking. It seems everyone knew he was a drunk.' Joe hoped she would be satisfied with that explanation. Elizabeth was too stunned to think, and never said a word. This reaction seemed worse than more questions to Joe, although he let it go at that for the time being.

Elizabeth was heartbroken, more so than when her family left her. She felt hollow, a hollow girl with a leg that had to be held together with steel rods.

Elizabeth turned it over and over in her mind, not really understanding how her hero could have died in the gutter like a dirty old man, to be remembered that way. The respect he had gained for his work would be lost.

Joe's parents came to pick him up the day before Elizabeth was to be discharged. There were mixed feelings, but getting home overrode the emotion of missing the companion that had been by his side through this terrible ordeal, an ordeal that had left scars that would go on, maybe for the rest of his life.

'I will pray for you every day as the sun goes down, Joe.' Elizabeth's sad eyes met his, searing her pain into his heart where it would be in a hidden place forever.

DAME Annie Jean Macnamara. 1899-1968
A medica; Scientist, her interest in Polio goes back to the 1925 epidemic.
Working with children's health and welfare at the Children's Hospital in Melbourne. 1935 she was honoured with the title Dame Commander of order of the British Empire. Dedicating her life to many causes and was credited with the development of the polio vaccine. The electoral district of Macnamara in Melbourne is named after her.

Sister Elizabeth Kenny. 1880- 1952
Sister Kenny as she was known (though not a registered nurse) used methods of treating the pain and paralysation from polio that were frowned on by many

in the establishment of medical science in Australia. Her alternative ways being accepted in the USA long before being used in the wards of Australian hospitals. Doing away with plaster casts and splints in favour of hot compresses and passive movement.

Dame Macnamara worked on a commission investigating Sister Kenny's methods and happily, they were accepted as useful.

Chapter 1

The Struggles of Abandonment
Elizabeth

'YOU CAN HAVE THE room down the back. The laundry can be your bathroom and you can use the lavatory off the back verandah.' Gerda snapped.

'Come back to the living room when you settle in and have some tea.' The expression on the old woman's face never changed.

That's obvious – down the back, Elizabeth thought. Old Gerda wouldn't want me anywhere near the master bedroom. There was a lovely spare room at the front of the house, and a fully tiled bathroom that was going to be out of bounds for her it seemed.

The old Georgian house had rooms everywhere that would have been nicer than down the back. Anything to make her more uncomfortable would have been Gerda's aim. Elizabeth knew her grandmother blamed her for her precious Werner leaving. She had thought he was precious too, until he deserted a sick child. Her grandfather smiled as she hobbled down the narrow passage to the back of the house.

The room was small with an iron bed against the wall. There was a wooden kitchen chair, a bedside table with one drawer, an oval mat, and a curtain covering one corner with four hooks and hangers to hang her clothes. The walls and ceiling were painted green, and even the floor was covered with a darker green lino all making the day another gloomy, dark experience.

The clothes Gerda had got for her were folded on the bed. Elizabeth could see they were all second-hand – a school uniform with someone else's name written on the tags inside, two sets of underwear, two pairs of socks, two hankies, two nighties, and a skirt and jumper for the weekends. She already had her orthopaedic shoes that the hospital had arranged for her. She wondered what would happen when her feet grew. Why hadn't her mother sent new clothes? She would never understand. Had they forgotten her existence?

It was at that moment that Elizabeth realised she was on her own. She would have to work hard to find ways to look after herself and survive.

The small window in her bedroom faced the backyard that was covered with pumpkin and potato plants that Otto Kasper grew. She watched as he harvested a large pumpkin and two potatoes. That was going to be the evening meal. It would be lucky if there was anything to complement the vegetables. At the hospital SOS aways said, 'You must keep up your protein. That's what gives you strength.' Elizabeth's strength wouldn't get much help at all with over-boiled pumpkin and potato every day, never the smallest piece of meat. The soup made her sick. She couldn't wait to get outside to vomit.

The ham sandwiches Gerda made for her school lunch were the highlight of the culinary day. The only thing that was better than the hospital was that she had almost forgotten the smell of antiseptic that surrounded the ward and everyone in it. Somehow, she missed it. The smell had seeped into her skin. She thought she would have it forever. It had drifted away. Fresh air became her friend now that her lungs didn't strain to spread oxygen through her body.

The kids stared at school. She was the only one there with a leg brace. Some of them had had polio, but hadn't been affected as badly, and didn't need a ball and chain. Every morning the teacher taped brown paper around her leg so the other children wouldn't be frightened by the sight of it.

The only friend she had was Peter Smith, and that was only because no-one else liked him. She was made to sit with him for that reason, and because he smelt so bad. Elizabeth started to feel sorry for Peter, wearing glasses with brown paper stuck on one lens and wearing the same clothes every day. He smelt like the wet straw that her grandfather put around the pumpkins.

Peter lived in a similar situation to her. He had been left with his grandparents too. There was a difference though, the grandfather used a leather strap on him most nights. Peter wasn't sure what he did to deserve the treatment but he seemed to accept it.

The only time Elizabeth experienced any aggression or more than usual nastiness, was when Gerda massaged her limbs. There were times, though, that she almost felt her tenderness, always pulling the softening hands back. Elizabeth wondered if granny Gerda had been hurt and had locked her heart away the way she had when Doctor Daisy left her world.

Peter and Elizabeth became friends, not that they liked each other that much. It was more the fact that no-one else wanted them. Peter was no replacement for Joe. That was never going to happen. Elizabeth got use to his smell and, as she listened to the stories of his miserable life, it made her feel better about her own situation.

Grandfather Otto started to tell stories about the love of his life, the merry-go-round. They would walk hand-in-hand to Luna Park. Elizabeth watched as other kids rode the horses and the more exciting rides, knowing she would never have that thrill. For the time being she was completely satisfied with her imagination taking over, seeing a world that took away reality for a short time. That's when her fantasy world began.

Becoming anyone she wanted, her imagination could see her sitting astride a prancing, bucking horse. Elizabeth was so exhausted on those days. The walk down to Luna Park and back home was hard for her, but she would never say no to escaping her reality. Some days Otto gave her money to go over to the Palais Theatre to watch a movie.

This was the best thing that she had ever experienced – watching the stars' legs and hoping that one day she would be able to discard her brace and look like Betty Grable. She dreamt she would dance like Ginger Rogers, and she would dye her hair like Rita Hayworth. Sometimes she had enough money for the movie magazine that was on sale at the theatre. She read into the night about the stars, what their next role would be, where they lived in Hollywood and who they were romantically involved with.

She fell asleep wishing she could be there in that famous world of stars that seemed to be on another planet, way beyond the earth in a far-off galaxy. She began to think of her bad leg as a detachment from her true self, an enemy, a separate identity. Why wasn't she born to be a star? That thought made her laugh. She could never be anything but herself in this world, so she would be whoever Elizabeth Kasper wanted to be in her own head. And that's the way it was.

IF GERDA WASN'T HOME when she came in from school, Elizabeth would sneak into the master bedroom and read the women's magazines that were hidden under the bed. She learnt about fashion, read the romance stories, putting herself into the shoes of the beautiful heroine. She imagined being kissed by the handsome hero. Seeing and smelling Peter brought her back to earth every day.

Elizabeth had never seen Peter smile. Perhaps there had been no belting last night, she thought.

'Me pop showed me some kindness. He gave me a fishing rod,' Peter said with the biggest grin.

A new adventure began for them both. Elizabeth would bring a tin of worms from Otto's garden and they would sit on the pier most of the weekend, rain or shine. If the rain got too heavy, they would go back to the merry-go-round and Peter would ride the horses. Otto always complained that he had to disinfect the horse that Peter rode to get rid of the smell. Elizabeth didn't care anymore. He was her friend and that's the way it was.

Elizabeth had another world she could escape to – the ocean that she had discovered while sitting with Peter on the pier, her legs dangled over the edge. As hard as it was for her to get down and up again with the anchor that she had to carry with her, it was worth it. The swirl of the water was calming, as she immersed herself into the movement of the waves, drifting into new dreams.

The water was never the same. She loved the white caps on rougher days, the wind blowing all her unsettling thoughts away. On the still days she could see the sand and the fish that were about to take the worm hanging off the end of Peter's line. The colours fascinated her. Some days they matched her mood: the darkest blue, almost black, were her bad days; the light aqua reminded her of the aura that had surrounded Doctor Daisy when he smiled at her. The ocean was never mundane like the regimented life of the disabled.

Elizabeth watched far out across Port Phillip Bay, wondering if she would ever see what laid on the other side. Sometimes she wondered where her mother and father were – over there somewhere? She concluded that they didn't care about their child with a limp.

She imagined herself swimming for miles until she came to an island that had no disease and everyone was happy. Then she would become a mermaid and she could go anywhere with her strong, jewelled tail and a fin that would propel her into a machine, diving, swimming, splashing. Some days her hair would be blonde, sometimes red with waves that matched the ocean. It was never straight dull brown like her own. When Peter spoke to her, she never moved away from her dreams until it was time for her to struggle back to her reality.

Elizabeth's schoolwork improved, although she and Peter were the dumb ones in the class and were told so every day by every teacher they had to endure. They always had to sit out when everyone else played games on sports days. She couldn't remember what it felt like to run, as she had done with her brother and sister before fate had paralysed her. Peter wasn't any good at sport either, but he was becoming a very good fisherman. He had decided that was what he wanted to do.

'Don't need all this brain stuff anyway. I will always be able to get by, catching fish and selling them. I will never be hungry, that's for sure. I don't need all that book learning. I will be out of here as soon as they let me.'

He reminded her of Joe sometimes. Thinking Joe probably smelt like a cow now anyway, Elizabeth laughed to herself. Joe never left her side in spirit. She prayed for him when the sun went down every day just as promised, never doubting he did the same.

School ended for the year. She had six weeks to fill in until her last year of schooling. Elizabeth wasn't sure if she could ever get a job, although it was in her mind to get away from Gerda as soon as possible. Otto gave her some pocket money for cleaning the merry-go-round most days. She spent a little and hid the rest in a tin in her bedside drawer – her running away money, she told herself.

HER CLOTHES WERE GETTING tight, and she needed a bra. She hoped that Gerda would take her shopping, but knew it wasn't to happen. Some days she caught up with Peter on the pier. Those were the days the mermaid was waiting, and they would float away into another life.

Peter was so happy with himself, having a customer who was buying all his catch. Getting rich wasn't out of the question. The last time she saw him, he was so distressed. His grandfather had found the money he had hidden so he could run away. The old man had taken it all off him and belted him with the leather strap that had gone around his legs all the years of his young life. 'Just to keep him in his place.' That's what the old bastard had said. Peter was devastated, holding back tears when telling the sad tale.

Elizabeth never saw Peter again. She imagined he took his fishing rod and ran away as far as possible from the grandfather, or that was what she hoped.

Elizabeth spent time on the pier by herself now and travelled the ocean as a beautiful mermaid. Peter's smell was gone, and the freshness of the salty air filled her lungs. She had wondered what it would really be like to taste the water. Negotiating the sand was out of the question. One day she might be able to get to the shoreline and put her bare feet into the magic ocean. When leaving the hospital, it was suggested that saltwater baths would be good therapy for her if someone would be able to carry her into them. That suggestion fell on deaf ears. No-one could be bothered. Would she have expected anything else?

She watched the seagulls fighting for titbits that passers-by dropped from their chips wrapped in newspaper. She saw the one with a limp miss out over and over. How does a seagull get a limp? she wondered. Elizabeth and the seagull had parallel lives. She watched as he kept trying, and eventually, he got the biggest chip of all. She almost cheered. 'We're battlers, you and me, little seagull with a limp.'

Just before school was to go back, she ventured into the St. Moritz ice rink. She knew she would never be able to skate, but it was another world. She could come and dream and swirl around in her mind and pretend. Elizabeth felt she would never leave St. Kilda. It was the world her human form would have to stay in forever, but her imagination would take her to every corner of the world.

Elizabeth had a small hope that Peter would be back at school on the first day, but there was a new girl at the desk that she had expected to share with him again. She looked a lot older than anyone else in the room.

The teacher introduced her to the class. 'We have a new pupil today. This is Phyllis Beal. She is joining us this year, having been in hospital, missing a lot of school. I hope you enjoy your stay with us. Elizabeth will look after you and help you settle in.' Mrs King walked away, leaving the responsibility to Elizabeth.

'Why were you in hospital, Phyllis?' Elizabeth asked.

'It was rheumatic fever. I have been sick for so long. Have you been sick too?'

'Yes, I had polio.' Elizabeth thought she must had missed the limp and the brown paper over her brace.

'Can we be friends?'

'If you can put up with my disability.' That was the first time Elizabeth had said those words aloud.

'I am very slow, nothing like I used to be. Maybe we will get better together.'

'That might not happen for me, but it will be fun trying.'

Elizabeth felt a little light-hearted for the first time since she had been ill.

Phyllis was taller than her and had short red hair. If she grew it longer, she might look like Rita Hayworth, Elizabeth thought. Phyllis's school clothes were better than her second-hand ones. Gerda had said they would last her until she left school and got a job. Then she could buy her own clothes.

Phyllis accepted her as she was, and that made Elizabeth happy. Their homes were in different directions, so after school they parted company. Last year, Peter had walked home with her. She missed him for the first time that first day, although she felt good. She wanted to skip but couldn't. In her mind, she took hold of her limping seagull's wing and skipped in circles all the way home.

Gerda was her usual grumpy self when Elizabeth entered the living room.

'When are you going to learn to cook so you can take some of the load off my shoulders? You know I have a bad back, but you never offer to help.'

'I do the dishes every night, I look after my room and do my laundry. I thought that was all you wanted me to do. I can help with the cooking if you would like, but I might not be very good.'

'You can start by cutting up the pumpkin.'

'Well, that has put an end to a good day,' Elizabeth said to herself.

Eventually she learnt to cook pumpkin soup and boiled potatoes. Sometimes there was bacon, cold cuts and ox tongue. If I ever get out of here, I will be trying some of the recipes that I have seen in Gerda's magazines, she thought.

The friendship with Phyllis was a blessing. She lived with her mother in an apartment on Grey Street. 'You will have to come home with me one day. But my Mum works at nights and sleeps most of the day, so it is hard having visitors.'

'That's okay. It is hard for me to have visitors too. My grandmother is so grumpy. I wouldn't want to inflict her on anyone. But when you are feeling up to it, we can go and ride on my grandfather's merry-go-round.' Elizabeth thought there would be other things that they could look forward to.

'Have you had a boyfriend?' Phyllis asked.

'No. Why? Have you?'

'You had Joe and Peter.'

Elizabeth laughed. 'Joe and I were pinned to a bed the whole time we were together, and Peter smelt so bad that it would have been just too much to bear.' Elizabeth laughed again. 'I have never really been interested. I know I will never be able to attract a boy, the way I am.'

'They don't always take too much notice about looks. That's what my mum says. One day we will get boyfriends, I bet,' Phyllis said, as if she knew what she was talking about.

Elizabeth wasn't about to tell her that she had all the romance she needed in her head with her Hollywood heart throbs, and that at times she had wished she could kiss Cary Grant or Robert Taylor, or dance with Fred Astaire. She realised that Phyllis might be past riding on Otto's wooden horses.

Growing up wasn't something Elizabeth was looking forward to. She wanted to get away from Gerda, but she wasn't sure she would be able to look after herself entirely. And where was the money going to come from? She had learnt to clean well, and her cooking was improving. Gerda had been bringing home some more interesting produce to cook, as long as she used Otto's specialties.

For the time being, that's the way it was.

Chapter 2

Beyond Childhood
Elizabeth

ELIZABETH'S TRANSFORMATION WAS TAKING place. Translucent blue eyes emerged, and the once mousey brown hair was now a striking deep auburn. She pulled the hair back off her face and tied it at the nape of her neck. Her maturing figure made her an attractive teenager. Wearing clothes that were two sizes too small seemed to accentuate her shapely figure. The only thing that detracted from her eye-catching looks were her orthopaedic shoes and the brace supporting her deformed leg.

Phyllis was becoming jealous of her new friend in a jovial way, always saying, 'You will take all the boys from me.'

Elizabeth didn't know what she was worried about. What boy would want to be seen with a cripple? Phyllis seemed to be obsessed with getting boys to like her and talked to every one of them that passed by, flicking her growing hair, moving her hips just like the girls in the stories that Elizabeth read about in Gerda's magazines.

Phyllis was still taller than Elizabeth and her red hair was going to be her crowning glory. She liked to dance around as though she was a movie star. Elizabeth still wasn't interested in boys but listened to Phyllis chat on about who she liked, and how good looking they were, or who she dreamt about. It seemed to Elizabeth that she liked them all. She just couldn't imagine why she was so keen to have a boy in her life.

It was the first time she'd had the pleasure of a girlfriend since she'd lost her sister and was enjoying her company. Phyllis had taken Peter's place, joining Elizabeth as the two dumbest kids in the class, another thing that held them together. She never told Phyllis about the way she escaped. She imagined that her leg was a different identity, and she went to the pier with the freedom of a mermaid, swimming all over the bay. The world of misery became a different place.

'That's the one I want to kiss first,' Phyllis would say. Elizabeth couldn't think of anything worse. She was still dreaming about Carey Grant and swirling around with Fred Astaire. Elizabeth never criticized her friend for her fantasies. They weren't much different to her imaginative world. Phyllis would be more likely to achieve her goals, Elizabeth thought. So that's the way it was, Phyllis chatting on about getting a boyfriend and Elizabeth listening.

The day came that Elizabeth was invited to Phyllis's house.

'Can you come over on Sunday? Mum is having Saturday night off, so she won't have to sleep all day Sunday. She said it was okay for us to spend the day together, if you want.'

'I will have to ask old Gerda, and tell her the address and do all my jobs first.' It would be a long walk for Elizabeth, but she was excited to meet Phyllis's mum. She sounded so cool.

Gerda wasn't happy when Elizabeth told her the address.

'Grey Street? You know the only women that live on that street, don't you?' Gerda yelled in her nasty tone.

'Not really. I think Phyllis's mother is a waitress. She works nights.'

'I'll bet she does,' Gerda snarled. 'Go at your own risk, that's all I can say.'

Elizabeth didn't understand what all the fuss was about. Phyllis never came to any harm living there, she was sure.

Phyllis met her on the corner of Fitzroy Street and Grey Street.

'There is a story about some old drunk that died here a while back. It gives me the creeps every time I stand where he carked it,' Phyllis said as Elizabeth came to the corner. Elizabeth thought she was going to faint.

'Are you okay?' Phyllis asked.

Elizabeth had trouble answering her, but finally got out, 'Yes.' She wasn't in any state to tell Phyllis about Doctor Daisy and was having trouble holding back tears.

'It's just the walk. I know I'm like an old lady at times.' She tried to laugh.

The visit went well. Phyllis's mum welcomed Elizabeth warmly and said to call her Beth. 'That's what all my friends called me,' she said.

Phyllis's room was small like Elizabeth's, but it was painted pale pink with floral curtains and bedspread and a lovely picture on the wall of a very glamorous couple dancing.

'That is a beautiful picture. Do you know those people?' Elizabeth asked.

'Don't you recognise Beth? That's Mum when she was a champion ballroom dancer. I don't know who the man is. She'll never say,'

'She was very glamorous. Oh! Not that she isn't now, but very young I suppose.'

'She had a bad back injury. That's why she walks a bit funny.'

'I didn't notice. She walks better than me. At least she has the memory of looking so great, and being able to dance – that would be a dream, something I will never be able to achieve.' Elizabeth's mood was getting morbid, and she wanted to go home to her depressing, green room.

'I have to get home early, to get the vegetables on the stove before grandfather gets back from the merry-go-round. I've had a lovely time. Thank you so much Beth, for letting me come. I'm so lucky to have Phyllis as my friend.'

'Do you want me to walk with you?' Phyllis asked.

'No, I will be fine now. I know where you live.' Elizabeth didn't want anyone near her when she had to walk past where Doctor Daisy lay dying in the gutter. Why had he done that to himself when he was so clever and caring? She could still see his droopy blue eyes looking down, wishing her to walk. If Phyllis knew how much she loved him she would laugh her head off. When she came to the corner her eyes misted over and her stomach ached. She thought she was going to vomit. She stood there for some time, almost hoping his ghost would appear, but of course it didn't.

For the first time, Elizabeth realised he had let her down. Why had he been so weak that he had destroyed his life that way and stopped helping the sick children? Even that realisation didn't change her feelings about Doctor Daisy with his pink bow tie and pink daisy just for her. She could never tell Phyllis how she had loved that old man that had died in the gutter.

'How was the visit with your friend and her waitress mother?' Gerda asked sarcastically.

'I forgot to ask if she was a waitress. Beth, she said her name was. She used to be a ballroom dancer, but hurt her back, so she doesn't dance anymore.'

'Oh, Beth Beal. So that's the story, is it?'

'Did you know her?'

'No not personally, but she was famous over at the Palais de Danse. She was a real beauty. The men loved her. She must be well past it now.' Gerda laughed to herself, as if she knew secrets about Phyllis's mother. None of this mattered to Elizabeth. Phyllis was the only friend that she had, and that's the way it was.

Phyllis never went with her to Luna Park, saying she wasn't allowed. Her mum didn't think it was a good place for young girls. Elizabeth didn't know why, having never seen anything that had scared her. Occasionally she saw some rough-looking boys having a scuffle, but nothing bad. Otto said sometimes they had to throw some of the boys out for being unruly, but nothing else. Elizabeth never asked why. All families had rules that had to be obeyed, and the kids never asked questions. Elizabeth still went down with her grandfather to the merry-go-round and helped, saving the wages. Sometimes she spent a little on a movie when there was one that was irresistible.

'Do you know anything about sex?' Phyllis asked Elizabeth one day at school.

Elizabeth was a bit surprised. It wasn't something she thought she had to worry about yet, or wanted to.

'I know how reproduction works. Well, in cows, anyway,' Elizabeth said a little shyly.

'Do you want to do it with a boy or a cow?' Phyllis laughed.

'I mean, Joe told me all about how the cow had to be served by the bull when her milk dried up. She had to have another baby so she would be able to give milk again.'

'Served. Is that what they call it? I thought it was called fucking.' Phyllis laughed again.

Elizabeth went red. She hadn't heard a girl say that word before.

'I only know what Joe told me about how the bull did it.' As far as Elizabeth was concerned, that was the end of the conversation.

'Oh, okay then. It is just that there is this boy who wants me to do it with him. I wanted to see what you thought.'

'No, of course. What did you expect me to say? Anyway, you don't need my permission, do you?' For the first time, Elizabeth walked away from her friend.

Their friendship wavered a little for a while, but Elizabeth missed Phyllis and soon they were best friends again. The subject of sex was not mentioned for some time.

Phyllis kept asking Elizabeth to come to her home and spend time together. She did go occasionally, but she just couldn't keep walking past Doctor Daisy's place of demise. Her mood would change, and she found it hard to enjoy her time with Phyllis and Beth. When she did go, Elizabeth would ask Beth about her dancing. Beth's eyes would light up and she looked ten years younger. She didn't understand why she wouldn't let Phyllis go down to the esplanade where she used to dance at the Palais De Danse. According to Gerda, Grey Street was a far worse environment than the beach area.

Elizabeth loved the playground atmosphere that Luna Park created with the big dipper, all the rides and Otto's merry-go-round. She loved the characters that were seen there and the sea breeze spreading its wings across the happy faces of the crowds. She also loved the Palais Theatre, the St Moritz, and her beloved pier where she sat and watched the world mingle and the seagulls waiting for a chip to drop from a daydreaming human's lunch.

When the sun shone, it gave St Kilda new life as the kids jumped into the waves off the sand, squealing with delight. Most of these things Elizabeth couldn't participate in, but watching nourished her. She started to go into one of the cafés on the Esplanade, Lottie's, it was called. She loved the atmosphere in there too. She would slide into one of the alcoves and order a chocolate milkshake. The sides of the seats were high enough that you couldn't see who was sitting in the next alcove, but you could hear. Elizabeth took her time drinking and listened to the chit-chat from the other cubicles.

Lottie was a roly-poly, jovial, middle-aged lady with rosy cheeks and the freakiest white hair that looked like she had never combed it. But everyone loved her, and she appeared to love them back.

Elizabeth heard things about the street girls that worked at night, and finally realised that that's what Beth did. It had shocked her at first, but the more she listened the more she realised they were just trying to make a living. She presumed that was what Beth had to do. It was weeks before she had enough courage to ask Phyllis about it.

'How did you work it out?'

'I listened to the girls talk in Lottie's. I heard all sorts of stories about what they have to do to keep their customers happy. I really feel sorry for them, and I hate to think about Beth doing those things.'

'She gets well paid. Sometimes she comes home with a black eye, or a bleeding nose.'

'I can't imagine how they do it.'

'Mum tells me it's not too bad. Sometimes she makes friends with the lonely ones.'

'I feel so sorry for her. She is so pretty.'

Phyllis laughed, 'That's why she gets the jobs.'

'Is that why you aren't allowed down to Luna Park?'

'No, that has nothing to do with it. There are more working girls up my end. There's someone she doesn't want me to see. I don't know who it is. I have a suspicion it is my father. I don't really care. One day I will get down there and you can show me around.'

That was the end of it for a while. They both stayed at their end of town, meeting in the middle to go to school. Elizabeth spent more time in the café. She and Lottie were becoming quite chummy. Lottie realised that Elizabeth was a loner for obvious reasons and started to care about her.

'I see you listen to the girls that come in on their days off. Don't fall into the trap of easy money. It's not really that easy, you know.'

'I don't think running a café looks easy either.' Elizabeth laughed.

'No, it isn't, but I can do what I want. I am free. I like hard work but, on my terms.'

'Don't worry Lottie, I could never get caught up in the sex trade,' of which she had learnt so much while listening.

Lottie had heard that many times, and seen many girls lose their way. She had high hopes for this lovely girl and didn't want her to go down the wrong path. It would be easy for her to be taken advantage of in her condition.

The school year was coming to an end and Phyllis never shut up about Billy Johnston – his blonde, curly hair and blue eyes that she gazed into, and what a good kisser he was.

'I let him touch my breast the other day, and he keeps saying that he can't wait to do it with me. I know I will give in soon. I really want to see what it's like, don't you Elizabeth?'

'No, not really. I'm too busy looking for a job that will pay more than what I am getting for cleaning the horses. I need to get away from Gerda soon or I will go mad.'

ELIZABETH WAS PUTTING ON the evening meal when she heard Otto storm in through the front door, almost running out to the backyard. She watched as he pulled out all the pumpkin and potato plants, smashing them all into the ground with his shovel.

He was screaming, 'Die, you bastards!' Over and over. Gerda just stood there like stone.

Elizabeth started to cry. 'Do something, Granny. Do something!' The stone never moved.

After he had destroyed the garden there was no evidence that there had ever been a plant in the backyard. Just a heap of mud was left. Otto walked inside, sat in his chair, and took his last breath.

Elizabeth was devastated. She didn't know what to do but cry. Gerda seemed to take it in her stride, calling the doctor and then the undertaker as if it was part of everyday life. Elizabeth had just lost the only kind person in her family. The merry-go-round would be lost to her. The money that Otto gave her would stop. Her world would only get worse. Otto had made living in this house and her green room bearable. The days passed in a blur. Maybe her parents would come for the funeral and take her away.

Otto was disposed of, and no-one came. Elizabeth didn't understand why Werner would not come to his father's funeral and comfort his mother.

Gerda didn't seem to want comfort. She just carried on as if nothing had happened. A man came to the door and Gerda signed papers selling the merry-go-round. Elizabeth was sure there wouldn't be money worries.

'You will have to get a job as soon as you leave school and pay board so we will be fine.' Gerda didn't have any idea that Elizabeth wanted to be as far away from her as she could get. Understanding Gerda Kasper was impossible for Elizabeth. The truth was, she didn't really know her, where she came from or what she thought. Her father's mother was like a stranger she passed in the street.

No-one seemed to care why Otto went mad like that. Elizabeth asked Gerda once and the answer was 'The Kasper family.' She expected it to happen, just like his father.

Great, Elizabeth thought, another thing I might be faced with one day. She wondered if her father would do the same thing, maybe he was going mad, maybe that's why he hadn't come for her.

The death of Otto had a profound effect on Elizabeth's mind. A deep depression took over her like a dark cloud. She had lost everyone she had felt close to.

Her parents, siblings, dear Doctor Daisy, Joe and Peter, now Otto. Was she poison to anyone who came near her?

She woke early and stared at her brace, leaning against the chair in her green room, the one thing that was constant in her life, the one companion that couldn't be taken from her – the thing she hated the most. Why did she have to live? Why didn't her parents come for her? They had abandoned her just because of her crippled leg. Nothing made sense. Bewilderment was eating into her soul. She got out of bed and did what she had to do to get through the day. Making plans to escape her reality was getting harder. Going to the pier later was always on her mind.

'We did it. Billy and me, we did it!' Phyllis was all about herself as if she had done some great good.

'So, what was it like? Was it as good as you expected?' Elizabeth asked but couldn't care less.

Phyllis hesitated. 'Billy's mate, Gerry, wants to do it with you and see you without your brace.' Elizabeth couldn't believe what she was hearing. Her depressed mind took a minute to calculate what Phyllis was saying.

'Why would you think I would be interested?' Elizabeth thought it was just another insult to a person who could almost feel her face buried in the ground.

'It takes you to a different place for a minute. I thought it might be good for you.'

Maybe Phyllis did care about her. At this time, Elizabeth was willing to grab any little piece of reassurance. That was where her depression was taking her. By the end of the day, Elizabeth had made up her mind. She would say yes. What did she have to lose? Her life was nothing to anyone, or herself for that matter.

When Gerry looked at her without her brace, lying on the grass, he said, 'My God you are beautiful! I have never thought of you as anything but a cripple. We only look at your leg.' Elizabeth couldn't take it all in for a minute. There was no time to think. He was on top of her and for that time, she was beautiful. Her red hair was flowing, she was Rita Hayworth lying there, hidden by the trees, behind the school.

She had given away her virginity with ease and that's how it was.

Chapter 3

Striving for Emancipation
Elizabeth

THEY WERE OLDER THAN the other kids that had finished school, because of their time in hospital.

'Do you think you will get a job?' Elizabeth asked Phyllis.

'I think Mum has organised a job at the grocers. It'll be okay for now.'

'Lottie has something for me. She would have had me at the café but didn't think I have the stamina for all the standing.'

'I hope that comes off for you, and you can leave old Gerda. She does sound like the devil.'

'I suppose she has looked after me – more than I can say for the rest of my family.'

'I will miss you, Elizabeth. I hope we can keep in touch.'

'I will always be at Lottie's now. You should be allowed down to the esplanade, grown up as we are.'

'I might just come. Mum will never know anyway; she still sleeps all day.'

'On your day off then. If I am not there, leave a message with Lottie.'

They made promises and crossed their hearts that they would see each other from time to time.

The girls parted. Elizabeth hoped Phyllis wouldn't get sucked into Beth's so-called "profession". She was still madly in love with Billy, and they did spend all their time together. Maybe that would be enough for her friend. Elizabeth thought that Phyllis would soon forget her, just like everyone else.

Lottie had found Elizabeth a job as a nanny. She wondered how she would pull it off, never having had anything to do with kids or babies. She had read all the magazines under Gerda's bed, so that should give her some information as a backup. Lottie gave her the address and sent her on her way to see if they liked her.

Elizabeth was so nervous. She didn't have any experience for any sort of job really. Cleaning a merry-go-round didn't count for much. Elizabeth had spent a small amount of the money she had saved on a new long skirt and jacket that she changed into at the café. She didn't dare let Gerda see that she had money. Her limp was more pronounced by the time she got there. That worried her a little. They might think that she would be incapable of doing the job.

She was sure that Lottie had filled them in about her disability. It was a modern, two-story, white, brick house with a large red door and a brass lion's head knocker. Elizabeth almost turned and ran. Well, that's what she felt like doing. The thought of not getting the job and having to stay with Gerda made her stand and muster as much courage as she could to take that lion's head in her hand and knock. The door opened almost immediately.

'Hi, you must be Elizabeth. Lottie said you had beautiful eyes.'

Elizabeth felt at ease. She had the smoothest voice, calming her straight away.

'Thank you. It is nice to meet you, Mrs Goldmann.'

'Call me Dolly. Come and meet my husband, Gerry.'

That threw Elizabeth off for a moment. That name reminded her of the day at school with Billy's friend. She had tried to put it out of her mind. It might be hard for her if she had to call Mr Goldmann, Gerry. Elizabeth didn't know whether to laugh or cry.

He was very tall with thinning hair. And looked much older than Dolly.

'Take a seat Elizabeth. Gerry and I will explain the job to you.'

'Our little girl is asleep at the moment. Her name is Maggie. Our jobs take us out of the house so much, we are looking for someone that will care for her as if she was their own.' Dolly was very definite.

'Dolly is still modelling, and I am at the office until late most days. No cooking or cleaning. We have others that will be in and out doing those jobs,' Gerry said with authority.

'You will have your own room and bathroom downstairs next to Maggie's room.' Dolly smiled.

'Have you any questions?' Gerry stood up and started to walk away. 'Dolly will fill you in with more details – wages and days off. I think you will do fine.'

He was gone before Elizabeth could think.

'So, when can you start Elizabeth? I have a big job next week. Would that be, okay?'

'Yes, next Monday then,' Elizabeth managed to get the answer out of her mouth.

'Oh, you can have Thursdays off, if that's okay. We will need you on the weekends. We always have people in.'

Elizabeth left in a daze, how was she going to tell Gerda that she wouldn't be living in the house with her and paying board? The excitement started to kick in – a real bedroom and bathroom in a luxurious home! If only she could dance, she would dance all the way home.

'I HAVE A JOB and I start Monday morning.'

'Well done! How did you manage that with all your problems? How much money are you going to get?' The old bat never asked what it was, or how she was going to cope; only how much money the job paid. Elizabeth was getting mad, making it easier for her to tell Gerda that she would be leaving.

'It is a live-in Nanny, so I will be moving out,' Elizabeth said with satisfaction.

Gerda laughed. 'How are you going to do a job like that? You know nothing about babies or children. So that means that you will not be bringing any money into the house.'

'You won't have to look after me, so the money from the merry-go-round should be enough for you.'

Gerda looked so angry, more so than normal. 'Yes. but your father will stop sending the money.'

'What money? Do you mean he was paying you all this time? I thought they had forgotten about me.' Elizabeth was stunned. How could the old bat lead her to believe that they never paid for any of her care, and it was all out of kindness that they had offered her a home, otherwise she would have had to go into a home for girls.

Gerda and Otto had always said that everything they provided for her was coming out of their pockets, and that she had to be grateful that they were willing to put a roof over her head. Confusion surrounded her. The situation with her parents and her grandparents never made any sense now. It seemed worse than ever.

Maybe her mother and father did care about her, but why didn't they write or ring? How could she believe that they ever gave her a thought? Gerda was still carrying on about Elizabeth leaving after all she had done for her, and what it had cost her to put up with an ungrateful girl. Werner had never sent enough money, she was saying. Otto had provided most of the food as it was, so where did the money go that her father did send? Maybe she spent it on her magazines. *If it wasn't so sad it would be funny*, Elizabeth thought.

'How did you get that new skirt and jacket? Where did you get the money for those? Not working with your friend's mother, are you?" the old bat yelled at Elizabeth.

'No, it is what I saved from the money grandfather gave me for helping at the merry-go-round. My other clothes are too small.'

'I didn't know he gave you money. Well, you had better give me what's left, seeing you are leaving me here alone.'

No way was Elizabeth going to give her any of the money she had saved. It was well-hidden in Otto's garden shed. She had put it there after his death. Elizabeth knew Gerda would never go in there, being so scared of spiders.

The webs covered the old tin shed now that Otto wasn't around. Some of the pumpkin and potatoes had started to reshoot. Soon the place would be over-run with spiders and spreading plants. Maybe Gerda would be consumed by spiders and vines. She would read it in the paper – a horrible old woman was swallowed up in her backyard. Elizabeth smiled to herself.

'What are you smiling about? Go and get me the money. You can go now. Don't wait until Monday. You're just like your mother, taking things that don't belong to you.' As she walked away, Gerda asked what the name of the employer was.

'It is Gerry and Dolly Goldmann.'

'Ha! What a joke, he will sort you out.'

'Do you know them?' Gerda didn't reply.

'You are a stupid girl.' Elizabeth could hear her laughing as Gerda turned her back. Confusion surrounded Elizabeth.

Elizabeth had two days before she was to start at Dolly's. She left the rags she had been wearing, only taking a few personal items and her new clothes. After dark she took a torch and retrieved her money from the shed and went quietly out the front door. Lottie was pleased to have her on the couch in her apartment above the café for a couple of nights. Lottie gave her a few tips about looking after a baby, things that weren't in the magazines. It appeared that she had a baby of her own, Elizabeth was surprised to hear. Lottie explained that she had run away with an American sailor, she wrote to from time to time. Elizabeth had never seen Lottie look sad before. She was always the happy one, taking on everyone else's worries.

'I am sorry Lottie, I never thought to ask you about your family. I am so selfish, as if I am the only one with problems.'

'No dear, my daughter is happy with her new family and new country. I might see them one day. Maybe when I sell the café, I will get over there and meet the grandchildren, two boys. They will be so grown up.' Lottie's voice wavered a little. Elizabeth realised everyone had something hidden away that wasn't seen by the outside world.

While Lottie was busy during the day, Elizabeth went down to the pier and went into her comfortable world where no-one else could invade her fantasy creation. She wondered what Joe was doing with his beloved cows. She prayed every day that he was happy. She watched the fish swimming around in and out of the timber that held up the pier, the ones Peter would never catch. She hoped that he was catching bigger ones some place far away.

She swam through the waves to the horizon with her mermaid tail splashing with the delight of freedom. Imagining that she would save her money and go many places. Her leg would not stop her becoming her mermaid self and swim. She would never think of Gerda again but would never forget Otto and his pumpkins.

She wondered what happened to SOS and would think of Doctor Daisy every day. She did her best to never walk past the gutter where he lay dying. On the second day just before Lottie was closing, Phyllis and Billy walked in. Elizabeth was pleased to see them. Lottie said they could sit and talk while she cleaned up for the day.

'We have some exciting news. We just had to see you before we went. Billy got a job on a cattle farm in Gippsland, with a cottage. We are going to get married. Mum said it was okay, better to be out of the city.' Phyllis couldn't wipe the smile off her face. Elizabeth didn't know what to say. She had to be happy for them, though she was unsure of the outcome.

'I am happy for you. When are you going?'

'We're getting married next weekend. Can you come?'

'Oh no, I have a job that I start tomorrow, and I'll be working over the weekends from now on. I will have to miss it.'

'Never mind. We wanted you to know.'

'We are so happy, Elizabeth. I wanted to thank you for your friendship. You were a great support to me. I wish you all the best things too.'

'Thanks. You did the same for me, but now you have Billy, and I will be moving on to a new life too. It seems our childhood is over.' The three of them laughed. 'Your mother will miss you,' Elizabeth said, thinking she was glad Phyllis would be out of Grey Street, and the temptation of the so-called easy money would be out of her mind for good.

It all seemed so simple – a new world was opening up to them.

'Oh, by the way, Gerry said he would like to see you sometime. Can I give him a message?' Phyllis asked as they were about to step out onto the footpath.

'No, I will leave that episode in my childhood too.'

She wondered if they heard her. They were so absorbed with each other and their future together.

DOLLY GREETED ELIZABETH AND took her down to her bedroom. It was a large room with a double bed and pillows everywhere. It had huge wardrobes with mirrors from floor to ceiling, and the softest cream carpet. The walls and ceiling were a pale grey, the furniture was painted cream, and the spread and curtains were a shiny deeper grey. Elizabeth thought she would die.

'I hope you will be happy here, Elizabeth. We want you to feel part of the family.' Dolly smiled.

Elizabeth couldn't speak, she was so overwhelmed.

'Now, come and meet Maggie.'

She opened an adjoining door to her bedroom – another beautiful room with the same décor as hers. The only difference was that the cot replaced the bed. The bathroom was set behind the two bedrooms with access from both. Stark white tiles line the walls. One wall was completely mirrored, and a bath was set into floor level. Elizabeth gasped. Her imagination could never have extended this far. To be living in such luxury.

Maggie was twelve months old, just about to walk. Elizabeth walked over to the cot and lifted her out, as if it was second nature to her. They loved each other at first sight, and that's the way it was.

Elizabeth soon fell into the routine that Dolly had set out for her and Maggie. She used some instincts and some of the things she had read, working in all her ignorance. When Maggie was asleep, she lived in her own head world, daydreaming about the movie stars. William Holden was holding a place in her heart at this time, and Elizabeth Taylor was taking over from Rita Hayworth. Her new surroundings allowed her to fall into the star role easier. They couldn't have a better bedroom than her, she was sure.

Sometimes when Gerry was home and they ate in the kitchen, Elizabeth was invited to join them. Most of the time, she had her meals when she was feeding Maggie. All the meals were prepared by the cook who came in most days.

Elizabeth had never known this level of happiness, even when she was with her family or that she could remember that is. When Maggie was two, she became more demanding, and Elizabeth was glad of her day off. Her leg still gave her pain, and fatigue was always lurking.

Most Thursdays she sat with Lottie, or listened to the girls talk about their pimps, or a trick they laughed about. A movie took her away too far-off places. Sometimes her Thursdays with all the activity, made her so tired she may as well have been looking after Maggie.

The Goldmann's home was in Balaclava, too far for Elizabeth to walk to Lottie's, she needed to catch the tram, which she had learnt to negotiate well. She was managing her leg with ease. It didn't seem to creep into her mind so much now. The Goldmanns never mentioned it at all, as if they had not noticed. She wondered why when her limp was pronounced after a long day.

After a sleep in her soft bed and silky sheets, she was always ready for her new life. Maggie would call out 'Lizzy,' when she woke, and their day would start with giggles and hugs. Some days, she thought her fantasies had taken over. Elizabeth Kasper was living someone else's life.

Dolly and Gerry worked long hours and didn't spend a lot of time with Maggie, making Elizabeth wonder if the little girl felt abandoned like she had been. They understood that Thursdays were the only day they were her parents. At least Maggie had that day, Elizabeth thought. She hoped that she was a better replacement than Gerda.

Elizabeth's work life was a dream. She loved Maggie more every day and she watched her development with pride, loving the thought that she was contributing to Maggie becoming a smart, well-mannered, beautiful child.

She still enjoyed her days at the esplanade. If it was raining, she would spend the time at the café or the movies. If the sun shone, she would become a mermaid and swim through the day.

Dolly was so kind to her, and if she ever needed anything, she only had to ask. Gerry was a little stand-offish, but polite and friendly, although he did make her feel uncomfortable at times. Not understanding why. Maybe it was all in her mind.

When it came time for Maggie to go to school, it was Elizabeth's job to get her there in the mornings and pick her up in the afternoons. The rest of the day was her own to do as she pleased. There wasn't enough time to go to the esplanade, so she became bored at times, and wondered what was going to happen when Maggie didn't need her anymore.

She saved all her money, occasionally spending on a new long skirt, blouse or jumper. Clothing didn't interest her very much. She was not able to wear high heels, so she felt that nothing looked good on her. Dolly always was dressed like she had stepped right out of a fashion magazine, making it hard for Elizabeth to imagine she could do any better than to stick with her comfortable outfits, hiding her orthopaedic shoes and limp.

Maggie was making friends at school and was having play dates. Elizabeth had the responsibility for meeting other parents and having them to the house. She was the Nanny and was accepted as nothing more. Polite hellos and goodbyes were all she got. She was never invited into the conversation or privileged to any gossip.

She became an outsider, knowing she would never belong in the upper-class world, even though she lived like one of them. The rich business world that Maggie would grow up in would take her away from Elizabeth eventually. Dolly assured her there would always be a place for her in the family, but somehow Elizabeth knew that would not be so.

Lottie was run off her feet without a minute to sit and talk the day Elizabeth really needed her company. She was lonely, something she had never acknowledged before.

'How much for thirty minutes?' the voice was rough and hard.

Elizabeth froze. 'Have you got somewhere to go?' It was her voice, but it was unrecognisable to her.

'I have a car. What's your name?'

'Rita,' she said, standing up. He didn't seem to notice her leg.

Lottie watched with tears in her eyes. She thought she had won with this beautiful girl.

'How much did you say?'

'It's free.'

Somehow, it did give her another freedom that took her to a different place, and as she became Rita with her rich flowing hair and beautiful smile, her fantasy world grew. And that's the way it was.

Three Thursdays of the month she became Free Rita. She had listened to the working girls for so long, she knew all their tricks, but she wasn't about to use the ones for the week of the bleed. That would be her day at the pier.

'I am sorry, Lottie. I know you never wanted me to go down that path, getting me the job and being my friend for so long, and I love you for all you have done for me. I will never be able to thank you enough.' Elizabeth's voice trembled.

Lottie put her arms around her. She loved this sad girl so much too.

'You have taken the place of my daughter. You will live in my heart forever.'

The truth was, Elizabeth knew she would never fit in, and this form of closeness was filling a gap for her, as much as the men that took advantage of her.

Maggie grew into a beautiful girl and called Elizabeth her second mother. She said she would never let her go. Dolly and Gerry knew that Maggie didn't need Elizabeth's help anymore. They invited her to stay on as long as she wanted to. It was her home. Her time with Maggie was so precious to her that she took what she could get.

Chapter 4

The Boy In-Between
Joe

JOE COULDN'T BELIEVE HE was home. The world looked so different, as if he had just been born, and the time he had spent in the hospital had not been him at all. The only thing that seemed real at that time was Elizabeth. Now she was gone, although she would never leave his mind.

The home wasn't as familiar to him as he had thought it would have been. All those long days and nights, dreaming about the kitchen with Nancy's meals on the table. Nothing seemed the same as the dreams that had been waiting for this day. Had Joe walked into a stranger's house? His disorientation was extreme.

Going to his bedroom, thinking that would be where home would be. Joe didn't feel that was the answer. It was Jessie and Dot – seeing the cows, then he would know he was home.

'It is too early to go down to the milking shed, Joe,' his over-protective mother was saying.

'I have been waiting so long to see Dot and Jessie. Please Mum, let me go down to the shed and see them. I have thought of them every day,' Joe pleaded.

'We will have to tell him, Nance,' Bill said, turning his head away from Joe's gaze.

'Tell me what?' yelled Joe's trembling voice.

Nancy took Joe in her arms. 'Dot is dead. She was very old and just couldn't hang on until you got home.'

Bill had to continue although it was breaking his heart. 'It wasn't long after that that we lost Jessie too.' Tears filled Bill's eyes.

The world stood still, as if someone had taken a photo and nothing was to continue.

'We didn't want to tell you before you were better, Joe. We knew how disappointed you would be.' Nancy was crying too now.

'Disappointed! Disappointed! You should have told me. That was what kept me going. That's what I was coming home for. That was the whole point of survival, to cuddle Dot and Jessie. You had no right to hide that from me. I am not a dumb kid that just laid around feeling sorry for himself!' Joe screamed.

He ran from the room, leaving his parents with tears running into the crevasses of their faces that they had gained over the time of Joe's illness. They thought they had done the right thing for their boy. They only wanted to protect him from the realities of life. He had suffered so much at such a young age.

Bill and Nancy had met at the local Saturday night dance, held in the community hall. The first time Bill touched Nancy's hand was when they passed in the barn dance. There were always girls sitting on wooden benches along the east wall and the boys along the west, staring at each other over the dance floor. It was three weeks before Bill had the courage to ask Nancy for a dance.

Nancy Thomas and her family had moved into the area a few months prior when her father was employed to manage a property about three miles from the Pike place. The young couple were so shy it was weeks before Bill asked Nancy if they could meet on Sundays sometime. Nancy would ride her pony into town and Bill would ride his bike, meeting at the deserted sports oval where the awkwardness of their romance began.

It was four years before they married, when Nancy would challenge Bill's mother for her kitchen. Joan Pike and Bill had been alone since Bert had died unexpectedly from a heart attack just after Bill had left school. Their routine was set. Joan would light the stove that was stoked the night before with just enough embers to start with ease and boil the kettle for her first cup of tea.

Then she would call Bill to wake up, and they would meet at the shed. The milking over, they would return to the kitchen. Joan would cook bacon and eggs with toast. She would have her second cup of tea while Bill got the wood in for the stove and lit up the water heater ready for Joan's bath. She returned to the kitchen and soon the aroma of freshly-baked bread drifted through the house.

Bill would head out to the paddocks doing jobs that had been piling up after his father's death. Then it would be time for the afternoon milking before they knew it. Both executed their roles with pride. Joan knew that Bill had to bring his wife to the farm, although she was not sure how she was going to cope. She liked the girl and was happy for Bill, but thought her role in his life was going to be replaced.

The cows were the main priority. From her long, painted fingernails Joan deduced Nancy wasn't used to hard work. So, Nancy took over the house and Joan helped Bill with the milking. And the various jobs around the dairy.

It wasn't long before Nancy was pregnant. Joan became more of an outsider in her own home, but did her best, and was looking forward to the arrival of her first grandchild. Nancy lost the baby. It died in the womb at nearly full term. This tragedy hit them hard. If it hadn't been for the cows, neither Nancy, Bill nor Joan would have ever got out of bed.

Joan's health deteriorated after that, and Bill carried the load alone. After his mother's death, Nancy lost another baby. The pair dragged themselves through the days like robots devoid of feelings. Two years passed until Joe arrived, the healthiest, most beautiful baby boy they had ever seen. They couldn't take their eyes off him. He sat in his pram, watching his mother and father milk until he could walk around doing small jobs that were invented for him. He was part of them, and the connection was so strong they felt it like a thread binding them together.

Joe knew nothing of his parents' hardships to save the farm, their battles to have a healthy child, or the devastation they felt when polio hit their boy. The trips to Melbourne and the impact of seeing him in the polio ward every weekend were exhausting.

Bill and Nancy worked through the week, anticipating seeing his face, even if it was pale, drawn, and lifeless. They anxiously waited for the doctor's report. This would become their life until they could bring their miracle boy home. Joe never knew any of the battles his parents had to endure over the time they had been together, or that he should have been the youngest of three boys.

As he laid on his bed that he had been waiting to get back to for so long, Joe sobbed. He hated his parents for not telling him about Dot and Jessie. He felt like a fool, loving two dead cows. He had told Elizabeth that when he got home, he would spend time with them and catch up, telling them the many stories that needed sharing.

He felt he was such a baby, crying over two dead cows. Farmers lose their animals all the time. It was part of being a strong man. Well, he wasn't a man, he was a kid. How was he going to become a man with parents that didn't give him credit to be able to accept the truth? He realised that he was arguing with himself. Was he a man or a child? No, he was in an in-between world that had crept up over the time lost in the polio ward. That had been his home, and Elizabeth was his friend. Oh, how he needed her now! He sobbed himself to sleep. Bill and Nancy were devastated again. What had they done to their beautiful boy?

JOE WENT BACK TO school. Everyone made him very welcome. He fit right back in, and it wasn't long before he caught up with the others in the grade. The teacher praised his hard work. Schoolwork was a diversion from his home life. The bond he had in the past with his parents was broken. As much as Bill and Nancy tried to break down the wall that Joe had built around himself, it couldn't be moved.

Joe started to play the drums at school and joined the dance band that was becoming the new love in his life. It helped him overcome his heartbreak over Dot and Jessie. The band master, Mr. Deer, encouraged Joe to practise after school. Sometimes he'd miss the bus, making it a long walk home.

They were the times Joe wondered what Elizabeth was doing, and how she was coping with that old bat of a grandmother. At least his parents hadn't deserted him. They'd only held back the truth to protect him. On reflection, maybe he was an ungrateful brat.

As the sun was going down, he prayed that Elizabeth was happy. He always felt a little guilty that he had walked away from polio without any disabilities, only tiredness that he dealt with easily. Poor Elizabeth had been left with her limp.

Joe was in a new world now. Music was taking over his mind. He was preoccupied with the band, and the songs that filled his head. Sometimes he went down to the shed and helped with the milking, only because he thought he was being selfish, and his guilt got the better of him. He was a self- absorbed teenager, that's what he told himself, as if that was allowed.

Bill nearly lost his patience with Joe at times. Though decided to let him come around in his own time. But it was taking longer than both Bill and Nancy had thought it would. They were heartbroken that such a simple thing had fractured their family. Bill would say to Nancy, 'Time will heal all problems, wait and see. Our boy will come back to us. Just wait.'

Joe became a full-time drummer in an adult band that travelled around the district, playing every Saturday night at local dances. Joe Pike was becoming famous. He was tall and handsome. His blonde hair was longer than most styles the young ones were wearing at this time. It made him stand out, and his piercing blue eyes were getting him the nickname, Paul Newman.

'He's getting too cocky for his own good,' some were saying. Joe easily got a girl – he was always the best looking in every town. He told each one they were the only one he cared about, spinning a web that was going to trap him before long. The older members of the band could see where his good looks and smart mouth were going to take him, and that trouble that was brewing for this talented young man.

Nancy adored her boy. If only she could tell him, or he would listen. When she tried, he was polite, but he turned away as soon as he could.

Joe could see his parents were getting older, and the work was getting them down. Some days his conscience got the better of him and he started to go to the shed every afternoon. He was too lazy to get up in the mornings. The weekends were hard work, and he had a lot of catching up to do. His image needed to be protected.

Joe Pike was becoming well-known. His fame was growing, reaching Sydney and Melbourne. Why did he have to milk the cows? They meant nothing to him now, just bad childhood memories.

As the sun went down, he never forgot Elizabeth, and prayed. He knew she would be doing the same.

Singing was the next step in his musical pursuits. He thought being a handsome singer would give him an edge. Nancy and Bill listened to him practising in his room, loving the sound of his voice. If that was the only part of him he would share with them, they had to be grateful.

The reason for the wedge that had divided them was almost forgotten. Sometimes it was hard to remember why Joe had divorced himself from them. He was the baby they had worked so hard for and doted on, watching his every movement from birth.

Nancy came down with the flu and was unable to get out of bed. Bill asked Joe if he could he please get up and help with the morning milk.

Joe did get up to help his father. The morning was frosty. Joe never remembered it being so cold.

'Gee Dad, of all mornings you expect me to get out of bed!'

Bill saw red. If Nancy had been there, he wouldn't have said anything, but this was the last straw. His son was the most ungrateful, selfish bastard he had ever met.

'Maybe it is time you got out and stopped taking advantage of your mother and me. You are holding one little mistake that we made against us. We thought we were doing the right thing, saving you the grief of losing the cows. Maybe we didn't know how much they meant to you, or what effect the polio had on your mind. All we did was love you. And you've repaid us with cruelty.'

'I will think about going then. That will solve all your problems. Let's get this milking done.'

Bill knew Nancy would have objected to any confrontation, and the attack on Joe about the way he was treating them. Years of silence, turning his back on his parents – a 'hello, goodbye, no thanks, yes please.' It was becoming so tense. Nancy's nerves were becoming raw. It was obvious that Joe wasn't going to discuss that whole affair, so Bill let it go. Maybe if he had to look after himself for a time, seeing the errors and the hurt caused to the two people that cared about him more than anyone else ever would, things might change.

Joe wasn't ready to leave. He was waiting for an opportunity to make it big in the world of entertainment. It was one thing to be well-known around the district. Waiting until an offer came from one of the big cities was the plan. His voice was improving, and he started to scribble words into songs. The more he wrote, the more he delved into his feelings. Before the songwriting everything was in the minute, on the surface, lacking deep thought, being impulsive. One of the older band members had said to him one day, 'Don't get too smart, Joe, before you can back up what you are doing and saying.'

That thought popped into his mind after Bill had made the point of the unkindness that he had been practising. Maybe Joe should try harder to put his coolness behind him and look at things from his parent's point of view. He had lost himself. Where had the Joe that they knew gone?

When he was lying in the hospital. That had been his true self, being Elizabeth's friend, a boy that had a heart that wanted to survive, walk, and run; to be worthy of the life that was given to him. For the first time after the encounter with his father, Joe really looked at Nancy. He had forgotten loving her cuddles, curling up on her knee, the good night kisses and the smile in the morning when she saw his face – all before the polio. Everything was before and after. Polio had stolen so much of his childhood. It occurred to Joe that he had taken it all out on his parents, blaming them when he should have been blaming the disease.

Nancy noticed the change in Joe; he asked her how she was feeling and hoped she had a nice day, sometimes he smiled. She hung onto every little piece of Joe that a mother craved.

He was helping with the milking now, sometimes saying to his mother, 'You have a rest today. Dad and I will manage.' The joy she got from his singing, muffled by the closed bedroom door, was the delight of her day. The house seemed to change, becoming a home again. Harmony and calmness were emerging, a laugh here and there, the mother instinct knew the waiting would pay off. Nancy never knew Bill had brought Joe to his senses.

There was a warmer feeling in the Pike home, although it would never be the same. How could it be? Joe was a man now. It was all before and after the polio. They did laugh again, and when Nancy ask Joe what he was up to, he answered and filled her in on all the gossip around the area. They were finally putting the bad dream behind them.

Joe worked in collaboration with the piano player from the band to get his songs together. When he wasn't on the drums, he would be the lead singer. Rock and roll was taking over the world. Bill Haley and 'Rock Around the Clock' was changing the beat of the drum. Elvis Presley was moving the music world in new directions too. Joe had to stick with what he knew – swing and crooning. That was the old-time dance world. The country people still didn't want to move into the rock and roll music.

Joe sang all his original songs. The slow waltzes were appealing. Everyone loved him, although the girls weren't flocking around the strong farm boy the way they had done before dancing had been spiced up.

Bobby Herd was the main man that did all the bookings and arrangements for the band. He soon saw that their popularity was falling. John Miles was on piano. Betsy Holland was an old girl. No-one could guess her age; her makeup was so thick. It was hiding years of secrets. She was on the clarinet and an overweight Jacky Munro was on cello. They had become Joe's friends, all having seen so much more of life than him.

Their common bond was music, and they had all taken Joe under their wing and helped him develop. Proud of his achievements, they had watched him grow from a boy to a fine young man, all hoping that the girls wouldn't be his downfall.

Bobby didn't play an instrument. He just managed the band Herd's Herd. That name was fine for country folk. It wouldn't go down in the big city so well and he knew it. Bobby was thinking of giving it all up. This modern world wasn't for him, although, how could he let the others down? He didn't know the other members were having the same thoughts.

Finally, the time came that Herd's Herd was to split. They were booked to play in their hometown, Little River. Everyone over the age of eight was there. The old hall felt as if it was moving off its foundations. Nancy and Bill had come. They didn't go out very often. The farm was sapping all their energy now. They were getting older.

Joe had told Nancy, 'You had better come. I have a surprise for you Mum. You had better be able to stay awake until the end of the band's final night.'

Joe wondered if there would be any country dances being held in a few years, not that it would be his worry. He had been approached by Albert Productions in Sydney to let them hear more of his music, with the prospect of a recording contract. He didn't tell anyone that he would be leaving within the week. His mum and dad would be disappointed, but Joe knew they wouldn't hold him back. It was the happiness of their boy that was important.

The last song was going to be Joe's surprise.

Joe trembled as he took the microphone. 'I would like to dedicate this song to a very special person who has always been there for me, even when I have deserted her.'

The band was to play their final piece together.

Joe sang from the bottom of his heart in the sweetest tone, showing love the best way possible.

'Oh, my dear Nancy, my lovely pretty fancy
A rhapsody of devotion,
Melodies of thankful reflection
There were times in my mind I drifted away,
The strength of your love made me stay.
The warmth of your loving embrace,
The thrill of seeing your loving face.
A mother's soft caresses,
Was the foundation for all my successes,
With the collaborating of our souls,
I am reaching my goals.
My lovely pretty fancy
Fiddle-dee-dee it's just you and me,
Your love is the key.
With your forgiving love, you are a blessing.
Our hearts beat to the same drum,
Because you are my beautiful mum
I love you my dear fancy Nancy.'

THERE WAS A HUSH over the hall that seemed to last forever to Joe, then everyone roared and cheered. No-one heard the lingering sound coming from the clarinet. Betsy had played her last note. The curtain came down.

Nancy couldn't move. Her Joe had taken her breath away. His charm had melted into the soul that had given birth to perfection in her eyes. The words and his sweet voice vibrated into a mother's heart that felt alive for the first time in many years. The pride Nancy felt was going to sustain her for the rest of her life. The heartache of Joe's childhood had vanished. Her boy had become a beautiful man.

Chapter 5

One Decision, One Mistake, One Lie, Would Turn to Many
Joe

NANCY WOULD DO ANYTHING for Joe, even give up her Austin A40 that she used to drive into town for shopping, visiting with friends or going to the other love of her life: the Country Women's Association.

There were only two vehicles on the farm, Nancy's Austin and Bill's paddock ute. Bill got to work on the old ute so it would be in a condition that Nancy could drive into town, thus allowing Joe to take the Austin to Sydney. Joe was putting an end to everything he had known, never going back to Melbourne since he left the hospital, as a child.

He didn't remember much of the city, this journey to a new world was starting to be overwhelming. His nerves were sapping his confidence. To be thought of as a talent in the country didn't mean he would make it in Sydney, and Joe knew it.

Bill and Nancy were convinced that the opportunity was too good to miss. After he had sung to Nancy, she thought he could take on the world, and sing his way into anyone's heart. The years of despair that the family had endured seemed to be forgotten.

The band had dispersed. With the death of Betsy, the others found it easy to retire, content to play their music alone, in their own space and time. Bobby Herd had given Joe a few names and addresses to check out if his deal with Albert Productions didn't come off. Bobby knew the industry, knew that the music world was so fickle, and more so in Sydney than the farming community that was Joe's world. Bobby had given it a go when he was young and naïve without much success. He had higher hopes for Joe.

Everyone wished Joe all the luck in the world. He was very popular in Little River. All Nancy's friends thought he was too handsome and charming to be a farmer. She had never told them about the disappointing time they had after the polio. They always put on a brave, happy face when going into town. So, in their eyes he was a perfect son, with his blonde hair and blue eyes, and the strength of a marble statue. Yes, Joe was what every girl and mother wished for. Nancy had wondered why Joe had never brought a girl home. She was sure there were girls around her boy. If asked, he would never say anything enlightening. They never meant enough to him to go out with them for long, or music meant more to him than any girl from around here. Maybe he would find love in Sydney. Nancy secretly hoped for grandchildren.

As Joe drove towards Melbourne, he thought about Elizabeth. He knew if he tried to find her and did, he would never make it to Sydney. They had written to each other, but the letters became fewer and fewer as they'd moved on with their lives. Joe knew why he wasn't as keen to keep in touch. He didn't think Elizabeth would approve of his casual attitude and lack of respect for the female sex. Most of the boys in the town paired up with a girl from school or the church and that was it – married before they knew it. That wasn't for him.

He had seen how easy it was to get a girl. They crowded around after the band had finished. He just took his pick and fooled around with the prettiest, always leaving before he got too involved. His virginity was still intact. He had seen too many of the older boys get caught getting a girl pregnant, and they'd be stuck with her for the rest of their lives. No, Joe had to be free to pursue his ambitions.

Some of the locals were saying Joe Pike was getting too big headed for his own good, and that Sydney would take him down a peg or two. Nancy didn't let the locals spoil her hopes for him. She knew her boy had talent and deserved to have success.

Joe had a lot of time to think, driving alone. He had never felt this depth of loneliness before. He sang his way through each mile. He was starting to see musical notes in the tall crops that lined the highway, seeing music in the trees that danced as he sped passed them. There were notes dotted along the power lines that hummed mysterious sounds. He opened the windows. The birds and the moving car all made music. Music was his world. He heard it everywhere. The cows, the farm, the country life. That was all behind him. Now he was free.

In between the songs, he started to talk to himself, trying to make sense of life. So far, there was so much that he had done that was to be never understood. The major stuff up was the treatment of his parents when he came home from the polio ward. He wondered why he'd cared so much about the pet cows. He went over his wretched treatment of the girls that had hung around in the early days of the band.

Joe stopped to give two hitchhikers a lift. It was the loneliness and the fact that he was starting to worry about talking to himself. The answers springing to mind weren't impressive.

'Where are you heading? Can I give you a lift?'

'We are trying to make it to Sydney. How far are you going?'

'To Sydney. Hop in then and see how we go. You might get sick of my singing.' There was no comment from the men. Joe had expected them to say they would like it if he sang a tune or two.

They were much older than Joe and didn't have much to say for a couple of hours. Joe was starting to think he should have kept going.

'I had planned to stay in a pub for the night. Are you doing the same?' Joe asked.

They had exchanged names but that was about all. Nothing had been asked or said to indicate as to what they were up to. Joe pulled into a pub at dusk, just in time to get a room and say a quick prayer for

Elizabeth. Why he prayed to a God he didn't believe in, or for someone he might never see again, was baffling. It was like cleaning his teeth. The prayer was part of the body memory. It just happened now. He wondered if she still prayed for him. There was a small inkling like a whisper. He knew that's what kept him safe, but he didn't believe in this God that hung from the sky.

He ran the tap in the basin in the small room, splashing water to refresh his tired face. He gave the hair a quick comb, then headed to the bar, expecting to see his two passengers there having a drink, but the room was empty, except for a man at the far end of the bar. He pulled up a stool and ordered a beer. He was not a big drinker, but the band always had one or two after a gig, just as a settler before heading home. Or that's the way it had been for Joe.

'On your way to Sydney, are we?' the bloke behind the bar asked.

'Yep, a new adventure. I have a meeting with a recording company,' he replied, feeling as though it would impress the barman.

'We see a lot of you young fellows passing through full of hope. Sometimes they call in on the way back.'

'I don't think I will be coming back. I'm out of Victoria. Might have to go back to see Mum and Dad some time when it suits me though.' Joe's voice was full of confidence. He wasn't going to let this grumpy bloke spoil his dreams. 'I play the drums and sing.'

'Rock and Roll, that's all they want now.'

'No, just can't get into it.'

'Well good luck then, but I don't like your chances of getting much work in Sydney. Though I hear the cabaret scene is still strong. You might fit in there.'

The bartender walked away, going to talk to the other customer. Joe felt a little defeated and he had just got over the border into New South Wales. He ordered a meal and sat at a corner table, missing Nancy suddenly. Maybe it was because of what was placed on the table – lamb cutlets. She always made them for him when he didn't feel well. He remembered the promise to ring when he got to Sydney. He felt like talking to her now. Joe was so mad with himself, acting, in his mind, like a baby. He had thought he was over being his mother's boy. Maybe he wasn't.

Joe felt guilty about the way he'd treated his parents after the polio, and his mother had forgiven him so easily for a few words he had written in a song. 'One day I will make amends.' He told himself over and over.

He slept heavily. It had been a long drive in the little, dark-blue Austin A40. His mother loved that car. In his half-awake state Joe realised that was another thing Nancy had given up for her ungrateful son. He was anxious to get on the road. He would have a quick breakfast, fill the tank with petrol and he would get to Sydney before dusk.

Joe hadn't seen the hitchhikers and was hoping they had got a ride with someone else. He was not in the mood for company today, beginning to doubt that the trip would be worthwhile, after the comments from last night's conversation with the bar tender.

The sun was shining, and the countryside was looking lush, a slightly different landscape from Victoria, but still had the Australian uniqueness. It was an adventure that would set him on a new path. He should be over the moon, not down in the dumps like a spoilt baby. Just as Joe was about to drive off, the back door opened, and the boot flew up. One of the strange men was throwing their bags in. Both hopped in the back seat. It took Joe by surprise.

'Oh, I thought you two must have moved on when I didn't see you around the pub anywhere,' Joe said, showing his surprise. He wanted to tell them to get out, but he was a country boy, and you never leave any one on the road if you can give them a lift.

'Where did you boys spend the night?'

'Under the stars,' Greg replied.

'Okay then. We better get going.' It was obvious to Joe they didn't want to tell him anything about their plans or what they were up to. He was becoming suspicious of the pair, and they were in the back seat of Nancy's car. Joe was becoming very uncomfortable.

'Would one of you like to ride in the front? You could take it in turns.' It was a small car and would have been a tight ride with two big men in the back seat.

'We're right in the back, it's all good.' Steve said in a cocky voice.

'Where did you get this heap of shit, anyway? I doubt it will get us there.'

Joe was about to answer but decided to let it go, his mood dropping lower. He wanted to sing, but knew it would offend the passengers, so kept quiet. The miles rolled by, and Nancy's car chugged along like a faithful friend.

Joe knew these men were Aussies. They definitely had the accent. They were dressed alike, both wearing a felt fedora, a blue shirt with a brown tie, tweed jacket and well-tailored trousers. They could have been businessmen but for their heavy black boots and their gladstone bags. Something didn't look right to Joe.

'Have you a job in Sydney waiting for you?'

'Just sight-seeing kid,' one of them said after a minute, as if he had to think about it. Joe knew they didn't want to talk, which didn't lighten his mood. The miles rolled by in silence.

'I'll be stopping to get a pie and to fill the tank soon. You two must be hungry.'

'You do what you like kid. We'll tell you when we need to stop. Just wish this heap of junk would move a bit faster,' Steve said in a muffled voice. Joe was starting to get nervous. He was a country kid who hadn't been around much by himself, and always had the older band members to shelter him from the outside world. If he couldn't cope with a couple of strangers, how was he going to manage in the biggest city in Australia? Butterflies flittered around in his stomach, as they drove on in silence.

They were in the middle of nowhere when suddenly Greg yelled, 'Stop!'

Joe slammed on the brakes and the little Austin skidded onto the gravel. Beads of sweat covered Joe's forehead.

Oh my God they are going to kill me, Joe thought.

They silently left the car and went into the bushes beside the road. Joe could see a large van parked up ahead. It seemed they were heading there. He was so scared, almost frozen. If he had wanted to drive away, it wasn't possible. Then he thought about taking off. They hadn't said to stay. Maybe they didn't want him to, but they didn't say to go either. Maybe they would get a ride with the van, then he would be free to go. His hands gripped the steering wheel. His knuckles turned white. The fear was stronger than he had ever felt. Even the polio had never put him in this state.

The men had reached the van, creeping towards the back door. Greg opened it slowly while Steve stood back. Joe heard two shots and saw a man slump to the ground from the back door. One of the hitchhikers was lying on the ground. It must have been Greg, because Steve ran to the cabin and took the van at high-speed north. Joe knew he had to try and help the men that had been shot.

He drove slowly towards them. Neither had moved, indicating they were dead. Joe had seen too many animals on the farm to know dead when he saw it. He moved the car as close as he could. He was not sure the van wouldn't return. He knew these two weren't going to harm him.

He could drive away, and no-one would track him down. One of the men moved slightly, leading Joe to think he had better get them to help or the police. The next town wasn't too far away. Somehow, he managed to get them into the back seat. Another thing that he learnt on the farm was how to move a carcass. He hated putting them in Nancy's beloved car and hoped she would never find out.

Joe heard a moan. He wasn't sure if both may be alive. Driving on until he reached the small town. He wondered if it was big enough to have a doctor. How lucky, he thought when he saw a sign for a nursing hospital. He rang the bell three times before a bleary-eyed old woman opened the door.

He explained that he had come across these men on the road,

hurt, or maybe dead. Joe had decided not to say anything about the passengers.

The old nurse looked in the car and felt both for a pulse. 'This fellow has a slight one, but not sure if there is any hope for either of them. All a bit out of my realm, gunshot wounds. We don't have them too often, or should I say, never. I had better wake the doctor. He won't be too happy.'

Joe thought she must have been joking as it was only mid-afternoon. It did seem to be a sleepy hollow all the same. It wasn't long before a battered old car came screaming up behind Joe's car, and a portly old man scuffled over to Joe and the nurse.

'What have we got, Gladys? Gunshot wounds? That's exciting.'

'I thought they both were dead, but one has a slight pulse. Do you want me to call in Jennifer? We might need her help.'

'Yep. We might have to call the police too.' Gladys moved inside to make her phone calls, leaving Joe with the Doctor.

'We don't see too much of this sort of stuff around here. How did this happen, do you know?'

Joe turned his head away, saying, 'No, I just came across them on the road.' He wasn't a good liar, but he didn't see the point of getting involved. It wasn't like he knew who these people were, or why this had happened.

Joe thought that as soon as they got the men out of the car, he would be able to move on and get to Sydney as planned. As soon as Jenifer arrived, the four of them got them inside onto a trolley and the doctor went to work. Joe was just about out the door when a policeman came into the hallway, blocking him from going.

'So, you are the one that brought them in then, are you?' He was younger than the others; a strong-looking fellow. Just what you would expect a policeman to be, Joe thought.

'Yes, that's right, but I don't know anything about them. I just came along the road, and they were in front of me. I am on my way to Sydney. I have an appointment tomorrow.' Joe was getting nervous, and it showed in his voice. He knew the policeman would pick up on it. This wasn't working out the way he'd thought. He hoped they would say 'go', and that would be the end of it.

That might have been the case in Little River, where everyone knew him. Why hadn't he told them the truth? It was still nothing to do with him, but now it would sound like he had something to hide. The doctor announced one dead. The policeman, Jackson the others called him, had started to go through his pockets for any identification. There was none. A wave of nausea overcame Joe when he remembered the gladstone bags in the boot of the car.

The one that seemed to have a chance of life started to come around. The doctor was sending the nurses into the operating room to set up, so he could get the bullet out. 'Hurry girls, we haven't got a lot of time. He's lost a lot of blood.'

Turning to Joe and Jackson, the doctor asked if they knew their blood type. The policeman said he was B positive. Joe wanted to say he didn't know so he could get out of the situation that, through no fault of his own, he now was stuck in. Joe couldn't do it when a life was in danger, so he told the truth.

'I am A positive.' He hoped that the almost-dead bloke didn't have the same.

'We will test the patient and let you know if we need your help.'

'Okay, Doc. We'll be here,' the policeman said.

Joe wished he hadn't remembered what his blood type was from his polio days. He sat there in this unknown town with this policeman named Jackson, wanting to spew. He looked at the green walls that surrounded him. Why was his adventure turning into a nightmare?

'Come on Joe, you're a match. If we're going to save this fellow, we need your blood,'

Joe sat there keeping his eyes shut as his blood ran into the near-dead man while the old Doctor poked around to find the bullet. When it was over, Joe had decided he had to tell Jackson the truth and go and get the bags out of the boot. He knew hiding the story wasn't going to happen.

'So, Joe, you might have to show me where you picked up these two. The one they have saved looks like a tradesman of some sort, but I am not sure. They're both a mystery. I can't pick their profession at all.'

'I have a confession. I didn't tell you everything that I know, which isn't much, but you might be able to make some sense of it. I am so out of my comfort zone I don't know what to do.' Joe's voice was breaking up. He thought he might cry.

Jackson could see he was an innocent kid and never made an issue of him not being up front from the start.

Joe went out and got the bags from the car. Seeing all the blood on the back seat of Nancy's car was hard to accept. What had he done? Why wasn't he content to stay home with the cows? That was more his world, not out here in this mess.

Joe told Jackson everything he could think of and gave him the gladstone bags. He hoped that would be it, and he could get on his way. He told himself never to pick up a hitchhiker again. Joe stood up to leave.

'Not so fast, Joe. We must go back to where this all happened. I will have a look in these bags first.' But Jackson found them locked. He would have to get the locksmith to have a go at them. 'Hop in my car and I will drop the bags off to the locksmith. Then you can show me where this crime was committed.'

Hearing Jackson say 'crime' frightened Joe. He didn't want to be involved in a crime. His head was spinning. This was a surreal situation that he could not comprehend. Joe showed Jackson the area where the men were shot. Jackson told Joe to stay in the car. Joe watched as Jackson picked up bits and pieces off the ground and put a marker there in case he wanted to come back.

'Did you find anything?' Joe asked on the way back to town.

'No, nothing really. It was as if there had been another car there though, Other than yours and the van, and the bloodstains had been disturbed, almost gone. There must have been a fair bit I imagine. This is a strange one, something to tell your folks about when you get home.'

Joe hoped he would never have to tell Nancy and Bill about any of it. All he wanted to do at this stage was get rid of the blood off the back seat of the car.

'Will I be able to get going now?' Joe sounded like he was pleading.

'No, sorry mate. There will be a few more questions. I have called the guys in from Sydney to go over it with me. They will want to talk to you and will have to go over the car. So, staying is the only option. It has to be the night here.'

'But I have an appointment tomorrow with a production company. It's my big chance.'

'Sorry Joe, this is what happens sometimes when you are helping out strangers – bit risky, hah!' Joe felt that this small-town cop was laughing at him. If he didn't ring Nancy tonight, she would be worried. If he told her that he didn't make it to Sydney, she would ask why. If he lied, she would know. He couldn't tell his mum what really was going on. Telling her that he would make it to the appointment tomorrow, that's all that mattered. Knowing he was okay, sounding happy and bright for the phone call would satisfy. Another night in a pub. Hungry and tired. He had never had a day like this one. Joe hoped this adventure wouldn't throw up more problems, all beyond belief.

For now, he ended the day with another bartender that knew everything.

'You the guy that brought the dead blokes in, are yah?'

'Only one was dead,' Joe replied. He didn't want to talk about it.

'Oh, yah, only half dead.'

Joe didn't answer. He took his beer and went and sat in the corner again. He watched the locals gossiping, looking over at him every now and then. It wasn't hard to know what they were talking about. The public phone was outside the hotel, so it was easy to make his call home, and to Ted at Albert Productions. He didn't sleep well and was very sluggish in the morning. It was only a short walk to the police station. He just hoped that they would let him go, though his enthusiasm for the trip was diminishing and his ambition for fame had faded. The detective that had arrived from Sydney was waiting as he walked through the door. 'So, you're the one that saw what happened. Come this way. Now tell me your story exactly from when you first met these men. Everything, every little detail.'

'Okay.' He took a seat, realising he wasn't going to get out of here any time soon.

Joe found out that the blokes' names weren't Greg and Steve. The information in the gladstone bags did tell the police the hitchhikers names. They had no idea who the other one was, no evidence as to which was which. They told Joe nothing about what they had found. There was a mentioned of contraband. Joe didn't want to know. It was all too much for him, coming from his sheltered country life. Jackson asked if he knew if the two men that had been shot were the hitchhikers. Joe hesitated. Would it be better to say, 'Yes', and that would be the end of the story?

'Are they both dead, or did my blood save one?'

'We would rather not say,' the Sydney cop said.

'Yep, they were the ones that got in my car. Can I take my car now, please?'

The answer was a sharp 'No.'

It was late afternoon when they finally said he could go, after leaving all his information and contact details, giving his home address too, which Joe wasn't happy about. What if they rang Nancy? He would have to tell his parents the whole story. He just couldn't do it today.

That wasn't the worst of it, leaving the car and being told to take the bus. Leaving Nancy's car behind was a wrench he wasn't prepared for. He was overwhelmed with sadness as he boarded the bus for Sydney.

Joe knew this was not the end of this nightmare.

He hoped that the room booked at the YMCA would be still available on his arrival, though he wondered if he would ever get there. Joe stared out the window, watching the countryside that had spoken with positivity when the journey started. Now it seemed to echo with impending gloom.

Watching the miles roll by, there was no tune, no melody in the landscape. Even the birds seemed to have lost their voices. Why had the music gone?

Chapter 6

The Expectations of Youth
Joe

JOE MADE IT TO the appointment with Ted a day late. Nerves were beyond his control. The past days had taken a measurable toll on Joe. Loss of confidence and lack of desire for the music were weighing heavily on Joe's shoulders. Surprisingly, he got through the audition with more confidence than expected. The country singer didn't feel too bad.

'Thanks Joe. I realise you must be tired after the long trip. I will go over the tapes and see what I can come up with.' With a kind voice, Ted said he would get back to him in a few days.

Joe felt composed after the meeting. Maybe there was a chance for him in this unknown world that he hoped would become his life. He set off to explore the city and get his bearings. The hustle and bustle were all a bit much to take in, and he wondered how long it would be before he could accept the noise as normal. He was Joe Pike, a farm kid from country Victoria and he was in Sydney. He wondered what Elizabeth would think. Funny, she didn't even know he could sing. On reflection, Joe wondered what talent she had now that she was grown up. It was so long since they had known each other, he pondered, remembering her beautiful eyes.

Joe was thinking that he had missed his big chance when he hadn't heard from Ted as the days turned into weeks. Getting a job was important. The money that he had saved and the donation from Nancy and Bill wouldn't last forever. He would have to check out the names Bobby Herd had given him. That became a challenge. A couple had died, and one had moved to Melbourne. He did find one chap, a lucky break.

Matt Thorpe was in his late fifties and was living in a back room of an old pub that he played his clarinet in most nights. Remembering his days with Bobby with lots of chuckles, Joe believed he was only telling him stories that would be acceptable to a kid he didn't know. Just by chance, the drummer of the combo that Matt played in had left, so Joe could step in if he liked, no strings attached. If something better came along, then he would be free to go. Joe jumped at the chance. He would be able to get out of the YMCA. Hoping to find a private room. However, he would like something better than Matt was living in. City life was hard after the farm.

He found a room with a window that gave him a view of a brick wall. It had a bed that had a mattress that looked a little lumpy, in a boarding house on George Street, not far from the pub. He still had to share a bathroom. There were many signs everywhere saying, 'Please keep clean for the next person.' But he could get a midday meal with the price of the rent, and it was an easy walk after closing from his night of playing, bringing music back into his soul.

The owner of the boarding house was a cheery lady about Nancy's age, with a ruddy, round face, indicating to Joe that her evenings may be taken up with a drink or two; but she made Joe feel welcome, and the smell that was coming from the kitchen reminded him of home. It seemed comfortable. He hoped it wouldn't be for long, all the same.

'Call me Ginger. That's what they call me, Joe. I'm happy to have you join the boarding house family. That's what you all are to me. I haven't got any family left of my own, so I pretend you lot are. So, I'll look after you good. Only boys though, no girls. They only come with trouble.' She giggled to herself.

'Thanks Ginger, that will be nice. I get a bit lost, missing my mum like a baby sometimes.'

'Come for a chat any time, love. I'm always here to help with anything. I like to look after my boys.'

Ginger's warm, animated smile baffled Joe. He had never met anyone like this lady before. Not surprisingly, she didn't look like she had ever been on a farm. Her hair was dyed black, a bit of a tangled mess really.

We do come from different worlds that's for sure, he thought.

The boarding house was like a rabbit warren. Passages and doors everywhere, most on the ground floor with stairs leading to Ginger's private quarters. There was a heavy chain across the open stairs hooked to the banisters, with a large sign reading 'PRIVATE'. Joe got the message loud and clear that no-one was going up those stairs uninvited.

Joe's room was right at the back of one of the long passages, and the bathroom was down another. It was a bit of a hike and, if it was occupied, it was most annoying. At this stage of his adventure, he had to suck it up. 'One day I will be in the money and get something better.' Joe was always dreaming.

Sydney was more advanced than Melbourne in those days. Bars stayed open until ten pm, although many stayed late into the night behind closed doors to listen to the music. Joe enjoyed his job and the members of the band, along with Matt, were taking him under their wings. It was very laid back, so Joe started to relax and put the van and the two murdered men behind him … until the day he saw Steve, or that was what Joe knew him as.

Joe was about to cross the road. Just as he stepped off the curb, he felt a hand grab his arm. Seeing this man that Joe believed had shot both Greg or whatever his name was, and the driver of the van, left him breathless.

'Let's talk kid.' The familiar voice scared Joe. He couldn't speak.

The killer led Joe to the back of a small café and sat him at a table against a wall, out of sight of other customers. Joe feared for his life.

'I suppose you think I killed those two blokes that day on the road. Well, I didn't. There must have been someone else in the bushes. That's why I took off. We were just going to check out the van and come back to you and continue to our destination.'

'So, what do you want with me then? I don't know anything.' Joe's voice trembled.

'I heard you took the men to the hospital and talked to the police. What did you tell them?' Steve, or what-ever-his name-was, squeezed Joe's arm hard. Joe almost yelled.

'Shut up or it will be harder, and you won't be able to make a sound again.' The man's eyes pieced through Joe like a knife.

'Did you keep the bags we left in the boot?'

'No, I gave them to the police.'

'Well, that was a silly move.'

'I didn't see what was in them. The police told me nothing. I know nothing about any of this and I told them only what I saw and that I helped the men. What did you expect me to do? Leave them there to die?'

'They are dead then.'

Joe realised that he didn't know whether his partner or the van driver was dead or alive. It had been kept out of the papers for some reason apparently. Joe had tried to put the experience out of his mind, and had done so, enjoying the band and the music for a time.

'The only thing I learnt was that Steve is not your name. But the police didn't tell me what your real name is. Was your real name in the bag?'

Joe's captor was quiet for a minute. 'Yes, that's right. So, you know nothing. You don't know if the two men you rescued are dead or alive, or if they told the police anything about what was in the truck?'

'No. They let me go after I gave them the bags. They knew I was staying at the YMCA, but I've moved now, so they won't know where I am anyway.' Joe was hoping that would be enough for this bloke to leave him alone. 'How did you find me?' Joe was brave enough to ask.

'Lucky break for me maybe. Not so for you though.' He smiled a smirky grin that scared Joe. 'Get out of here kid. I will be in touch.' He stood up to walk out.

'So, what was in the van that had caused two men to be shot then?' Joe surprised himself having the courage to ask.

'You don't want to know kid, or you might be next on the list.'

Joe couldn't move. He sat there in a daze; his healthy country skin was turning grey. He felt weak and was finding it hard to breathe. What if this bloke found out that it was my blood that saved the van drivers life? He was trapped in a deep, dark hole that he couldn't escape.

How was this happening to him? Joe sat there for some time, wishing he had never stopped and taken those two injured men to get help. If he had driven on, no-one would have known he was ever there at the scene of this mysterious crime. How he wished he had someone he could tell this story to and share his misery with.

He remembered the cows, how he'd talked to them. That thought made him realise that had been the reason his mind exploded when he found out that Jessie and Dot were dead. They were the keeper of his childhood secrets, his guilt, his pain when he was in the polio ward. He knew they would have been listening. They had taken the burden from him and given him comfort.

Now a man, he felt more vulnerable than he did then. Elizabeth, that's who he needed, Elizabeth. Did she ever need him? He buried his head in the comfort of his hands. Tears filled his eyes. He wanted to scream like a baby in this café in the middle of Sydney. Was this payback for hurting Bill and Nancy so much when he was a boy?

Joe wandered down to King Street, making up his mind to go into Albert Productions and see if Ted would talk about the future. He thought he would have to go home if nothing better came up. He wanted more than working at the pub, as much as he was enjoying it.

He was looking over his shoulder the whole time in case Steve popped up. It was making him jittery. He had to get Nancy's car back. He rang the police a couple of times, but the answer had been 'No not yet.' Joe felt like he was walking into quicksand every day, just waiting to sink.

Greeting Joe warmly, Ted took the boy into his office.

'I lost your contact number, Joe. I thought you must have moved on.'

Joe had let the girl at the front desk know he could be reached at the pub, so he started to get the message that there would be nothing for him here.

'We are not ready to take a chance on you now, Joe. The music scene is moving so fast, with the television and the international bands taking over the world. We are not sure where it's heading. If you could get out there and make a bit of an impression on the young ones around town, that might help.'

Joe explained that he was only drumming with a band in a pub on George Street and hadn't had a chance to sing. Ted said it was up to him to make it happen. Joe left dejected. The mood was becoming darker. He was lonely, scared, and yearning for home. Singing wasn't something he was in the mood for now. And having a pretty slim repertoire didn't help. Joe just wasn't up for the work that would be needed. He wished for someone like his old pal John Miles, the piano player from the old band, to get him on track again.

He wrote to Nancy and Bill, never giving them a hint about what was happening. He always sounded full of the good things that were on offer in the city. He told them he loved the place, and there were so many opportunities to aim for. Lie after lie. It was becoming easier with every letter.

Joe did have a love-hate feeling for the place. He was becoming more familiar with city life. When the sun shone, he would take a walk in the park and marvel at the harbour and the surroundings. He started to scribble lyrics. The words came easily, but the tunes evaded him.

Joe contemplated posting songs to John back in Little River for help. But then he thought that might be seen as a failure, a backward step. Pride was really his failing. He wrote to John saying that he had all the help needed from his new friends. More lies upon lies.

Joe finally revealed a couple of songs to Matt, asking if he thought he could get help with a tune and music.

'Do you think the fellows would let me sing some time?'

'Sure, Joe, let's see what they sound like when we rehearse. We have to get some music to back up your lyrics first. It could be fun. Don't expect much though. The crowds we get in here don't do much listening in depth to the words. It's the music they crave.'

Joe saw Matt's acceptance of the fact that he could put a song together was a step forward. It gave Joe a little confidence to keep going. Joe's mind was completely on the music and was putting the shooting in an abyss.

There were only a few chaps that stayed to have lunch with Ginger. Most had day jobs, so Joe didn't get to know many of the boarders. Stan was a night manager at an ice cream factory on the other side of the harbour. Joe asked why he didn't live over there near his work and not have to catch the ferry. He just said there were benefits, living at Ginger's place.

Joe didn't know what that was all about and didn't ask. They became friends and often spent the afternoons together. They chatted about their families and why they had come to Sydney. They were the same age but had come from completely different backgrounds, growing up with many different experiences. But somehow there was a bond that came with their age group. Both were born in the same year. They were a product of their time and that was what held them together, as if they understood each other – same code of manners, respect, and rules, whether it be the hypocrisies of life or not, that was their stamp of existence.

Ginger ran a tight ship. The rules were: Monday morning the bottom sheet of the bed and the two towels that were allotted for the week were to be left outside the door to be laundered. When the fellows got back to their rooms, they had to make their beds. The clean sheet was to be put on the top and the old one on the bottom. Once every two weeks she would vacuum, rotating the rooms. All doors were always to be left unlocked. There was never any theft. It was the manners and respect of the time.

If there was ever a problem, Ginger soon gave the culprit a quick kick up the bum and they were gone. It was a smooth operation, this quaint boarding house in the middle of Sydney. Joe thanked his lucky stars that he called Ginger's place home. He was coping better now that the music was back in his heart and the beat of the drum ran through his veins.

When he wasn't with Stan or at work, he would find a quiet place and sit under a tree or on a park bench and ponder. The lyrics would come to him. They didn't always fit into the song he was working on, but if they felt good, he put them in the back of his journal for another day. Finally, Joe was enjoying Sydney, even if there was a tree that reminded him of the paddocks at home.

Chapter 7

Dark Shadows Persist
Joe

JOE SINGS...

'Tender voices whispering low,
Memories drift away.
Secret mistakes the dark shadow
Melting hearts will sway.
Joining our velvet hands
Together floating through regrets
Voices with no demands
Leaving behind resentments.

Tender voices whispering low.
Memories drift away.
Secret mistakes the dark shadow
Melting hearts will sway.

Our trembling lips meet,
Gazing eyes dreaming

Hear the drumming of a heartbeat,
Both emotions steaming'

JOE SANG HIS HEART out on and on, delivering the love song. The band was placed right behind the performer. They gave him their support and the boost needed along the way. Joe felt so alive, jumping out of his body, never wanting to leave the stage. This was home. The crowd seemed to listen and that was proven when finally, the noise faded, and Joe took his bow. The drunk audience clapped and cheered.

I am on my way, Joe thought, stepping down from the stage with eyes on the floor. There was only one person that would wear work boots like that to a night out at the pub. He knew it was Steve before looking up.

'So, this is where you hang out, singing for your supper.' The smirk was all over this pest's face.

'Leave me alone. I don't know anything about your problem. Get out of my life.' Joe couldn't contain his anger and was about to walk away when Steve grabbed his arm.

'Not so fast, I have a few questions.'

Joe looked around. No-one seemed to be taking notice. There was fifteen minutes before the next set.

'Okay. Come outside and tell me what you want.' Joe wasn't about to tell him any more than had been said the last time this dark shadow had appeared.

'Why can't I find out if my partner and that bloke that was driving the truck are dead or alive?'

'How would I know? The police never told me anything more than I told you last time. I suppose if you haven't heard from Greg, he must be dead or hiding from you. I still can't get my car back.' Joe was mad with himself for telling Steve about the car.

'So, the police have your car. Why, what was in the car that they would want?' Steve seemed to panic.

'Because of the blood, I suppose.' *Oh God, why did I say anything about the blood?*

Steve grabbed Joe's jacket, pulling him up close, their faces almost touching, breathing the words that Joe had to swallow.

'I'll fucking kill you if you put me in this mess.'

'I think you got yourself in this mess, not me. I didn't want you to get in the car the second day. That was your idea. You were only using me, an innocent country kid who had never been to a big city. I know nothing of your world. Were you hoping to put the blame on me? What are you up to anyway? I am starting to think you got in my car for a reason. Are you ever going to tell me why you picked me to get a ride with, of all the cars on the road that would have been much faster than my mum's little Austin?' Joe was stunned that he had the guts to talk back to this bully.

'Just watch yourself. I'll be seeing yah.'

The best night he had since being in Sydney was now ruined. He now realised that he may be in danger, being a witness to a murder.

The boys in the band couldn't believe that Joe wasn't over the moon when work had finished, and they were on their last beer.

'Your song went over well, Joe. You should be happy with the audience's reaction.' Matt tried to get a smile out of Joe.

'I am, really. It is just that I have something else on my mind. Sorry, not in a party mood. I'll call it a night. Thanks for your support. I do appreciate it. We'll have another go at stunning the crowd. I have more songs that need music if you're all willing to give it a go.'

He got up to move away from the boys that had become friends. There was no way could he tell them about the stalker, or why he was being harassed.

'That's good, Joe. You did a great job. We're right behind you.' Matt was saying as the others lifted their glasses in a well-done gesture.

Joe walked home, jumping at every sound, car horn, and shadow. He didn't know what to fear. He wondered when Steve would appear again. He did believe Steve when he said he didn't shoot anyone.

He'd never seeing him with a weapon. Somehow, Joe knew Steve was involved in something. Why the men got into Nancy's car was a mystery that Joe wondered if ever would be answered.

Stan and Ginger had come to see Joe's debut song with the band, making him feel special, the start of a fan club maybe. Because of the upset, he hoped as he entered Ginger's Place, that they weren't around. He was not in the mood to talk after his visit from Steve.

As he entered the front door, Joe saw Stan hooking the barricade across Ginger's private stairs. He stayed in the dark hall until Stan turned down the passage to his room. Strange, seeing Stan coming down from Ginger's private apartment. Maybe they'd had a night cap.

Joe didn't sleep well. The image of Steve's face never left his mind. The success of the evening had been forgotten. Only nightmares circled, reliving the shooting over and over.

Joe heard Stan knock on his door before lunch. His shattered body couldn't move, exhausted from last night's drama. He decided to spend the day in bed and hide away from the world.

Joe found himself longing for the days in the polio ward when they laughed away the days, strength allowing. Why did he think more about Elizabeth when he was in a low mood? These days she was a woman, and if he passed her in the street, she would be unrecognisable to him. 'Maybe you should find yourself a real woman instead of relying on a childhood memory to keep you sane,' Joe almost yelled at himself. He wondered whether the memories were as true and wonderful as lingered in his mind.

What miracle was it that praying for Elizabeth at sunset, seemed to give the power needed to renew his strength? It was late afternoon when finally, Joe struggled out of bed and down to the bathroom. His reflection in the full-length mirror showed a naked man that stood over six foot tall, the strength of a giant and the physique of an athlete.

He was a handsome man with blonde hair and blue eyes. Joe felt he was looking at someone else. He only saw a scared child with one leg slightly slimmer than the other. He wished his mother was there as a protection, the mother that had been rejected as an enemy for so long. He stood there, disgusted with the image that had been given so much, but had given nothing in return. He turned around, looking into the mirror to see if he had a backbone.

'Grow up, you wimpy bastard!' Joe yelled at the image of a man he wasn't sure he wanted to be.

By the time Joe got to the pub, the bad night seemed to have vanished, and the beat of the drums took over. It was decided that every Friday night Joe would sing. As the weeks passed, the patron numbers doubled. Joe started to gather girls like in the old days. They clamoured to touch him, asking for an autograph, smiling, telling him how handsome their hero was. He could have had whatever he asked for.

Joe always went home alone. A couple of times he thought, she doesn't look bad, but he quickly changed his mind, not wanting the involvement.

The boys in the band started to joke about Joe's lack of interest in girls. They asked if he wanted a boyfriend instead. He wondered about himself at times, but no, Joe liked girls. It just never seemed to be the right time or the right girl. Joe kept writing love songs that seemed ironic. He had never been in love. The words were all pure fantasy. He was living off imagination. Maybe that was the real world.

If it wasn't for the fear of Steve showing up, Joe's life wouldn't have felt half bad. Living at Ginger's Place, having Stan and the boys in the band as friends was filling the day-to-day needs. Not hearing from Ted for some time was a downer.

Joe had a plan: writing and singing for a few months, then inviting the agent to the pub one Friday night to see what would happen from there. Joe could only give so much. If it wasn't enough to make it big, so be it. Steve hadn't bothered Joe for weeks, although the feeling that he wasn't far away gave Joe the creeps. He never heard if the truck driver had survived. His blood was running through this stranger's veins. He'd looked dead when Joe had left the operating room.

Joe scanned the papers for some time after coming to Sydney. The shooting had never been mentioned. Steve had the truck or had driven it away. He deduced that the cargo in the back of the truck must have been worth taking a life to someone. Maybe Joe's ignorance was his saviour, having no knowledge of the criminal world. As much as Joe tried to forget that a crime had been committed, he couldn't put the scene out of his mind. At the most inopportune moments the horror would flash in front of his eyes.

Joe was right. As predicted, Steve emerged from the shadows one night after the pub had closed. There was a cold, brisk wind. Joe wanted to get home into his warm bed and catch up on sleep.

'What the hell, Steve? You frightened me again. I know nothing more than I told you.' Joe's anger was hard to hide.

'I just can't stop thinking that you are not telling me everything you saw that day when the men were shot. If my partner is alive, I need to know.'

'I told you that the police have your bags and have your real name. Why haven't they contacted you, or have they?'

'No, no. I wondered that myself. I wouldn't be hard to find, living at the same address that was in the information. Another thing I find strange is why they haven't come after me.'

'You are asking me? I know nothing, as I keep telling you.'

'My boss can't move on the project until he finds out what the police know.'

'Look Steve, or whatever your name is, why are you involving me in your problems, scaring me half to death, creeping up on me all the time?'

'It's my boss. He keeps wanting me to put pressure on you to tell us more about the shooting. It had nothing to do with us.'

'Well, you were there. You drove the truck away. What do you mean it had nothing to do with you and whoever you work for? It appears to me that it had a lot to do with you.'

Joe was getting so aggravated, thinking maybe he should tell Steve that his partner was dead, and the truck driver could be alive. Then he thought better of it.

'You drove the truck away. Why did you do that if it wasn't your deal?'

'I can't explain that at the moment.'

'What was in there that you had to have? Why won't you tell me? It's incriminating, isn't it? You confuse me so much. What are you up to? Stop trying to pull me into your crime. I want nothing to do with you.'

'I did not shoot that gun. The shot came from the bushes beside the road. Really Joe, I didn't do it.'

'Okay, even if I believe you, what do you want from me? I know nothing. Leave me alone. Get out of my life.'

Steve walked away with his head low, as if he had been offended or hurt. Joe started to feel a little sorry for this criminal. Maybe Steve was caught up in something out of his control.

It was later than usual when Joe reached the front door of Ginger's Place. He had made sure everyone would be asleep. The hall light was spreading a dim glow across the entry. He heard footsteps and waited before he walked in. It was Stan coming down from Ginger's apartment, sneaking across to the passage, heading to his room.

Strange, another night cap? Joe thought Ginger must get lonely and need company.

Joe asked Stan the next day on their walk. Stan smiled saying. 'You're just a country kid, so innocent. You'll have to grow up sometime soon.'

Stan slapped Joe on the back, 'Ginger is a good sport. Maybe you'll take my place when I move on.'

It finally dawned on Joe. Stan was sleeping with Ginger. 'How could I be so dumb?' He chuckled. *What a fool this country kid is,* Joe thought.

Chapter 8

Secrets from Beyond
Elizabeth

THE UP-TURNED GLASS MOVED slowly under the three fingers resting on its base. Elizabeth's eyes widened as the word 'Otto' was spelled out. 'Is there one of us that Otto would want to communicate with?' Lottie's friend Lucy asked. Elizabeth found it hard to speak.

'It's me. Otto was my grandfather.' Elizabeth whispered, 'Gerda.' She didn't know why she'd said her grandmother's name. The glass went wild all over the board. They couldn't pick up on any of the words it was spelling. Their fingers were having trouble staying on the glass. Lucy realised it was a foreign language.

'Can you speak to Elizabeth in English?' Lucy asked.

The glass began to move slower, as if the mood had changed. The anger seemed to be gone.

'*Gerda is the host of the devil.*' The glass moved to spell those words. The three sat and stared at the board.

'Do you want to ask Otto a question Elizabeth?' Lucy wondered if this experience was getting too much for her.

Elizabeth knew that Gerda had a bad side, that was for sure, but she'd never seen Otto disapprove of her.

'What did she do that was so bad?' Elizabeth asked.

The glass spun around the board spelling out a disjointed sentence. 'A baby not hers or mine, came to this country, running away fast, bad things, Gerda very bad, the baby not hers, not mine, poor mother, so sad for mothers losing their babies. We have a son now. Gerda steals.'

The three sat as if they had been turned to stone. It was obvious to Elizabeth that Werner was not their child. They had escaped Austria to avoid giving the stolen child back and being charged with kidnapping. Otto would be seen as guilty as Gerda.

The glass moved again, saying that he had told Werner about it all when she was in hospital with polio. Elizabeth felt drained, not knowing how to take this news that there was no blood connection to Gerda. Her father knew and never had the courage to tell her.

Lucy was saying, 'We had better leave it for tonight. I am sure you have had enough for now. We can do it again if you have more questions.'

Lucy and Lottie had been friends for years, and Elizabeth had come to know Lucy too, over coffee when the café was quiet. One of their chats resulted in the decision to have a séance and try to communicate with the spirit world. Lucy said it was fun, having done it from time to time. Elizabeth didn't have any expectations, regarding it as a bit of a joke. She now was left with a heavy heart. Why was this happening again? She did not want the feeling of the unknown to take over her existence. More questions invaded her mind.

Her mother was right, always saying it was as though her in-laws had escaped from a crime. There must have been a reason they came to Australia at that time, long before war had invaded their country. That was why her father had turned his back on the couple that he thought were his parents. But why had he done the same to her?

For weeks Elizabeth went over the séance in her mind, reliving every word. There was much that didn't make sense. It was like putting a jigsaw puzzle together. There was only one way to get more of the story: confront Gerda with the information that had come to her, hoping for answers.

Elizabeth didn't visit Gerda often, only when her conscience dictated it. Gerda had aged and, without Otto or Elizabeth to look after her, she had let the house deteriorate. Otto's backyard hadn't been touched since the day he had pulled out the pumpkins and left.

She opened the door with her key and found Gerda asleep in Otto's old chair. There were soup cans all over the kitchen and paper plates spread over the table, with crusts and crumbs everywhere. Elizabeth wondered if she had been eating the soup straight out of the can. There was a foul smell coming from the front room. Elizabeth discovered a dead cat that had its throat cut some time ago. She shook Gerda awake, yelling at her to get out of the chair and clean up the place.

'What are you doing here? You must want something. You are never here when I need you, ungrateful bitch.' Gerda was slurring her words.

'Have you been sick? Do you need a doctor?' Elizabeth's guilt was kicking in.

'Why would you care? You would like me to die so you can get your hands on my money.'

'I wouldn't have thought you had any money.'

Gerda broke into a laughter that Elizabeth had never heard before, sending shivers down her spine. Otto was right, this woman was hosting the devil. Even if the rest of his story was false, that part was true.

'Why is the dead cat in the front room? Where did that come from?'

'I didn't have any food. It was hungry and wouldn't stop meowing, so I cut its throat.' A deep, devilish laugh came from the depths of her being.

Gerda was scaring Elizabeth now. She wanted to escape from this house of horror.

She rang a doctor, who in turn contacted the welfare, and it was decided Gerda needed to be assessed for mental health problems. An ambulance was called. They asked Gerda who her next of kin was, and she pointed to Elizabeth, saying, 'That cripple there.'

Elizabeth signed some papers, and her grandmother was gone. There wasn't a chance for Elizabeth to ask about Otto's allegations. She wondered if there would be another time.

Retrieving a shovel from Otto's shed and burying the cat was her first job. It was after dark when Elizabeth got home, exhausted. She just wanted to fall into her silky sheets and sleep; to be able to forget about the old bat, knowing how bad Gerda was, and the crimes that had been committed.

The house was in darkness. Usually there were lights on everywhere. Elizabeth knew Maggie would still be out at a girlfriend's party. Everything seemed strange. As she entered, she noticed that the lamp was on in the living room. In the soft glow Elizabeth could see Dolly and Gerry sitting on the couch. She was not sure she should intrude on their privacy. She thought she heard Gerry weeping. She crept slowly, trying not to be noticed.

Dolly called, 'It is okay Elizabeth, you can come in.'

Elizabeth didn't want any more drama today.

'Gerry has just had some bad news. His sister passed away.'

A tension filled the room for a minute while Elizabeth acknowledged the news. She didn't know Gerry had a sister. Gerry had always been very pleasant, but Elizabeth wasn't always comfortable in his company. The relationship was different from the one she had with Dolly. Dolly had become a friend more than a boss. Even when the three were together, Elizabeth felt a remoteness in Gerry as if he was keeping secrets. It appears that this was one – a sister hidden away.

'I am so sorry, Gerry. That is sad news.' She gave Gerry a hug.

Elizabeth didn't think it was her place to ask questions. She went to her room. The day had been a nightmare. She had to lie down. Her whole body ached, and her mind was drained. Elizabeth could not stand another minute of this horror. The guilt, the mysteries and the uncertainty of what more lay ahead regarding Gerda, niggled at her consciousness.

The next morning Dolly and Gerry seemed to be waiting for her at the breakfast table, looking the same as if it was any other day.

'Ah, there you are. Come and sit. We would like to tell you about Gerry's sister.' Dolly seemed cheery this morning, Elizabeth expected them to be mournful.

'I wanted to tell you all these years, but I wasn't sure how you would take it.' Gerry said, smiling at her.

'My sister Suzanna has been in an iron lung all these years. I visited her every week, telling her about you and how well you cope with your life after polio. She would say that it was gratifying to know that I had someone who had suffered like her that I could help.'

Elizabeth was stunned. She had always been thankful to the Goldmanns for the family life they had given her, and their life of luxury. Elizabeth knew she would never belong in their world though. She had learnt to enjoy it from the fringe.

'You may think it was strange that Gerry wanted to help you enjoy life as much as you possibly could. It gave him comfort that he was doing for you something he couldn't do for Suzanna.' Dolly was so sweet, but her words weren't helping Elizabeth.

'I loved my sister. It is a sad time, although there is a joy that she no longer has to endure the life that was bestowed on her.'

Elizabeth knew that she could have suffered the same fate and was always grateful that she did leave the hospital despite her limp. Elizabeth thought of her dear Doctor Daisy, Sister Kenny's methods, her loving nurse SOS, the Dame that had come to the hospital that day, and how they had all worked so hard. But there were always the ones that escaped their healing hands.

'Thank you, Gerry, for telling me your story. I am sorry that Suzanna didn't escape the disease as well as me.' She smiled as she rose from the table and took refuge in her room.

Elizabeth lay on her bed and cried. She wasn't crying for Suzanna, but for herself. Elizabeth had taken Suzanna's place in Gerry's life to appease his conscience and guilt that he was enjoying life while his sister was confined to a jail that was unimaginable.

Elizabeth cried for the years she'd thought she was given the job to bring up Maggie for her own worth, when she knew Suzanna should have had the privilege. That was why Gerry had always been aloof with her. There was a distance that Elizabeth could never break through. When he looked at her, he would see his sister. It was her that should have been walking with a limp. She should have been playing with Maggie and watching her grow. It was Suzanna that should have had the pride that Elizabeth felt; a pride that was Gerry's sister's right.

Gerry had never said that she was doing a good job. It was always Dolly that complimented her on her work, and made her feel at home, part of the family. The fact was, it was Gerry who wanted her there, to prove he loved his sister by giving charity to another victim of polio.

Elizabeth loved Dolly more than ever, knowing the truth. But she felt contempt for Gerry. She just couldn't help it. In her heart, she knew that it wasn't meant to be seen that way, but the hurt seeped through her soul.

Maybe Dolly and Maggie would love her for herself, not seeing her as a victim, but as the strong woman Elizabeth Kasper was becoming.

Elizabeth's problems were mounting. She didn't know how to handle the Gerda situation, and now she felt Gerry had deceived her. One step at a time, or one limp, she thought, just before falling asleep in the lavish room Gerry had provided.

Elizabeth had given the authorities Dolly's and Lottie's phone numbers if they needed her regarding Gerda. She had to fill them in on the story so they would be up to date on the old bat's condition. She did not tell Dolly about the séance. On top of Gerry's sister's death, it wasn't the right time. Dolly gave her a cuddle and said she would do whatever was asked of her. Lottie understood everything, like she always did. For the first time in her life Elizabeth thought she was lucky, having both these women as friends.

It would break her heart to leave the Goldmanns, this place that Elizabeth felt was her home. Her love for Dolly and Maggie would never die, although there was a rift that had been created that was hard for her to dismiss from her mind. She was sure Gerry had noticed her indifference towards him since he told her about Suzanna.

Elizabeth knew Gerry could never understand that in her eyes, he had belittled her. He would never understand that when you are looked down on and snickered at for being different, help can be seen as an insult. He would never believe he had done anything wrong. In his mind he had accepted a disabled girl into his home for no other reason than kindness.

After many hours of going over and over all of Gerry's words on that day at the breakfast table, the decision to stay was made. Elizabeth would try to understand why the grief of having a sister locked away in a tunnel for life had made him think being kind to a cripple and providing her with a home and a job was making up for the life Suzanna would have led.

Elizabeth felt that she was compensation for Suzanna's life. This was beyond Elizabeth's comprehension. Elizabeth would never tell Dolly that Gerry's actions made her feel unworthy, a charity case, another victim needing support from a wealthy, strong man.

Maybe she was overreacting. Maybe she was carrying a big chip on her shoulder. If only she didn't have this limp and be referred to as a cripple. Oh, to be seen as normal.

It did occur to Elizabeth that perhaps she was letting the limp define her.

Chapter 9

The Cruelty of Madness Deserved
Elizabeth

GERDA WAS PUT INTO a mental facility. 'She may need shock treatment,' Elizabeth was told. She knew that wouldn't change her personality or her mental state; those having been cemented into her at birth. Elizabeth now knew that Gerda couldn't pass this affliction on to her as she had no blood ties to any Kaspers – Werner wasn't Gerda's son and Gerda wasn't her grandmother. The person that was her mother and an unknown father was the blood that sustained her. The old bat had been landed with a child that had no blood ties.

Waves of the old guilt crept over Elizabeth, remembering Gerda's rough hands that massaged her frail body when she came home from hospital. Those times were almost loving. Maybe there were reasons she had turned into the sour person she was.

Elizabeth laughed with Lottie about how the old bat was getting what she deserved. One day when she got the courage there would have to be a visit. It seemed Gerda was her responsibility, and there were so many questions that were taking over her mind.

Life at home was running smoothly. Dolly was becoming closer to Elizabeth, though Gerry was pulling away from the girls since his sister had passed, for some reason that no-one understood. Maggie was becoming more independent, needing her mother and Elizabeth less. This gave the two mothers more need for each other. They spent their time over coffee more than they had in the past, chatting about what their day was going to entail, what they wanted to achieve and why Gerry was retreating into himself more every day. Elizabeth joked one day that he would wind up with Gerda soon if he didn't watch it. They both laughed, though both were secretly scared that it could happen.

Maggie's beauty grew with her maturity, taking the best parts of her parents. Dolly's long legs and flowing blonde hair and Gerry's dark eyes turning her into a stunning woman. It was only natural that she became a model and carried on in her mother's footsteps. Occasionally, she would come to one or the other with a problem, choosing the one that she thought would have the appropriate knowledge and the right answer.

'It's so good having two mums. I am bound to get the answer I like that way,' she said as she danced away into a world that was only meant for her.

Elizabeth had never told Dolly anything about Lottie and what happened on Thursdays. She never wanted Dolly to know about Free Rita. Dolly knew Elizabeth had a friend called Lottie who owned a café, and she spent her days off there and at the beach. That was her time to do as she pleased, so Dolly had never asked. Elizabeth was more a member of the family than a Nanny, a tag that had long gone.

Dolly didn't think it was right that Elizabeth should only have Thursday as her only day off. She could come and go as she pleased. Her wages would still be earnt. There were always jobs for her to do around the house, and she did look after all of Maggie's shoes and clothes. Some days Maggie's clothes took Elizabeth to another place, just like her mermaid swimming through the water. Looking in the mirror, holding a special dress over her body, Elizabeth would daydream. If only she didn't have her limp to hide, maybe she could have a dress like this and feel glamorous. Her life was filled with her daydreams that no-one would ever know.

It was getting harder to keep all her secrets from Dolly. They were sharing so much of their emotions and time together. Their main worry was Gerry, not that Elizabeth had the same depth of feeling about the situation as Dolly did, but she still found it hard to understand his deception and the reasoning behind having given her a job and a home.

Elizabeth had to keep her Thursdays at Lottie's, not sure she could retire Free Rita, still needing the escape from reality. The addiction to the moments that she was someone else was something that sustained the spirit to carry on. Loneliness wasn't the main reason any more for the need to drift above the world into the clouds, leaving the feelings of uncertainty, inferiority, and her disability behind. Elizabeth would have to work harder to gain a perspective on human nature to achieve peace of mind.

'What's going on with Dad? He is so grumpy these days,' Maggie asked after one of Gerry's moods.

'He seems to be having a rough time getting over Susanna's death.'

'Lizzy, we didn't even know that she existed. It is all so hard for me to understand why he never said I had an aunty, or he had a sister. I think he is weird.' Maggie was crying now, clinging to Elizabeth.

'Grief is a funny thing. It affects everyone in different ways. We are not to judge. Your Dad will be okay soon. Don't worry. He knows we are here for him.' Elizabeth surprised herself that she seemed so passionate about Gerry when she was having trouble with the issues around Gerry herself.

Elizabeth almost asked Maggie to the beach, hoping that would be a calming influence for her. Luckily, she pulled back from the suggestion. The idea of sharing her other world with anyone was unthinkable.

Elizabeth needed her day on the beach by herself, taking her mermaid self into the ocean, riding the waves, smelling the freshness, the salt covering her skin, the sight of the ocean with a life that held mysteries unknown to man. She wanted to wash away the grime that was accumulating around her soul, tearing down the walls that had been her protection.

'DO YOU WANT ME to arrange another séance? You don't seem the same since the message from Otto, and Gerda being put away.' Lottie asked, worried for her friend.

'No, not now. It is more about Gerry. He is making us all miserable at home – down in the dumps all the time, never talking, not even to Dolly. The way he looks at me … It is as though he hates me.'

'Why would he hate you when you might be the one that could understand what his sister may have been through?'

'Oh, I never had that level of pain or disability.'

'Well, I am glad of that. I may have missed out on knowing you. You do enrich my life, my darling Elizabeth.'

'Thank you. You have saved me, Lottie, you really have.' Lottie put her arms around Elizabeth. They both had a tear trickling down their cheeks.

The only way Lottie knew how to help was to be there for her friend.

Dolly relied on Elizabeth more even as Maggie needed her less. Elizabeth felt that she was letting Dolly down as she had her escape to the esplanade. It was like going to a different world, her world, her ocean, her Luna Park. It was her family. The sights ran through her veins. It was her lifeline, not to be shared.

Elizabeth now wore tailored slacks and blazers. Dolly had convinced her to do away with the long skirts and jumpers that she thought hid the calliper and limp. On Thursdays she couldn't bring herself to wear the slacks though. She was so sure the skirt hid all her disabilities. The men were too preoccupied by the time she took off the few clothes that she would remove, to notice much about her. Elizabeth felt that the skirt was Free Rita and that was the way it would stay.

Her new persona gave her another identity to hide behind. Somehow it made her feel more confident. Dolly couldn't get her to change her hairstyle. She kept saying, 'It would soften your face if you didn't tie your hair back, and let it fall naturally.' Elizabeth held firm. The hair was staying. Dolly never would know that it flowed across the pillow when it belonged to Free Rita.

Of course, Lottie knew about Elizabeth's Thursday activities, but they didn't discuss it much; only if Elizabeth had a funny story to tell, like the man running around the room naked, pretending to be catching butterflies. Then they would have a good old laugh. Lottie still wished that her dear friend didn't have the need for that so-called comfort.

The sunset was particularly beautiful this afternoon. Sitting on the pier, watching the sun disappear behind the horizon, Elizabeth wondered why she was still praying for Joe. Was he even alive? Did his birth date come up when the marble was pulled from the barrel? Did he have to go to Vietnam? Was he killed in a war that wasn't Australia's war? Did Joe even know her name any more? Did he care if she was dead or alive? Why hadn't he ever tried to contact her? Why hadn't she tried to contact him? Why was this sunset making her exasperated? Praying for Joe just in case it might work, that's what Joe had said, and while she did, they were both alive. Joe faded away into the other world that only they both knew.

Dolly and Gerry were having their evening meal when Elizabeth arrived home after her Thursday ritual. The cook didn't come in now unless the pair were entertaining. Dolly's work had dried up as much as her looks, so she was cooking more these days. Elizabeth thought she was still beautiful, she just wasn't making her way on to the magazine covers any more. It was Maggie's turn now.

'Have you had dinner?' Maggie called as Elizabeth came through the front door.

'Yes, thanks. I will head to my room unless you need me to do anything.'

Gerry got up from the table and walked across the room so fast that Elizabeth never had time to move. He slapped her so hard she hit the floor and skidded into the wall.

'You, ungrateful bitch. After all I have done for you, and you treat me like I am nothing.' Gerry's anger was something that neither of the women had ever seen.

Dolly didn't move for a minute. She couldn't take in what she had just seen. Elizabeth was dizzy. Her head was swimming around like a merry-go-round. She saw Otto's face and the pride he had in his moving horses. Dolly rushed to her side, taking Elizabeth in her arms. 'Gerry, what are you doing!?' Dolly screamed, fearing she might be next.

'Why is she alive and Susanna is dead? My beautiful sister lay there like stone and this bitch was allowed to live, walk, and breathe. Why didn't the same thing happen to her? She must have made a deal with the devil.' Gerry's face was dark. His eyes were sinking back into his head. He was going mad. Dolly called an ambulance.

Elizabeth was ten years old again. As her eyes opened, she saw white lights, white walls, white nurses fussing around.

'Is that you SOS?' There was no reply from the figure standing before her.

Elizabeth drifted back into the glow of white.

The next time her eyes opened it was Dolly standing, staring down at her. She seemed so tall. Her hair falling over her shoulders was tinged with grey. Elizabeth usually coloured Dolly's roots. Elizabeth wondered who would do her hair now.

'How are you feeling? The doctor said you are on the way to recovery from your nasty fall.'

'I fell? Is that what happened to me, a fall?'

'Yes, it was like your leg just went from under you.'

It was weeks before Elizabeth remembered what had happened, and what Gerry had said. Her heart was breaking again.

Maggie came to visit often, saying how she missed her so much and asking when was she coming back home. Elizabeth knew it was no longer her home. Her dream and her silk sheets were over. She would never tell Maggie the truth. She knew what it was like to be disillusioned about parents. It was better not to know.

Lottie was her strength. After hearing the true story, her heart broke for her friend.

The injury had done more damage to her bad leg, so her rehabilitation was slow. Elizabeth had a lot of time to think. Why wasn't Joe Pike here in the hospital with her? It was so lonely without him. She was sure she saw Doctor Daisy walk through the door many times, and how she wished that SOS would come and hold her hand.

'You will be able to go home soon,' one of the doctors said, smiling.

Elizabeth was sure he didn't understand why she didn't smile back. Dolly had never said she wasn't welcome back in so many words, though Elizabeth knew that what she'd thought of as her family and home was gone. Her love for Dolly and Maggie would be no match for Gerry's hatred of her, and that love was no match for her hatred of him. Elizabeth never asked after Gerry. She didn't want to put Dolly through the discomfort of having to answer. It was obvious that she hadn't told anyone what really happened and was ready to make an excuse for Gerry's assault.

Elizabeth talked about her predicament over and over with Lottie. A small flat near her would be ideal, although without her job there was no way she could afford the rent. Lottie said she would give her some work, but it wouldn't be enough. As Elizabeth had only worked for the Goldmann's she had no experience to offer. With her disability, the hope of getting a job was negligible.

Maybe Suzanna had been the lucky one after all. Elizabeth dismissed that thought from her mind immediately, as she did when she thought about Free Rita not being so free.

Elizabeth had known all along that she would have to go back to Gerda's house. There was no other way. Gerda wouldn't be there. The doctors had told Elizabeth that she would never be well enough to return to her home. The house couldn't be sold until Gerda died, so that's what had to be. The memories of the place would be hard to go through but there was no other way.

When the taxi pulled up to the house Elizabeth found it hard to move. A paralysis of a different kind – fear and disappointment took over. Only for the fact that the taxi's clock was ticking over, and the price of the fare was escalating, made her move. The sight of the old place scared her. Since Otto had gone, no-one had attended to the garden so it was overgrown.

The windows were covered with ivy and the grass was reaching the windowsills, reminding her of a spooky childhood story. That would have to be the first job – spend some of her savings on a gardener. When she opened the front door, the smell that hit her was almost unbearable.

Elizabeth could see her savings dwindling. She walked through the rooms, images popping into her head as the memories flashed before her. She would have to work hard to make this place a home. Elizabeth couldn't bring herself to go into the green room. That would be just too hard today. She went into Otto's garden shed and sat on an old bag of something and cried and cried.

Having told Dolly that it was time she looked after the old place and would have to give up the job, she expressed her gratitude for the years she shared with them. Dolly didn't protest, and Elizabeth said that a courier would pick up her belongings if Maggie could pack them up for her. Dolly had tears in her eyes when she said that would be right. She would see that everything was there for her. The two women had too much respect for each other to go into details. Guilt hovered in both their minds. Neither could comprehend life without each other but knew there was no other answer.

Elizabeth longed to hold Maggie in her arms and tell her the true story but couldn't do that to Dolly. However, she didn't want Maggie to think she had deserted her, so had asked Dolly to tell her that she had family matters to attend to and would catch up with her soon.

Dolly had agreed. Anything to save Maggie from knowing the truth. Another part of Elizabeth's heart died that day, the part that held the love for Dolly, her friend, and Maggie the child she had nurtured and helped to raise, to grow into a beautiful, strong woman.

Somehow, Elizabeth had always known this day would come, but could never have imagined the way it had happened. She wondered how long it would be before she lost Lottie. Why did everyone she loved abandon her?

Chapter 10

The Cruelty of Madness can eat into a Person's Heart
Elizabeth

ELIZABETH SEARCHED THE CUPBOARDS for some clean sheets to make up the bed in the spare room, the room that should have always been hers.

She knew there would be some cans of soup left from when Gerda was in the house alone. They would fill in until tomorrow when shopping would stock the pantry. The power had never been disconnected. She had paid the monthly accounts for some reason, now knowing why. She opened the windows that weren't stuck from one thing or another, to freshened up the place a little. The one thing Elizabeth could do was clean. She wanted to get rid of the old bag's rubbish and her stink, and the place would be hers.

Elizabeth didn't know how she was going to manage cleaning out her grandparent's bedroom. That was a task she wasn't looking forward to.

Gerda had never moved any of Otto's belongings. It was as though he would be home at any time. Elizabeth could see weeks of work in front of her. With her bad leg it would be a slow process, one step at a time or limp at a time, with persistence as always.

Elizabeth had climb so many mountains. This one was going to take endurance. Where was the strength going to come from? She wasn't sure.

It was a week before her boxes came from the Goldmann's. Two pairs of silk sheets were on the top of the first box Elizabeth opened. Tears flooded her eyes. Maggie knew they were her favourite things in the whole world. How was she going to live without this darling girl in her life? There was a note: *Mum and I miss you. Come back soon. Love and kisses to my second Mum.* Maggie deserved an explanation for Elizabeth's sudden departure, though there was no way of explaining the situation without implicating her father, which would probably hurt her in a way that would turn her against Elizabeth. After all, blood was a stronger tie than friendship.

The old musty wardrobe was in better shape now that Elizabeth had cleaned and disinfected it over and over, waiting to hang her clothes. The new look clothes had pride of place, and the Thursday skirts and jumpers were hung at the back. The large tallboy with deep drawers held the rest of her things comfortably. The small dresser displayed her makeup and hair accessories nicely. Elizabeth stood back with satisfaction. Yes this is my room. I will make it my home.

Lottie had convinced Elizabeth to apply for social benefits, which she had always been entitled to, but having a job and the generosity of the Goldmann's, the need hadn't been there to do so. With that and the money that she would earn from the café, managing would be easy. Elizabeth just had to learn to live with the horror that came into her mind like waves of torture, of the times that Gerda made her life unbearable.

As the weeks went by, the house became sparkling clean and the air fresher. Gerda was being pushed further into the past with every day. Elizabeth was falling into a new routine of her own for the first time in her life and enjoying it.

Missing Dolly and Maggie was becoming easier, though she did wonder what new and exciting things Maggie was up to. Elizabeth's hope was that one day they would be together again. She placed it in her basket of dreams.

The new independence gave Elizabeth a power that was new to her. Why hadn't she realised before that nature had taken some abilities away but had replaced them with a fortitude that would not be broken. She started to have pride in herself, taking more care of her appearance.

Lottie never asked Elizabeth to work on Thursdays. Why did she want to slip back into that old Rita with the long skirt and jumper? The men that came in on Thursdays would never recognise her when she was her new true self, or that's what Lottie liked to believe.

'When are you going to give up Rita, my darling?' Lottie asked one day.

'When I am old and worn out,' Elizabeth laughed.

'I want to be here to see that day.'

'I might decide to marry one of these faceless, nameless creatures that are always asking. That would be a day that would be worth being here for.'

'You get proposals?'

'All the time. I'm not sure they remember the next day, when they go home to their wives.' Elizabeth laughed and laughed.

'I know some of them are serious, the ones that haven't noticed the calliper.'

'Oh, don't put yourself down that way. You are a beautiful woman. There will be a good man out there for you one day.'

'Well, it won't be one that Free Rita attracts, that's for sure.' They both laughed until they cried.

Life was good again, although the cloud that hung over Elizabeth was closing in on her. It was the visit to Gerda that she had been putting off for so long.

Elizabeth knew that time was running out to get the answers to the questions that only Gerda could give her. The hospital had kept her informed of Gerda's condition, and Elizabeth had paid for any of her needs not met by the facility.

When Elizabeth walked into her ward, Gerda didn't know who she was for a minute. The new look threw her. She could almost admit to herself that the girl was beautiful.

Gerda sat as if already dead. The dark hair of her younger days had gone, leaving a mop of unkempt white. A head covered in snow, never able to melt away from this icicle woman with an ice encrusted heart, a woman without a drop of warmth in her body. Elizabeth painted this picture in her mind, walking towards her grandmother.

'Well, you have finally come to gloat over the old woman, have you?'

Elizabeth had made up her mind that she wasn't going to let the old bag upset her, although it was going to take every ounce of nerve not to lose her temper.

'I have been checking with the doctors all the time, hoping you would be able to get home soon,' Elizabeth lied. 'I have been looking after the house. It is looking just the way you like it.' Lying again.

Gerda was suspicious of Elizabeth but chose to say nothing about the house.

'So, what have you come for? Still working for those Jews, are you? Or have you woken up to that husband and moved out?'

'Yes, I have moved out. What do you mean about the husband?'

'How do you think he gets his money?' Gerda almost snarled.

'I didn't ask exactly. He went to the office every day, insurance, I always thought.'

'You are so naïve. Haven't you learnt anything about men and their dealings? Nobody gets rich unless it is against the law. He launders money through his so-called insurance business.'

How does the old bag know all this? How did she know about Phyllis's mother and other people that had no connection to the family, unless she just spied on everyone. Elizabeth's head began to spin. Did she know about Free Rita? Her face went red. Panic was making her weak. The old bat wasn't losing her mind. She was calculating every move.

'Are you feeling sick?' Gerda asked, with a smirk on that ugly face.

She was starting to unnerve Elizabeth, a talent Gerda had when knowing she had the upper hand. Elizabeth remembered her new power. I can't let her get to me, she thought.

'I heard that you aren't my father's biological mother.'

It was Gerda's face that turned red now.

'How did you hear that?'

Elizabeth could see the rage rising like a volcano.

'Otto told me.' Elizabeth was never going to tell her that Otto sent her the message from the grave.

'He was busy before he left, wasn't he? Telling Werner and you. Well, what about it? I gave Werner a good life and he never thanked me for it just like you. Bastards, the pair of you!'

'What do you mean, the pair of us?' Elizabeth was thinking she might find out more than she bargained for.

'You made your way into your mother's womb from another man's sperm,' the satisfaction on Gerda's face was horrifying.

Elizabeth took a minute, staring at the floor. What other secrets could this terrible person have hidden away, waiting for the right time, with a force of the devil to bestow on to her victim?

'You mean the only blood tie I have in this family is to a mother that deserted me and left me with you?' Elizabeth almost felt sorry for Gerda being stuck with another child that she had no blood connection to.

'Why did you feel obligated to look after me then? Why wasn't I sent to an orphanage?'

'Otto liked you, and he said you would look after us in our old age. I don't know why he would like a cripple so much, why he expected me to put up with you when you probably would take after your mother, such a slut, cheating on Werner the way she did.' Gerda took a breath, losing the little stamina that was left in an old, withering body.

'Werner didn't want anything to do with us after Otto told him the truth. It was his stupidity telling Werner about the way we got him, and how we escaped to Australia. What did he think? That Werner would accept it and carry on as if it didn't matter? Otto was an old fool.'

Elizabeth was shattered once again. What was her comeback going to be, coping with this new information.

'Who is my father?'

'How would I know? Your mother never said, and Werner was so devastated that it was never spoken of again, not that he knew for some time that you inherited your lying from your mother.'

Gerda started to laugh. 'I do have my suspicions though.'

Of course, Gerda would have some idea. Her spying methods would have worked overtime to find out what Ingrid had been up to.

'I think it was Werner's best friend, Barry. They always seemed so close. After you were born, he was never seen again. That pretty much gave me the answer.'

'What was his full name?'

'I don't remember. I'm in here because I have lost my mind. Did you forget? Maybe you shouldn't believe anything I say.'

Elizabeth couldn't move. She wanted to get away from this evil witch but was sure her legs wouldn't hold her. 'Why are you leaving me the house? You must hate me so much.'

'Otto made me do it. He thought you had your share of bad luck, and you would never get anyone to support you with that withered leg. "She will never get anyone to love her the way she is, the poor thing. It is our responsibility to look after her," That's what he said.'

Elizabeth wanted to shout, shut up, you miserable bitch!

'Why did you steal Werner? Didn't you think of his mother and father, about their feelings, the devastation that you caused? Destroying lives. Is that your aim? Does that give you purpose? Do you think you were put on this earth to bring down everyone that crosses your path?'

'I had my reasons, many in fact. I needed the love of a child.' She paused for some time. 'I had three miscarriages and I thought Otto would leave me. I was unworthy to be a woman, or that is what I was led to believe. I was young and naïve. Was it too much to ask for a child to hold in my arms? I did the mother a favour anyway. I don't think she even asked the father's name. She was such a fool. Hah, if she had only known.' Tears rolled down her ugly, worn-out face.

Maybe she wasn't always so horrible. Elizabeth tried to imagine her as a young girl full of dreams, losing babies one after another, coming to a strange land with only Otto and a child that wasn't hers. Both she and her husband, criminals. Elizabeth looked at the old woman that the years had turned into a lunatic. Maybe kindness was all that was needed between them, neither having the ability to express because of the deals that life had thrown at them.

Confusion, guilt, and disappointment overwhelmed Elizabeth. Maybe she could put her arms around this old, ugly, demented woman as some kind of retribution, or slight understanding. She stood with her leg that had been abused, her separate identity, she stood with a strength that was stored for such an occasion, walking forward, putting her arms around the old bat with as much feeling of care as she could muster. The old woman cried.

Elizabeth turned and walked away. Before reaching the door, the words came strong and loud penetrating like an arrow bouncing off the undeserving back.

'Goodbye, Free Rita.'

Elizabeth would never see Gerda again.

Chapter 11

The Afflictions of Others' Secrets
Elizabeth

IT WOULD TAKE ELIZABETH weeks to absorb the truly devastating information that Gerda had so much pleasure in passing on to her. Elizabeth wondered how she had kept it to herself all these years without wanting to make life more uncomfortable for this girl that she had been forced to care for. Having this cripple invading her life night and day, stealing Otto's attention and devotion away, must have deepened the hatred she harboured for the bastard child.

The fact that she was a result of an affair between her mother and maybe Werner's best friend, took the guilt away from who she thought was her father. Werner had good reason for her being palmed off to his so-called parents. Elizabeth didn't understand how her mother could have turned her back on her the way she did. Even if it was for the betterment of her brother and sister. Cutting off a child without a word or explanation was so cruel. Elizabeth was the innocent party. She was a child, a very hurt and damaged child, physically and mentally.

Elizabeth had written to her mother in the early days. There were times when she'd received a card saying how the family hoped she was well, and still enjoying living with Otto and Gerda. When Elizabeth was brave enough to write how unhappy she was and that she did not want or enjoy living with the grandparents, and that being with her own family would make her happy, there was never a reply. She was so hurt by this rebuff so many times, it was easier not to bother. The expectations of her going back and being with her brother and sister were just another dream to put into the ever-growing dream basket.

The day would come to confront Ingrid and Werner, and with luck, she would get to know her siblings. Having neither the strength nor the will to do so at this time, that satisfaction would have to wait.

Elizabeth rang Lottie, saying she wasn't well, and she would be in soon. She lay on her bed for days. Depression set in, taking her to a dark place, something she had never known before through all her bad and unhappy days. She was lying there waiting for some kind of intervention, a stillness in the room. She had created a safe place in this house, even knowing that Gerda still stalked in the darkness.

Why had the medical staff and Doctor Daisy worked so hard to save her from a death that now she craved? She did not want to let their hard work be wasted on an ungrateful child. Elizabeth had always made some kind of effort to be happy. She and Joe had decided that would be a salute to their work and kindness. Now her world had lost any glimpse of lustre that might have peeped through. She pulled her silk sheet over her head and cried. She cried for Maggie and Dolly, the ones who had given her hope that she had a purpose, a life with meaning. Elizabeth looked over at her calliper leaning against the wall, the only thing that she would never lose or could be taken away from her, her crutch that was her companion. She wondered if they would bury her with it. That brought a smile to her face. Maybe she would get out of bed tomorrow and try again to make the best of whatever lay ahead.

Never having the support of her so-called family hadn't stopped her before. Slowly the time Elizabeth was spending in bed became less, and she started to do the jobs around the house that she had let go. Having almost starved herself while neglecting her needs, she even spent some time in the sun, thinking about fixing up Otto's garden. Flowers instead of vegetables would be nice. The day Lottie knocked on her door was the day Elizabeth turned herself around.

'My darling, I have been so worried about you, and missing you so much. Even the customers have been asking, "Where is that beautiful Elizabeth's smile?"'

Elizabeth felt a little guilty for not letting Lottie know more of the story. She never wanted to hear the word spoken: illegitimate. She probably would never know who her father was and would not been wanted by anyone.

'I am so sorry, Lottie. I sank into a deep hole, and it took me some time to crawl out of it.'

'Why didn't you ask me for help? You know I am always here for you, my darling.'

'Shame, maybe. I have a lot to tell you. It will slowly come out, but for now I must work through it all and try to make some sense of my life that seems to be sending me one disappointment after another.' Elizabeth was close to tears.

Lottie respected her friend's privacy and didn't ask questions.

'When you want to talk, I will be here for you.' Lottie put her arms around Elizabeth and held her tightly, hoping she could pass on her love, and Elizabeth would know that her feelings were genuine; she was the one person that wouldn't let her down.

'Give me another week and I will be back. I miss you. Thank you, Lottie, my one true friend.' Elizabeth felt the dullness move away, and her mind was clear for the first time after her visit to Gerda.

She felt a little alliance to Werner. He had no idea who his mother and father were, and he was in a foreign country to that of his birth. Elizabeth had a choice. She knew who her mother was and had a chance of finding out the name of her father if she wanted to pursue the hunt for the evidence. Would she ever have the desire to do so? She thought about writing to Werner but made the decision to leave the matter for another day. Maybe she was better off not knowing or caring. What had he or her mother ever done for her? It was her brother and sister that Elizabeth would like to know. They could look for her, if they had the need. Elizabeth put it all to rest and made herself get on with trying to get the best out of the predicament, concentrating on the house and Lottie's café. And, of course Free Rita. The boys must be missing her.

By the time Elizabeth got back to work at the café, she looked like her old self, or as others knew her, that is. To be back on the esplanade gave her an excitement only a few would understand. Seeing the ocean meet the horizon, feeling the freshness of the sea air and watching the clouds mysteriously drifting past, gave her back her lifeline.

This is my world. To hell with the rest of those who are supposed to be connected to me. I divorce you all, and never want to think about any of you again. Elizabeth wanted to shout this to the world, but who would care or listen? It was clear now that she would do the best she could with what she was given. Her mind was the strength that she would rely on. If that meant becoming a mermaid swimming to the horizon, or seeing herself as Rita Hayworth on Thursdays, that was the way it was going to be. Elizabeth laughed to herself when making this last resolution. That poor old Rita was a bit out-of-date now. Many new stars had taken over from the actresses of the 40s and 50s, though in her mind, she would still be Rita.

Lottie was surprised to see Elizabeth arrive on Thursday in her long skirt and jumper. She was hoping that her lapse into depression over the last few weeks might have made her see that Rita wasn't necessary to create happiness.

Elizabeth hadn't told Lottie what the visit to Gerda was all about. Because of the way she had bounced back, Lottie wasn't about to bring the subject up. Elizabeth would tell her if she needed to, and it was clear that she didn't at this time. Lottie was leaving it alone, not wanting to rock the boat, although knowing it must have been overwhelming for it to have had that effect on her darling friend.

Robert was waiting for her when she arrived. They were all Robert to her. If dreams came true, it would have been Robert Taylor sitting there. He was one of her favourites. So, they were all Roberts. Knowing any of their names would have spoilt the illusion, and the whole exercise would be lost. Being in their world was her make believe. They were just bit players taking directions. Elizabeth Kasper was in command. As long as they didn't see her take off her calliper, she had control.

Lottie had tears in her eyes as she watched Elizabeth get in the car and drive away with some lost soul that had a need that no-one else could meet but Free Rita. There was always a working girl that would get put out when she watched her take one of the tricks away. Their pimps would have given them a black eye or worse if they didn't bring in their regular amount of money at the end of the day. They couldn't give themselves away free like Rita. They never understood why she indulged in this inconceivable practice. Sometimes they tried to get Rita out of the place, but Lottie always stepped in and said it was them that needed to leave. But they enjoyed the milkshakes, and now coffee was becoming a thing in Melbourne. Lottie's was so good they all ended up sitting back in disbelief that any girl would work for free.

Elizabeth's dishevelled hair flew all over the pillow in this Robert's bed, as they tossed around in a less than organised sexual frenzy, with closed eyes. Who was this person that was making her want more than she had ever wanted before? Was it magic? His touch exploded through her body like lightning. Elizabeth never equated sex with love.

Today was confusing her, moving her to a new plateau, one she had never reached before. She cried out. 'This one is for you, Gerda; I hope you are watching.' Elizabeth wasn't sure if the satisfaction was because of this Robert's commitment to the passion of the moment, or that she wished that Gerda had watched every minute of Free Rita's ecstasy. The old witch of a spy. Elizabeth wondered if love was a possibility.

A new sense of freedom of being unincumbered by the burden of a family that had dragged her mind into a place, making her believe she was nothing. She always thought it was because of the disability. Now she knew the real reason behind the cruelty she had suffered was because of her mother's infidelity. Gerda was dead to Elizabeth now. The memory of her childhood was becoming fainter with time. Not having many good times to fall back on was making it easier to put Werner and Ingrid in an outer circle of her mind, so that their presence never appeared.

It was as though Elizabeth had put Gerda to rest before she had stopped breathing.

The only person that she had a longing for was Maggie. Elizabeth had been so grateful that the Goldmanns had entrusted their only child to her. She never had the slightest idea what being a mother would have felt like, and to be able to nurture this child was the greatest gift that was given to a girl with a disability.

Dolly had disappointed her not to acknowledge the fact of the assault, though knowing it would have been too hard not to stand by her husband. Elizabeth was hurt all the same. It would have been nice if they had talked about her injury and decided what to do about it together. In her heart, she knew that wasn't possible.

After Gerda's story about Gerry, she realised that there had been a lot going on with the family that she didn't know about, all of which was none of her business anyway. Dolly was so used to the luxury and lifestyle to put it at risk. Years living in that dream, which now was becoming harder to imagine, had been her life. Letting go of the Goldmanns wasn't going to be easy.

There were nights that Elizabeth woke feeling lost, but by morning the load magically lifted as if she flung it away and was back to her bubbly self. Lottie noticed that her friend was happier than she had ever seen her before.

'Has Gerda died?' Lottie asked one day when it seemed that Elizabeth might grow wings and would fly.

'No, isn't it a shame? Why did you ask?'

'You seem to be walking on air today.'

'I am just happy. The breeze was clearing away the cobwebs, the sun was shining, the birds were singing as I walked down to Lottie's wonderful café at Saint Kilda beach. Everyone is smiling in here. What more could I want to make me happy?' Elizabeth laughed and hugged her friend.

She wondered if Lottie would think her friend was more unstable than she already thought, if knowing that Free Rita wasn't the only fantasy hidden away in her secret life. What would Lottie think if she knew Elizabeth prayed at sunset for a boy named Joe, that was now a man? If they passed in the street, he would be unrecognisable to her.

Becoming a mermaid swimming to the horizon, wanting to know what was on the other side was another of her secrets. Elizabeth knew if she let the world know about her secrets they would disappear, and she would vanish with them. She wanted to need no-one.

Elizabeth had to prepare herself for the day that Lottie would get enough savings to go to America to be with her daughter. That was a time that was unthinkable, so she tried to put it out of her mind. Elizabeth was learning to deal with problems when they arose, not in the anticipation of them happening as she had done in the past. This made the daily load easier.

Gerda finally passed away, and the house was Elizabeth's. The solicitor took care of everything. He did warn her though, that the son might dispute the will. Elizabeth waited. Neither was contacted. Not a word of sorrow, nor of wanting a keepsake from the house. The solicitor didn't understand. Elizabeth didn't bother to explain.

One problem she never envisioned was Jonas Kasper walking into the café.

'I am looking for Elizabeth Kasper. I went to her address, but she wasn't home. A neighbour told me she worked here.'

Lucky it isn't Thursday, Lottie thought to herself.

'She is in the back. I will get her for you. Can I say who is here to see her?' Lottie had a feeling it was him, something about him resembled Elizabeth.

'Tell her it is her brother, Jonas.'

Elizabeth had heard Jonas's voice and froze. Has he come to take my house? went through her mind, knowing that he couldn't. Trembling, her trust wavered.

Chapter 12

When the Depth is Overwhelming
Joe

STAN HAD BEEN GONE for a few weeks. Joe was missing him, their walks and chats, the one thing he enjoyed outside the pub environment. Benny had moved into Stan's room. He was different from Joe's friend, cheery with a ruddy, round face, always smiling, with pink cheeks. You would think he was blushing. He had a mop of red hair. Joe wondered if he would take Stan's place in Ginger's bed too.

Ginger introduced him at lunch, 'Benny is going to be here for a short time, so let's make his stay with us a happy one.' Ginger had a way of making her new guests feel welcome.

Everyone said, 'Hi Benny, good to have you fill Stan's seat.'

And maybe Ginger's bed, Joe thought, then wondered why he seemed to care.

Joe kept his distance from the new lodger. There was something about him that put him on edge. Behind that smiley face Joe felt, were hiding a million secrets.

As he was the first of Ginger's boys to sit down for Sunday lunch, he picked up the paper to catch up on the news. Benny came in and sat next to him. Damn, Joe thought, I will have to talk to him now.

'How's it going, Joe? I hear you're a singer in a band. I must pop in some time and have a listen. The gossip is that you are pretty good.'

'I only sing on Saturday nights. I am just waiting until I get a record deal.'

'So, you think you are that good, do yah?'

'That's my plan, anyway, still living in hope.'

'Maybe you don't know the right people.'

'Probably the case. I'll keep trying all the same.'

'That's the spirit. I hear you have plenty of that.'

Patronising bastard, Joe thought, as a couple of others came in and took the seats next to Benny. Joe was glad the conversation was over. It wasn't until after lunch and they had all gone that Joe wondered about Benny's comment about him having plenty of spirit. That made him wonder how he would have come to that conclusion.

Joe was still trying to get Nancy's car back, to no avail. He couldn't imagine what the police were doing with it, and why they wouldn't give it back. The guilt weighed on his mind. Nancy had given up her car so he would be able to get around Sydney. There were days that heading south and going home seemed the best option. He knew his parents would understand, although he couldn't bear to see their disappointment and sad faces. He had done that to them before.

Joe desperately wanted to tell someone about this predicament he had found himself in. Now Stan was gone, there wasn't anyone he was as comfortable with to share this surreal story. Sometimes he was not even sure what had really happened. It seemed like a bad dream. Only for the fact that he didn't have Nancy's little car, he might have been able to put it out of his mind.

And then there was Steve, always in the shadows, lurking, waiting for answers. Why he had never told Steve that Greg, the other guy, was dead Joe wasn't sure. Maybe he liked the mystery of it all, seeing himself as a spy or a double agent. That might be the way to go.

Joe laughed. Yes, a good way to get a bullet in your head, like the truck driver and Greg, or whatever his name was. Steve and his boss must assume Greg was dead. Why would the police still have the car otherwise? There were so many things that didn't make sense to Joe. He had tried to get a take on it, but it was so far out of his realm that his mind couldn't grasp why anyone would want to kill.

Benny was always hanging around, no matter what time Joe walked in or out. He always seemed to be there.

'Don't you have a job?' Joe asked one day.

'I am on an assignment that doesn't take me away from here much.'

'Oh okay.' Joe decided not to ask any more, knowing he wouldn't get an answer.

Joe felt Benny's eyes following, piercing his back, as he walked out onto the street. Joe decided that if he saw Benny at the lunch table, he would eat elsewhere.

It had been a busy night at the pub and Joe stayed behind later than usual. He also had more to drink than usual too. As he was coming through the front door, Ginger was at the bottom of the stairs, waiting.

'Are you okay, Ginger?' Joe asked in what seemed an echoey voice.

'Sure, Joe, just waiting for you. You're late tonight.'

God, she knows what time I come home. Is the whole world spying on me?

'Would you like to come up for a night cap?' her voice was thick. Not her normal self, Joe thought. Oh God, does she want me to take Stan's place? What about Benny? He would be more suitable to satisfy her needs, surely? Joe's mind was racing.

'Come on, it will do you good. You seem tense lately.'

'I have had a busy night. I would like to go to bed.'

'My thoughts exactly,' Ginger laughed.

I've saved myself for this, all the young girls I have passed up waiting for the right one and I am summonsed by an old woman whose bed needs warming. Joe couldn't believe he was heading up the stairs to Ginger's apartment.

Ginger had already taken off her clothes before Joe entered the door. She stood there in all her naked glory, a huge smile on her face.

Joe was trembling. He didn't know if it was fear or excitement. He would be so clumsy. His experience was so limited. He had never gone all the way with a girl. He wasn't sure what she would expect.

'Come on Joe, don't you like what you see?' She was coming for him like a raging bull.

Joe thought Ginger was in pretty good shape for her age, and he could see why they called her Ginger. Joe had to tell her.

'Ginger, I'm a virgin.' He could feel the redness on his face getting brighter and brighter by the minute.

'Well now, I would never have guessed. You are so popular with the fans at the pub, the opportunities you must have had with girls. You could have had your pick. So, into men, are you? Get out if that's the case. I don't want to waste my time.'

Oh God. Now I've offended her, not falling into her arms. 'No, no I like girls. It's just that I wanted it to be a true love situation, never wanting to make use of a girl the way most boys do.'

'Oh, a saint are we Joe? Come on, I'll change that for you.'

Ginger slipped under the bed covers. Joe wasn't sure why. He had seen everything and now she was covering up? A signal to follow. Maybe I can't offend her again, he thought. He was getting excited about the idea. The sight of Ginger in her birthday suit had made him very interested, to put it mildly.

Ginger took Joe to places he never knew existed. He knew he would never look back. Sex was going to be his new companion.

'Okay Joe, you can get back to your own room now. I'll let you know when I need you again.'

'Thank you, Ginger. I'll be waiting. I hope I wasn't a disappointment, I'll do better next time,' he said, almost pleading there would be a next time.

Ginger laughed. 'You are lovely Joe. Who is Elizabeth?'

Oh no, I must have called out her name, Joe thought. 'Just a girl I knew when I was a kid. I don't know why I said her name. I haven't seen her,' – Joe hesitated – 'since we were in hospital together.'

'You had polio then, did you?'

'Yes, we shared a couple of years together. I can't imagine why I would have mentioned her name.' Joe wondered how Ginger knew he had been a polio victim.

'How did you know? About the polio, that is.'

'I could see one of your legs was compromised, not that it mattered Joe, you are just what I need.'

Joe left Ginger's room in a state of confusion. He wanted to shout that he had just had the best night of his life with a woman older than his mother. All his values went down the drain. He couldn't remember why he had been so pedantic about falling in love. It would be ridiculous to think he was in love with Ginger, but he did enjoy the softness of her breasts, her long fingers creeping over his body and the sweet smell of her scent. He would never forget how she'd led him to paradise.

Joe had never thought his polio would be detected by anyone. It was a mystery as to how Ginger could pick it up in the dimly lit room. He went over this new experience many times through the night. It took the place of the Steve nightmare. Ginger was amazing. No wonder Stan found it hard to leave. He wanted to go back again tonight. He tried to remember how often Stan went up to her apartment. Joe would have to wait for his next invitation. He broke out in a cold sweat, thinking she might not want him again. And she was older than his mother...

When Joe got to the pub the boys knew, slapping him on the back saying, 'At long last Joe, it has happened for you. Good on you man!'

'How do you know, or what do you think you know?'

'That you spent the night in the bed of someone that gave you that glow on your face,' one of the band members said.

Joe laughed. 'I didn't think it would be so obvious.' He hoped the boys would leave it at that. They pressured him for details. Joe couldn't tell them that it had been an older woman, who Joe was sure had once charged for her pleasures.

Joe became a regular visitor to Ginger's bed, much to his delight, and it became inconceivable that he could ever leave a lover. He imagined being with her until the day she died. This was another secret to hide from Nancy and Bill. Joe's pleasure outweighed his guilt.

It was a Saturday night. The pub was buzzing. Joe had just finished his first set. Lifting his head from his bow, he saw them sitting there together grinning. Joe walked to their table, horror surging in his gut. Steve and Benny stood with hands extended as if to welcome a friend. It was all Joe could do to speak. He couldn't shake their hands. His arms wouldn't move. Finally, the words came,

'So, you two know each other then? What a surprise!'

'Yes, what a coincidence. We work for the same firm. I had no idea that, um, yes, Steve hung out around here.'

'Funny coincidence, Joe. Do you have any news for us? Have you got your car back yet?'

Joe was sure they would have known if the car had been returned. They probably know I am sleeping with Ginger too, he thought.

'Yep, really funny you two know each other. I thought you were hanging around for some reason Benny. Bet that's not your real name, is it?'

'It'll do. So, you haven't heard anything about my partner then?'

'He must have died after I left the police station, I suppose. Wouldn't you have heard if he was alive? Do you know his family, why not ask them? Anyway, you have the truck. You must have the treasure that was in there, I presume.' Joe was shocked with himself. Why did I say that? Now they will think I know what was in the back of the truck. He said quickly, 'Not that I know what this treasure was.' Joe thought the damage was done. He could almost feel the gun in the back of his head.

'Well, it's complicated. Anyway, that's none of your business.'

'No, it isn't any of my business, so why do you keep harassing me?'

'We like you, Joe. Just wanted to catch up. Are you going to sing again? We might stay. We like you, Joe.'

Joe felt sick. Was this nightmare ever going to end? It occurred to him that they knew that Greg, or whatever his name, was dead and they were using that as a weapon to get to some other secret they thought he was harbouring. There must have been something in the truck that the authorities didn't want known. Convincing them he knew nothing was the hard part.

By the time Joe got home he was in a fragile state. Part of him hoped that Ginger wasn't waiting for him, but she was. Joe started to tremble.

The pair never talked much, just got on with the job that they both needed.

Tonight, Ginger could see that Joe wasn't himself.

'Not in the mood tonight? I can live for another day if you aren't up for it.'

For some reason this made Joe cry.

'Oh, I am so sorry Ginger. It's just that things weren't that good tonight. You must think I'm a baby. I just don't know what to do.'

Ginger put her arm around Joe, as a mother would, and let him rest his head on her shoulder.

'Maybe you had better share your problem with me. I am sure it can't be that bad. Come on, tell me. I might be able to help.' Her voice smoothed Joe a little.

Before Joe could stop himself, the story spilled out, leaving nothing to the imagination. Every detail was as vivid as if on a movie screen.

Ginger seemed shocked. She held him closer and stroked his hair.

'You poor boy, coming to Sydney, wanting to be a star, and having to witness a murder, and then these thugs creeping in the shadows, feeling threatened all the time. Oh, my darling, my darling boy.'

Joe was disgusted with himself when the story was over. How could he be such a blubbering baby when he wanted to impress this woman who was becoming the love of his life?

'I'll ask around. I know some people, if it is guns or drugs.'

'Oh, be careful Ginger, please. I shouldn't have told you. I don't want you to be in any danger.' Joe almost started to cry again.

Ginger let Joe stay in her bed for the night, putting him to sleep like a baby in her arms.

Days went back to normal, or normal for Joe and Ginger. Sex and singing. Joe was living a dream. What more could he ask for? To get Nancy's car back and never see Steve and Benny again. Would that be too much to expect? he thought.

The mates at the pub pulled him into their inner sanctum now that he was experienced with the fairer sex. Joe hoped they would never find out that his lover was an older woman, not that he was ashamed of Ginger. In fact, he admired her. Joe knew the boys would never understand, when he could have any of the young attractive girls who swooned over him after he sang.

'It seems it's not guns or drugs, Joe. Your friends must be into something that my connections know nothing about. I'll keep my eyes and ears open all the same.'

'Ginger, I hope you are not taking any risks. That's something I couldn't deal with, you being hurt in any way.'

'So, you care about me, Joe.' Ginger laughed, tussling his hair.

Joe would never know if Ginger cared for him, or he was just a toy that she had fun with, filling a need.

Chapter 13

The Enigma of Grief
Joe

MOST NIGHTS JOE HOPED Ginger was waiting for him. Their relationship had taken on a different meaning now. It was like Joe had a partner in the crime that he was involved in, although it wasn't his to answer to. Maybe Ginger was treating him like a cause now, rather than a necessity. Joe didn't care much. He needed her and that was that. Funny though, he hadn't seen the two men since the night Joe had told Ginger about the predicament he was in.

He had asked Ginger why Benny wasn't around. She just smiled and said he must have had to leave. He knew she must have got rid of him some way or another, but decided it was best not to ask. Joe didn't really know Ginger. There was a lifetime between them. She never talked about her past. Joe knew that it was out of bounds. 'All best left alone,' was her answer the only time he did ask.

The night came when Joe finally saw Ted sitting at the bar, watching him sing. The fluttering wings of a thousand butterflies gathered, turning Joe's stomach into a whirlpool. Had he finally come to offer him his big break? He was singing one of his new love songs. They were coming easier now. The relationship with Ginger was the closest feeling that he had had to love. It gave Joe new inspiration. But he knew for sure it wasn't true conventional, romantic love he felt for Ginger. He knew if he wasn't there, he would be replaced by another. Their need for each other was a powerful force, whatever it was that passed between them. 'His muse' he had called her one day. Joe saw tears spring into her eyes.

He stepped slowly over to Ted and took the stool next to him.

'Hello Ted. It is so good to see you out of the office.' Joe didn't want to be seen as over-anxious.

'Nice to see you too, Joe. I hear you're drawing in the crowds with your songs.'

Joe took note of the fact he didn't say his singing.

'The Beetles are taking the world by storm. Sometimes I think their lyrics are a grab as much as their rock-pop beat. There's so much rock these days, and the world is getting closer, making local music hard work. It's not what it used to be, Joe.'

Joe knew this was a nice way of saying, 'Your voice is old fashioned.' His heart sank.

'Joe, would you consider writing new lyrics for a rock and roll band that is on the way up? They're in need of help in that area. Your words are very moving, with an understanding that penetrates, just what the young fans are looking for now.' Ted put his hand on Joe's shoulder, as if he knew that Joe's disappointment would be hard to bear.

Joe was just getting over the shock of being rejected for his singing, and then the shock of being asked to write lyrics for another band.

'The money will be good, and they look like getting overseas, so it'd be a big step forward for your career.'

'Thanks Ted. I will get back to you. I'll have to sleep on it.' Joe had trouble responding. His head was spinning. A songwriter for someone else was something he had never thought of up until this moment. The members of the band had expected Joe to come out bouncing with good news. Joe's glum face told them that he had been rejected once again.

'Ted wants me to write songs for an up-and-coming rock band.' Joe wasn't taking this offer as a step up and was visually upset. The band's reaction was different. They slapped him on the back. Congratulations were in order. Joe was seeing this as a failure for some reason, thinking that if you weren't the one on stage, you were nothing. Listening to the boys made him think he might be wrong.

Telling Ginger, her beaming smile made Joe realise that he would take the offer.

'I am so proud of you, my beautiful boy. I wonder how long it will be before you will be off to claim your fame and fortune and get out of this old boarding house run by an older woman.'

'I won't be leaving you Ginger. I need you as my inspiration, my beautiful girl.' They both laughed. Joe couldn't imagine leaving Ginger, but Ginger knew it wouldn't be long before they would be without each other.

Joe met the band that he was to work with a few weeks later. There were three young boys, Cedar, Basil and Sorrel and one girl called Blossom. Joe was sure they weren't their real names and had been chosen to coordinate the band as one, becoming 'The Flowers'.

It seemed to work for them. They were full of ambitions and dreams, not to mention talent, of which they had plenty. The group had met at school a few years earlier and were a close-knit group, though Joe felt at home with them straight away, and was happy to be part of their team. The Flowers practised in Blossom's parent's garage. They had soundproofed it for the band when they were younger, in hopes that they might develop into something big.

Now with the backing of Ted as their agent, it just might happen for them.

Joe stayed with the band and the pub writing his lyrics when they came to him. He was paid nicely when his songs were accepted. He was getting a bulging bank account, which put a smile on his face when making another deposit. He felt satisfaction when he heard The

Flowers singing one of the songs he had written over the radio. It was amazing.

Joe had told Bill and Nancy about his songwriting, occasionally ringing, although he corresponded mainly with a lengthy letter. He found it easier to lie in a letter about the situations he found himself in. He was sleeping with an older woman, had been involved with a murder and lost Nancy's car. These were the secrets Joe hoped they would never know about. His parents wouldn't have understood how their son had got into a lifestyle that was so far out of their comprehension. Sometimes he wondered about it himself. It wasn't a vision that had entered any of the plans when he'd contemplated a future of stardom and glamour.

Now and then, Joe Pike was mentioned along with The Flowers, giving his ego a boost. Even at the pub the girls would call out, 'Love your words,' in The Flowers songs, giving him a small taste of fame.

Ginger had suggested that living in a boarding house wouldn't be a fitting place for a man with the status he aspired to. Joe just laughed and gave her a hug saying, 'You can't get rid of me that easily.' Ginger smiled up at him, her eyes full of gratitude, which surprised Joe. She always seemed so independent, never needy. She hadn't been herself, Joe thought, a second hug lasted longer.

Elizabeth heard the name one day while listening to music and wondered if that was her Joe Pike that she prayed for at sunset.

Blossom was always looking at him with longing eyes, something he avoided constantly. He was quite satisfied in that area. Ginger was demanding enough for any man. Joe chatted with all the members, but tried not to give Blossom any signals, or give her any idea that he was interested in the sparkling eyes that were trying to get his attention. That became Joe's added mission, to discourage Blossom from being interested in this songwriter.

'Have you got a girlfriend, Joe?' she asked, her head on the side. Smiling, looking at him with those longing eyes.

'No, but I'm not looking.' He didn't know what else to say.

'Are you gay Joe, why didn't you say?'

'No, I'm just happy the way I am at the moment, that's all.'

'You just don't like me. Is that it?'

'No, I really like you Blossom, just not at the moment.' Joe was getting himself into trouble the way the conversation was going. To his surprise Blossom seemed to accept this feeble excuse and moved away. She started to play one of his most popular love songs. Joe was hoping that would be the end, and she would set her sights on another.

Ginger wasn't waiting for him as much as usual when he got home from the pub. It didn't worry him at the time. He was always tired too, these days. The songwriting was becoming more important now The Flowers were getting gigs everywhere, all over the country, and there was talk of an overseas tour. We need some new songs Joe, 'Get your finger out,' was the cry every time he entered the garage. They could have moved into a city studio, but they preferred to stay in Blossom's home and the suburb that they were comfortable in.

Joe noticed that Blossom was becoming moody. Some days she was so happy and sang as if on stage, performing to an audience that the Beetles would attract; and others it seemed she was singing without a soul. Joe asked Basil, the unofficial leader, if she was okay. He just smiled and said, 'Yeh, good man. She wants to go psychedelic. That's the way to go. Your words will be a bigger hit when we reach that level.'

Joe never asked again. He had seen the drugs that were working their way into the music industry, destroying lives. The band was good enough without the hype of lysergic acid, and his words didn't need any help either. He did not want to go down with them when their world collapsed. It worried Joe.

He declined the invitation to accompany The Flowers on their overseas tour. Ginger hadn't been feeling well, and the thought of leaving her was something he couldn't do to his favourite old girl. That thought made him think of Nancy. She would be so proud of him. She would be telling the girls in town at the butcher's and the greengrocer how her son was doing so well in Sydney. Joe thought she would add that he hasn't got a girlfriend though. I will never have a grandchild. Even though he had hurt her so much over the years, she still thought the sun shone out of his arse.

The tour was a remarkable success. The world was at their feet. Joe's words drifted across the oceans to new lands. He had an offer from an agent in the United States. Getting to Sydney was an important thing for a country boy who had turned his back on the best mother anyone could wish for. He remembered the hurt he had caused over his love for two favourite cows.

It seemed to Joe that it would be too much for both his parents to imagine him in another country. He was not about to take that giant step. He was afraid of leaving the world that he knew for a place that would keep him behind-the-scenes, not enabling the steps necessary to gain the fame he craved. Joe would leave that for another day. Hearing his words playing through the radio would be enough until he was ready to explore the world further than Sydney.

Finally, the call came. He could go and pick up Nancy's car. Joe thought Ginger might like the two-hour drive south to get out of the city. However, she still didn't appear to be her normal, cheery self. He decided not to make the suggestion, realising she wouldn't be up for the drive back, following him in her car. It was a selfish thought, wanting her company.

So, he went off by himself to retrieve the little Austin A40. As the bus hurtled along, the landscape quickly changed. Joe was homesick for the pasture meeting the blue sky, the waving grasses going to seed, the wind whistling through the trees, giving them their own identity. Each one seemed to speak to him as if he had been missed. This wasn't his bush landscape, but it was Australia, New South Wales, a cousin to Victoria. They smelled the same, had the same DNA. This was his land, and he would be loath to leave it.

Joe reflected on the time he'd had in Sydney. Strange, it hadn't met his expectations, although he did not want to go home. That wasn't for him anymore, even though knowing the bush would never leave his psyche, and the true mother of the earth would always be there to pull him into her arms.

When he arrived at the police station, he recognised Jackson, the policeman that had been there on the day of the crime, Joe's nightmare.

'Hi, Joe. Finally, they are releasing your car. It has been a while. You must have missed it.' Jackson was his friendly self.

'Yes, I don't know why they would have needed it for so long.'

'This is a complicated case, not that we at this unimportant station know much about it. They kept us pretty much in the dark. Something to do with a couple of mining companies and the government. Oops, I might have said too much.'

Joe thanked Jackson for the keys and decided not to ask any questions. He didn't want to hear any more in fear of knowing something that, whoever Steve and Benny were might appear and the whole stalking affair would begin once more.

The drive back to Ginger was full of dark thoughts about the killings, bringing that day alive again. Maybe the government was behind the whole thing. That's why nothing was reported in the papers. It started to make some sort of sense.

'Oh my God, maybe I really am a spy!' Joe laughed to himself. In between the memories of the murder, or murders, there were new words that the open air along with the sight of the distant mountains and Joe's beloved countryside were bringing to life.

A million ideas for new songs were swimming around in his head like never before. Just out of Sydney, Joe pulled over. The sunset was stunning, with the fierce red, orange, and yellow merging into gold. Elizabeth's name seemed to be written all over it, praying, hoping she glowed in every sunset, with every prayer bringing her happiness. If only Joe could see her face. He thought of the only image that was left; the little girl lying next to him in a hospital bed.

Joe drove Nancy's car down the lane behind the boarding house, parking it next to Ginger's steel-grey Jaguar. Ginger will laugh when she sees the little Austin. Joe just knew what she would say: 'Do you call that a car?' And they would both laugh.

Nancy needed her car back. He must think about getting it down south soon. Joe didn't like thinking about his mum driving the old ute into town. He now had the use of Ginger's car if need be. Joe didn't like driving in Sydney anyway, far too busy for him. There were no dirt tracks around the city.

Ginger seemed back to her old self when Joe returned. He had only been gone for the day; it was not much different to being away at work. He didn't care why there was improvement. It made him happy to see her back, fussing around with her usual vigour. Seeing Joe with a beaming face, she threw her arms around his neck. Joe hoped no-one was around to see her open affection. He still thought the other boarders didn't know about the relationship with the landlady. Joe was still a boy from the bush, worldly wisdom eluded him.

Joe spent every minute he could writing down new songs. The words were flowing, unscrambling as they escaped his brain, lightening the load he had brought back with him from the drive home in Nancy's car. When he shared the songs with Ginger, she encouraged him, saying he was the genius that she had waited a lifetime to discover. Joe laughed, but secretly he was happy that she thought so highly of him.

Joe loved Ginger with a passion that was unexplainable. How could a young, good-looking man with the world out there for the asking, be madly in love with a woman older than his mother? He didn't try any more to pretend to himself that it was anything other than true love, shameful as it would be seen by others. His guilt was subsiding. He was almost proud that Ginger would want him in her bed. There was an electrifying intensity between them that scared Joe sometimes. How would he ever face life without her?

Weeks later Ginger told Joe, 'Your murders are all about uranium. It is best that you say nothing about any of it. It's a very tricky business that. Don't involve yourself. Never say another word to those men.' Ginger was so serious. Her words scared Joe. Her connections must have found out after Joe came back with the information he had received from Jackson. It worried Joe that Ginger knew people that would be able to access this type of knowledge. While the stalkers weren't bothering him, Joe was glad to leave it alone and concentrate on his work and Ginger. She was becoming a more important part of his day, or more so nights that he spent in her arms. That's where his mind and body were content.

The Flowers continued to be successful, and Joe happily rode on their coat tails. A couple of his songs nearly made it to the top of the charts. 'We will make it next time,' was the band's cry. Joe secretly hoped that day would come. Ginger would be so thrilled. Just seeing her face when it happened would be something; all the reward Joe could ask for and a gift for his muse.

Joe noticed his old girl was looking tired, wanting to go to bed earlier than usual, sending him off to his room some nights.

'You had better pay the doctor a visit. You are looking worn out,' Joe said as gently as he could. He was starting to worry about her.

'No, I just need a couple of days to get over it. I will be as good as new. You keep me going Joe. Don't leave me.'

'You know I never would do that. Don't think of it for one minute. I love you, Ginger.'

'Thank you, my beautiful boy.'

He'd never really said that he loved her before. He wasn't sure that was what she wanted to hear. But now he wasn't ashamed to admit it. *Why didn't she say she loved him back?* Joe wondered. Maybe that was too much to expect. They had a bond that bound them together. Joe didn't think it could be broken. He thought of Elizabeth. It was nearly sunset. He was bound to her too.

As he followed Ginger up the stairs, he noticed that she seemed slower tonight. He helped her with her clothes, lifting her onto the bed. They laid together for some time.

'Could I call the doctor? Please let me,' Joe pleaded.

Ginger smiled. 'I have left the number by the phone downstairs. I will tell you when. Just hold me tight my beautiful boy.'

Joe held her. They melded together. They seemed to become one.

Ginger's hand that had been squeezing Joe's so tightly relaxed. It took Joe a minute to realise that she was gone. Her hand slipped out of his grip as they lay beside one another on the sheet. Joe stared. A hand that didn't seem to belong was beside them. He wanted to brush it away. It had no life. It wasn't Ginger's hand. Her hands had a gentle strength, touching his young body, running her fingers through his hair down his back, tickling him if he wouldn't smile, saying, 'Come on laugh, no-one is grumpy in my bed.'

Joe told his heart to stop beating. 'Don't break the thread that holds us together,' he pleaded to the air that surrounded them. As he lay back on the pillow, the glow of the bed side lamp started to flicker, almost like morse code. There was a message he couldn't read. 'Oh God, I am losing my mind.' Joe was drowning, sinking to depths unimaginable.

Finally, he struggled to the phone. He rang the doctor, not knowing what else to do.

'You must be Joe. Ginger said you would be looking after all the arrangements, and I am to give you her solicitors card, so you can get in contact with him to get the instructions.'

The doctor shook Joe's hand. Joe couldn't speak. He led the doctor to Ginger's room, although it seemed he knew the way.

'Didn't Ginger tell you that her heart had been failing for some time? You are in shock. I will prescribe you some medication to get you through the days ahead.' The doctor was a kind man, Joe thought through the fog invading his world.

'No, no she didn't say.' Shock after shock. Why didn't she tell him? He may have been able to help her more.

'She was a tough old thing and had endured so much, but always made the best out of what life dished up, good and bad. We all loved Ginger. I knew this day wasn't far away.'

Joe looked down on the woman lying there in the place that had led him to his paradise, looking so peaceful. An angel. He wondered who she really was. His Ginger belonged to him, not them.

'Ginger never got over losing her two children, a boy and a girl, five and six. Did she ever tell you? What the doctor was saying hit Joe's ear drums like an explosion of firecrackers.

'No, she never said,' he managed.

'It was polio, way back. I will call the undertaker and give him her information.' The doctor gathered up his bag and walked away down the stairs.

Joe knelt down next to his beautiful old girl, taking her cold hand and cried until his heart turned inside out and broke into little pieces. How could he go on…

Chapter 14

Holding on to the Invisible
Joe

JOE CALLED IN SICK. He couldn't face going to the pub. His stomach churned every time he tried to make sense of Ginger's death. She had been taken away. He wandered around the room, smelling her clothes, spraying himself with perfume that sat on the dressing table, touching special trinkets, picking up the book she was reading a light-hearted romance that surprised Joe. Maybe that was her way to relax, waiting for the prince of her dreams to come home. The prince hoped his queen didn't need that type of story to put her in the mood. Joe cried.

It was like someone took a foreign hand and made it open the bottom drawer in her dressing table, where she would sit at the mirror, hoping to see her youthful self just once more. Ginger had told Joe about it one night and they had rolled on the bed in laughter. There was a tin box. Joe opened the lid. Two faces stared up at him from their hospital beds, sad, little, grey faces that should have been smiling, wanting to run and play. He turned the photo over. There were the names, Tippy and Hope, Ginger's children. Joe's heart broke. He stared and stared at the children. They became Joe Pike and Elizabeth Kasper. Joe cried.

Joe was to meet the solicitor the next morning in the dining room. He was still amazed that he had to take responsibility for Ginger's affairs; she had many old friends that could have stepped up to the mark.

'Good morning, Joe.' Dan Collins greeted him with a firm handshake.

Joe was in a dark place and could not smile, but managed to say, 'Have a seat, Dan.'

'First of all, I must congratulate you. It is a fortune that is coming your way.'

'What are you talking about, for helping with her affairs?'

'Didn't Ginger tell you?'

'No, Ginger like to keep secrets, it appears.'

Joe was in no mood for any of this cat and mouse carry on. He just wanted the funeral over and done with, so he could go into a deep hole and bury himself.

'Ginger named you as her next of kin. You are the sole recipient of her Will.'

Joe took a minute to understand what Dan was saying. He knew she owned the boarding house and the Jaguar parked out the back. His head was spinning. Why did she do that? Joe was bewildered.

'So, all the assets go to you, Joe. It is all yours to do with as you please; all of Ginger's estate.' Dan was talking fast, as if not wanting Joe to asked questions that couldn't be answered, or tell him things that he wasn't supposed to know. A new nightmare was looming. Joe started to tremble.

'I'm not sure why Ginger has left it to me. There must have been others that would be more deserving,' Joe stammered.

'It was you she loved, Joe. Ginger was a loyal friend to many, but it was you she loved, and she wanted you to be happy and safe. Those were my instructions.'

'She really loved me, she really did?' Joe sounded like a halfwit. He just was so surprised. She had never said, and how he had wanted her to.

'I think she has proven that she certainly did. Her wealth could have been spread around, but she wanted you to be free of financial worry, to be able to pursue your career and maybe help your parents out when they wanted to get off the farm.'

'Ginger told you all about my parents and my ambitions?' Joe didn't think Ginger listened to half his drivel, and was surprised that she would pass it on to this Dan.

'I have looked after Ginger and her finances for many years and have given advice too many times to remember. She was a good stick and will be missed by all the Sydneysiders who have crossed her path. She helped many along the way. Everyone loved her.'

Joe sat and stared at his hands, turning them over and over, looking for something, although he didn't know what.

'I need your signature on these documents, and then you can organise the funeral. Would you like me to come to the undertaker with you? I can see you are having trouble coping. Ginger was so proud of you, Joe. She will be happy with whatever you decide to do.'

'Thank you. That would be helpful. I have never had to do anything like this. My only grief in the past that I have suffered was the loss of my two cows.' Joe wished he hadn't said that. Dan must think he is dealing with a child. Joe didn't know what he was doing, or how he would get through the next few days.

'Okay I will pick you up later this afternoon. Look after yourself, Joe. That's what Ginger would have wanted.'

'I hope you will be able to look after the finances for me, Dan, like you helped Ginger.' Joe wondered how he had the forethought to ask that question. Was greed and the love of money already pressing his buttons as it did to others that used wealth as their lifeline?

'She was hoping you would ask me to do just that. I will be happy to look after you, Joe. Funny though, you never asked me what you've inherited.'

'I thought it was the boarding house. Is there more?'

Dan held Joe's arm. 'That's right the house, car and two million dollars in cash, stocks and bonds. Ginger loved you, Joe, don't ever doubt it.'

Joe was paralysed, sitting there like stone. There had never been any indication that Ginger was a multi-millionaire, not that he had given it a thought, and she would never have talked about herself anyway. His Ginger was unknown to the world. They'd danced a duet that no-one else would understand, living on an island, an existence that no other entered. It was their escape from reality. She would be judged as a predator, devouring a young boy, turning him into her toy, to be played with at her leisure. Joe questioned her love for one moment. Was she replacing her son, the child she had lost, with any young man that came her way?

Joe expelled that idea. She'd never treated him as a son, only as an equal, admiring his talent, encouraging, supporting like a partner. That's what they'd been: partners. That is what Joe believed and that was the way it was.

'That's why I'm her beneficiary. She did love me,' he told himself over and over. Joe was convinced it was what Ginger wanted, and he would honour her wishes and carry on and make her proud. He finished arguing with himself and laid on her bed, soaking in as much of her as was left, hoping it would last for his lifetime.

The days that followed were like walking through a mist, sometimes so heavy that Joe found it hard to break through. For some reason, every one of Ginger's old friends seemed to know who he was. Her social life away from the boarding house must have been extensive. Joe wondered how she was always there at lunch and when he was coming home after closing. Even if he didn't stay behind for a drink, she was always there. Only in the early days. Maybe she was out on the nights he didn't get invited to the apartment.

In the beginning they'd never talked about anything. With the appetite they had for each other there was never time for chit-chat. Then he'd started to sing, and Ginger would ask how the gig went, and their conversations became more like friends having a chat until the passion got in the way. Joe realised now that Ginger made sure there was never an opportunity for Joe to ask questions about her day.

He shook hands with people from all walks of life – a sea of faces he had never seen before, all telling little stories about how Ginger had helped them out of some jam or another. His head was spinning. Joe didn't care. This wasn't his Ginger that they were burying, it was theirs, the one he didn't know, the one he didn't care about. They didn't know what the softness of her body was like against his skin. They couldn't have inhaled her sweetness or known the feel of her gentle touch that took his breath away.

He wondered if they knew she'd given all her money to this stranger. Did they know she had so much? How had she come by all this wealth anyway? Joe's mind was in turmoil. Would some vulture try to take the money? Joe was becoming paranoid. Was it losing Ginger or was it her money? Was that going to change him into a greedy fool? His thoughts raced. Music, he needed his music. Joe formulated a plan in his head: As soon as this funeral is over, I will escape to the pub and hide behind the music.

Everyone had left. Only Dan Collins and the doctor remained. They were the ones that seemed to know all about his relationship with their old friend.

'Joe, will you call into the office next week and we can discuss your plans? It will take some time to get everything sorted, but it will be easier if I know what's on your mind.' The doctor didn't say a word, though Joe could see he had been crying. Funny when he came to see Ginger dead, he didn't seem to have any emotion. Maybe he'd loved her too.

'Okay, I will do that, not that I have given the future much thought. It is so overwhelming. I am not sure when I will be able to think straight. I don't know how I am going to live without her. She kept me in line, so to speak. She was my muse, you know.' Joe could see the two men standing like statues, now wanting to cry like babies. Joe couldn't think of what he was going to tell Dan. The only thing that kept going through his mind was getting a new car for Nancy. Yes, that's the first thing he would get Dan to organise.

'Before you go Dan, not that I want to ask, but is the money...' Joe paused.

'Ginger never broke the law, Joe, she made some very wise deals when her husband died, just after she had lost her children. I'm not saying that she was as pure as the driven snow; Ginger had some very hard times over the years, but I think her last ones with you were the best. Her estate is your reward. Accept it as it was given, with gratitude, and handle it with care.'

The day after Ginger's funeral Joe headed to the pub. His head down, watching the cracks in the footpath, he didn't notice if the sun was shining, or the clouds covered the blue. It was just another day he had to get through. The music was helping. It took him away, drifting into space, but the earth was always waiting to hit this grief-stricken fool with a thud.

Later that night, he happened to look up as he was about to bump into someone. It was Steve or whatever his name was.

'Hi Joe. I hear you lost your woman.'

'Shit, get out of my way, you bastard. I know nothing. Leave me alone.'

Joe hurried on, getting away as fast as he could. He realised that Ginger must have had someone protecting him. Now she was gone they were back, and they knew about his relationship with the landlady. Did the whole world know that he'd been sleeping with Ginger? Did they know about the money? Would they try to get it off him? Joe trembled when he got to the boarding house. He sat in a dark corner and stared into his misery. Joe wasn't sure how he was ever going to manage anything. He felt like an empty shell.

The days rolled into months. The boarding house ran as if Ginger was still there. The cook and cleaners stayed on. Dan handled the wages. The only thing Joe had to do was book new boarders in, and the old ones out. He had no problem doing that in the fog he still walked around in.

He expected Ginger to appear any minute. Maybe he needed to get away for a while, get out of Sydney. He couldn't go home. How would he explain all the money? He couldn't tell Bill and Nancy. They wouldn't understand how anyone would give him the wealth that had been bestowed on him. Not that he had any of it yet. He really wanted to get Nancy a car. She might believe he had earnt enough from his music for a car, but anything else was unexplainable.

The guys in the band knew that Joe's landlady had died, although they couldn't understand the depth of depression that he was in. Even the music wasn't giving him the vibe that it usually did. He was down in the dumps. As much as they tried to get him out of it, nothing worked. They soon gave up and accepted that he had to get over it in his own way and time.

The Flowers had missed Joe and wondered where he had got to, not seeing him for a few weeks. Blossom was nominated to ring the boarding house and check.

The phone rang in the hallway and whoever was walking past lifted the receiver. Sometimes it went unanswered. It was Blossom's lucky day. Joe picked up. Blossom didn't recognise his voice for a minute.

'Is that you Joe? We have been missing you calling in with some new words. We need you, Joe. I need you. Where have you been?'

'I haven't been well. Sorry, I should have let you know. It's been hard.'

'Your voice seems strange. Have you had a sore throat?'

'Yeh! That's right, a sore throat.' Blossom had given him an out. There would be no more questions. 'I'll get back to work soon. I miss you guys too.' Funny, Joe thought, I do miss them. That was the first time Joe had felt any sign of normality since Ginger had gone.

'I really miss you, Joe. I will be waiting.'

'Are you sober, Blossom?'

'For you, I will be. Don't stay away too long.'

'A couple of weeks. See you then.'

Joe hung up and stood looking at the phone as if he could see Blossom's face, young and pretty. He wondered if he had ever really looked at her properly, as he climbed the stairs to Ginger's apartment, well, his apartment now. He would have to change some things. Yes, maybe paint the walls a darker colour. He liked navy-blue. He wondered if Ginger had liked navy-blue too.

They had never talked about their colour preferences. Ginger always wore pink, but he couldn't do that, just too girly. They had accepted each other as they were. Joe had learnt not to ask questions, and thinking back, Ginger found out all she wanted to know about him in a way that didn't seem like prying. Joe was happy to tell her all about Elizabeth. He'd never thought about the reason why she wanted to know about a childhood friend. It became clear the moment he was told about her two children.

How he wished she had shared the tragedy with him. Their relationship would have been seen as strange to the outside world, the conventional world, but to Joe it was the truest, most loyal and meaningful connection two people could have. No-one was going to take that away from him.

Slowly Ginger was leaving the room as Joe moved more of his belongings in and hers out. He was losing his old girl. He had placed a portrait that he found stored in the back of her wardrobe, a photo she must have had taken a few years back, on the opposite wall to the bed. She was looking down on him just the way he liked it.

He didn't have a concept of the amount of money that would be his to control, the only thing he wanted was to buy Nancy a new car, a latest model Holden. That was his plan. Joe had instructed Dan to organise it to be paid for and delivered to the farm as soon as possible.

'There are just a few more details to finalise, Joe, and it will be there.' That was Dan's latest message. Joe had to be patient. He only wished it was possible to see the look on his mother's face when the bright, new, shiny car arrived.

In his melancholy mood, he started to jot down words, hoping they might get his mind back into some sort of working order. With luck, a song might be born out of his grief. 'True love' came together between his tears. It was the darkest days he would ever know, or so he thought.

'True love'
My true love watching from high above
A love so strong it cannot die
angels carried you away into the sky
Ginger oh my Ginger, I will for ever cry
I didn't have the strength to hold you close
Though I was the one who loved you most
Why can't you stay, just for one more day
Ginger oh my Ginger don't go, don't go away
The glowing embers of love will never fade
To be continued in our masquerade,
We danced in our own parade,
Oh, Ginger I love your smile,
Oh, Ginger I love your style.
Ginger oh my Ginger my true love, my only love
I was your hand, and you were my glove
Unforgettable Ginger you will be my only true love.

THE DECISION TO SHOW 'True Love' to The Flowers was hard to make. It was Ginger's song, although he felt that it was the only way he could express his grief without making a fool of himself – yelling to the world how much he missed his true love.

The Flowers were pleased to see Joe, and noticed that he wasn't his confident self, almost introverted. Blossom planted a kiss on his cheek.

'Come on Joe, get over yourself. Everyone has a sore throat now and then. Oh, I see that the old pro that owned your boarding house kicked the bucket. Not a good time around you now. We'll get you back on your feet. Have you got any new songs for us?'

Joe wanted to hit her across the head and watch her bleed. It took all his strength not to walk out and turn his back on the band. The boys patted him on the back, saying they were hanging out for him to get back. It took Joe a minute to regain his resilience. He wished he'd given himself more time in his dark hole before facing the outside world.

The band was riding high. Their popularity was gaining momentum. They needed a new song to get them to the top. Reluctantly Joe showed them 'True Love', and they thought it was his best. Joe knew it wasn't going to sound like it did in his head when their rock beat regulated the tune, but his words would convey his thoughts and the meaning of his true love.

'I wish you had written those words to me, Joe.' Blossom almost drooled. 'You must have known true love. The words are from one lover to another. So, are you free again? You know I'm waiting.'

Joe felt sick. He thought, If I don't get out of here, I will make a fool of myself.

'Yes, that's right, but I wouldn't say I am free. I will be tied to that love forever. Sorry Blossom, that is just the way it is.'

'One day, Joe, one day.'

Chapter 15

Holding on to Lost Smiles
Joe

NANCY'S NEW CAR WAS on its way. The money was filtering through to Joe's bank account as Dan was getting all the finances sorted. Joe's mind boggled, knowing the business brain Ginger had and the achievements that she'd made. If he didn't have Dan, he would've been in big strife. He still did not think of the money as his. It was as though it still belonged to Ginger.

Joe had rung Nancy and told her there would be a surprise arriving by the end of the week, giving her no clue as to what it was. He couldn't remember being so excited, except seeing Ginger at the end of his day. Hopefully his mum wouldn't ask too many questions as to where the money came from to buy the car. More lies would be required.

The phone rang in the hallway. One of the boarders called, 'It's for you Joe. It's your dad. He sounds upset.'

Joe froze. His father never used the phone. He knew the car wasn't due to arrive for a couple of days. With wet hands he picked up the receiver. Sweat was running down his body; the clean shirt was sticking to his back. Something had to be wrong.

'Is that you Joe?' Bill's voice was trembling.

'Yes, Dad. What's the matter? Is Mum sick?' Joe had trouble getting the words to leave his throat.

'She is dead.' Bill burst into tears.

Panic overtook Joe. He had trouble holding on to the phone. The little voice he had seemed to disappear. 'What are you saying Dad? That can't be true. The car will be there in a couple of days.'

'What are you talking about, Joe? Didn't you hear me? Your mother is dead. You must come home.'

'Mum is dead. How could that have happened? She was always so fit and healthy.'

'Joe, the brakes failed on the ute. She never had a chance. The ute went off the road and hit a tree.'

Joe couldn't believe what he was hearing. The old ute that she should never have been driving! It would have never happened if he hadn't taken her car.

'Are you there? When will you come home? I need you Joe, my boy. What am I going to do? Joe, please come home,' Bill pleaded.

'Yes, I will be there as soon as I can. Just hang on. I will be home. Hang on, Dad.' Joe's mind spun around and around. He wanted to cry but there wasn't time. He had to get a bag and get going.

Joe went over the conversation with Bill while he was getting himself organised. He would drive, taking Ginger's Jag. If he drove through the night, he would get there by midmorning.

In his daze when leaving the boarding house, who should be waiting on the foot path but Steve.

'Going somewhere, Joe?' he asked.

Joe had brought the car around to the front door, so he didn't have to carry his bag around the back.

'What's it to you? Do you watch every move I make?'

'Sorry Joe, I was just passing.'

'Like hell you were.' Joe threw the car keys to the little Austin at him.

'Here, have the car. It's out the back. Maybe what you are looking for is in there. You might find something you left behind that the police never found. Just take it. It's yours. I never want to see that car again, or you either Steve, or whatever your name is. Get out of my life.'

Joe didn't wait for Steve to answer. He was in the car heading south out of Sydney, as fast as the speed restrictions would allow. He had told the boys at the pub that he might be gone for a couple of weeks. Also, he rang Blossom to tell her that he wasn't sure when he would be back. He would ring Dan when he got home to Little River.

He was talking to Ginger, mile after mile. Sometimes he sang her favourite song. He told her all about the farm. She might have heard most of it before, but she wouldn't care, Joe thought. Then he talked to himself, wishing that he knew more about her life.

Why didn't she tell me more about her kids? I would have loved to hear about my old girl's kids, Tippy and Hope, and their father. What about their father? Did she love him like she love me?

He loved someone he hadn't really known. Dan and the doctor would have known her better. But they didn't know his Ginger. Maybe he'd invented the Ginger he wanted to be in love with. He wondered if she was ever real. The money was his proof that her life before him wasn't where she belonged.

When he reached the farm gate, Joe had come to terms with the fact that his Ginger only lived during the years they were together. Dan and the doctor's Ginger had died before Joe was in her bed.

Joe told Dan what had happened, and that the new car hadn't arrived. Dan said it would be there later today, and assured Joe that he would be looking after everything until he got back to Sydney.

'Maybe you might have some ideas for new investments. The money is there for growth. Money makes money, Joe.'

'I will have my hands full for a couple of weeks. My mind is on my mother and father now.'

'I understand. Do what you must do. Look after yourself. I'll be here for you when you get back.'

Joe thanked him and wondered why he'd thought he could think of money at this time. Maybe money dominates the mind once it gets a hold of you. Joe would ask Ginger what to do; what suggestions she had for a new money-making venture.

Bill had not moved from his seat at the kitchen table, staring at his cup of cold tea, since Joe had arrived home. After greeting him, Joe had gone straight to the phone to ring Dan.

He sat down next to his father, taking his hand. Bill had aged more than Joe had expected. He was stooped over, with almost white hair. He hadn't washed a dish since Nancy had gone.

'We will have to go to the undertakers, Dad. You'd better go and have a shower.' Joe was sure he hadn't washed since it had happened.

'I'll wash up while you go to the bathroom. Off you go. Do you need me to get your clothes?'

Joe sounded like Nancy. They both thought the same thing, but neither said it. It didn't seem as if Joe would be getting back to Sydney any time soon. He was already feeling trapped.

Joe stood at the sink, washing and scraping the dishes just as Nancy would have done for all those years. He looked out the window, seeing the view Nancy would have watched every day, caring for her family. The seasons would have come and gone through that kitchen window, but her days would have been the same as she stood in this same place, at the same time, every day of her married life. Joe felt a wave of nausea go through him. Why had he just accepted that was her job? He'd never thought that she might have needed more out of life.

Now it was too late. His selfishness had taken so much from her. He took her car to Sydney, so that she had to drive that old broken-down ute. He might just as well have taken a gun and killed her in cold blood. And before that, the way he had treated her over those damn cows was appalling. Joe dropped a plate on the floor. The smashing sound brought him back to the present. It was no good feeling sorry for himself. Helping his dad was the important job now.

The car arrived just as Bill had finish getting dressed.

'What is this, Joe? A new car is getting unloaded in the driveway.'

'That was mum's present, a new car so she didn't have to drive the old ute into town.'

Tears filled Joe's eyes for the first time since he'd heard of Nancy's death.

'A few days too late, Dad. It was mum's surprise.' Joe's disappointment almost made him crumble. It was only a few days ago that the only thing he could think about was what the look on Nancy's face would be like.

'Where did you get the money for such a beauty from Joe?'

'Oh, I'm doing pretty well with my music Dad. Don't you worry about that. It is yours now.'

'No, I'll have to get a new ute. A farmer has to have a ute. I couldn't take that up the paddock and throw a sick calf in the back. The insurance will pay for a good second-hand ute. You get your money back, son.'

Joe wished that he would stop saying ute. It was grating on his brain every time he said it; all he could think about was the old thing smashing into that tree.

'Nance would have loved it though, and would have been so proud to drive it into town and say, "My boy bought me this new car." And you picked her favourite colour.'

Joe hadn't known that green was Nancy's favourite colour. That was just lucky, not that it mattered.

NANCY'S FUNERAL WAS SO different to Ginger's. Joe knew everyone there. The whole town was grief-stricken. Everyone loved his mum. Just like Ginger, Nancy had helped so many. As the stories reached his ears, he realised that most of what Nancy had done, he had never known about. In all her friends she'd left part of herself behind, for them to remember. Joe listened to her friends as they told him how proud she was of him. If they only knew. Joe's guilt deepened.

One thing: on the day he'd buried Ginger there had been so much he hadn't known about the love of his life, and now he was finding out things about his mother that were alien to him. Had he really known either of the women his heart was breaking over?

Joe and Bill were exhausted after the day that was like the darkest nightmare. They had both put on a brave face. That was what was expected of two strong men, and they played their part well. But now at home, they became a blubbering mess, neither knowing how to comfort the other. Joe went to his childhood bedroom and looked at the ceiling, not wanting to remember anything of that day, or any of the days he'd spent in this room in the past. There were cracks in the ceiling that had not been there when he had last laid on this bed. He wondered how much more the property had deteriorated. Exploring the place would have to wait for another day. It was time for the afternoon milking. He would have to help Bill, as much as he wanted to get away back to the dark corner, the hiding place Ginger would share with Nancy. Joe wondered if he would ever come out of this grief cave.

'I'll give you a hand with the milking Dad,'

'Thanks Joe. That will make the day a little easier.'

'The cows don't know that we are having a bad time. They will want their discomfort dealt with. Do you think they'll know Mum's not there?'

'They won't notice. She didn't always come down to the shed these days. She had slumped into a bit of a depression. She never said why she was so sad.'

'I hope it wasn't because I wasn't here.' That's all Joe would need to add to his guilt, he thought.

'Who knows? Just could have been sick of milking, morning and night.'

'How will you manage Dad? By yourself, I mean.'

'You won't come back then? I shouldn't have said that. You have a career that will make you famous. Of course you won't come back. The cows are my life. I will be okay.'

'I'll get back as often as I can,' Joe said, knowing that was not true.

Lie after lie was becoming a way of life that he never gave a second thought to.

The week after the funeral was the longest seven days of Joe's life. He had helped Bill with as many jobs as he could while there was daylight. Bill had let so much go. He was getting past doing the heavy work, although the cows looked as good as ever. They were his main priority. Joe was satisfied with that and thought the farm would go on until Bill joined Nancy.

Arrangements were made with a local Holden dealer to exchange the sedan for a ute. The look on Bill's face was almost compensation for Joe not getting the pleasure of seeing or hearing about Nancy's reaction when she had got her car. Bill thanked Joe and felt like a kid with a new toy.

'A brand-new ute! Thank you, Joe. Your mother was right about you, you are a good boy.' Bill couldn't wipe the smile off his face.

Bill's comment gave Joe another reason to add to his guilt list.

'Before I leave, can I arrange for a rouseabout to come in and help you with the work? Just the heavy stuff?'

'No, I don't want anyone interfering in my affairs. I will leave anything I can't handle until you come for a visit. I have the cows. They will be there for me. Joe, I have some knowledge now that I gained when Nancy was away in her mood, internalising her world, how much your pet cows meant to you when you were a young boy.'

Joe stared at his father. The emotion that surged up in his chest scared him. How could the feeling of Dot and Jessie still hold such a special place in his heart?

'That's okay Dad, I did cause a bit of a rumpus, didn't I? I've felt so bad over the years for blaming you and Mum, making life hard for us all.'

'I understand, Son.'

'I'm heading back to Sydney in a couple of days. I have commitments I have to take care of.' Joe was relieved when Bill never asked what his commitments were.

'That's okay. You get on with your life. You are young and your talent can't be wasted.'

Joe wasn't sure whether the world needed what he had to offer. But if it made his father justify the reason for him leaving, well, let it be.

Joe felt some comfort sitting in Ginger's Jag on the way home. As he thought of Sydney and the boarding house now, he felt her there in the passenger seat, smiling.

He was sure he heard her say, 'Turn the boarding house into a boutique hotel.' By the time he had reached King Street he had redesigned the boarding house from top to toe. He couldn't wait to tell Dan his ideas.

'Do you think that is a good idea, Dan? A boutique hotel, Ginger's place? The classiest accommodation in Sydney, with all the trimmings?' The excitement rose in Joe's voice.

'Well, that could be just what Sydney needs. It'll take some time and you'll lose the boarders for the duration of the renovations.'

'Yes, will we be able to manage with the cost involved? I mean, I can still live there, and with my jobs at the pub and The Flowers I'll be all good.'

'Did Ginger mention her idea before she died Joe?'

'What idea?'

'To turn the boarding house into a small hotel.'

'You mean she had that idea too?' Joe knew now that Ginger was still by his side.

'Yes, a couple of years back, but we decided it wasn't the right time.'

'Are we ready now Dan? It would be like a memorial to Ginger. I really want to do it. I know it will be a big chunk out of her money, but I am sure it will pay off.' Joe was hoping that Dan agreed.

'Let's do it, Joe. For Ginger.'

They shook hands and the deal was done. Dan would get onto an architect in the morning. As he turned to leave Dan waved, saying, 'Hope Ginger gives you some ideas. There will be many decisions to be made,' with the biggest grin.

Joe rang Blossom to say that he was back and would call into the studio in a few days.

'I'll be glad to see you. The others will be too. We have a bit of celebrating to do.'

'Oh, what for?' Joe didn't feel like anything would be worth celebrating.

'True Love' is heading up the charts. Ted thinks it might make it to the top.'

Joe was slow to respond. 'That's good. It'll put you on a good footing for your future.'

'You too, Joe.'

'Yes, I had better get back to writing. I am a bit stale at the moment. I'll see you, Blossom.' Joe couldn't talk any more. Blossom rang straight back. Joe didn't have time to move away from the phone.

'I forgot to tell you. Your friend, Steve, called by the studio and told us your mum had died. That's why you were away, and he would check on you when you got back.'

Joe was speechless. Did he know everything about every day of his life? And why did he care so much?

'Thanks for the message, but he's no friend of mine. Don't talk to him again if he comes by.'

'Okay, if you say so Joe. See you. I will be waiting.'

Chapter 16

The Joy of Finding Lost Connections
Elizabeth

THE ONLY THING ELIZABETH had wanted all these years was to see her brother and sister. Why wasn't she jumping for joy? Lottie put her arms around Elizabeth and encouraged her to go out into the shop and meet her brother.

'If I could stop shaking, I would. What do you think he wants? He can't take my house, can he?' She had waited for this day. Now she wished it would vanish with the past she had learnt to live without.

When Jonas smiled at her it was obvious they had the same mother or father, but Elizabeth knew it was the mother.

'Hello Jonas. It is so nice to see you after all these years. What brings you to Melbourne?' Elizabeth spoke as if talking to a customer.

'It is good to see you, my long-lost sister.' He smiled with Elizabeth's smile.

Elizabeth guided him to take a seat and asked if he would like a drink.

'Thank you. I've just had my lunch, so not for now. Do you own the café?'

'No, it's Lottie's baby. I just work here. She's my long-time friend, one of the best things that has happened in my life, her friendship.' The words came easily. She couldn't deny the sibling connection made her relax.

'You didn't say why you are in Melbourne.' However, she realised that she didn't know where he lived. Why did she presume that he still lived with the parents?

'I've come down for a Butchers' Convention.'

'So, you're a butcher then.'

'Yes, I have my own business in Bairnsdale. I don't live at home. I moved out when I was fourteen and started working for old Calvin. When he retired, he sold me the whole lot, business, shop and flat above. I consider myself a lucky fellow.'

'I thought I might have heard from someone when old Gerda died. I expected a challenge to the Will. I didn't think that Werner would want me to have the house.'

'They didn't even tell me she'd gone until months later, and just in passing. They never said anything about a Will or the house.'

'She was a rotten old thing, rotten to the core, as they would say.'

'So, you didn't like her then. They always said you loved her and wanted to stay at the family home with her and Otto. The fact that you never answered my letters, I took the hint and left you alone.'

'You wrote to me? I wrote to you and when I never got a reply, I thought you wanted me out of your life. Who wanted a crippled sister embarrassing them?'

'I never thought that. I don't think I realised you had a limp until I saw you just now.'

'They must have kept the letters from us for some reason. It was cruel. To think I could have had you in my life all this time... Oh Jonas, what sort of people have we come from?'

'I've wondered about a lot of things, but I was always treated very well and had no reason to enquire about you and the grandparents. If I had only known! I am sorry Elizabeth. When I said I might look you up while in Melbourne, they did act a bit weird. Mum said, "Don't believe anything that Elizabeth tells you. She's probably crazy." I wondered why she would say that.'

Elizabeth was shocked by all this information and found it hard to take in for a minute. Jonas must have felt the same, as they both seemed to be lost for words. Was it the right time to tell Jonas that she was only his half-sister?

'Are you married, Jonas? You would be such a good catch for a nice country girl.' Elizabeth giggled.

'No. I've never been in love enough to make that commitment.'

'What about Emma, is she happy?'

'She has had some ups and downs. She left home at about fourteen too. Maybe you were the lucky one, Elizabeth. Emma is okay now. She has two boys and a good husband. Neither of us go to the parent's place much. They are always bickering. It becomes draining. There's never any laughter, depressing really. Everyone is happier if we stay apart. Elizabeth wanted to tell Jonas so much about her miserable existence with Gerda. Being so happy now, it seemed pointless to revisit her childhood.

'I must get going. There will be a meeting in an hour. Would you be able to meet me in the city tonight for dinner at my hotel?'

Agreeing, they exchanged their details and would meet around seven. Elizabeth was swept away with excitement.

'By the way Elizabeth, I never imagined that you would be so beautiful,' Jonas said as he waved, stepping out onto the street.

'It seems by the look on your face, you had a nice get together, and you have no worries about losing the house.' Lottie was pleased Elizabeth looked so happy.

'He is delightful, Lottie. It's sad that we have been kept apart, probably because of my mother's affair.' The friends smiled at each other with an understanding that only true friends can have.

Over dinner Elizabeth explained everything to Jonas, sometimes finding the reflecting intimidating, telling her story as envisioned through her child mind. She told him of the trauma of the hospital, not elaborating on the pain; how Joe had saved her every day, owing him her life. Some of Gerda's cruelty had faded, almost seeming trivial now.

She told him how Otto had made her life more bearable. Otto and his merry-go-round. Elizabeth smiled, remembering her days cleaning the horses. She explained that her expectations of life weren't that high. She learnt to get satisfaction from her own company, and Lottie had taught her to be confident and proud of who she was.

She told Jonas about the Goldmanns; how they had given her a dream life. It was like living in a wonderland after the time with Gerda. She told him about why that life had come to an end, and her deep love for Maggie, the child she had the privilege to raise, now a beautiful model. She also mentioned that, apart from an occasional photo in a magazine, she had no contact with her.

'Maybe that was a bigger disappointment than being rejected by her own family,' Elizabeth concluded, touching Jonas gently on the arm.

Jonas had tears in his eyes when Elizabeth paused. The telling of her story had been strenuous, leaving her depleted. When she had composed herself, she asked, 'Was your childhood wonderful Jonas, the childhood I should have been a partner in?'

'I am so sorry Elizabeth; I have no idea why they deserted you. We grew up almost like you never existed.' A wave of guilt washed over Jonas.

Jonas told Elizabeth that her name was never mentioned after the first year they had moved to Gippsland. 'Emma wasn't old enough to take much notice, and I believed what they told us – that you loved Gerda and wanted to stay with her. Polio was never talked about, or how you had to stay in hospital for so long; only that you were happy with Gerda. After there was no reply to the letters, my kid's mind took over and I forgot about you, I am ashamed to say.'

Jonas went on, saying that he never had any reason to complain as he always thought he had a normal family. Having schoolteachers for parents gave both him and Emma a certain amount of status in the school yard, and then in the community as they got older. Both parents were respected, involved with charities and the like, and had their photo in the local newspaper all the time for work they had done, all for someone else, as both siblings realised as they got older.

They were well fed and clothed. They had a nice home, a three-bedroom, white weatherboard house that the government provided, and the school was a short walk away. Jonas asked if Elizabeth remembered how they walked to school, reciting tables and spelling. That was the only time they spent as a family. It wasn't until going to high school that they noticed how other families interacted more with their parents than they did.

Their parents never came to anything involving the children. Once out of sight and on the bus, it seemed as if their job was done. They never even asked what Emma and Jonas were doing unless there was a bad report, or they had mucked up over something. The parents bickered all the time. Jonas thought marriage was like that until he spent time at a mate's house and saw a happier situation. Both left school as soon as they could. Emma went to live with a friend and her family, and Jonas got a job in the abattoirs at Traralgon. That's where he learnt his trade and boarded with a workmate.

The funny thing was that their parents never objected to the siblings leaving school, nor leaving home, and not getting a trade or wanting to further their education in any way. The siblings just left. Jonas had gone some time before Emma. She became so lonely, telling Jonas, she felt like a stranger in her own home. Looking back, Jonas thought their parents were glad to get rid of their children.

When old Calvin advertised for an apprentice after Jonas had been away for over a year, he thought going home might be the right thing to do. Thinking there should always be some comfort in your home, and he had always felt safe there. Coldness was all he knew. He stayed with the parents until he acquired the business and had his own home.

'As I listen to your story, my dear sister, I know now just how bitter and hard they really were, the pair of them, our parents.'

Elizabeth knew she had to tell Jonas the reason behind her dismissal from the Kasper family. But after listening to him she realised the life that she'd always thought may have been an improvement on her green room and Gerda's grumbling, might not have been so. Was it living with Gerda and Otto that made Werner the way he was? It had nothing to do with the genes he was carrying.

Elizabeth knew her mother had a repulsive streak running through her veins. There was never any love between them from the day they took her to the hospital. That was the day her mother's love had abandoned her. Through caring for Maggie, Elizabeth had learnt what that love could have been.

'Jonas, there is something that I must tell you about the family. I am sure you have never been told. It is the reason that I only have feelings for you and Emma. I was pushed out for no fault of my own or the fault of the polio. I always thought that it was my withered leg that was the embarrassment; not wanting a cripple spoiling the perfect family image.' Elizabeth moved around in her chair to bide her time. This was a story she thought she'd never have to tell.

'Our mother had an affair after you were born, of which I was the result.'

Jonas was silent for a moment, staring at the table that was covered with the remains of the dinner to celebrate their reunion.

'Do you know who your father is?' Jonas asked with a trembling voice.

'No. Gerda said she thought he was Barry someone.'

'Barry Harwood, maybe. He came to the house a couple of times.' He thought for a moment. 'Funny, now I think about it, not long after we had left the city I think, I heard them in the kitchen talking, whispering. I remember Dad wasn't home. He was away on a school camp with his grade. Mum called out that she would be out for a while, and to get something to eat out of the fridge for our tea. It is all coming back to me. It was strange, but I was a kid. It meant nothing to me then. I never saw him again, though I heard his name mentioned sometime later. They were having an argument and dad screamed his name. They had plenty of fights, but this one was very heated, and this Barry's name rang in my ears. I bet he's your father.'

'I don't care about who he is. As I said before, I only care about you and Emma. I didn't want to have to tell you Jonas.' Elizabeth was distraught, destroying Jonas's belief in his parents.

'They have been living a fake life just so they are regarded as model citizens. It makes me understand them a little better, I suppose.' Jonas's face was drained of colour.

Elizabeth wasn't about to tell him anymore at this time. Finding out his father had been kidnapped by his grandparents… It wouldn't have been fair to burden her brother with old Gerda's crime. He would have enough trouble processing their mother's affair, and that she was only his half-sister.

'I wonder what else they've hidden from us.' Jonas was getting more than he'd expected from the meeting with his long-lost sister.

'Elizabeth, let's make up for all those stolen letters and write every week.'

'Yes, I would love to hear more about your everyday activities and get to know you, my brother. I want to be part of your life, Jonas. Thank you for finding me. It is a dream come true.'

'Next time I come to the city I will get Emma and the children to come too.'

Elizabeth realised that she was now an aunty. As slight as the blood tie was, she was an aunty!

Jonas kissed her on the forehead as they hugged and parted. 'I think I love you, Elizabeth. I hope we meet again soon.'

'Oh Jonas, we have lost so much time! How can we ever make it up?' Tears sprang into Elizabeth's eyes.

As she rode the tram home, Elizabeth felt numb. It would be weeks until she would tell Lottie about her precious time with Jonas, and how they were so connected that she never wanted to let him go again.

LOTTIE HAD NOTICED THAT Free Rita had not appeared since Jonas's visit. She was hoping that Elizabeth had buried her at long last.

'I haven't seen Free Rita lately, Elizabeth. Has she retired?' Lottie asked with her fingers crossed behind her back.

Elizabeth smiled. 'Maybe.'

Elizabeth later admitted that after meeting Jonas, the guilt was extreme.

'What if he had come on a Thursday and I was sitting there as Free Rita? I would be so ashamed. I've never had any reason to feel that way. Even when I found out that Gerda knew, I didn't care. But I would never want Jonas or Emma to think of me in that way. Knowing them has given me a reason to find my true self.'

A week later, Elizabeth came into the café with her makeover, surprising Lottie and the customers; the new haircut, and shorter dress took the eyes away from the therapeutic shoes and brace. Lottie almost cried. 'You are beautiful my darling! Why has it taken so long for you to believe in yourself?'

'I have a brother and sister now. They have both written to me since Jonas went home. They are what has been missing my whole life. One of my dreams has come true.'

'You can do anything you want now, my super woman. I am so proud to be your friend,' Lottie said, throwing her arms around Elizabeth and squeezing her so hard, they both fell about laughing.

Chapter 17

Daring to Dream a Dream
Elizabeth

LIFE RAN SMOOTHLY FOR Elizabeth. She was happy that there was no more evidence of Gerda at home, or so she thought. She loved the café and the letter writing to her new-found family. These all filled in her days without a load weighing on her shoulders. Her time off was now spent at the pier, watching the waves roll in and out with the yachts drifting along to the rhythm of the wind. She absorbed the sun that brightened her smile. She imagined becoming a mermaid and swimming to the horizon. Now that Free Rita had disappeared, Elizabeth, with her short hair that blew in the breeze, seemed to have a freedom that released the noose that had been strangling the hidden beauty. This light-heartedness gave her the peace of mind that she had been missing for so many years.

That was until the day that Elizabeth had always dreaded, the day that Lottie wanted to leave. It was in the middle of July. The days were dark, thick with cloud cover. Most days drizzled with fine rain. Elizabeth's trips to the beach were limited. Fewer customers flocked to the café. Elizabeth enjoyed the leisure of being able to chat to the regulars who still popped in for the cake and coffee.

Lottie had received a letter a few days before, Elizabeth remembered, and she had been quiet, which wasn't like her. Lottie hadn't been herself since the letter had arrived. Why hadn't Elizabeth realised something was wrong? The café was quiet. It was almost closing time when Lottie asked Elizabeth to come and sit down.

'We need to have a chat, Elizabeth.'

'What's wrong? You look so worried,' Elizabeth said with anxiety.

'I've had a letter from my daughter, saying that she isn't well and has to be hospitalized for some time. I really want to go to her. Our time might be running out.'

Elizabeth had never seen Lottie so down before.

'Just for a short time, do you mean?'

'No. I'm sorry, but I will have to sell the café. I've saved some money, but I will need whatever I can get for this place to get by. I don't want to be a burden to my daughter and her husband, even though the boys are working and away from home. No, my independence is so important to me, as you know.'

Elizabeth couldn't speak. It was like the world that had been created for her was crumbling again.

'I wish I could just hand it to you, but I really need the money. Oh Elizabeth, I am so sorry.'

The friends parted with a hug, both saying they would think about it overnight.

Elizabeth couldn't bear the thought of losing Lottie as well as the café, although she'd known the day would come that Lottie would have to go. She was happy for her friend, but oh so sad for herself. There had to be a solution.

That night, she fell asleep thinking she would ask someone tomorrow. But who? Dolly? She would have the answer, a friend who was outside the situation. But why had she thought of an old boss who had let her down in the end? She had been let down so many times, she said to herself as she drifted off into her dream world.

The new day dawned with the sun shining through the old-fashioned lace curtains that Gerda had left behind.

Why haven't I got rid of those dusty old relics? Elizabeth thought as she opened her eyes. It doesn't matter now. It won't be long. I won't be seeing them soon.

Her problem was solved. She felt it was Otto. He had saved her again. Elizabeth had no recollection of anything that had happened while she was asleep. The answer was just there. It all seemed so easy. It was like Otto had planned this all along.

The first thing Elizabeth did was to go to the real estate agent and arrange to put the house on the market.

'Lottie, I have put old Gerda's house up for sale. If you will accept what I get from the sale, I will be able to keep the café.'

Lottie burst out crying.

'Oh, Elizabeth, that is the best thing that I could have hoped for.'

'I will be very happy in your apartment upstairs. In fact, getting out of that old house will be the best thing that could happen.'

Lottie had stopped crying and was smiling, taking Elizabeth's hand, stroking it like you would an exquisite fabric.

'The agent wasn't sure how long it would take to sell. I thought you could start your trip with the savings and when the house is sold, we can finish the transaction.'

'Well, your mind has been working overtime my darling.' Lottie was almost speechless.

'All set then? I sound like I want you to go, but I don't. I will find it so hard to be without you Lottie. I don't know how I will be able to carry on.' Tears welled in Elizabeth's eyes. The pair sat in silence.

So that was the way it was going to be. Lottie would achieve her dream of being with her daughter and meeting her grandsons, and Elizabeth would have a new home and own her beloved café.

Elizabeth couldn't wait to tell Jonas her news, that they would be travelling in parallel paths; him in his butcher shop living above, and her in her café living above.

Lottie packed as much as she could take with her and asked Elizabeth what she wanted from the flat that she had called her home for so many years. She gave the rest away to anyone that would take her old belongings. It was the biggest clean up the flat had ever had. Lottie's heart sank a little as she saw the years of the past drift away like dust. Before Lottie left, Elizabeth signed a contract for the sale of the house, and Gerda was out of her life forever.

The day Lottie left; the doors closed for the first time since Elizabeth had been going to the café. It was such a strange day. Facing customers would have been too hard. With respect to Lottie, Elizabeth didn't want to change anything. She was planning to keep the décor just as it was and always had been from that first day they had met. Elizabeth had been a baby that day she'd walked into the café. It became the place of an education, learning so many life lessons, Lottie being the closest thing to a mother that Elizabeth had known. Elizabeth reflected on all those years. Even when Dolly took over her life, Lottie was still her strength. Lottie had prepared her for this day. She was now in charge of her own destiny.

The day was full of hugs and tears that never stopped for either of the two woman that had meant so much to each other. Lottie had seen Elizabeth through so many problems and watched her nearly destroy herself as Free Rita. Lottie consoled her over and over, listening to the way she was treated by the world around her. Elizabeth felt like she was losing part of herself. The tears finally stopped, and life went on.

The apartment had two bedrooms. Lottie had the smaller one set up as an office, where she sat at closing time, documenting her takings for the day. Elizabeth had asked her to leave it as it was, and she would follow in the same manner every night. After deciding to buy modern furniture, she would wash down the walls before it arrived, making the little place sparkle. With new cutlery and plates and the latest utensils, she felt like a princess. If this had happened without losing Lottie, she would have really swum to the horizon.

Elizabeth had little time to herself now. Days off and getting away to the beach were a rarity. Most nights after counting the takings and writing up the ledger she fell into bed, thankful for her day.

Lottie had left behind two girls who had worked for her for some time. Luckily, they had decided to stay with Elizabeth, and they became as loyal to her as they had been to Lottie. So, to the customers, the only thing missing was Lottie's jovial persona that seemed to linger at times around the café.

When there was time, Elizabeth did her letter writing to Jonas, Emma and Lottie, and only opened their return correspondence when she had time to sit and enjoy their words.

Lottie was looking after her daughter now that she was home recovering. She wrote that she'd felt at home as soon as she held her daughter and grandsons in her arms. She was able to find a small bungalow a few doors down from Helen's home, enabling her to come and go as the need may be. To Elizabeth, Pinehurst Carolina USA could have been outer space. The concept of being so far away was too much for her to cope with. She imagined Lottie was just away. Although Elizabeth missed her friend, she was happy that Lottie was getting more out of life than she had dreamt, after working hard all alone for many years, just as Elizabeth would be doing. Elizabeth smiled to herself and wondered when her dream that was waiting behind the horizon was going to arrive. Until then, she enjoyed fitting into Lottie's shoes.

IT WAS A SUNNY day with a slight breeze. The aroma from the ocean was fresh and salty, just the way Elizabeth liked, a perfect Melbourne day. She hadn't sat on the pier for some time. The café had been quieter for a time after Lottie had left. Elizabeth had to put in extra effort for a couple of months. It was paying off now and was busier than ever. But today she found her way to escape. She stared at her missing horizon and wondered how far Lottie was away. Could anyone swim that far? She giggled to herself, thinking how glad she was that no-one in the world could guess what went on in her head. She watched as her mermaid tail swished in the water, dancing with the waves. She was thinking about Otto, wondering how he was coping without his beloved merry-go-round.

As the sun was setting, she prayed for Joe and wondered if it was her Joe that had written the words to the song she would play in the café. She thought he must have had a 'True Love' to be able to write those words. She prayed he was happy.

He didn't recognise her as he walked into the café, looking around, wondering where she was. It was Thursday. Free Rita was always here on Thursdays. Elizabeth came over to his booth to take his order.

'Hi, sir. What can I get you today? We have some tasty cakes that you might not have tried before.'

'It isn't cake I was looking for, but I will have a coffee thank you, ah.'

'It's Elizabeth. You haven't been in before. I hope you enjoy my little café. I aim to please.'

The voice. He recognised the voice. 'I have been in some time ago, and yes, I did enjoy the service.'

A chill ran over Elizabeth's body as she realised that he must've been a Free Rita customer. Did she go and hide in the kitchen and let someone else deal with him? Or confront him and hope that he never came back?

As Robert watched her walk away, noticing her limp, he had second thoughts about it being the girl he had dreamt about, waiting for the day he was free.

She would accentuate her limp, and he would be confused and leave. That was Elizabeth's plan. When she took his coffee to the booth, she saw him look down at the orthopaedic shoes. Elizabeth was sure that had done the trick. She walked away with confidence.

It was two weeks before he came back. He is handsome, Elizabeth thought to herself.

'So, is it the coffee you like, or do you work around here?' Elizabeth asked, surprising herself with her almost flirtatious voice.

'It is the coffee; I will give you that. Let's say I like the scenery.'

Elizabeth felt herself blush. She moved as quickly as she could to the kitchen. She thought about asking one of the others to take his coffee to the booth but didn't.

'I've never forgotten the time we spent together, Rita.' His voice was low and smooth.

'My name is Elizabeth. You must have me mixed up with one of the other street girls. Sorry.'

'Funny, I don't remember you as a polio victim though. You must have distracted me with your charm.'

Elizabeth had a feeling he was the one – Robert, who had made her feel that love could be found, but only for a slight moment. So why did she remember?

'I could never forget those eyes; the one thing that has been on my mind since that afternoon. I can't forget.'

Elizabeth's palms were becoming hot, and the perspiration was running down her fingers. She had to get away. His name was really Robert. What would he say if he knew she called all her men Robert, he being only one of many? Why was he pursuing her? There were other working girls in the café. He could take his pick. Maybe she should be truthful and tell him she wasn't interested any more, not being able to hide being Free Rita. Or maybe she could become Rita Hayworth and do the dance of the Seven Veils; or maybe have his head severed and served up on a silver plate. Elizabeth smiled to herself. Maybe Rita would never really leave her.

'I would like to take you out to dinner and get to know you, the real you.'

'Why, I am a café owner, and my work here is what I am, and, yes, I am a victim of polio. When I was ten it happened, so I know no other way of life.'

'Please, Elizabeth, sit. Let me convince you to come out with me.'

There was no way she could stop herself from obeying. His voice intrigued her, the smooth depth penetrated like a mystical spell.

'I know there were many men who took advantage of your willingness to be available to the desperate creatures that came looking for the girl that was giving herself away for free, no questions asked. You were so beautiful; well, you still are.' Robert paused. 'I am sorry that I was one of those who took advantage of you. It was a bad time in my life, and you gave me hope.'

'I did it all to feel the closeness of another human being. I knew no-one would ever want me the way I was. And also to spite my grandmother, I suppose.' Elizabeth couldn't believe she had opened up to this stranger.

Robert touched her hand, and a spark ran up her arm, right into her heart.

There was no turning back. She knew she would do whatever this handsome Robert asked of her.

Robert was a movie buff, just like she was. Their first date was at the Palais, holding hands, watching Elvis Presley in 'Viva Las Vegas.' Elizabeth thought she had died and gone beyond the horizon.

After the movie they walked through Luna Park as it was closing. Elizabeth told Robert about her life with Otto and the merry-go-round, and how she'd cleaned the horses, saving the pennies he would give her, hiding the money from her grandmother. Robert told Elizabeth that he'd never been to Luna Park. It was full of germs, his mother would say. It was clear they had come from different worlds.

Elizabeth had three unanswered letters waiting for her to come down to earth. Her reply to each filled Jonas, Emma, and Lottie in on what was happening in her world. The closest to the feeling she had for Robert was her great love for Doctor Daisy, although it was completely different.

Thinking of old Daisy always made her sad. The two loves couldn't be compared, and she would never tell anyone of her thoughts. Joe would be the only one that would be close to understanding. The day would come, and she would sit down and tell her pen pals that she was floating on air.

Robert told Elizabeth about his disastrous marriage, and how his Catholic upbringing wouldn't allow him to divorce. He knew his wife wanted out as much as he. The only way she could escape was the illness that caused her death. He was ashamed to say that her death had been a relief to them both.

It had taken Robert some time to come to terms with the fact that his freedom came about in the worst way. So, guilt weighed heavily on his mind. He knew the only way he would be able to get on with his life and enjoy love and happiness, was to find the girl who had given him hope for his future on that afternoon. He had never forgotten that little old-fashioned café along the St Kilda esplanade.

Elizabeth and Robert absorbed each other with a hunger that had been dormant, waiting to be awoken by love – a love that was strong enough to break through the walls that they had both built up to protect themselves from life itself.

Robert spent Saturday nights at Elizabeth's place. On Sunday mornings they walked to the beach. Robert paddled in the shallow water if it wasn't too cold. He would ask Elizabeth to take off her brace and come with him. That was the one thing that her love couldn't overcome – her disability. 'One day, I am going to carry you, just so I don't have to be without you.' Robert would say every Sunday morning, both laughing.

Elizabeth would never tell Robert about her secret life at the beach: becoming a mermaid, swimming to the horizon, or praying for Joe; the boy that was now a man, that she didn't even know, who may have written the song 'True Love.'

Chapter 18

Indulging Devotion
Elizabeth

MARRIAGE WAS NEVER MENTIONED. Both Elizabeth and Robert were happy with the way their relationship flowed, having established a routine that suited them both that did not interfere with previous commitments. Their love took the empty space that had been waiting to be filled.

Robert was an accountant, working for one of Melbourne's top firms. Before losing his wife of many years, they had lived in an outer suburb. Robert travelled by train into the city daily, welcoming time to himself coming and going, making home life a little more bearable. As a dedicated employee, the firm rewarded him for a job well done time after time over the years. Now Robert lived in the city. He walked to work and took a tram ride to visit Elizabeth. Robert's life was full of satisfaction.

Elizabeth wished she could tell Dolly and Maggie about her handsome, successful man. She knew they would be proud, as she had her own business and a man to adore. If the day came that Gerry was out of their lives, she was sure Dolly and Maggie would make contact.

Occasionally, Elizabeth went to the beach alone, even though she treasured every moment that she shared with Robert in her special place. Time with her dreaming was still a need that no-one else could fill. She never told Robert how much the beach had been a lifesaver during the misery of childhood. She imagined becoming a mermaid, floating on gentle waves that would whisper a mystery of jumbled words that brought her peace. How could you share something that had no explanation?

Elizabeth's letters were full of positivity, the recipients feeling her joy.

When Jonas and Emma visited Melbourne, the thrill was overwhelming for their lost sister. How could the excitement of her world last? That chilling thought ran down her spine many times.

Both of Elizabeth's siblings liked Robert. They each asked Robert and Elizabeth to come and stay. A holiday in the country would do them good, was the cry. Elizabeth would laugh, saying, 'One day we will make it,' although she knew that day would never come. Going anywhere near Werner and her mother was never going to happen.

Robert never had children, so Elizabeth made light of her experience bringing up Maggie. She never let him know the anguish and suffering she endured, not been able to know what was happening in Maggie's life.

Neither had ever driven, so travelling away from the city had to be on public transport. This never stopped Robert from taking his special girl on many adventures. He showed her a world outside of St Kilda. To Elizabeth's amazement, everything became more interesting.

Robert never asked about Free Rita, although Elizabeth felt she was always lingering in the background of their relationship. At times, she smiled to herself, thinking of how Rita had brought them together. Elizabeth had never had the expectation or hope that she would share her life with another. She'd thought romance like that only happened in the movies. This lover made her world something Rita could never have given her.

Robert became her teacher, bringing the outside world to

Elizabeth's doorstep, broadening her mind, and giving her knowledge that previously seemed beyond her reach. She believed the café was a successful business with a profit at the end of the week. As she listened to Robert, new ideas popped into Elizabeth's head.

'Have you thought about modernizing the café?' Robert asked one day with trepidation, recognising that the place was so out-of-date that his suggestion may offend Lottie's boss.

Elizabeth didn't answer for a minute. Robert felt he had stepped over a barrier that was not allowed to be crossed.

'I will never change Lottie's,' was all that she said.

Elizabeth was thinking of changing bits and pieces but never the décor. She might redo the booths that were looking worn, with new burgundy velvet fabric; paint using the same cream that had always been there; update the kitchen, but never take Lottie out of Lottie's.

The menu could be modernized: Take away chips and sandwiches and add a new specialty – Otto's pumpkin soup. Who would have thought Otto's pumpkins could come to life in this way? Elizabeth smiled every time it was delivered to a customer. Combined with the drifting merry-go-round music and the smell of Otto's soup, some days Elizabeth felt him as if he was there, knowing all the drama over those pumpkins was worth the hard work.

Elizabeth was comforted by the thought that Otto might feel a snippet of pride; he'd been the only family member that was ever kind to her. It was her small way of giving thanks. If he hadn't made Gerda leave her the house, Lottie's would never have been Elizabeth's, and the fairytale existence would never have been possible.

Maybe Elizabeth had been too tied up in her wonder world to notice that Robert had been looking weary and struggling to keep up with her on their walks.

'Elizabeth, I have to take a break. Let's sit for a minute.' Robert was almost gasping for breath. Elizabeth looked around with concern. She was usually the slower one.

'Don't you feel well? I'll get you a drink.' She moved as quickly as her limp would allow to a nearby kiosk.

Robert had recovered by the time she got back, but was glad of the drink, The incident had scared them both. The explanation was that it had been a tough time at work. Robert had been weighed down as a couple of staff were off sick. He had to attend to their clients. So, the incident was put down to overwork, and all seemed back to normal.

Elizabeth did notice some days her lover looked a little grey, although, as he was his cheerful self, she dismissed it. Elizabeth had never mentioned anything about Werner not being her father, or that Otto and Gerda had kidnapped him because Gerda couldn't have a child of her own, fleeing from Austria to Australia before the war. That story that sounded too fanciful to believe. It was another secret that would be kept hidden.

Elizabeth was grateful that Robert was past the age for any involvement in the Vietnam war. Jonas missed out also. There were times when she wished she knew if Joe was safe. She prayed harder at sunset on those days. Many women came into the café fearing for their sons who had been drafted. Robert made her more aware of the conflict, so she was able to converse with her customers freely. The world had become closer with the broadening of her interests.

Robert was her lover and mentor. Some days it was like she was living her childhood dreams, having Robert Taylor, one of the Hollywood film idols, by her side. The young Elizabeth used the gift of imagination to fantasize about being in love in a romance that took away the horror of the life of a child who lived with a wicked grandmother.

Although the time with her grandparents was becoming dimmer as time went by, it could never be forgotten when the limp and the ball and chain were there as a reminder. Robert's pretence that her limp didn't exist made it easier for the intensity of their romance to become stronger every day. Maybe there was truth in the saying that 'love is blind.' Elizabeth smiled to herself. She was blind to any fault that

Robert may have had. In her eyes there were none. Little did Elizabeth know that her great lover had secrets too.

The young Robert had idealistic beliefs. He'd joined the communist party and applauded equal rights for all; everyone deserved to be as rich as the next man. Wealth should be divided so that comfort was afforded to the community as a right. Robert marched with comrades, went to meetings, shouted the party doctrine on street corners. He was trying to expel the teaching of his parents and the church that had invaded his childhood and which, as a young adult, he constantly fought.

The priest that seemed to be behind every waking hour, there when he was sleeping, tapping him on the shoulder saying, 'Come to confession. You must have done something wrong.' On waking, Robert wondered how a child could be born with the guilt of a sinner. He saw the hypocrisy behind everything he had been told. 'It was a guide that would make him a better man.' That's what was said.

He wanted the freedom of thinking for himself – to get rid of the rules and commitments that had been imposed upon him by others. He watched the atrocities that men used to gain power and wealth against others. He read how history repeated itself year after year in an endless circle of untruths and injustices, when only a small number would rise out of the ashes to gain rewards. How was the destruction and cruelty possible? Robert saw that justice didn't exist.

He looked for an answer, and that seemed to be communism. That would be the way to right all the wrongs the world before him had created – the abolition of the innocent while the mighty, powerful ones took away their dignity, sapping the strength from the willing, breaking the spirit of the kind soul who only wanted to do good. Robert's young, idealistic mind was full of fire, wanting to change the world.

It wasn't until Robert had finished studying and gained employment, In an environment where he watched the hard worker get promoted and the idle justly getting the sack, that he reassessed the thought that all are equal. He realised that the freedom that he craved for mankind was unattainable for the nonconformist.

He found it hard to readjust his thoughts of the perfect wonderland; that survival was not for dreamers, and hard work was the only way to be rewarded. He almost reverted back to his parent's morals that had been instilled in him. The old conscience would reappear from time to time. Even the priest's voice penetrated his thoughts, like a past echo engraved into his weak soul. The strength that was gained when he believed there was a way to have a level balance had disappeared. There were parts of Robert that would never be mended. Freedom was not to be for the conformist.

To Elizabeth, Robert seemed to be full of confidence, a 'do anything, go anywhere' kind of man of the world. Little did she know of the many nights he would wake with the fear of falling into a dark pit of despair. He felt he had never escaped from his parent's words that were embedded into his brain: 'You can't be seen doing that, what would the neighbours say? What would the priest say? You will have to confess.'

He felt sure he had never committed a sin, never stolen, nor lied. Some days he wondered if taking another breath would be considered a sin…

He wanted to find his own path, not one that was chosen for him by others. This was his aim behind joining the communist party, he realised. It all came to a head after he fell in love with a protestant girl. His parents had locked him in his bedroom and didn't let him out for over a week. They made him promise never to see her again and to go and confess the sin of loving a sinful girl. The weight of humiliation of locking a young adult in his room like a baby, nearly destroyed Robert. That's when the rebellion started. Somehow, his parents never found out about the party connections.

Robert ended up marrying a girl of their choice that he had no love for. It was a form of escape, only to go from one jail to another. Over the years of the marriage, he had asked the devil to take his wife away many times, to save him from the internment of the sentence. Divorce was out of the question, a bigger sin than being unfaithful, as Robert was sure his wife had been many times. The day she died, guilt set in. He believed that the wishing had bought about her demise. He blamed himself for hatred he had felt for the woman whose life he had shared for many years. He thought it was too late for him to gain the true spirit of his being.

The day after the funeral was a turning point; the first step to becoming his own man. Robert met Free Rita and a new dream began. It was some time before he found himself in a place where he believed that the beautiful girl with the translucent blue eyes and auburn hair that flowed over the pillow like a web that drew in her prey would be interested in him.

Finally, the time came when two lost souls were salvaged with a love and happiness that both had thought was beyond their grasp.

Some days they never spoke. It was as if each knew what the other was thinking, not living in the past or the future, only for the moment. Elizabeth worked hard every day. The café became busier. Customers were spreading the word about the little old-fashioned café with the huge reputation. The street girls were happy. Free Rita was serving customers coffee and pumpkin soup these days and not taking their tricks away. This was one of the reasons Elizabeth liked the booths, giving privacy. The rich, the naïve, the girls, could all sit without knowing who was beside them. The new boss always acknowledged that it was Lottie who made the place successful. Her small contribution helped it along. Elizabeth's letters to Lottie never elaborated on the success, in fear of hurting her feelings.

It had been seven years. Robert walked through the door just before closing every Saturday. They would wander down the esplanade to one of their favourite restaurants, before heading to the Palais to enjoy the latest show. Both were starry-eyed, even at their age. Hollywood always had new surprises.

Elizabeth had been busy in the kitchen and hadn't noticed he hadn't come in. Panic shook her body with a jolt looking at the clock. She thought he must have been held up, but why hadn't he rung, as was the normal procedure? It all seemed so out of character. With her stomach churning, Elizabeth took the tram into the city. She had a key to the apartment as she sometimes did spend time there with Robert when the chance arrived. Just as she was about to open the door, a neighbour appeared saying that Robert had been taken to hospital, the Fairfield, he thought. Elizabeth froze.

She walked into the hospital, a place she'd never wanted to experience again. She saw Doctor Daisy and sister O'Sullivan as plain as day, almost calling out to them 'S.O.S, my Robert needs you.' She was ten years old again, pleading for help. Somehow her legs carried her to the nurse's station.

'Do you have Robert Rigby here? He was brought in by ambulance this afternoon.'

'Hang on while I check. It was this morning. Is your name Elizabeth Kasper?'

'Yes, that's right. He is here then.' She was a little relieved.

'He has named you his next of kin. Is that right?'

Shocked Elizabeth said, 'Yes can I see him?'

'He is on the second floor – Ward 3. You take the—.'

'Thanks. I know the way,' Elizabeth hurried to the lift.

The woman at the reception realised why she knew where to go, watching Elizabeth walk away. Her heart sank for her, knowing there would be another reason to hate this place once again.

Robert's heart stopped beating minutes before she reached his bed. The doctor explained that her beloved Robert had come in with meningitis earlier in the day. 'With his heart condition, we couldn't save your friend.'

'My friend!' Elizabeth wanted to scream.

'What heart condition? I didn't know he had a problem with his heart.' Elizabeth almost shouted at the bewildered doctor. The doctor tried to comfort this distraught stranger. She was thinking of Doctor Daisy again. Oh, how Elizabeth wished he were here.

'The arrangements will be up to you now. Can I get someone to help you with the details? Robert will be in the mortuary until you have made plans.' Elizabeth only heard 'arrangements' and 'plans'; her mind and body couldn't function. Finally, the doctor got someone to arrange a taxi to take her home, telling her to ring tomorrow. That would be the last act of kindness for this one. He was a busy man. He moved on to the next patient.

Elizabeth wasn't going home, not tonight. She couldn't face looking at her bed without Robert, not on their Saturday night. As she opened the door, she took in the scent of Robert's last movements that were left behind. It was obvious he hadn't been well. The bed was unmade and the remains of the evening meal from the night before were spread all over the table. Robert was so meticulous about the tidiness of his surroundings. There was an envelope on his pillow reading, 'Elizabeth'.

Standing in the middle of the room, she stared at the at the letter, transfixed, not able to move for some time. Reaching out to open it took all the strength that was left in her grief-stricken body. Elizabeth fell onto Robert's pillow, trying to read the words he had written through a flood of tears.

My Darling Elizabeth, the love that I was looking for my whole life,
I am so sorry I didn't have the strength to tell you that I was sick; that I had a limited time to spend on this earth with you. I know my effort to save you pain is now causing you more, now that I have gone. I was too weak to tell you, too weak to see you face-to-face to say that our time together would be short. Please forgive me. If only we had met when we were younger and had more time.
Like your Joe, I would never have let you go. I know you prayed for him. I was so envious of the time you spent thinking about the boy you once knew. I wanted to fill that space in your mind. I

wasn't born with the courage that you have. Please forgive me for leaving you this way. I love you; you are my life. I wanted to be with you forever. I tried so hard to survive this failing heart that was full of love for you. Now I can only live in your memory, the way Joe has been. My darling, be the brave, courageous person you are. Go on and enjoy your ocean waves and float with me in your imagination. I will be waiting on the other side of the horizon. In my death I will cling to you for eternity.

I have left all instructions in the desk with my will, and the solicitor's contact information. What was mine is now yours, my darling. You have made my life worth living since the day I laid eyes on you.

Goodbye my darling. Thank you, for giving yourself to me, enriching my life beyond all expectations.

Yours forever,
Robert.

Screaming like a wild animal had invaded her body, Elizabeth fell back on Robert's pillow, unconscious. Shards of sunlight pierced the room when her eyes opened. It would be the first day of her life without Robert. How was she going to get through this day, the next, or the next, or any day from now on? Automatically, she walked to the desk. Shaking hands opened the folder. The formality of the information was explicit, making it all too easy for Elizabeth to follow her lover's instructions. A copy of the Will was in a separate envelope. The personal note pinned to the front said, 'What is mine is now yours, my darling.'

Elizabeth stared at the brown envelope for some time before her trembling hands were steady enough to open it. Through the blur of tears, she made out 'The Melbourne Apartment' and 'five hundred thousand dollars goes to Elizabeth Kasper'. She heard his voice over and over: '*I want you to get the best out of the life that you will be forced to live without me, without me, without me.*'

It was hours before Elizabeth had no more tears to shed.

She knew that the girls would be waiting on the doorstep, needing to prepare for the day. Through the fog that clouded her mind, Elizabeth needed to get to the café, knowing that would become her stability. She told the girls she'd had a busy morning with some legal matters. They would have to manage on their own. They had been doing that quite a bit since Robert had been around, so thought nothing of it.

Elizabeth was broken apart, reading Robert's letter over and over, storing every word and their meaning in her heart, a heart that broke little by little every time the words floated through her mind. The fact that she was now a wealthy woman hadn't occurred to her. The grief that was eating into her soul had not allowed thinking further than today and the job that had to be done.

Just before sunset, Elizabeth managed to get to the beach. Sitting alone on the pier she prayed for Joe, wondering how Robert knew about her prayers. He must have caught her out one day, not that she had tried to hide the ritual. It just seemed too childish to tell him that part of her story. Now she thought she should have explained. Maybe their minds were one. She searched the horizon for any sign, pleading with Robert to give her something to hang on to. There was nothing.

Chapter 19

Uncontrollable Destiny
Elizabeth

THE WAVES CONTINUED TO roll in and out. The seagulls still squawked, stealing chips when heads were turned. How could the world not know Robert had been engulfed into the nothingness of death? How dare others go about their daily lives not knowing he was gone? Elizabeth wanted to drown in the deepest water at the end of the pier. It would be so easy; the anchor that was attached to her leg would make sure she would go straight to the bottom of her beloved ocean. A smirk crossed her face as she thought, *Maybe it has a use after all.*

She escaped to the beach as much as possible. The staff understood but when they thought their boss could handle a little criticism, they asked her in the kindest way possible not to let the café suffer. Elizabeth was enormously popular with the customers, some regarding her as their friend. They watched her mourn for Robert over the months, helpless to change her mood. It was too much for some. More and more stayed away. The business started to decline, along with Elizabeth's missing friends.

It was a Sunday night. As Elizabeth looked at the takings she recorded in the ledger, she realised that if Robert were looking over her shoulder at the figures, he would be disappointed that the café was sliding into debt.

When the staff arrived on Monday morning, they were surprised to see the transformation. Elizabeth seemed almost happy and on top of everything. By the end of the week, the café was back to normal. The word spread. Lottie's was back to its cheerful, prosperous place with its regular customers once again. Elizabeth had regained her strength. No-one would know that her grief was masked behind the façade that was known as a beautiful face.

It wasn't long after that a letter arrived from Lottie's daughter, telling her that Lottie had passed away peacefully. The details weren't given. Elizabeth knew that Lottie had been getting on and had enjoyed the time with her family. Her legacy would live on in the café.

Strange, she wondered why she wasn't sad about another dark shadow of death crossing her path. In her heart, she knew that Lottie had left the day she boarded the plane for America. No grief would compare with the loss of Robert.

Saturday nights were the hardest. She often thought she heard him coming through the door. She believed he was there. She said 'Hello,' and waited for an answer that never came. It was like the days she sat on the beach, watching the clouds drift over the varying-coloured skies, waiting for a sign beyond the horizon. Waiting. One day there will be an answer. Elizabeth's new focus was dreaming; waiting for a sign that would make her life worthwhile. She never forgot Joe; she was hanging onto Joe.

The news item on the second page of *The Age* caught her eye. 'Solomon Tobias Goldmann Arrested.' The article went on to disclose that he was accused of crimes including espionage, fraud, blackmail, and being involved in an international network of organised criminal events, including several murders, some of them taking place in Australia. She read the article over and over, trying to take in the depth of meaning of the tremendous implications of crimes that were incomprehensible to her. She finally realised that this was Gerry, and he must be in jail.

Her thoughts went to Dolly and Maggie. What would happen to them? They would be so ashamed – or did they know? A wave of guilt washed over her. She had benefitted from the wealth that had been received from these horrific crimes. Old Gerda's words came back into her mind: 'Nobody gets rich unless it is against the law. He launders money through his so-called insurance business.' How did the old, demented woman know about the Goldmann's crimes?

She asked herself, *Did everybody know that I was living in luxury from the money gained in this way? Did Lottie know? She wouldn't have sent me to work for a criminal if she was aware, surely?* Elizabeth's mind was reeling with questions. She wished Robert was by her side to share this story. He would be able to explain what it was all about, and to assure her that there was nothing to answer for, not knowing her wages were coming from money gained illegally.

That day's newspaper was close by. It would be bound to give any new information and details of the crimes Goldmann was being prosecuted for. Elizabeth was sure assault or abuse weren't among the charges. There was never another word. The case seemed to be forgotten. Elizabeth tried to put it out of her mind, along with the feeling of guilt for the lifestyle she had enjoyed, living in the home of a monster. She worked harder every day so, when falling into bed, sleep came easier with exhaustion. However, sleep couldn't take away the dreams that plagued her darkest nights. The nightmares persisted.

She'd wished that Gerry would be out of the picture so that her relationship with Dolly and Maggie could continue. Elizabeth now knew that her wish was wasted. They both knew where to find her. She always excused them because of Gerry's domination. Elizabeth went cold, thinking that they had known about his criminal activities. How could she have not known that she was living under the roof of this vile man, although she had no trouble believing every word that had been written in the newspapers.

Why hadn't the police ever questioned her? It seemed some of the crimes had taken place when she had lived with the Goldmann's.

Elizabeth went over the time, trying to remember if there were any signs that she was living with bad people. How did old Gerda know, that old bitch! Elizabeth never took any notice when she had made derogatory comments about her bosses. Elizabeth realised that her response would have been that Gerda was wrong. They were so good, kind, and she loved them.

Why wasn't Robert here to share this story? How many times a day did she make this wish? She always turned a blind eye and deaf ear to any sort of crime and had never been interested. It was the best way, living in St. Kilda. Funny, she thought, growing up with a kidnapper, she must have known how to beat the law. Elizabeth thanked God she didn't have the old bitch's blood running through her veins. Her blood ran cold again, knowing Maggie might be in danger. She couldn't stop caring for the only child that would ever be in her life.

The letter writing continued to flow back and forth between Jonas and Emma. Elizabeth never wanted to lose contact with her siblings. After Robert's death she wrote about everyday happenings, never letting the true effect of his passing or of his inheritance be known. Elizabeth was a secret-keeper from way back. The trivia of life kept her interested in going on. Emma's stories about her kids' antics made her smile, as did knowing that one day, everything she owned would belong to them.

The parents were never mentioned. Their understanding of the situation was limited. Elizabeth had made it clear that after Robert's death that coming to Bairnsdale would never happen while Werner and her mother were alive. Jonas had promised to come to Melbourne as soon as possible. He had a new lady in his life and was keen for her to meet Elizabeth. Knowing that Jonas wanted to introduce his new love to his sister pleased her. She wasn't completely alone.

Lottie's Café became Elizabeth's everyday life again. Some days were harder than others. Climbing the stairs and falling into bed had lost the comfort that had been gained from her silky sheets now, knowing that her love for those sheets came from Goldmann money.

She smiled to herself. Robert had learnt to love snuggling into the silky-smooth softness. It was a wonder world that this beautiful girl had created. It was a space that was theirs.

She woke early and stripped the bed. She took the spare set of sheets out of the cupboard. Elizabeth hurried down the stairs as much as her limp would allow. She stuffed the sheets into the incinerator in the yard at the back of the shop. They burnt easily. That was the last of Gerry Goldmann, burnt to ashes. She told the girls there were some things that she needed and would be shopping, going off to buy some cotton sheets. Elizabeth's life was changing, or her bed linen, at least.

Another hard time was when a letter arrived from America. Lottie's daughter had found it among her mother's possessions when cleaning up Lottie's home. She sent it on, unopened. Elizabeth's hands trembled. The envelope had been stuck down long ago, dated the week after Lottie had arrived in her new country.

It read:

My dear girl,

I already miss you, having watched you grow into a beautiful woman. It was cruel fate that took away the life you deserved. Your unique eyes, auburn hair and a figure that turned heads until they saw your calliper. That damn thing that you had to drag around, resembling a sack of potatoes over your shoulder every day. I watched you as you destroyed that beautiful young girl and became Free Rita. I saw a lot of myself in you and wanted you to have a chance to be able to respect the person you could be proud of. The only pride you had was that you gave yourself free, taking no payment for giving that beautiful body to anyone that asked. It broke my heart as I watched.

I had people that dragged me out of bad situations, so that's why it was important to help you, my dear girl, to get you out of that café. It was my way of getting you away from every derelict man who needed to relieve himself at your expense. My plan didn't work the way I had hoped, as you kept coming back. I realised it was your way of punishing yourself for having a disability. I wish I'd had the knowledge at the time to make you believe that there was no need to atone for something that wasn't your fault. Please forgive me for sending you to Goldmann's place. I knew they had a shady background, not that I knew why, or what they were up to, just that they did deals with underworld thugs. There were so many in the city that had to get by during the war. People had to take chances when there was an opportunity. Easy money was very tempting back then, so I never judged. You have to understand that I needed money too, so I didn't care where it came from or how it was obtained.

I have to confess that I knew Gerry Goldmann was a bad man, a crook with all sorts of connections and had control over people in all walks of life. I hoped that you wouldn't have to be exposed to any of that side of his business. I was so pleased that you never did. Part of me was glad when you had to leave, although it was very sad, the way it happened, hurting you that way. My wish is that you never know or have to bear the brunt of anything the Goldmanns have done. The problem was that I didn't expect you to fall in love with Dolly and Maggie the way you did. I was grateful that the wife treated you well, until the end. I wanted to tell you when I saw you getting so involved with the family, but you loved the child so much, and I could see how happy you were. Elizabeth, you are so kind and innocent in many ways. I knew how devastated you would be that I had deceived you. I just couldn't bring myself to say the words. I hope you can forgive me. To my relief, you are now safe from any of the Goldmann's doing. He will get what Is coming to him one day, I am sure. I know that you will look after my café and learn to love it the way I did, well still do until my new life takes me far away from St. Kilda. Here's hoping you find what you are looking for and have the happiness you deserve. I love you Elizabeth, almost

as much as my daughter, only wanting the best for you always. I
am sorry my weakness let you down.
    Your lifetime friend,
    Lottie.

Elizabeth took some time to process the letter that should have come to her years ago. Poor Lottie had never said anything, not one word that Elizabeth could remember about Gerry or Dolly, knowing all the time that Gerry was a criminal. It was obvious her guilt for arranging the job had played on her mind, clearly taking it to her grave. Lottie's guilt made her write the letter, but she'd never had the courage to send it. Elizabeth didn't know how to feel. She was so grateful to Lottie for so many kind and helpful acts, that she could never feel anything but love for her. It was herself she was mad with. How dumb, not to know what was going on, even though her instincts had told her from that first day. She put it down to his name being the same as the boy at school, having both used each other as an experiment. Anger erupted in Elizabeth's heart. Did they drag Maggie into their world too? She hated herself for the hours of anguish spent over the need for Dolly and Maggie in her life.

The beach would solve all the problems. The horizon glowed as the sun seemed to rest on the straight line that met the sky. The breeze delivered the music from the merry-go-round, surrounding Elizabeth like an armour of protection. The ocean with its white-capped waves carried away the dregs of society, the scum of the earth and all the hurt and pain. Her ocean swept them all away to the other side of the horizon.

Feeling that others were unreliable, having trust in another would be impossible. Even Robert had let her down, leaving the way he did, like Lottie. Both lacked the courage to tell the truth. The grief, anger and doubts that had been accumulating as if in a basket that was becoming too heavy to carry any longer, were thrown into the waves. Elizabeth watched the basket bob up and down as the tide drove on.

She saw the parallel lines coming together with the vanishing point taking her load away.

Now, it was time to enjoy what she had gained. The gift from Otto, his pumpkins and the house, the gift from Lottie, the years of care and love bestowed on her. And Robert for his love without judgement, loving Free Rita and the memories he had left that would be with her for life. And the money. She knew that security and wealth was something that would never have to enter her mind. How lucky to have such friends pass through her life. They seemed to make up for all the shit she had endured. She wondered if Otto was walking beside her as the music drifted past. She smiled, knowing that the people you least expect can be your saviour. Elizabeth had come to another stage in the journey, with new twists and turns. There was an acceptance that this was how it was to be for now.

A year had passed when Elizabeth read a report in *The Age* that a date for the Goldmann trial had been set. The headlines read: 'Solomon Tobias Goldmann to be Tried.' He was to be tried for multiple crimes in two weeks at the Supreme Court, Williams Street, Melbourne. The list of crimes in bold print was there for everyone to see. Elizabeth found it hard to believe that these crimes were going on while she lived with the family.

She'd adored her time living in the beautiful house. Her room was a sanctuary away from old Gerda. Looking after Maggie was a delight most days – how she loved that child that wasn't hers! Elizabeth shuddered when the thought that Gerry, or his real name, Solomon, may have hurt her baby. She thought that if she went into the court, she might catch a glimpse of Maggie. She could have children of her own by now. Reading the list of murders made her almost feel the pain being inflicted on her. No, as much as she hated the abuser, he couldn't be a murderer, not Maggie's father.

The trial was all over the newspapers and television. Elizabeth watched and read everything, after deciding not to go near the court, not sure if she wanted to see the Goldmann women after all. So many of the full implications of the crimes were hard for her to understand. How had he got away with these horrific, complicated, mysterious crimes?

How she wished Robert was here again to explain. It appeared that Gerry was the mastermind behind an international network through Asia and Europe, involving theft of anything that was illegal and lucrative – minerals mined in Australia, including uranium, that the world wanted on the black market. Elizabeth realised the investigation into the Goldmanns had been going on for many years, including the years she had been living under their roof. A chill ran through Elizabeth's body, realising she could have been in so much danger or arrested.

Goldmann had recruited an army of conspirators, including politicians and people in organisations of importance. They were a protective barrier against the law. Every one of these people had something to gain from knowing this devil. Once they had received one gain, they were bound to the cause of Goldmann for life.

The dedication of the law enforcement agencies worldwide, who had worked tirelessly over the decades with determination, resulted in catching the degenerate with enough evidence to prove he had committed a lifetime of crime.

Seeing the names of Gerda and Otto Kasper printed in black and white took Elizabeth's breath away. After she had regained her composure, she read on – Solomon's father, old Goldmann, had helped the Kasper family escape from Austria to Australia, giving him an insight into this lucrative new country. He soon came to take advantage of the land the Kaspers had told him about. There was no evidence that the old Goldmann had any involvement in crimes that took place in Australia, or why the Kaspers had to escape from their home country with their young child. Seemingly, their friendship wavered after the old Goldmann emigrated with his family. There was no connection to the Goldmann in later years or to any of the crimes committed by either the long-dead old man or his son. The Kaspers were guilt free.

Crying through the night, Elizabeth sank to a new low.

It was hard to read the newspaper the next day. However, the fear of not knowing got the better of the innocent girl who seemed to be carrying the curse of others. Turning the page, she almost thought there was nothing about the trial, but her eyes widened when the name of Joe Pike jumped out. He had been an eyewitness to a murder that had taken place in NSW many years ago. He would be cross-examined today. Elizabeth wondered if it was her Joe Pike. Maybe she would get a glimpse of him on the news. She probably wouldn't recognise the boy she prayed for every sunset.

The implications of Goldmann's Network of criminals, the ones that were destined for that life, the ones for whom that life was second nature, the ones coerced into illegal acts because of the threat of blackmail and others who concealed their guilt, amazed Elizabeth. How did the bastard get away with it for so long? Her mind went over it again and again, as if Hollywood had created this story, a movie to capture an audience. That's where Elizabeth's mind belonged, not in reality.

It was obvious that Goldmann had never killed anyone. There would be a henchman for those jobs. It appeared that that these men didn't know who they worked for. The mob chain was strong, with any weak link being disposed of. Elizabeth understood that this was what would have happened to Joe Pike if he'd witnessed a murder. There was never a photo or footage on the television about this man, Joe Pike, to Elizabeth's disappointment. She wished it might be her Joe Pike, that he might come to find her. Why was her life so tangled up In this trial that had nothing to do with her? How she wanted to tell Robert!

The beach was her need. She would morph into a mermaid and swim to the horizon.

Chapter 20

Entrapment
Joe

JOE WOKE AND STARED at the mother of his two children.

He loved the twins. He had almost forced Blossom to call them Tibby and Hope, never saying why the names seemed so important. Blossom had convinced him to marry her after becoming pregnant, and really, he'd had no other choice. It wasn't bad, the life they had together, although he would never love her like he still loved Ginger.

The band was at its peak. 'True Love' had put them up there with the best, riding the wave of fame, getting bookings all over the place. Then came the big one – the USA, and Joe went along for the ride. Ginger's Place was finished. Joe was so proud of the hotel. The décor was French Provincial, with a touch of Aussie thrown in. It was just the recipe for attracting the fine clientele that filled the rooms most nights. Joe and Dan had established a reliable team to keep the place running to a high standard.

There was nothing to stop him going with 'The Flowers.' He was so excited to join in the adventure. Joe thought that Blossom would never get him into her bed, resistant as he'd been to her flirting, ever since Ginger had gone. The intoxication of Las Vegas, the success, the fun nights, the partying that never seemed to end, took Joe far away from normality. It wasn't long before he started to enjoy the comfort of Blossom's body next to him. Joe was sure she'd planned the pregnancy, her last-ditch attempt to tie him to her. His lost soul was now tied to another. Joe felt a sadness that Nancy would never know that she had become a grandmother. Bill was happy when Joe wrote and told him that he was going to have twins. (*Maybe they will take on the farm one day,* he thought hopefully).

The babies weren't born until they were back home. Joe couldn't have taken them to his apartment. There were many reasons for that. Blossom didn't know that he had retained Ginger's room just the way it was, and he would never want her in there. That was Joe's escape, lying on Ginger's bed, dreaming of the days when they'd been together; trying to recapture the past.

They bought a small place near Blossom's parents' home. Blossom would go and practise with the band and Joe would look after the babies and write. The words didn't come as easily as they did when he was really in love. Romance was no longer running through his veins as it had when Ginger was by his side. Domestic life didn't feed his creativity the way freedom had done.

The time came when the band was having trouble keeping up the momentum. They weren't getting as many engagements as they had in the past, so Blossom was home more. Joe became suffocated and made excuses more and more to get away. 'There is a problem at Ginger's place. I will have to get down there,' he would say, hoping that Blossom wouldn't ask questions. Joe knew that every time he said, 'Ginger's Place', Blossom would recoil into her shell, and it would be days until she would be herself again.

As a family they functioned well enough to the outside world, but as individuals they were missing their true selves. For some reason, Joe chose to conceal the fact that he was wealthy and had no need of her money, always making out that Ginger's Place struggled to make a profit. This suited Blossom, thinking she was the main money earner, giving her the upper hand. Joe became less of a man than ever. If it wasn't for the joy the kids gave him, he was sure he would've run home to Little River.

Things became smoother when Blossom began singing with another band that had more gigs. She was working between the two and Joe was left alone more and more. With all his home duties he thought he may as well be at home on the farm. He would imagine Nancy's sink and gaze out at the changing seasons. The kids would like it there, for sure.

Joe had come to Sydney with the dream of being a singer, recording songs that would filter through the airwaves. His name would be in lights, his face on billboards. Instead, it was his wife that was having his fame. He was becoming a behind-the-scenes backup, hidden in the background, a house dad. His words were out there, but not his face. How had he let that happen? No-one knew who he was when he walked down the street with Tibby and Hope. He was so proud of them and loved them more and more every day. He hoped that Ginger knew he had replaced her babies.

Joe hadn't realised what a relief it had been, not having Steve (or whatever his name was) watching his every move while he was overseas. Now that he was home, he was sure the pest wouldn't be far away. It was still a mystery as to why.

Blossom did know some of the details because of the day Steve showed up at the garage when the band was rehearsing. Joe never felt the need to let her know too much about the crime, given it wasn't his crime. He was always in the background in Steve's crime, in Blossom's career, and in his mind, sometimes he almost believed that the twins were Ginger's, not even his.

Joe was losing himself, becoming a robot on remote control, taking orders from others. The twins didn't resemble him much, only Tibby's eyes were his eyes, and sometimes he caught a glimpse of Nancy in Hope. They took after Blossom, but there was no doubt they were his. Blossom made sure of that. That's how life was, good and bad. Joe had no choice but to follow the part that fate had placed in his way.

He saw Steve through the front room bay window, sitting in a car across the road. 'Let him sit there all day. I am not going outside,' Joe said to himself, laughing. He had the day planned: cooking with the kids and catching up with the laundry. He wondered if he would ever know what happened that week he left home, looking for fame and fortune.

Who was paying this stalker to spy on him? 'There would have to be big money involved in it some way,' Joe was thinking again.

Joe was lucky Blossom didn't care about the house too much. It seemed that her mother was fastidious about having the house clean and tidy all the time. Blossom was happy to live in a mess, just to spite her mother. When her kids' grandmother did come to visit, her discomfort made Blossom happy.

Joe never had to do housework. Nancy made sure of that. The 'home dad' just fumbled around and did things his way. The home was for Tibby and Hope. If they were happy, he felt satisfied with his day. That's how life was for now.

If Joe had a chance to get away and had the day to himself, he would head to Ginger's Place, take the stairs to her apartment and lie on her bed, hoping she would somehow send him a message if he stared at the ceiling long enough. He was sure that someday something would materialise, knowing his old girl was watching.

Joe never forgot to pray for Elizabeth at sunset, even when he was in the US. Knowing that they wouldn't be seeing it at the same time never stopped him from the duty he had undertaken over all these years.

So, life went on until the day that Steve came to his door at sunset, disturbing his thoughts of Elizabeth. The babies hadn't woken from their afternoon nap. Joe knew he'd been hanging around but seeing him at the door was a surprise.

'Can I come in, Joe?' Steve asked as if he was an old friend.

'If the babies wake it might be hard to talk. I presume that is what you want to do.'

'Yes, we've solved some of our concerns. We now know that you saw nothing that we can use against … Ah, our opposition.' Steve wasn't giving anything away.

'I wondered when you'd realise that I knew nothing. It was all your doing, your deal. You forced me to drive you. I was an innocent kid. You've wasted all these years stalking me, scaring the daylights out of me. All the time I thought I was going to be harmed or killed. Why were you and that other creep that lived in the boarding house, always there to invade my privacy? There must be big money involved in whatever scheme you are in.' Joe had trouble controlling his anger.

'Joe, someone you once knew could've been involved so we had to be sure that you never had any knowledge of a man called Gerry Goldmann. We have now proved that you've never known him.'

Joe found it hard to believe that he had put up with this stress for the fact that he might have known someone in the past.

'Did you get in my car that day because you thought I might have known this person?' Joe was bewildered. 'Why didn't you just ask me? I've never heard of him.'

'I won't be bothering you anymore. I really like you, Joe. I wish we'd met under different circumstances, a different time. I was hoping that you would have become successful. I knew your ambitions. I know writing was not where you wanted to go, but you seem to be happy the way things have worked out for you.'

'I will be a lot happier now that I know you won't be hanging around anymore.' Joe didn't know whether to laugh or cry. A load had been taken off his back. He was free, well, from Steve anyway.

'Well, what was it all about?'

'I am not able to say.'

'Why didn't you ask if I knew this Goldmann? Oh, I suppose you thought I would lie. Well, you certainly took your time proving it.' Joe's frustration was beginning to show. 'What is your work, apart from harassing innocent people?'

'Sorry Joe. I really like you and have watched your life go in many directions. I know you have had some hard times, and in those times, I would've liked to help, but that was not my job.'

'Will I ever find out what the shooting was all about?'

'It might be in the paper one day.' Steve stood up and shook Joe's hand. As he left, Steve said, 'Au revoir, Joe. Sorry you didn't get the life you were looking for.'

Joe sat and stared at the wall until he could pull himself together, feeling that this stranger had known more about him than any other person in his life. And for what? Why had this happened to him? Would he ever know?

Chapter 21

Hero Dad
Joe

JOE KEPT WRITING, HOPING for another number one hit that never came. His head couldn't get into the right space; doing the dishes, cooking, and mopping, along with the babies, took away any inspiration. It was killed, being a housebound man.

Blossom and Joe were growing further and further apart. The marriage was a sham. They had never relied on each other. There was never a dependence of need. A true connection of two hearts beating as one would never happen. Joe took every day as it came. Cuddling his kids was enough to feed his emotional needs. Blossom had never really filled that role. The role she was supposed to fill became less with every week of this façade of a marriage. Blossom thought Joe needed her because of the money. She was making a mint. Joe had never told her how wealthy he was. That was between him and Ginger. Tibby and Hope kept them together, neither needing the other.

Joe was sure she was spreading her sexual favours around. She never looked for that comfort at home, so the distance between them grew. They were becoming strangers. They worked together as if they were running a business. Looking after the house and kids suited Joe just fine for the time being. It was all about the kids for Joe. Of course they were Blossom's. She had given birth to them. She had plan to bring them into the world for whatever reason she had at the time. But to Joe, she had given him a gift that he never imagined that he wanted.

Blossom's fame was deserved, along with the accolades that came with her hard work and talent. The Flowers were her first love. They finally took over her life. The admiration for Blossom and the band had audiences spellbound. Joe thought they'd reached their pinnacle. Then came the call from Las Vegas again.

The kids had just started school. Joe didn't like the idea of them being moved and going to school in America. Strangely, Blossom agreed. It was only a six month contract, so neither Joe nor Blossom could see a problem with her being away. The amount of time that Blossom spent with the kids was minimal, they would hardly know she was missing. Joe wouldn't pine for the pleasure of her company either. They parted with an embrace, both wishing the other happiness, as if that was the end of their life together. There was no need for words.

Tibby and Hope said, 'See you, Mum. Have a good time,' and ran off to play.

'If you come up with any credit-worthy songs, send them over,' Blossom called back as she got into the hire car.

And that was the end.

Joe's routine didn't change much. He thought about going to see Bill, a trip back to Victoria in the school holidays. The kids would love the cows. Nancy wouldn't be there. A darkness crossed his mind. He knew he would never put the plan into place. It was never the right time. He would go into Sydney and spend time with Dan, making changes to the hotel. It had to be the smartest boutique hotel in town, and it was. Business boomed.

Tibby and Hope had no problems at school and gathered a nice group of friends that Joe readily invited around to their home to play after school. There was always a birthday party to attend on the weekends. Joe got to know all the mothers and would chat before and after school, sometimes going to coffee mornings. Of course, they knew he was Blossom's husband, so he was never sure if they liked him, or it was the thought of having the husband of a famous entertainer as a friend that was the reason they wanted him in their group.

It is for the kids, he would tell himself. If they had a good social life this dad was doing a good job. Blossom had sent him some clippings with reviews of the show all being excellent, and it looked like the band would get a longer contract. Joe wasn't surprised and felt relieved that Blossom wouldn't be coming home soon. The kids didn't seem to care. All was well in Joe's world. The time he spent with the kids, and the days he spent on Ginger's bed day dreaming was enough for him at the moment. *When the kids are adults, that's when I will catch up for myself.* He laid on Ginger's bed and laughed and said to her, 'I think I am turning into a woman.'

Twelve months later, Joe received a letter from a solicitor. Blossom wanted a divorce. Joe agreed provided he had custody of the children. Blossom made no claim on the kids, the house or money that she never knew Joe had. It was so cut and dry. No-one asked questions. The band had only ever paid Joe for the songs they decided to produce. The rest would be in a case under some bed somewhere. Songwriting wasn't giving him any satisfaction. He would put it in the past. The kids and Ginger's Place filled his days.

Joe's good looks had matured with age and, with a slight whisp of grey creeping through his hair, he still dazzled a room as he walked in. Once the women at the kid's school heard he was divorced, the game was on. Married or not, he could've taken his pick. It reminded him of the old days when he could have any girl everywhere he went. Funny how he had no interest in gathering more problems regarding the opposite sex.

Steve was out of his life, although he did keep a vigil over the newspapers. He didn't want to miss any reports about the crime. He wanted to know if there was an arrest or any article that might give him a clue to what it was all about. Joe never knew what the hell he was looking for, except now he had the name Goldmann. Blossom had deserted him, and he would never feel the affection of Ginger's blissful comfort and love again.

The type of relationship that would be on offer from the school mothers was never something he wanted to engage in. Maybe there is another Ginger waiting for him out in the world that he had not explored. Some day he might go searching, but not now. Now there was always the kids. One day he would make plans like going back to the farm. He might even tell the kids about the cows that he'd loved and lost. Joe laughed at the thought. They would think their old man was mad. Joe was content.

It wasn't long before the school found a way to make use of Joe's talent as a singer. They asked him to take charge of the school choir. Tibby and Hope were both interested in singing and pleaded with him to take it on. What choice did he have? Secretly, he couldn't wait to help his girls excel, hoping they didn't get the hunger for show business that he and their mother had.

Joe started to go to the school a couple of times a week, although it wasn't long before he was there almost every day. He had a new love. The girls were becoming more like Blossom as they headed for puberty. Blossom's parents had always helped Joe with the twins, as they lived nearby, and they could see Tibbey and Hope becoming as famous as their mother. They encouraged them to bring their friends and rehearse in the garage. They had both learnt the guitar from an early age. That was one thing that Blossom had done for them, letting them pluck away on her old guitars that she left lying around, and teaching them easy chords.

Joe was the only father that went on school trips with the choir when they performed away. They did well in most of the competitions. Joe was becoming almost a hero, always being congratulated at school assembly and other parent meetings. This was making him more desirable to the mothers than ever.

Joe was so proud of the twins. Some days he thought he would burst. He wondered if Blossom ever thought about them, other than the birthday card with a new head shot of herself, and sometimes a Christmas card, if she remembered. The girls never seemed to care. It is hard to miss something you have never had. Joe consoled himself with those thoughts.

The weight of his lingering guilt still dragged him down. He rang Bill on the odd occasion or sent a card or letter; similar to the way Blossom treated Tibby and Hope – adding to Joe's guilt. He just couldn't bring himself to endure going home again without seeing Nancy. His mother had forgiven him over and over for the way he had treated them over those damn cows, such a trivial thing. Why had he been so ignorant of their feelings? He would never know. It was hard to go back to his child mind now and forgive himself for being a fool. It was the polio. He was furious with the disease. There was no-one else to lash out at. It was the polio. Why was it Nancy and Bill he targeted? He was a child that had endured the hospitalization, an innocent child. Someone had to pay.

He wondered how he would cope if the girls turned on him in the future. It was hard to imagine, as the parent-child relationship had always been harmonious between the three of them. Maybe rocky times would come as they get older and want to go their own way. He knew they would always have each other – 'Two bodies with one mind,' he often said to them. They always answered together the same words any time they wanted to leave an uncomfortable discussion. 'We love you Dad,' and disappeared into their room.

Joe never felt alone. If he did, he spent more time at sunset praying for Elizabeth.

He wondered if he would ever see her again. Maybe she had forgotten about that country kid that laid in the bed next to her, now seemingly a lifetime ago. *Maybe one day*, Joe thought.

Chapter 22

Redundance
Joe

THE SCHOOL CHOIR BECAME Joe's passion, and Tibby and Hope loved having him around. Joe wondered how long that would last. Teenagers didn't want their father watching their every move. They would be off to high school next year, so they would have their freedom soon enough. Joe tried to back off as much as he could, remembering those years with Bill and Nancy and his moods, thinking no-one understood, yelling abuse some days at the top of his voice. If he could only take back the words that he had spoken to his parents; more regrets for him to hang on to. Joe was determined to try and see the world through the girls' eyes. Being with the young ones gave him an insight into a younger universe that otherwise he would not be privy to. For now, everything went along with only slight bumps here and there, which Joe handled with ease.

Joe started to sneak some of his own songs into the choir with the help of the girls backing his lyrics with their music. This small achievement in this unimportant place and time meant more to Joe than the days with the bands and all the gigs, the applause and cheers he'd gotten trying to reach great heights in the entertainment industry.

Some days he felt like an old man. He laughed to himself. It was the days he lay on Ginger's bed that he realised that he was lonely. The girls were spending more time with their group of friends in the garage, practising their music just as their mother had done. He could see a band emerging. He was never invited to go to give advice. He didn't expect they wanted him interfering, although it worried him that Blossom's parents were encouraging them to follow in their mother's footsteps.

It wasn't that they didn't deserve a chance to reach for their dreams. He had no right to stop their desired destiny. He wondered if the girls saw him as a failure. Some days he saw himself that way, although he'd never had those thoughts when the girls needed him, when they were younger. Now there were times their needs required a mother, and the closest thing they had to one was their grandmother. The grandparents and Joe had always got on with each other in an off-handed way on both their accounts.

Joe had never told the girls much about Bill and Nancy, and they had never asked. He'd told them a little about the farm. Any more had been too painful, only bringing his guilt to the surface. It was easier to keep quiet. Joe was losing the girls. What was new? Elizabeth, Ginger, Nancy, Blossom. Not that Blossom had ever been his to lose really; now, Tibby and Hope. The twins had places to go that wouldn't include a father.

Joe had always known there would come a time when they would drift away. Now he watched with a sullen realism as it started to happen. Joe's job wasn't finished. They would be with him for a while, although they didn't need him the way they had in the past. The days became longer. He went to town more often, finding more work to do around Ginger's Place. He smiled to himself. *You will always save me, my beautiful old girl.* Joe still felt Ginger floating around the hallways, and he was sure she was there when he went to the apartment and whispered her name.

Joe wandered the streets of Sydney, drank coffee, stared at the harbour, sometimes running into old band members doing the same as him; the ones that were left. They chatted about the days when they could drink all night and sleep all day. Joe wasn't as old as them and wondered what he was doing. There was no need for him to work. Ginger had seen to that, but he was turning into an old man before his time.

Steve wasn't hanging over his shoulder. Strangely, Joe missed him sometimes. There were nights he stayed over in the city if the girls had a party or a sleepover at the grand parents. One lonely night he wandered down to the old bar to listen to the band – all new faces, though a couple of people did recognise him, calling, 'Where have you been Joe,' as if it was only weeks that he had been missing.

'So, you used to come in here?' the barman asked.

'Yep, a while back. I was in the band, and I sang a bit.'

'Is your name Joe Pike?'

'Yes, how did you know?' Joe was surprised the barman would know his name.

'I haven't been here long, but I have heard others talk about the famous Joe Pike.'

'Nah, I wasn't famous, just had a lot of fun. I think that's what it was, hard work but fun.'

'The band needs a bit of a boost. You should come back. I'll tell the boss you're here.'

The guy moved away from the bar. He came back a minute later, saying, 'Yes, he wants to see you.'

Joe had a new gig: the choir during the week and the band on the weekends. Life came back into Joe's face. He was a bit rusty, but he didn't take long to get back into the swing. With the adrenaline kicking in, Joe was his old self again. It was as if the last twenty years had not happened. He was back in the place in which he started. Joe started to tread water.

While waiting for another big chance, Joe couldn't get help thinking that Blossom would be back to take the girls away with a promise of fame, bright lights and all the glitter that came with stardom. How could he tell them it wouldn't happen when they'd watched their mother's name appearing everywhere. Blossom's parents had always passed on to the Sydney papers any new work that came her way, any new hit song. They didn't let Australia forget their girl and the fame that came her way in America.

Joe had never hidden Blossom's talent or achievements from his girls. Their mother deserved that. The fact that she was happy to leave them to further her career was forgotten. Joe was never to forget but wouldn't say as much when they decided to go. If Blossom cared for them, after all she knew of the pitfalls of show business surely, she would protect them from harm.

They hadn't seen Blossom for twelve years. She came at the end of their school year, waltzing into the house as if she still owned it. Joe wondered if she remembered she had been away so long, or if she would know what the girls looked like. Of course, they were a mirror image of her. The little bit of Joe's likeness in Tibby's eyes was still there, though he had begun to think he was the only one that had noticed, apart from Tibby.

Tibby knew. When they looked at each other they saw themselves looking back. It was like a secret code they had between father and daughter. Losing one another wasn't an option. Joe hoped they would remember the nights he'd held them when they were scared or sick; when Tibby fractured her arm and Hope's pain was as bad. Together, the three of them cried through the night. When they did physically go, they would stay in Joe's heart. No ocean could separate them, and the moments that they shared no-one could take that away. The bond the years of love he had given and received would be ingrained in his whole being forever.

Joe was right. Blossom filled the twins' heads with all the highlights of her life, telling them that when they were ready, she would send the plane tickets and they could live with her in her desert home that she had built and designed, with two spare rooms just for them. What was

Joe going into battle with? There wasn't anything like that he could counteroffer, nothing.

The girls and Blossom stayed over with Blossom's parents for the rest of her visit before she had to go back to her glamourous Las Vegas life. When their mother dropped them back to the house, saying goodbye, she called back, 'See you in twelve months my lovelies! Oh, and Joe, I love you.'

Joe couldn't speak. The power of fame had more strength than love for another, be it lover or child. Joe understood, though knew he could never have done what she had, walking away from her flesh and blood, even if she trusted Joe to look after them. Joe wasn't sure he was going to have that trust in Blossom when the girls left him.

Joe's heart sank; she had won. The best he could do was to enjoy as much of his babies as he could until the plane tickets arrived. He put aside a room at Ginger's Place for the girls and took them into the city as much as he could, even got them to sing with him and the band at the pub. He always took them home early, before the crowd got too drunk and unruly.

He was having a hard time seeing them as adults. He wondered if Nancy had the same feeling when she saw her boy turn into a man. The girls enjoyed their Sydney trips, seeing Joe in different surroundings, playing the drums, and singing away from the choir. He took on a persona they had never seen before. Their dad was almost a stranger, a tall, handsome stranger. Away from the washing up and sweeping the floor, they were shocked to see their talent had not only come from their mother. Joe did still fit in all the washing, cleaning, and meals. He had spoilt his girls, they might get a shock when they get to their mother, who he was sure, wouldn't lift a finger to clean. He supposed she would have help in the house. That would make the girls less self-sufficient. Maybe he had better do a bit of boot camping so they could look after themselves. That became his mission for the time he had left with them. His loneliness became forgotten, Joe's days were full.

The day came. By chance, he spotted a newspaper on a hall table at the hotel. The headlines read, 'Federal Police Investigation.' It went on to expose an international crime syndicate involving the illegal exporting of stolen uranium to a network of mercenaries and leaders of warring countries, along with fraud, murder, and embezzlement.

Somehow, Joe knew the story was the crime that wasn't his crime. The memory of the truck full of rocks started to make sense. Maybe Steve would appear again.

Joe waited.

Chapter 23

Back to the Comfort of the Past
Joe

HE WAS WAITING FOR the day the girls would be gone; waiting for the police or Steve, (what- ever his name was) to appear and change his world again, or worse, a summons to court for this cold case that should have been solved years ago. This crime had happened so long ago that the memory of the details were fading from Joe's mind; whether it was because of the time span, or for the want of getting rid of the whole nightmare, Joe didn't know. The only thing that he knew that would stay the same was his time with Elizabeth at sunset.

It was getting closer to the end of the girl's school life. They would not consider the thought of further education, having their minds on bigger things: The glamorous life that their mother was living, not a stinky pub in Sydney, when sometimes the crowd didn't even listen to the music; singing with their father, not understanding why the crowd wasn't interested in their performance; or staying in a room in an old-fashioned boarding house.

Joe was disappointed when they had described it as that one day. It was fun, but not for the ambitious, as the girls were. Blossom and her parents had made out that Blossom's fame had come easily with no sacrifices or hard work. The girls would never understand. They would have to experience what the world would throw at them. The one thing Joe gave Blossom credit for: she worked hard, but he wasn't sure about her parenting skills. He feared that she would see the girls as a thorn in her side before long. Then where would they be, with nothing to fall back on? Joe worried about everything.

He knew the tickets would come as Christmas presents. Around September, he went into a deep depression finding it hard to get out of bed. The choir had performances for end of the year concerts and graduations. Everyone noticed he was not himself, thinking he was ill. Some offered help. Even some of the mothers he had rejected in the past tried to comfort him. Tibby and Hope knew what the problem was. They were keeping very quiet about it. They were going no matter what. It was their big chance. In their young minds, they had no appreciation for what their father had done for them and didn't seem to care that their mother had deserted them, running off to the other side of the world to quench her hunger for fame.

Suddenly Blossom was their hero, Joe, just a babysitter. Joe grieved for Nancy. If only he could tell her about the girls. He did not know how he was going to go on without them. He wished he could ask Ginger how she coped when she lost her Tibby and Hope. if only all his girls could be still with him. If only he had been the famous one instead of Blossom. All these 'if only's were becoming Joe's life.

Somehow Joe did get through the next few months. The choir had many successes and Joe took his bows as if he was on the stage in Las Vegas. The girls were proud of their under-achieving dad in a patronising way. Having a mother that was so talented spending her days in the kitchen or washing dirty laundry, gave her the right to leave her babies. Maybe the girls in their juvenile ignorance thought they had a good reason to get on her bandwagon now, due to the fact she had neglected them. She had to pay for fame. They saw it as their pathway to success.

The tickets arrived as predicted in a Christmas card for the 1st of

January. Joe felt his life ebbing away. He tried not to let the girls see how devastated he was, helping them with their packing. Joe hoped he had prepared them for what lay ahead, although he knew there would be so many things that he could not even imagine. He laughed internally, remembering that when he left home, he was a witness to a murder. Nancy would never know or probably have believed such a thing could happen to her boy. Thinking about Bill and Nancy was adding to his guilt. Bill had never met his granddaughters nor his daughter-in-law when he had been married. Maybe Bill would see a poster of them in a magazine when Blossom introduced them to the world. Joe's guilt grew.

Why had he never taken them back to Victoria? Why couldn't he bring himself to go to the farm? Was it because he couldn't bear to go into the kitchen and not see Nancy standing at the kitchen sink staring out the window? Or was it that his guilt was so huge now that he couldn't face his father? Why had he deserted Bill, just the way his girls were about to desert him? Was this karma or pay back for the pain he had put his parents through?

Joe strained his eyes, watching until the plane turned into a dot in the sky. The twins had disappeared; gone into space, flying away into their dreams.

He wanted the best for them. If Blossom could hand out those dreams, he would be happy for his girls. He doubted it would be so easy. He had a terrible premonition that he would never see the girls again; like everyone else that had left him. He made the girls promise to let him know every week what they were doing. He knew that wasn't going to happen. It didn't stop him from hoping that they might miss a dad who had made them his life, and keep in touch. The one thing that held him together slightly was that they would always have each other.

He called into the closest real estate agent on the way back from the airport, to put the house in their hands to be sold. He was wiping away the best years of experiencing the life of a father bringing up two beautiful girls. He wondered if they would remember their childhood home. After the girls' comments regarding the hotel, Joe felt he had to renovate. It was looking a little neglected. He would keep the girls' room as it was. Sydney would be Joe's home again. He planned to grow old in Ginger's apartment.

Chapter 24

Journeys End. Journeys Begin
Joe

THE TWINS HAD SETTLED into their mother's home in the Nevada desert with ease, or that was what Joe was told. He had received a letter from Blossom the week after they had left, assuring him that the girls were happy with their new home and were enjoying their mother introducing them to her friends. Joe accepted this news in good faith or preferred to believe his girls were happy.

He finally received a letter from Tibby, that sounded as if Blossom had told them the truth. It was full of excitement. Joe could almost hear her talking faster than her usual even, flowing tone. It seemed the house was always full of stars and interesting people, and they liked Blossom's long-time boyfriend who also called Blossom's place home.

Tibby was disappointed that they hadn't seen Blossom's Vegas show. She kept saying she would take them one night soon. In closing, Tibby said that she missed him. Joe's heart sank a little further. The love he had for his girls was indefinable. He wondered if Nancy and Bill had felt the same way about their ungrateful son. Joe's guilt grew with every thought about family that came into his mind.

The months became a year, and he'd been wandering aimlessly

through the days, getting a moderate amount of satisfaction from running Ginger's Place and playing with the band, although he seemed to be walking through a fog most days. Ginger was fading away. Walking into her apartment was losing the sensation that once inspired him to keep going. Joe's ability to hold on to her was waning; his power to grip onto her spirit was no longer strong enough to keep the great love by his side.

The band members were getting younger. The pub was in the process of being sold. The old boss had died. Everything was changing. The old trends were becoming obsolete; Joe wasn't sure he could change his ways. He was always wondering how Blossom was keeping her popularity at a level that she was accustomed to. Maybe she had changed with the times. Perhaps the girls were keeping her young and in tune with the new wave of music. Her confidence and talent would sustain her.

Joe's mind was always in a turmoil, not making sense. Many days were spent thinking he was going crazy. The days became a blur, somehow Joe managed to make it to the pub for the gig. Most nights he would have a drink with one of the regulars. Often, they would ask, 'Are you okay Joe?' He would say, 'Yes,' and that would be it. No-one really cared.

The drink started to become his companion. He always woke up in the bed that he had shared with Ginger, although never remembering how he got there. He carried out the same ritual the next day. The days merged into one. The pipe dream of hearing from his twins was a fantasy that lived in the head of a desperate father left alone. An occasional note would arrive saying they were okay. They never told him what they were doing – if they were singing with Blossom.

He wrote back asking questions but not prying, being so aware of not overpowering or intimidating Tibby and Hope. He never asked anything personal, never denigrated their mother. The forgotten father tried so hard, only wanting answers that never came, or if they, did it was only a few words that gave no information as to what they were doing.

Telephoning never gave him any satisfaction. There was never an answer. If he ever saw a paper from the USA he would buy it and scan through every inch, just in case there was a mention of Blossom and her show. There never was.

A few months later the new management took over the pub and it was closed for renovations for a few weeks, giving Joe no reason to get out of bed. That's when the forgotten father nearly hit rock bottom. The days passed into nights. Ginger's Place didn't need him. The staff held the place together like a well-oiled machine. Money didn't matter to Joe. He had so much – his bank balance grew and grew. The only thing that was taken from him was the tax he had to pay, and the money that he put into the girl's accounts, that they had never touched.

It seemed Blossom was taking care of all their expenses. They didn't even need his money. There were long nights when Joe cried himself to sleep, feeling so sorry for his miserable existence. There were days he couldn't eat or drink. He just lay in that bed, staring at the ceiling. Waiting.

Joe remembered staring at the ceiling when Ginger had died. It was as though Blossom and the babies had never happened. He was losing the music, the fragments that had always kept his soul together. Music was a place that he could rest and regain strength, being swept away on the waves of rhythm, the beat, the melody, the vibration swirling through his body into his brain, taking away the pain of life. It was no longer working. The beat had changed. The vibrations grated on his psyche. The rhythm that was once his had vanished. The past had zapped Joe's life away.

There he was, leaning in the doorway of Ginger's Place. The years had change him little. Steve dipped his hat as Joe stumbled out onto the footpath.

'What the hell! You are just what I need in my life.' Joe staggered slightly.

'We have him Joe, we finally have him.'

'What do I care?' Joe started to move away. Steve grabbed his arm.

'Wait up man, I wanted to warn you that you will be getting a summons to appear in court over the murder. As you know, we know you have no connection to the crime. But you did witness the murder, Joe.'

'So, when will this happen? Will I have to go back to Melbourne?'

'Soon and yes, back to Melbourne. That's where the trial will be held.'

'Okay, I will be there then.' Joe started to walk away. Steve grabbed his arm again.

'Are you okay Joe? I know I haven't seen you for some time, but you don't look well.'

Joe was startled for a minute. Why would he care what was going on in my life? He made it uncomfortable for long enough. 'Why would he care now?' Joe wondered with a foggy brain. 'I've turned into a drunk that's all. I am alone, lonely, alone.'

'Let's have a coffee and we can talk. I will fill you in on the case and you can tell me what has been going on.' Steve sounded as though he cared.

Joe said, 'Okay,' and led the way to his favourite sobering-up café.

Steve could only tell Joe a small fragment of the evidence, as there was still so much that had to come out at the trial, and Steve wasn't able to divulge any details that would prejudice the case. 'The mystery of the whole affair was complicated. It was a crime that had taken nearly three decades to solve. The network went all over the world. Our Australian based Interpol played a big part in the covert operations to catch these criminals.

At the trial you will be examined on what happened in front of your eyes, and as you are a witness to one of the many murders, there was no way of saving you from this ordeal. You will be asked about what you saw and the shooting; how you got the two wounded men to the hospital. You did try to save their lives, or one anyway,' Steve explained to Joe in an almost caring way.

'So, what was your role in these years of investigation? Are you with the Federal Police, or are you a spy like I thought you might have been? I never knew whether you were a goody or a baddy, Steve. You scared me.'

'Believe me, I am on the right side of the law, Joe. My job doesn't allow me to make friends. I would have liked a meaningful relationship, a helping hand for you, like when Ginger died. I felt for you then Joe.' Steve almost sounded like any bloke he would meet at the pub.

'Will I ever know your real name?' Joe laughed for the first time since the girls left.

'I'm Steve; it's best left that way. I must be examined at the trial, but it will be from behind a screen, so I won't be recognised. Sorry Joe. I am sure this is hard to understand. These covert operations are hard work. I don't have, or can't have, close connections.'

Well, that saves you from a lot of heartache, Joe thought. If he had never had anyone in his life, he could be free of pain now.

'We all make choices, Joe, and we must live with the consequences. That's how it goes.'

Joe stared into space. His mind was blank. It was all too hard to get his head around. *Did anyone ever have the answers to the messes they found themselves in?* Joe was thinking. He almost missed Steve getting up to leave.

'I won't see you in Melbourne, Joe. It wouldn't be appropriate.' Steve was putting out his hand. Joe felt that he really wanted to give him a hug, another inappropriate action. Joe was glad about that.

'Thanks Steve. I might see you again sometime. Oh, by the way, who was the connection that I was supposed to have had with this Goldmann?'

'It was a long shot, but we had to cover all our leads. When you were a kid and had polio, you knew a girl. We had to make sure you weren't still friends with her.'

Joe went cold. Did he mean Elizabeth? She would have been so young. She couldn't be part of a crime. 'She worked for the Goldmann's. Sorry Joe, we had to look at every one that he had anything to do with. One link led to another. In this case we were on the wrong track.'

'Is that why you got in my car, I was a suspect?'

'You and the girl. We had to be sure.'

Joe was having trouble getting his head around this information.

'Elizabeth Kasper, you mean? We were in hospital together as kids. I haven't seen her since then. What the hell Steve? You have caused me so much grief over the years because I knew someone when I was a kid.'

'If you hadn't seen the murder, Joe, it would have been different. It was because of the dead man. We wanted to protect you. We had to watch in case they came after you. Sorry Joe. We just couldn't say a word about anything.'

'Did you do the same to Elizabeth? Did you harm her?' Joe was getting mad now, firing up. Hurting him was one thing, but hurting Elizabeth? That wouldn't be tolerated.

'No, we knew very early that she knew nothing about her boss's criminal activities.'

Steve explained that it took all these years to catch Gerry Goldmann and get enough evidence to convict him.

'Elizabeth worked for his family when she was young. She was a home help and brought up the Goldmann's child, Maggie.'

'You know everything about her. Do you know where she is now?'

'Goldmann was a pig, an abuser. She finally left. She owns a café on the esplanade in St. Kilda.'

Joe was stunned. He knew about Elizabeth, his Elizabeth. She had a café. *Good on her!* Joe thought.

'You loved this girl,' Steve was saying, when Joe realised he was talking.

'No, we were just kids. We shared a lot of things that no-one else would understand. We kept each other going, that's all.' Joe smiled a warm smile that Steve had never seen.

'The man's a bastard, Joe, a user. He hurts everyone he meets. Your friend was lucky to be free of him, but he was also very clever and had so many offshore connections. It seemed the network around

Melbourne was extensive – politicians, people of influence, all kept their mouths shut in fear of either losing money or their life. It made it hard for the authorities to catch him. It took almost a lifetime for some; we've all aged, trying to nab him.'

Steve stood to leave again. 'Sorry Joe. It was my job. We had to be sure.'

They shook hands again, Joe watched until Steve was out of sight. *Everyone leaves me*, he thought.

Suddenly Joe felt sober. His head was clear. His focus turned to Victoria. He would go home to Bill and tell him everything. Why hadn't he thought to ask Steve if he knew Elizabeth's address?

'I will be able to find her. I will find my Elizabeth. She won't be that little mousey kid now, but she will have her blue, translucent eyes. I will know her.' Joe felt like yelling this revelation to the world around him but whispered the soft words into his heart. *I will find my Elizabeth.*

Chapter 25

Finding New Joy
Joe

JOE WASN'T LOOKING FORWARD to the trip to Victoria. The memories of his last trip haunted him through every mile. Driving into the farm and not seeing Nancy waiting for him was a devastating thought. It was another load for his diminishing power of mind. He didn't really care if he got there. It would be so easy to run the car off the road and the world would go black, taking away his pain.

There were things that were holding him back. He had driven Ginger's Jag. Having sold the family sedan when the girls left, he didn't have a lot of use for a car when he was living in the city. If he did, the old Jaguar was waiting in the back of Ginger's place ready for an outing. She was such a faithful, reliable old girl, he could never destroy her to benefit himself. A smile crossed his face. He had an excuse for everything. It was as though Ginger was sitting on one shoulder and Nancy was on the other. When Joe had phoned Bill to say he was coming down at long last, Bill's voice had a weakness that Joe was shocked to hear, until he realised his age. Life would have taken its toll.

'Oh, I should have been more caring. He was such a good man and

I let him down.' Joe wondered who he was talking to, maybe his guilty conscience. It was always present.

Joe would stay with Bill for a week or two before he had to be back in Melbourne for the trial. He might have to tell Bill about his involvement. 'I should have told him years ago. I never thought it would come to this – me standing in a witness box in a court of law.' Joe was talking to himself again. He screamed out at the lonely road ahead 'I am a shit of a son!' Joe was the only one to listen. *Maybe I was a shit of a father too*, he thought. *I'm getting what I deserved.* The words invaded his mind.

Joe could see the farm had deteriorated almost before he came to the entrance of the long drive to the house. The sadness that had travelled with him deepened. There wasn't a cow in sight.

He found Bill struggling with a trailer, trying to attach it to the tractor. Bill waved when he saw him coming. Joe called, 'Hold on Dad. I will give you a hand.' Bill stopped. He looked at Joe as if he didn't know who he was.

'It's Joe, Dad. You knew I was coming.'

'Joe, oh yes, Joe.' They put the trailer onto the tractor without a word.

'What are you up to Dad?'

'Not much these days. I was just going to load up some firewood. There are a couple of dead trees in the west paddock. Bring the chainsaw will yah?' Joe obeyed. The chainsaw was where it had been when he was a boy. They decimated the old dead gums and carted the load back to the woodshed in silence.

Joe showered and put his things into the drawers as he had done as a child when Nancy had left the clean clothes on his bed. He lay on his boyhood single bed and stared at the ceiling, remembering the days in the past that he had spent many hours wasting time doing the same thing. How many hours had he spent ceiling watching as a boy, and as man here and in Ginger's apartment, never seeing anything? Joe never thought he would be here, waiting to go into court to be questioned about a murder he'd witnessed so many years ago. He lay there wanting to cry, like the day he found out he'd lost his cows. He was becoming that boy again.

Bill had sold off the herd a few years back and was now living off his savings. It would be no good trying to get him to sell the farmland. Joe was sure that he must be nearly broke. Joe would be able to support him as long as he lived but wasn't sure how he could get him to take the money. He stared at the ceiling now, coming up with a plan to save his father.

Over breakfast Joe asked, 'Have you been well, Dad?'

'Oh, lots of aches and pains, Joe – old age.' Joe realised Bill was very old, and if he had been here maybe his dad wouldn't have deteriorated so much; another thing to add to his list of guilt. 'Are you going to stay now? You know, I never met your girls. Have you some photos to show me?'

Joe went off to the room to bring back an album of old images of his babies. He would have to explain why there were no recent photos. It was going to be a long day.

As he took the dishes over to the sink, tears ran down his cheeks. Why wasn't Nancy standing there? He wanted so much to tell her what a mess he had made of his life. Joe wanted his mother to save him from himself. He wandered out to the yard, remembering his favourite spots around the farm, remembering Nancy's morning ritual of taking scraps to the chooks, talking away to her egg-givers as if they were her best friends. There were only three in the pen. Bill mustn't be replacing them these days. Everything was so run down.

'I should have been here to help,' Joe said to himself.

He strolled to the tree, a schoolboy friend. All farm kids had a tree that held all their secrets. He touched the trunk, feeling its life seep into his hand. 'If only God had given me your strength,' he said to his old friend. *What God?* Joe thought. They pottered around the farm, Joe following Bill as if he was ten years old. He went back to the tree at sunset to pray for Elizabeth. He made a pledge to himself that he would find her when he was in Melbourne.

'How come you're still driving that old Jag? I would have thought that you would have upgraded your car by now. You should have kept that Holden that you had delivered here the last time you were home.' Bill couldn't bring himself to say, '*home for you mother's funeral*.'

'Oh, I don't know. I love it I suppose.'

'Needs some work.'

'I don't have much use for a car these days, living in the city. I walk most of the time.'

'I'm surprised it got you here. How many years has it been since I have seen you?'

Joe was too embarrassed to answer.

'I want to help you while I am here, Dad.'

'While you're here.' Bill's voice trembled.

'I have commitments in Sydney. I will have to get back some time soon.' Joe wondered what commitments he really had. 'I have the trial first. That's in two weeks, so let's get some work done before I must go and endure that unfortunate experience.'

'What was that all about, Joe? I did read about a crook called Goldmann. Did you know him?'

'No, no I didn't. I witnessed a murder that involved his henchmen.'

'So, you said something like that on the phone. I didn't really understand. I'm sorry you had to see something like that.' Bill sounded a little sympathetic. Joe hoped he didn't ask questions. He didn't feel like talking about any of it. No questions were asked.

'How long has it been since you have seen your girls then? Have they deserted you?' Bill wasn't a sarcastic man. Though there it was, or was it just Joe's guilt? 'Do they ring often?'

There it was again. There was a wedge between father and son that went deeper than either was equipped to repair.

Joe would do as much as he could physically to help Bill. He hoped his father would agree to the plan he had devised in his mind.

'I have some money that I want to invest Dad, and I thought that this farm and land would be a good business. The way it was before it would be an interest for me too. We could do it as a memorial to Mum. You could put a new herd together and employ a couple of farm hands. One could live in, and one would come in daily. There would be enough work for three. You can manage the boys. What do you think? The one that lives in could help you with the house. I'll stay until we can work it out.' Joe thought the last comment sealed the deal.

Bill seemed to come to life, looking for the best-priced cows to put a herd together, and applied for a new milk contract. Joe went to the bank and transferred money into the farm account. Bill never asked how Joe had enough money to throw into the farm, when he knew it would never make a fortune. He knew if he asked too many questions, there was a chance Joe would change his mind.

Bill's face lit up for the first time since Nancy had left. He would be a farmer again. Nancy's house needed a good clean. She would be ashamed of the way Bill's neglect had spoilt her immaculate home.

Joe noticed he seemed to be moving around better as the days went on, wanting to get jobs done that hadn't been done for years. Joe congratulated himself for bringing Bill back to life, not realising that he had a spring in his step too. He sat under his tree at sunset every day and looked forward to the day he would find Elizabeth.

'The trial starts in a couple of days Dad, so I will head into Melbourne tomorrow and find accommodation. Not sure how long I will be gone. I might be away for a week or so.'

'Okay, do what you have to.' Bill smiled. He had things to do.

'We will talk to the guys that applied for the jobs when I get back. Look after yourself while I am gone, Dad.' Batting Bill on the back. Moods were changing.

MELBOURNE WAS QUIETER THAN Sydney, and Joe found somewhere to stay easily enough, comparing everything to Ginger's Place. There was nothing like his boutique hotel to be found – well not at the quality of his, of course. Joe's self-esteem was growing.

He went into the witness stand with confidence, answering

questions with ease. He stepped down. Joe was sure he wouldn't be called again. He didn't see Steve or anyone else that had crossed his path connected with the murder. He walked back to his hotel, sure that it was all over. The years of the unknown were all behind him. To Joe's surprise, he was looking forward to getting back to the farm. First to find Elizabeth.

He sat watching the gulls diving into the waves, smelling the salt settling on his face. Port Phillip Bay had a freedom that he hadn't seen in Sydney Harbour. Joe had taken a tram down to St. Kilda, not knowing the area. He walked along the esplanade. That would be the best way to find her. A café on the esplanade was all Steve had said. Joe never thought to ask if she had married and changed her name. Nerves were hitting Joe's stomach for some reason. What if she didn't want him to intrude on her life?

Why hadn't he asked Steve more about Elizabeth when the chance was there?

He had peered into a couple of cafés. Joe realised that they seemed to be becoming commonplace in Melbourne. They were all small, intimate, unique places he found intriguing. A light bulb popped into his head: A café-come-coffee shop off the foyer of Ginger's place would work wonders. The farm was out of his mind for the rest of the day. He wandered down the esplanade with touches of Kings Cross. Joe was full of motivation. The man who had lost the music from his soul, suddenly found himself humming.

In desperation, Joe decided to go into the next café he came to and ask if they knew Elizabeth Kasper.

This handsome man had lost none of his stature. The only signs of age were the grey streaks that were lightening his hair. He walked through the door of this old-fashioned café on what started out to be a very ordinary day.

Instinctively, she knew it was her Joe Pike. Elizabeth couldn't move. It was as if her shoes were stuck to the floor with glue. Joe felt the same. He saw her eyes. No-one else could have eyes like his Elizabeth.

They didn't speak. When they both could move, they just hugged each other until they had no choice but to get out of the way of customers. Tears ran down their faces like babies. Elizabeth led Joe to a booth, holding his hand. They both found it hard to speak. Finally, Elizabeth said, 'So it was you in the paper, a witness in the Goldmann trial.' The words were disjointed, soft and low, almost a whisper, as if their meeting was a secret.

'Yes, I live in Sydney and had to come down because I witnessed one of that creep's murders.' Joe was as nervous as a child.

'You are here to stay. How are the cows?' Elizabeth felt so stupid. His cows would be long gone.

'Oh, not good.'

'Joe, you grew so big. It's been so long, I missed you, my Joe. I always thought you must have gone away, not ever seeing you.'

'I don't know why we never kept in touch. We were kids. Life took over, I suppose.'

'Have you had a good life?'

Joe couldn't answer.

'Are you staying in Melbourne? Do you have to go back to Sydney? Oh, I never thought. Are you married? Do you have children?' The questions were pouring out. There was so much to know about what Joe had been doing over the decades.

Joe couldn't take his eyes off his companion that he had shared one of the worst times of his life with, although he had forgotten so much of what they had endured. Melbourne was bringing it back to him now.

'I was married, but not now. I have twin girls, but they are with their mother in America. I haven't seen them for a sometime. They must be so grown up.'

'That's sad Joe. I am sorry.' Elizabeth realised that they weren't going to cover what had happened in their lives in a few minutes. 'I have to know everything about you, Joe. I have imagined what you were up to so often. I even thought you were that famous songwriter that had written 'True Love.'"

Joe laughed. 'Yep, that's me.'

'Really? I pretended that I knew a famous person. Oh Joe, that is wonderful! You have a talent I didn't know about. Are there other songs that I missed out on? I played 'True Love' in here all the time.'

'I never got around to doing that well again, I am ashamed to say.'

Elizabeth could see sadness in Joe's face. Neither would ask if the other had prayed at sunset as they had pledged so many years ago.

The chatting went on until it was time for Elizabeth to close the doors. The girls wanted to leave. She had left all the cleaning up to them.

'Can we meet tomorrow?' Joe asked with anticipation.

'I would love to spend more time with you. I want to hear about every day we have been apart.'

'Do you want to spend the rest of your life listening to the story of my pathetic life?'

'Only if you'll listen to mine.' Elizabeth tried to laugh, but these words were no laughing matter. 'Joe, can we meet on the pier at sunset?'

'At sunset. That will be the best place for us to get together.'

The answer was clear. They had both remembered the sunset ritual.

Chapter 26

Together
Elizabeth and Joe

JOE WAS THERE BEFORE her – sitting in her favourite place. The sunset was going to be early tonight. It had been a clear day, not a cloud to be seen. Elizabeth had been anxious all day, meeting Joe after all these years. The boy that was now a man who had a lifetime of unknown things to tell her. She wondered if they would even like each other.

'How did you know this is where I usually spend my time watching the sunset?' She smiled at Joe, exploring his face, seeing the boy from their childhood.

'I've never been to St Kilda before. I remembered so much that we spoke about in the ward. Somehow, I knew.' There was no need for more questions.

Joe had noticed the calliper as soon as he walked into the café. He had considered the most accessible place that Elizabeth would be able to negotiate without a problem. They both knew that was the reason. No explanation was needed.

'I never thought I would see you again, Joe. I tried to imagine what you looked like as a man, but never really got past the kid that saved my life.'

'I thought it was you who saved mine.' The child in them laughed.

'Have you had a good life, Joe? Have you been happy? Was it worth the struggle that was ahead of us to overcome?' Elizabeth's face darkened.

'I've had some good times,' Joe had to pause before he could go on. 'And some bad. This murder that I had to witness has been a burden to me for so many years; it seemed unreal at times.'

'I've followed the trial in the paper and on the television. I had an interest in the outcome.'

'I know that you did. The guy who followed me for years told me only recently that you had worked for the Goldmann's. That's how I knew you had a café on the esplanade. Didn't you wonder how I found you?'

'I didn't think. My mind has been swimming since you walked into Lotties, so I never questioned the reason you were standing in front of me. Did you notice that my grandmother knew Goldmann's father when they had lived in Austria? Not that I knew any of the story until I read it in the newspaper. I worked for the Goldmanns for so long, I'm surprised that I was never questioned.'

'Steve, the fellow that followed me, told me they did investigate your background and knew you had nothing to answer for. This is all so confusing it will take forever getting all our stories shared.'

Joe put his hand in Elizabeth's. 'Just seeing you is enough for me now. I won't be going back to Sydney for a while. I must get the farm sorted out. Dad's getting on and now, without Mum, he's lost.'

'Oh, I am sorry Joe. Your Mum was so lovely. I always wished she was my mother when she came into the ward. Some days I pretended that she was.' Elizabeth didn't want to look at Joe in case they both started to cry. 'There is so much I want to share with you. A lifetime has passed by since we laid there in the horror of our disease. No-one else could understand unless they had the same experience.'

'I was the lucky one, not being left with any tell-tale signs. I wished it had been the same for you. With those beautiful eyes, you are stunning.' Joe smiled at this girl he had prayed for every day at sunset.

'I call it my ball and chain.' They both laughed again.

'Do you think that our praying to a god that probably doesn't exist kept us together?'

'How will we ever know? In death. Maybe that might be where the answers are.' They laughed again.

Elizabeth hadn't laughed so much since Robert had gone.

'The funny thing is that a murder has brought us together. I often wonder why we never kept in touch.'

'We were so young, and we had lost two years of our young lives. We were in different worlds.'

'I was so upset about my cows. It took over my life for some time. God I was a stupid kid.'

'Your cows... Weren't they glad to see you when you got home?'

'They were dead. It is along story. I don't want to waste time talking about two old cows. God, I was a stupid kid!'

'We all were. That's what being a kid is.' They laughed again.

The sun was setting. They watched as it disappeared, both praying in silence, giving thanks for the mystery of them being side by side again.

Joe walked Elizabeth back to the café. There was always a light left on, just as Lottie had always done.

'Would you like a snack? There is always something left at the end of the day.'

'That would be good. What's your specialty? Do you have an 'Elizabeth Queen Cake'?'

'What a great idea! Queen of the café world.' They laughed again. They sat in one of the booths. Elizabeth warmed up her 'Otto's soup special' and made Joe a coffee.

'You have this game sewn up then. This is a very inviting café. What made you stick with the forties-fifties style?' Joe was showing more than a passing interest now that he had the idea to incorporate a coffee shop at Ginger's Place.

'It's another long story that will wait for another day.'

'I'm sorry, I never asked you if you were married or had children. I was just so pleased to see you. In my mind you are still ten years old.' The laughter was louder this time.

Finally, Elizabeth answered, 'No, nothing like that. I am still all yours.' More laughter.

'Can we spend the day together tomorrow? I can pick you up. Have you a place you like to go and relax?' Joe didn't know his way around Melbourne well enough to suggest a suitable venue for the old friends to chat.

'That would be lovely, Joe. I will think of somewhere.' Elizabeth didn't want to go to any of the special places that she had been with Robert. The girls would be delighted that the boss wouldn't be hovering around for a day.

'I will pick you up at 10. Is that okay? I'll have my old Mark 2 Jaguar. I hope you don't mind driving around in a bit of a rust bucket...'

ELIZABETH WAS WAITING ON the footpath when Joe arrived. She had taken extra care of her hair, doing her best to hide the few strands of grey that had started to appear. Her face was free of wrinkles and still she didn't need glasses. When she looked in the mirror, the woman looking back didn't seem too shabby. She'd never had a full-length mirror in her flat. Her image could compete with any beauty. Elizabeth felt good for the first time since she'd lost the only man that her heart and soul had been given.

It was like they both had been reborn into a world that no-one else could enter. Elizabeth had decided that the Dandenong Ranges might be a nice drive. Something that she and Robert had never done. Joe was happy to oblige. Elizabeth read the map while Joe followed instructions. The sky was clear again. Elizabeth felt alive for the first time, even though she wished it was Robert that was taking the trip with her. Looking over at Joe, her heartbeat rose. Joe was her saviour once again. The old Jaguar took the twists and turns like the old trooper that she was.

Joe thought Ginger would have loved to take this trip into the hills.

'You must love this old car, Joe. Have you had it for a long time?'

'I do love the old thing. I don't think I could ever give it up. It belonged to someone I loved more than life itself.'

'I always thought when I listened to 'True Love' that the composer of that work must have had a great love.' Before Elizabeth had the last word out of her mouth Joe was reliving his life with Ginger. Elizabeth felt the highs and lows as if she had been there with Joe, being a part of his life, an extension of her childhood friend.

'I am so sorry that I have spent so much time talking about Ginger. It is the first time I have ever spoken to anyone about her. She surprised me, knowing that I had polio at some time.'

'How did she pick that up? You have no signs of being affected. You haven't got a ball and chain.'

They didn't laugh this time. Joe told Elizabeth about Ginger's children and how she had lost them due to polio. Elizabeth could see that Joe was still affected by the loss of Ginger.

'But you said you had been married and had children.'

'That was some time after I lost Ginger. It should never have happened, although I had my girls.' Joe couldn't go into his life with Blossom now. Telling the Joe and Ginger story had taken so much out of him. Things that he'd never resolved over the years had been brought to the surface. He'd shocked himself.

'Thanks for listening to me ramble on. I shouldn't be off-loading all this on you. I want to hear about what you have been up to all this time.'

Elizabeth didn't speak immediately. She wanted to tell Joe so much, and there was so much she wasn't sure he could accept; that might destroy his image of her.

'I had a torrid time with old Gerda. She hated me. I didn't find out the reason until years later. It was the same reason that my mother hated me too. You must have noticed the way she treated me on the rare visits. I didn't have much of a life really, until I went to work for the Goldmann's.' Elizabeth had trouble going on. 'I had hoped to see them on the news – Maggie and Dolly at the trial. They didn't seem to appear or were well-hidden.'

'The rumour is that they live overseas somewhere and have done for years. I just happened to hear someone outside the court say.' Joe could see the trauma that remembering her stories was causing for Elizabeth.

'Otto was so kind to me. He did his best, seeing what was happening most days. I don't think he like Gerda much either.' Elizabeth then told Joe about Otto's pumpkins and the way the pumpkin soup became so famous. Telling Joe about the Goldmann's was easy. Her years there were more than she could have hoped for, and Joe noticed how her face lit up when she told him how she'd nurtured Maggie from a baby into a beautiful woman. Joe suggested that they have a break and have lunch at the next town they came to.

Sitting in a cute out-of-the-way restaurant, Joe couldn't take his eyes off the girl that he'd never thought he would recognise as an adult. How silly! He would have known her anywhere. She was his Elizabeth.

'You are beautiful, Elizabeth. This will go down as one of the happiest days of my life.'

'Oh, thank you Joe. I bet I wouldn't be able to compete with Ginger.' They laughed.

'Have you had a great love too?' Joe asked, not knowing if he should go there.

'I was lucky enough to be blessed with a wonderful man that cared about me. Yes, I have had a great love.' Elizabeth couldn't bring herself to say another word. Joe seemed to understand.

'Let's enjoy our lunch and ignore the past for a while.'

Elizabeth agreed. They enjoyed experiencing driving past the giant eucalypts that lined the winding roads; the aroma of the dense bush that was so different from the odours of the city. The wildflowers danced, swaying with the breeze, sun and sky, and the drifting clouds. The comfort of being with each other was magic. On the way back to the city there were some quiet moments. Joe wished he had been around to help Elizabeth through the tough times. He could only imagine. Elizabeth was thinking the same; that the scars that Joe must be carrying seemed to go deep. They were approaching the esplanade, coming past the corner of Gray and Fitzroy streets.

'I hate coming past here.' Elizabeth was overwhelmed. She couldn't control herself as she usually did and started to cry.

Joe couldn't understand what had happened. 'What is it, my dear girl? What is it?' Joe stopped the car near the curb.

'Oh, I am so sorry, Joe. I don't know what came over me. I try never to come past this corner. This is where they found Doctor Daisy, dead in that gutter.' Joe put his arms around the child he remembered.

'You are the only one who knew what he meant to me. You would understand how I would feel, knowing he lay dead, and to be regarded as nothing but a drunk, when he had helped so many kids,' she said.

Joe's comforting was appreciated. Elizabeth kissed him on the cheek.

'He did mean so much to me. Thank you, Joe, for understanding a little kid's fantasy.'

'I do know how much you thought of the old guy, not that I understood how, with his cauliflower face.' They both laughed. There are meaningful experiences good and bad that were stored away in the back of the mind that appear when least expected.

'Are you coming in for Otto's soup, now you know the story? There will be cake left over too.'

'How could I refuse such a royal invitation?' He bowed as he helped Elizabeth out of the car.

'Thank you for today. We still have many years to cover. Will you come to my hotel tomorrow for lunch? Can you be done without again for another day?'

'Yes, the girls will think it is Christmas, not having me around again. I will have to answer their questions about why I am going out with this handsome stranger. It will be like your trial. I'll get the third degree.'

'Do you get the tram into the city? Are you sure that is okay?'

Elizabeth laughed, 'I have managed all these years without you, Joe. I get around. You might be surprised.'

Joe laughed. 'Don't forget I know how strong you are. I will come home with you and if there are clouds in the sky, we will watch them until the sun sets.'

Elizabeth felt she was in a different world that she couldn't get enough of, although, as much as she wanted to tell Joe everything that had happened to her, Free Rita might have to stay hidden.

Elizabeth felt Joe's grief when he told her about Tibby and Hope, and how he had convinced Blossom to give them Ginger's lost children's names. He was sure she had never known why he wanted the twins to be a ghost of someone else's children. Joe had always told himself that it was a way for Ginger's babies to be remembered. Elizabeth wondered if anyone else in the world knew what a soft heart Joe had.

That soft heart went out to Elizabeth when the story of Maggie was related, between tears that this admirable girl had held back for so long.

'Now that you think Maggie and Dolly are overseas somewhere, probably hiding away from the law, I will never know. Just maybe Maggie was forbidden to see me.' Somehow this made Elizabeth feel calmer. Joe got word that he was exempt from the Goldmann trial as all the Australian evidence had been completed. There would be a higher court hearing with many worldwide arrests to take place. After what seemed to be a lifetime, his long-term relationship with Steve (whatever his name was) would be over.

'So, until tomorrow then.' The old friends hugged as long as they could. It was a comfortable place to be for them both.

Elizabeth closed the door of the café. *If only I could tell Lottie about this time in my life,* she thought as she turned, looking at their creation.

Joe was waiting for her again at the doorstep of his hotel. The smile on his face was nearly as big as the door opening. Elizabeth smiled to herself as Joe held that door open for her, directing her to the dining room. She had been fearful that he may have been staying near Robert's apartment and she would have to eat at one of their favourite places. That wasn't so. Before the waitress had taken their order, Joe asked about her great love. Elizabeth had been grateful that he hadn't asked about Robert up until now. What if Joe asked how we met? Will I be able to save the reputable state of my childhood virginity?

'His name was Robert. I had been alone for so long I had really given up on the possibility of marriage or any relationship. My disability, or that's what I blamed. Robert was the best thing that had ever happened to me, Joe. I loved him just as you loved Ginger. He never told me that he had a bad heart, and our time was limited. When you were telling me about your Ginger dying, it gave me chills. They both kept their health problems a secret from us.'

'Do you ever see your family? You haven't mention them. I know it must have been hard for you the way they left you with the grandparents the way they did. I could never understand how they could do that to you, how any parent could.' Elizabeth told Joe the whole story, that Werner wasn't her biological father and how Gerda had kidnapped him as a baby and escaped to Australia from Austria and, as we now know, with the help of Gerry Goldmann's father.

'Gerry, is that what he calls himself?'

'That's what he was known as. His whole life was a lie.'

'Did you leave because you found out he was a crook?'

'No. He hurt me one night. It was too dangerous for me to stay.' Elizabeth could see the anger in Joe's eyes.

'He has been a thorn in both our sides. Oh, my darling, I wish I could have saved you from the many hurtful things that have happened to you.'

Elizabeth told Joe how she had got the job with them in the first place. And filled him in about the other best person she had in her life, Lottie.

'That's how I ended up with the café. It has been in my life forever.' Elizabeth explained how it all came about – Otto's money, Lottie going to America, Gerda and Otto's death, only leaving out Free Rita.

'I do keep in touch with my brother and sister. We write and ring. Jonas isn't married but Emma has two children that I love to hear about. They seem to be great kids. They are always asking me to visit. I never will while they live near the mother and father. They respect my problem with the situation; not that they know the full story. I will tell them one day.'

They had talked into the afternoon – not another diner in sight. 'I'll drive you back to the beach. You haven't shown me Otto's merry-go-round. Can we do that?'

'I haven't been into Luna Park since the old witch sold Otto's pride and joy, but we can do that. It is like we are getting rid of the things that we have been carrying around, weighing us down like a bag of bricks. Speaking of, Joe, you haven't told me anything about your music career, and why you went to Sydney.'

They sat on the pier and Joe told Elizabeth about his dreams and the bands. How Ginger was his muse, and when she'd gone the music left with her, or that was how it seemed to him.

'I know I should have gotten over losing her. I never will, but really, I made that my excuse. I'm just not good enough. I can't blame anyone, not Ginger, Nancy or Blossom. That's my weakness – blaming.'

Joe went on and told her about how he'd treated Nancy and Bill over the cow saga, and all the other things that filled his mind and soul, accumulating in a mountain of guilt. They sat quietly, watching the birds fly overhead, trying to reach the clouds.

'What do you see in the clouds Joe, do you remember?'

'Of course! How many days do you think we wished for a fine day so we could be wheeled outside?'

'I can see a big question mark up there in the sky. Why did we get polio, and others didn't?'

'Why did you get a limp, and I was left with nothing? You are a much better person than me and you have those enchanting eyes.' Joe's remarks made them both laugh, though they wanted to cry.

'You are so good for me, Joe,'

'You are so good for me, Elizabeth.'

The sun was setting. There was a quietness for a time.

'I watch the horizon. That's my escape. I turn into a mermaid and swim until I reach it. One day I will go behind it. That's where the answers are.'

Joe never said anything for a minute. 'I have great admiration for the survival strategies that you put in place – to have an escape plan in your head.' They laughed again.

'Can we walk over to the merry-go-round, or is that too far for you?'

'No, I will be fine.'

Hand-in-hand, they enjoyed the bustling of the coming and going, both feeling more alive than they had for so long.

'Will we have a ride?' Joe hoped she would agree.

'I never rode around. I only cleaned. I loved the pair of greys side by side. I will have to go side-saddle and you will have to help me on.'

'It will be my pleasure, Madam.' They climbed aboard, having trouble because of their laughter. Elizabeth felt like she was a teenager and didn't care.

'We will only have tomorrow. I'm going back to Little River to help Dad get the farm together, so he'll have some incentive to keep going. It's never going to make much money, but he will never leave. I could buy him anything he wants. His pride won't have that. He is a stubborn old coot.'

'Then will you go back to Sydney?' Elizabeth's eyes filled with tears.

'Now that I have found you, I will be around in between my commitments.' Joe put his arm around this woman that had brought life back into the realm he walked in.

'Let's make the best of tomorrow. Then we can make plans.'

'I never want to lose touch. You've brought a bright light into my world, Joe.'

'Can I pick you up then? Are you allowed to sneak away again?'

'We can go a little further down the beach road. There is still more you haven't told me. I want to know more about Blossom and the twins.'

'There is more you have to tell me too, I am sure.'

Elizabeth didn't want to let him go. She was hesitant to invite Joe up to the flat, not because she didn't want him there. It was her struggle to get up the stairs that she didn't want him to see.

'How do you manage the stairs climbing up to your flat?'

Elizabeth got a fright. *Can Joe read my mind?* she thought, unable to speak for a minute.

'It is getting harder – must be old age. One day I might have to sell the café and retire to a small cottage somewhere.' She answered, a tremble in her voice.

'Sometimes I struggle to get up to my apartment too. Yep, old age!' They both laughed.

Joe left Elizabeth after seeing her safely inside the café, watching her through the glass windows for a moment before leaving.

ELIZABETH AND JOE DROVE along the bay, parking not far down from St. Kilda on a cliff over- looking the ocean. The sun was shining. They walked, finding a bench where the warmth was comforting. They gazed out into the distance. The horizon stared back at them. Joe was starting to understand Elizabeth's fascination with the mystery that was challenging them.

'How long is it since you have seen the girls, Joe?'

'I haven't heard from them for so long. I have no idea what they are up to. I just can't take the rejection anymore. I gave them sixteen years of what could have been my prime time of life. Every minute of that time was for them, being a mother and father combined is a full-time job. Then they were gone.

'When I went back to Ginger's Place some days I felt like my life as a father never happened. Their mother had the fame I wanted.

She never cared about them while she lived her dream life – career, glamour, freedom, men or lovers, whatever they were to her. If that's what my girls wanted, who was I to stand in their way? Well, I didn't have the power or strength to oppose their plans. I'm a weak coward sometimes.' Joe hung his head.

'Why don't you go to America? They might want to see you. It could be a nice surprise for the three of you.' Elizabeth saw the gravity of the situation. Her heart went out to her friend. She understood how he must feel. It would be more hurtful than her losing Maggie.

'I've never given it a thought. Maybe it could work. At least it would give me the information that I have sought after for years – just to see their faces and to know if they are achieving and happy, and if their mother has been kind and loving. I never wanted more for them. I just might do it.

'Are you financially safe, Elizabeth? I hope you don't mind me asking. I have been very lucky, and I have so much money I don't know what to do with it. I can see Lottie's is a success. I would like to think if you needed to retire that you could. Sorry to be so personal.'

This was something that Elizabeth hadn't expected to be asked.

'Thank you, Joe. No, I am very cashed up, as they say. Robert saw to that. He left me with plenty and as you say, I have the café too. I own it all – the land and premises. In that regard, I have been lucky.'

'That's how I have so much. It was Ginger's. She left me with millions, and I've built on that with smart investments, and Ginger's Place. You've given me the idea. Now I am planning to incorporate a coffee shop off the foyer. I might ask for your input.' They smiled warmly at each other.

'Partners, hey Joe? That will be nice.' Elizabeth was happy to think that Joe thought he might need her help.

'Sounds like we have both have had some very low times. A lot of my problems have come from my own making. Not you, my lovely girl, you have been a victim of bad circumstances and very rotten people. It is painful to me that I wasn't around to help.'

'I had Lottie and Robert. I treasure the wealth of life they gave me. Nobody should be completely responsible for another adult. My mother was the one that let me down. Well, I think Werner made her choose between me and his two children. It is hard to apportion blame. I don't know the truth behind why, and I never will.'

'You never told me how you met Robert.'

This was the question Elizabeth had dreaded. She could make it all sound simple, clean and nice, or she could tell the truth. Joe wondered why she wasn't answering.

Finally… 'There is a side of me you might find hard to believe or understand. As you have seen, I live in a fantasy world at times. It takes me out of the reality of my disability and the heartache I've had to endure. I am not trying to make excuses for myself. I always knew what I was doing.'

Joe sensed it was going to be hard for Elizabeth to tell him this story. 'You don't have to tell me if you would rather keep it to yourself. Some things aren't meant to be shared. I am such a baby. That's why I blurt everything out.' He smiled at Elizabeth.

'No, I think it is time for me to offload that ton of bricks from my shoulders. Another escape to hide behind, that's what it was.' Elizabeth told Joe the whole story of Free Rita and how her love for Rita Hayworth and wanting to be her, was how it had all began.

Maybe if she hadn't lived in St. Kilda, it would never have started. It was all so easy. It got rid of Gerda, her mother and her limb, if only for a short time, giving her the strength to face the world that wasn't meant for her to enjoy. Free Rita and the ocean were how she survived. 'Lottie got me the job at Goldmann's and hoped Free Rita would take her last breath. I couldn't let her go Joe. It seemed that was my life, not the reality of the truth.'

Joe took Elizabeth in his arms and they both wept like babies.

'How I wish we had been there for each other. I will never let you down again.' Joe's love for this girl was as it was the day they had met when they were sick children.

'I was different from you. I deprived myself of any intimate connection with the opposite sex, or anyone. We were a mixed-up pair.'

'Were?' Elizabeth wasn't sure they had changed. They both laughed. Neither had laughed so much in, well, forever.

'Ginger taught me to be human and get the best out of myself. Also teaching me who I was and what I had to give, and how to receive.'

Elizabeth could see the pain Joe went through when speaking of his true love.

'Robert had come to Free Rita when his wife had died and remembered her for years. He finally came and found her, and he loved me more. That was our lucky break, meeting Ginger and Robert. It was deemed that we could only have them for a short time.'

They sat in silence, drifting into the past, taking their eyes to the horizon.

'It seems we were on a self-destruction campaign.' They laughed again. There was a lightness in their step as they walked back to the car.

'I feel free for the first time since I lost Robert. Thank you, Joe.'

'I do too. We are good for each other. That load of bricks might be offloaded now. I think I must go and see Tibby and Hope before I am completely free. Thank you for your suggestion. I'll go to Las Vegas soon.'

'Will I see you again?'

'I will call in on my way back to Sydney and we can make plans. We can never stop seeing each other, not ever. I love you, Elizabeth.'

'I love you, Joe.'

Joe headed back to the farm the next morning to amend another mess he had left behind. Bill looked five years younger. Joe was pleasantly surprised. Having a purpose was all that he'd needed. *I should never have let the music leave me*, Joe thought.

He phoned Elizabeth every day. Some days their chats were short. The connection was enough. No-one else had an understanding that the pair shared.

Bill asked him one night after they had put in a hard physical day about his songwriting. 'Other things get in the way. I suppose maybe it will revisit me again. To be ready is the main element. I should wake up to myself. Things are looking up for me, Dad. We will get this farm moving before I get distracted with daydreams.'

Joe employed a boy to do the yard work under Bill's instructions. And girl was going to live in, taking over the kitchen and revamp Nancy's vegetable garden. Her name was Pixie.

Elizabeth laughed when Joe told her, not thinking she sounded like a farmhand. Joe assured her she had all the requirements. The name didn't match her appearance or farming strengths. The first time Joe saw Pixie standing at the sink, holding back his tears wasn't easy. It was the same when he introduced her to where the vegetable garden that was now reduced to weeds. It was hard to see another standing in Nancy's spaces.

Pixie and Jack seem to be up for the challenge.

'Time will tell,' Joe told Bill, hoping he wouldn't be too hard on them; not that any sort of hard was in his nature, only hard work. It was two weeks before Joe was satisfied that Bill would be able to cope for a time. He was getting on, Joe had to remember. A lesser man would be in a retirement home. Joe felt proud of his dad. If only his kids felt the same about him, and not the weak man Joe imagined was their opinion of him, thanks to Blossom.

Elizabeth couldn't wait until Joe got back to Melbourne. The invitation to stay in her spare room was there as long as he didn't think she was an old woman getting up the stairs. Elizabeth had told Joe that Robert hadn't lived there full time. They had kept their own space and it had worked for them. Joe had told Elizabeth Ginger would have liked to have done the same thing. 'Until we got so passionate that she couldn't wait for me to get home, and I felt the same way.'

Elizabeth knew no-one would ever replace Joe's Ginger.

'She never told me she loved me. Maybe she thought the magic would disappear. Or it was because she knew we wouldn't be together for a long time? I found out everything she did after we were tied to each other was for me. Another guilt to add to the pile. I told her all about you. She heard me call your name at times in my sleep – my ten-year-old mystery girl.'

They laughed.

'Well, I can see why she wouldn't have been able to resist your charm all those years ago. You are very handsome Joe.' Elizabeth always knew he would be.

'You are so kind. Why haven't we been backing each other up all these years?'

'As I am to you, you are to me, a mystery.' They laughed again.

'Are there any jobs I can do for my keep while I am here? Not that it will be long. I have to get back to Sydney, not that the staff miss me. They are like yours. Makes me feel redundant at times.'

'I know the feeling. My girls have the same effect on me at times too. I have never let them know how I make Otto's pumpkin soup. I have all the ingredients in my head, so they still need me.'

'My smart girl. That's what I need. Something that only Ginger's Place has, and no-one else will be able to copy. Oh, I do need you in my life, Elizabeth.'

'I will try and come up with a unique recipe that will be a new challenge.'

'Something gingery I suppose would be great.'

'Leave it with me. My customers might get a few ginger fluff's, to put it mildly, while I experiment on them.' The friends laughed.

They went to the pier and watched the horizon, filling in more blank spaces of their past. A quietness settled at sunset. Joe pottered about, doing odd jobs that Elizabeth didn't have the strength or knowledge to do. Lottie's was looking brand new by the time Joe had planned to go home. The pair parted making promises to ring and never, never to be strangers again. Joe would need help with the new project – a name for the coffee shop. Maybe he would call it a coffee bar. That would be different.

Elizabeth suggested that it be called 'Hope and Tilly's' and Joe had like the idea. Elizabeth and Joe had saved each other once again. They talked for hours most nights. They both wondered what their dead partners would think of their friendship.

Elizabeth wouldn't see Joe again until he came back from America.

Chapter 27

Obscurity of Solace
Elizabeth and Joe

THE WEEKS THAT JOE had spent in Melbourne were like a dream. Elizabeth couldn't believe the elation that she felt during their time together. It was different from when she was with Robert. Oh, how she missed him – his embraces, his gentleness, his arms folding her into him. It was the safest place she had ever been.

The world was different with Joe – a history that didn't need words, a realm that no-one else could enter. Their meeting had rejuvenated them both. Elizabeth wrote to Jonas and Emma, telling them about the boy that had helped her during her time in hospital, knowing that they wouldn't understand, but rambled on anyway about how happy she was they had come together.

They both said they were pleased for her, and both told her that Werner was sick and that she should come and see him because it might be the last chance she would have for father and daughter to make amends. Elizabeth almost laughed when she read the words 'make amends'. She loved Jonas and Emma, and she had no right to destroy any feelings they had for their parents. This was her torture, not theirs. She would leave them with their naivety. Jonas rang a few weeks later to say that Werner had died and when the funeral was. He hoped she could make it. Her reply was a simple 'No.'

Joe and Elizabeth spoke on the phone most nights, lying on their respective beds that they'd shared with their lost loves. Both wished that they could share the experience with their partners of the past. But they knew that Robert and Ginger would not understand the deep connection between Joe and Elizabeth; a bond that was theirs alone. They were having fun, talking about Joe's project, 'The Tibby & Hope Coffee Bar'. Elizabeth sent recipes for Joe's kitchen to try in the guest dining room.

Joe said, 'No sweetheart. You haven't hit the mark yet.'

Elizabeth laughed, saying, 'I will try harder boss.' So, it was to be, for a time.

Elizabeth finally did come up with a cake that everyone was happy with. Joe called it 'Intoxication.' Joe wanted Elizabeth to fly to Sydney for the opening of the coffee bar. As much as she wanted to, she just didn't have the courage to get on a plane. Joe explained everything in the smallest detail: the room, the colours they had chosen together, the fabrics, the chairs and tables, the floor coverings – all very plush, in keeping with Ginger's Place.

Elizabeth could visualize it most nights when Joe told her about his day and the work that had been completed. The renovations were taking much longer than Joe had expected. He didn't plan his trip to find his girls until he was sure that the Coffee Bar was working without a hitch.

It had been nearly twelve months since Joe had been to Victoria. The farm had been chugging along; the occasional call he had to Bill was encouraging. Jack and Pixie had become an item, and Bill asked them into the house. Joe's father had taken Joe's old room and the young lovers had taken over the main bedroom.

Joe felt that for the first time he had made a payment off the debt of guilt to his father in a small way. Maybe Bill had the grandchildren that Joe didn't give him. The guilt remained. It seemed Bill was the farmhand now.

He worried about Elizabeth's vulnerability. He had seen how much she struggled to keep up with her everyday commitments. Lottie's was her life. Joe knew she would never give it up; just as Bill wouldn't give up the farm. He laughed to himself, wondering why he seemed to be the weakest person he knew. They both had a fortitude he didn't possess.

JONAS HAD COME TO Melbourne for business not long after Werner's death and rang Elizabeth, asking her to join him and the lady he planned to marry for dinner. She worried that the meeting might be strained. She prepared herself for confrontation over Werner but being able to see Jonas made up for any anxiety.

Her brother was a kind man; Anne was a lovely country girl, just right for Jonas. The three enjoyed having a light-hearted chat, relieved that Werner wasn't mentioned. It was easy to see that Jonas wanted to understand his lost sister so much, but just couldn't imagine her life, even when he had listened intently as she told her story. Elizabeth managed to ask about her mother, although she was not really interested. It seemed the right thing to do, for Jonas's sake.

'Funny, I think she might be relieved in a way. When I called in, she was sitting, having a wine, watching the television. She told me she can watch what she wants now.' Jonas's face darkened. 'I'm not sure that's the way it is supposed to be when you lose your lifelong partner. Relationships confuse me sometimes.' Jonas smiled at Anne. 'I would be devastated if I lost you, my love.' Turning to Elizabeth he said, 'I am sorry that you lost Robert. I think we loved deeper than our parents.'

Elizabeth realised that her half-sibling didn't accept that she wasn't Werner's child. She decided to leave the matter alone; Jonas was like an overgrown, sweet boy.

'Will you ever come and see Mum? Not that you have been mentioned. I told her we would be catching up. There was no comment. I can understand that you wouldn't be bothered. If only she could see how beautiful and successful you are, I am sure it would make her proud. However, does a mother that lets her child down have the right to that pride?' Jonas tried as hard as he did to make Elizabeth feel some comfort, knowing all the time he would fail.

'It is all too late. I will never forgive her for making me live with Gerda, whatever reason she had. I don't care if Werner asked her to do it. A mother should stand up for her child. I would like to be able to do it for you and Emma. I just can't.'

Jonas could see the injury that had been done to Elizabeth's soul. Her face told him that it was irreparable. He would never ask her again to speak to their mother. Jonas filled Elizabeth in about Emma and the kids. It sounded as though she had done an admirable job bringing them up, considering the role models she'd had.

'We've all survived, despite our parents.' They both smiled, secretly glad neither had to be responsible for another human being. Despite the sibling enjoyment of each other's company, saying goodbye, they knew it would be the last time a face-to-face meeting would take place. Jonas and Emma's alliance with their mother was too strong.

'I will always love you Jonas and remember the times we have shared here in Melbourne. Finding you filled the empty space I was saving in my heart for you and Emma.'

'I feel the same. Elizabeth, you will be with me until the end. Thank you for being my sister.'

'Half-sister, remember.' Elizabeth had tears in her eyes that Jonas didn't acknowledge.

Elizabeth cried all the way home, not concerned with those around her on the tram. She wondered why everyone left her. In her mind there was a fight going on as to who the worst person was, her mother or Gerda.

Joe felt for her when he listened to her story, realising their lives ran in parallel lines in so many ways.

IT WAS EASY TO spot. It was the eyes. They were her eyes, looking at her, asking to meet Elizabeth Kasper. 'I guess your name is Barry somebody. Am I right?'

'Barry Harwood, that's right. You know about me then.' He had a kindly persona, with Elizabeth's eyes that seemed to take over the slightly greying face.

Elizabeth thought, *He looks older than my mother*, and immediately remembered that she had no idea what age her mother looked, or even what her age was for that matter.

'Yes,' Elizabeth found it hard to say father. 'You had an affair with my mother, of which I am the result.' Barry's only child could feel the anger rising from a deep place that had never been able to appear until now. Elizabeth wasn't sure that she had the strength to go any further with this conversation. They both stood there staring at an image of the blood tie that held them together. Finally, Elizabeth asked him to sit down.

'Thank you. I always wanted to meet you. It was part of the agreement with Werner that I never did, nor Ingrid either. I thought it would be better never to cause any more trouble.'

'Well, it is nice to meet you, I suppose. I'm not sure how I am meant to feel. I really feel nothing, I am sorry.'

'I can't expect anything else. I wanted to see if you have had a good life. I see you wear a calliper.'

'No-one told you that I had polio when I was ten?'

'No, I was forbidden to contact anyone that knew you. It was lucky that I heard Werner was dead. We're all so old now. What can it hurt, talking to you? I never had another child. It didn't happen for my wife and me. I couldn't tell her about you. If only we could have looked after you. By chance I heard many years later that you were sent to live with your grandparents. I never knew anything about them. They were never spoken about when I was with your mother.'

Elizabeth could hardly get her breath to answer. Her emotions were erupting. She could feel her face going redder and redder by the minute. She wanted to kill someone – her mother or this man that sat passively, looking at her as if he cared.

'I had a terrible childhood. Everyone was cruel. My grandfather was the only one that I could say did anything nice for me.' Elizabeth's voice was slow and hard. She hoped he hung on every word, and that those words would eat into his soul and create a dark, deep guilt.

'The funny thing was that I didn't like Ingrid that much. She wouldn't leave me alone. It was easier to give her what she wanted. I think she had a reason to hurt Werner, and I was her way of doing it. As you can see, I'm a weak man and when I was told that they had a connection that would be happy to murder me, I took off.'

Elizabeth started to feel sorry for this pathetic creature that was another victim of the Gerda Goldmann underworld. Suddenly Elizabeth was glad to have this stranger's blood running through her veins, rather than anyone else's. If only she had never known who her mother was, she could have been anyone she pleased. Maybe the mermaid wasn't out of the question. She pulled herself up then. Was she going mad?

'I am sorry, my dear, that I had a hand in giving you a life other than the glorious one that was what I wished for you.' Barry's voice wasn't as strong as it was when he first introduced himself.

'Can I get you something to eat, or a coffee?'

'Thank you. Do you own this café?'

'Yes.' *Oh no, he wants my café*, Elizabeth thought.

'Have you any children? I can tell you would make a beautiful mother.'

Elizabeth analysed every word into a negative and was sure he had an ulterior motive, not thinking he could have any interest in her or the life he had given her. The one thing she didn't understand was why was it that she had a perfect life with Werner and Ingrid until she got polio.

'Didn't they know you were my father until the polio? Why was it then that they discarded me?'

'Ingrid and I knew, but somehow Werner only knew about the affair, not that you were my child. Your mother and I were the only ones. When he found out about the affair, he and two other men came to my door and gave me the ultimatum. Barry's face became pale. Elizabeth hurried to get his coffee. He seemed to regain his strength after he had the drink.

'When did you stop seeing my mother? Did you ever see me?'

'She put a stop to it after you were born. I never knew why. It all seemed like a nightmare. I never did understand what it was all about, the game she was playing. I was lucky that my wife never found out about any of it. Werner was the only one. Maybe she told him. I will never know what was behind it all. I am so sorry. It seems you were the one that suffered.'

'It seems so. Often the innocent ones take the brunt of others' careless actions.'

Elizabeth's anger was starting to subside a little as they chatted. Barry and his wife had moved away, and he had done his best not to think about the child that was his, knowing he had no right to claim. Barry had lost his wife a year ago and set out to find Elizabeth. He had remembered the Merry-Go-Round at Luna Park, so went there and asked around. It was all too easy.

'Where are you staying Barry?' Elizabeth asked, already making up her mind that he wasn't staying with her.

'I am in a boarding house up the road a bit. Could I come and see you tomorrow, dear? I have enjoyed meeting you so much.' When he smiled at Elizabeth, she couldn't stop herself from having the feeling of a slight connection.

'Pop in for breakfast and stay as long as you like.' As she said it, she wondered why those words had come out of her mouth.

'You are a beautiful woman. I can't imagine anyone rejecting you as a child. See you tomorrow then.'

Elizabeth watched as he stumbled out the door. He was an old man. She could see that at a younger age he would have had her stature. She was not surprised that her mother had found him attractive.

Letting another person into her life only to be let down again wasn't a consideration at this time. It came to her in the night that Werner must have found out from her blood group after she was admitted to the hospital, that he couldn't have been her father. He mustn't have known until then. *Funny, when I had his friend's eyes. Ingrid must have been a good liar. To* be rejected because of their mistakes was unforgivable. Maybe Barry was a better person than Werner and Ingrid. Elizabeth hid her head under the pillow, thinking she was just in the way; garbage that should be disposed of.

Barry arrived at the right time. The café was bustling with the breakfast rush. At least he could see his daughter had a successful business even with a deformed limb. After it quietened down, Elizabeth took a break. She went and sat with him, her father. Their chatting came easier today. Elizabeth found that she didn't blaming Barry for any of the mess he had been dragged into. The more she learnt of his circumstances, the more evident it was that Barry was a victim too. He had been plagued with bad luck. Just when he had a good job in a new town, a rumour would circulate of a misdemeanour or crime that he had no knowledge of, which ended in a dismissal, and he had to start again. It wasn't until the later years that he realised Werner was behind it.

'I wouldn't have said anything about Werner, but it seems you didn't have any respect for the man. I hope you aren't disillusioned with this information.'

'Did you read about the Goldmann trial that was heard in Victoria some time ago?'

'No, I was living in Queensland up until a few months back.'

'I am getting a strong feeling that Werner may have been connected to him in some way.' Elizabeth's mind was working overtime. Gerda knew Gerry's father. What if Werner was his son – Gerry's brother? The kidnapping wasn't a kidnapping after all. It was an arrangement. And debts had to be paid. What Barry's role in the affair was, she couldn't imagine. Maybe it was just lust on Ingrid's behalf.

'Have you any Austrian relatives?'

'No, only Scottish. All my ancestors came from Scotland. Why do you ask?'

'Oh, just a hunch.' Elizabeth would keep her ideas to herself.

'Are you going back to Queensland?'

'No, I plan to buy a place around here somewhere. I need to be by the beach.'

'Me too,' Elizabeth said without thinking.

'It is the beach and the eyes we have in common then,' Barry said, as if that was it. They were tied together for eternity.

'Well, we will be able to keep in touch. That will be nice for both of us.' Elizabeth genuinely felt very comfortable with this stranger who was her father. And so, it was to be for a time.

The days they met at the beach, the gulls and waves spoke to them, interpreting what they heard in their own way. After Elizabeth told Barry about Joe and Robert, they never revisited the tangled web of the Goldmann's or old Gerda again. Their enjoyment was the ocean.

It was late Sunday night. Elizabeth wondered why a call would come after eleven and was surprised when Jonas was on the other end of the line. She was expecting it to be Joe.

'Sorry to ring so late. The news isn't good. It is Mum. She hung herself. She is dead.' Jonas was quiet.

'Oh, I am sorry, Jonas, that you have to be in that predicament.' She had to collect her thoughts. She felt nothing but didn't want Jonas to know.

'Emma found her hanging in the shed. We called the police.'

Elizabeth could hear the fear in Jonas's voice. She felt for her brother and sister, but nothing for her mother.

'I thought I should let you know. She left a note, sort of – words scribbled on a piece of old board written with lipstick. "This is for the ones I loved, although they never knew."'

'Thank you for calling. Give my love to Emma and the boys, and you too Jonas. We will never understand why. Maybe she had demons that haunted her. No-one is to blame.'

When she had finished the call, relief overwhelmed Ingrid's second-born child. Her mother must have carried a load of guilt that finally engulfed her. And Elizabeth didn't care.

Tuesdays were the days Barry and Elizabeth met on the bench overlooking the ocean. They always greeted each other with a hug. Elizabeth told Barry about the phone call and the note.

'Maybe her conscience got to her in the end. Do you think it was us that she loved? It's all a bit too late for us to give a shit,' Barry laughed.

'I agree. It's another story that will never unfold. The truth will be hidden forever. She never wanted me to be friends with my half brother and sister. She destroyed the letters we wrote to each other after I came out of the hospital. Jonas tried to find me when we were adults, after all the damage had been done.'

'I am sorry I was part of the foundation that formed your miserable existence. If only I hadn't been so selfish in not wanting to destroy my marriage. We all lost, even Ingrid, it seems.'

'There are so many things that I will never understand. I blamed it all on my limp for so long, and it had nothing to do with it, except if I hadn't gone to hospital, they would never have known my blood type. An unlucky break, I suppose.'

'See you next Tuesday, Barry,' Elizabeth said as she struggled to stand up.

They walked away together, arm in arm. When they parted, Barry thanked her for letting him into her life. Elizabeth was content that she had some answers, and Barry was a big part of the mystery that had surrounded her all the years of her adult life.

Joe was excited for Elizabeth as she relayed the Barry and Elizabeth story after their meetings.

The one thing that Elizabeth couldn't get out of her mind was why Lottie sent her to work at the Goldmann's. Joe found it hard to believe too, but had no answer or suggestion to help. That was another mystery. Elizabeth didn't like to think Lottie had any affiliation with them, but it did seem very strange that she had found out that Lottie had known that he was a criminal. She finally put it down to the fact she had borrowed money from him in her early days, and if he helped in any way you became indebted to him forever, it appeared.

Why Gerry wanted her there was another mystery. Was it a debt Gerda had to pay, or was it a debt he had to pay her? *It would be like the bitch to put me in that situation.* Was it Dolly that spoilt it all for them? Elizabeth went over and over her whole life. There may have been clues and connections from the start; a web that she was caught in but had no active part to play. Vendettas went on through generations – it seemed someone had to pay. Elizabeth would never understand, and there was no-one to answer the questions. If only she could find Dolly and Maggie…

The headlines in the Herald read: 'Solomon Tobias Goldmann Convicted.' The article went on: Solomon Tobias was convicted of extreme fraud, along with six murders to date. He has been sentenced to life in prison, along with others in the worldwide syndicate he created.

Elizabeth's reaction was relief; not that she was sure why. He was past hurting her, and all the others in the family were gone. She was running late for her meeting with Barry. She wanted to tell him the good news, not that Goldmann could hurt him anymore either. Well, he'd never known who had caused his life to be out of his control really.

Barry was already waiting on their bench. Elizabeth could see the old brown hat pulled down over his ears, and the gabardine coat collar turned up. Elizabeth called, but he didn't hear. As she got closer, she called again. 'Did you see the news?' Barry still didn't hear. When his daughter slid into the seat beside him, she thought he had fallen asleep. It was a minute before Elizabeth realised Barry had died watching the horizon.

The short relationship with her father was over. Barry had left the ground floor apartment he had purchased in Grey Street to her. That came as a surprise; not that she could ever live in Grey Street, knowing her doctor Daisy had died there. It would be too hard. When the time came, she would sell it and buy a cottage nearer the beach.

That night the phone call to Joe was a long one, going over the Goldmanns again, and the effect of Barry coming into her life, giving her some peace. They were both happy: Elizabeth was resolving questions in her mind. Her life was making a kind of sense. Joe was happy that the coffee bar was what they had both dreamt of. It had worked its way into a favourable routine, and the profit was more than he could ask for. And most customers came back for a serve of 'Intoxication'.

'Did you see the article about the man who had followed me around for years? I recognised his photo. You know, the one I said named himself 'Steve.''

'No, Joe, I didn't see it. Was he one of Goldmann's men?'

'It seems he was a double agent, working with the police, although loyal to Goldmann at times. Well, he was rewarded with a jail sentence too.'

'Joe it's becoming like the end of a story.'

'Not yet for me. I am going to book my plane fare tomorrow. Are you happy about that? I will finally get there.'

'I do want the situation resolved with your girls, Joe. I will be patient until you get back. I will be happier when you are in Victoria again, and we can be together. I'm sorry that I am such a wimp; that I won't get to Sydney.' Elizabeth was worried the girls would hurt Joe. There was a bad feeling that wouldn't leave her, even though the trip had been her suggestion.

'Me too. I can't wait. I love you, Elizabeth.'

'I love you, Joe.'

If Elizabeth hadn't the burden of the calliper, she would be dancing on her way to the pier. Her mind had never felt so free. The answers that had come about over the last year had a degree of satisfaction, giving some peace. She was trying to remember when that feeling had been there before.

Lost in her thoughts, she stepped off the curb into the path of a fast-moving car.

The lights were blinding, as she struggled to regain consciousness. Elizabeth was ten years old again. She was in limbo. There had been nothing. It must have been a dream, that cruel life. She could see Robert's face but didn't know why he was there. Lottie's face looked sad. Otto's face was going around and around like a merry-go-round. *Why are these people smiling at me? I don't know these faces. I am only ten years old.* She looked through the bright light, wondering why Doctor Daisy wasn't there to hold her hand. Her legs wouldn't obey her mind. Elizabeth couldn't move.

She heard the nurse saying, 'The poor girl. She's paralysed for sure this time.'

Elizabeth called out S.O.S. No-one came running or understood.

Chapter 28

The Tricks Fate Plays
America

JOE HAD TRIED TO call Elizabeth when he embarked in Honolulu, then again before boarding the flight into Las Vegas. The call rang out again and again. He was worried. It would have been lunch time at the café. Elizabeth was always there. If not, why hadn't one of the girls answered the phone? It wasn't engaged.

Joe had booked a room in one of the lower-class motels along the strip, not sure why he didn't go up market. There was not a doubt he could afford more opulent accommodation. When he had been there with 'The Flowers' many years ago, he didn't like the fake society that mingled with vile intentions. Now his girls were probably part of that society. The thought gave him a bad feeling. This was no town for a country boy from Little River.

Sydney was no comparison for this evil place either, or not the Sydney Joe knew. Before leaving his room the next morning he tried to reach Elizabeth again, to no avail. Joe was really worried now. He had left a message on the answering machine hoping she would ring the number of the motel.

There had been no evidence of Blossom or the girls on any of the billboards that lined the road from the airport into town. He scanned the strip to see if there was any trace of the girls working in one of the clubs. There was nothing of Blossom nor his girls to be found. Joe tried the old number he had, just on the off chance someone would answer. Nothing. He would have to go further than the strip on the hunt for answers. Joe despaired that he couldn't reach Elizabeth or the girls.

The heat was depressing. He couldn't wait to get into an airconditioned bar; to sit down and order a drink. He realised that he didn't have a photo of Tibby or Hope that he could show anyone for help. They weren't kids anymore. Their maturity could have changed them so much that he might not even recognise them himself. He wandered, hoping he would stumble over a clue as to their whereabouts.

Joe walked in and out of every bar, club, show room, and casino all over town. There was nothing. No word came from Elizabeth. Joe had started to drink too much. He blamed the heat, not the hopeless search. He desperately wanted to get home to find Elizabeth, but he couldn't leave until he knew where his girls were. It was a week before he left his room sober. He knew he wouldn't get home if he didn't find the girls. He went to the police station, hoping there might be a clue there. Someone might know of Australian twins singing. That must be a rarity. Surely Blossom couldn't be forgotten already.

'Blossom's daughters, yes we know them, Sandy and Rusty,' the Sergeant was saying, as he called out to his mates: 'Do you know where Sandy and Rusty are playing? There is a fellow here who's looking for them, saying he is their dad.'

'Lucky guy to have had Blossom in his life,' someone yelled out from behind a wall. Joe heard laughter from around the station.

'Do you know where my girls are, or not?' Joe was getting very uncomfortable.

'I know Blossom is in the south of France with her fancy fellow.' The Sergeant could see Joe wasn't in the mood for jokes.

'They're playing out at the Golf Club. Get a car and go out there.' This voice came from the cell area.

Joe thanked them for their help, hoping it was true. So, he was looking for Sandy and Rusty. He thought they must have decided to use those names for the stage. The next day he made his way to investigate.

There they were, singing away, looking like they were enjoying every minute of the performance. Joe's heart nearly jumped out of his chest. The love and pride he felt was overwhelming. There was no way he could stop the tears. He clapped so loudly that the girls couldn't help but notice the lone, overexcited man. Neither recognised their father.

'That guy that was clapping like a maniac. He wants to come backstage. He said he's your father, Joe Pike, is that okay?'

'Shit, shit, just give us a few minutes.' Rusty sat down with her head in her hands.

'What are we going to tell him, Sandy, or should I say Hope?'

'Do you think he saw that our names are changed?'

'I don't see how he couldn't have.'

'Let's tell him the truth. We didn't like our names and Mum said he made her agree to use Hope and Tibby. I'm not sure why she didn't like the names much.'

'Okay, we will say we just didn't like the names, and Mum said they belonged to someone that meant something to you. It had nothing to do with us.'

'We will upset him I suppose.'

'Did you think we would ever see him again?'

'No, Mum said he'd never come, he's such a wimp.' They both laughed, putting their arms around each other.

Joe knew they would always have the strong sibling connection to rely on.

There was the strongest urge to scoop his babies into his arms and hold them close. The minute he walked into the dressing room there was a chill that swept across his face, almost like a warning. He stepped backwards, surprised that the girls didn't move to greet the father they hadn't seen for so long.

'I had trouble finding you two, my babies. I think you are more beautiful than your mother. I have imagined what you would look like in my dreams.' Joe was stunned that he wasn't getting any reaction. Why didn't they want to see him? His mind buzzed. Was it unreasonable to think they might be a little glad that he was there?

'Can I sit down?' Joe finally asked.

Tibby came to him first. She still had Joe's eyes. She took Joe's hand as if to shake it like a new acquaintance. Joe was confused. These were his girls.

'You're a long way from home,' Hope was saying in an American accent, confusing Joe more.

'I wanted to see how you were. I can never reach you.'

The girls looked at each other as if they didn't know what to say. Joe wanted to cry. That was the moment he knew he had lost his babies.

'I could never find any information about you two. I searched newspapers and magazines thinking you mustn't have followed in your mother's footsteps. I now can see you are very successful. I am so pleased for you.' Joe felt the girls soften a little.

'Yes, Mom makes it easy for us and has been there all the way along our path to fame. We have a part in a movie next year. We're off to Hollywood. Can you imagine?' Tibby sounded excited.

'Do you use Sandy and Rusty as your stage names?' The girls looked at each other as if they wanted the other to answer.

'Well, no, Joe. We had our names changed. These suit us and our image better.'

'Mom said she didn't want Hope and Tibby anyway. They came out of your past. That's what she said, and they never meant much to us. We are happier now.'

Shock after shock. Joe was having trouble comprehending the conversation that was going on between the twins, as if he was a stranger.

'I suppose you changed "Pike" as well?' He didn't expect them to answer, but yes, they had.

Joe couldn't help himself, he had to ask, 'Did you ever give me a thought?'

In unison they answered, 'No.'

Joe wanted the ground to swallow him and send him back down under.

Why did Blossom do this to him? He never stopped her from having a career like she had stopped his attempt to take his further. Joe could see the girls had been poisoned against him. They had forgotten his years of care and devotion.

'What about your surname, as Pike was out of the question to keep.'

'Yes, we are Mathews now after Grandma and Grandpa. They were so happy. It was lucky we did it before they died. Anyway, Mom said you only married her because she was pregnant,' Hope said, laughing.

Joe couldn't get words out of his mouth to protest. The damage was done, and they didn't care about him or anything he might say. Joe stood up to leave and the girls made no effort to keep him there.

'Well, it was nice to see you. Are you happy? That is all a father wants for his children.'

He hoped for some positive response, but there was none. Joe's girls watched him walk out the door.

Joe turned back and faced the girls. 'The bank account I set up for you has never been touched. There is a substantial amount in it. Maybe you should give it to charity.' Joe turned his back to them again.

In unison they said, 'What bank account?'

Joe called out, 'Ask your MOM!'

The girls were dead to him. He had lost them just as Ginger had lost her Tibby and Hope. Joe didn't go to a bar. He got the alcohol delivered straight to his room. The sunset came and went. Sometimes he thought of Elizabeth. It was the first time that he neglected his prayers for her since they'd parted at the hospital as children.

He took another drink, thinking before he passed out, *She has deserted me too.* Finally, the management of the motel called the police. Joe was arrested and placed in a cell to dry out. It happened to be in the same station that he had asked about his girls. After a few days, when Joe could comprehend what he was doing in a cell although still being confused, he was able to answer questions. The guy asked him if he'd found Sandy and Rusty. Joe told the big guy in the uniform how they had treated him, and that they didn't want to know the father who had looked after them while their mother was off getting famous.

He was sober enough to know not to say anything about Blossom. Joe was sure they would see that she could do no wrong. All the guys seemed to take pity on Joe. Maybe they'd been down the same path. They helped him get back on a plane, homeward bound. He tried the phone in the café while waiting for his flight. To his surprise someone answered. 'It's Joe. I haven't been able to find Elizabeth, is she there?'

The phone was silent for a minute. Joe thought he had lost the connection. 'Oh, Joe, I didn't know how to reach you. We've just reopened the café.' Joe was starting to feel his legs fold under him.

'Why?' he yelled, knowing something was wrong.

'Elizabeth had an accident. She's been in hospital ever since you went on your trip. She was asking for you at first. She is a lot better now. We got your message to ring the motel, but they said you had gone. Are you on your way home Joe? She needs you.'

'Yes, I will ring the minute I land in Sydney. How bad is it?' Not that he wanted to know. Maybe he was a wimp.

'Wait till you get home. Elizabeth will tell you all about it.' Sally was a long-time employee and seemed very concerned for Elizabeth.

'Are you keeping the café going?'

'Yes, we are all back almost to normal, just missing our boss so much.' Joe could detect a tremble in her voice. Joe's flight was being called. Walking to the gate he was shaking with fear. Was Elizabeth dying? Losing her was an unbearable thought – *not Elizabeth, not my Elizabeth. It couldn't happen, not now when I need her.* Things were going through Joe's mind that he couldn't cope with.

As he found his seat, stumbling into it with a thud, tears ran down the face that looked ten years older than it did when leaving for America. He realised he was only thinking of his needs, selfish thoughts taking over his mind. Maybe it was because he couldn't bear to think about what Elizabeth must be going through. *My girl is alive. We can conquer anything*, Joe thought, before exhaustion took over. He didn't wake until he hit Sydney.

Before falling asleep, Joe had decided to check out Ginger's Place, and if he wasn't needed, he could be in Melbourne the next day.

THE SMILE ON ELIZABETH'S face was all Joe wanted. His beautiful friend was alive. Tears flowed before they could speak.

'What happened? I turn my back and you end up in hospital. Do you think this is where you belong?' Joe was trying to make light of the situation, a situation he was yet to find out about. 'No-one will tell me what is going on. You look so good. Why are you still in here?'

'I am sorry, Joe. I wanted to tell you myself.' Elizabeth hesitated. 'My rehabilitation will take some time. I have to learn to manipulate my wheelchair. I'll never walk again. My injuries were so bad I'm lucky to be alive.'

Joe couldn't speak. He stared into her translucent eyes, trying to understand why. Hadn't she had enough pain and been hurt by so many? It just wasn't fair. That was all Joe could think. It just wasn't fair.

Elizabeth relayed more details of the accident calmly, as if she had expected the meaning of her existence was not to be able to walk. She had got away with it once before and now fate had caught up with her.

'What are we going to do? You can't live at the café.' Joe was beside himself with grief, forgetting the urgency he'd felt to tell her about the rejection that had occurred in America.

'I thought I would live in Barry's unit for a while until I can manage, then I will get a small place somewhere near Lottie's.'

Joe couldn't believe the fortitude of this woman. Her strength astounded him. Maybe Blossom was right. He was just a wimp, not deserving of the women that had come across the same path that he was treading. *Not even my daughters.*

'I will sell Ginger's Place and come and help you.' The words came out of Joe's mouth like someone else had said them. Elizabeth didn't say anything. It was as if she hadn't heard what Joe had said.

'Joe, how did it work out in America? Did you find your girls?' Elizabeth noticed that Joe looked drained, putting it down to jet lag.

'Oh, I found them. They are doing okay – lots of work. Their mother was away. They are great singers.' Joe couldn't load his heartache onto his friend. Her load was heavy enough.

Joe stayed at Elizabeth's flat and helped out with jobs around the café. He visited Elizabeth every day. He went to Barry's unit and gave it a coat of paint, tightened up a few screws here and there, and had Elizabeth's bedroom moved there, as if it was above the café. Joe made sure the wheelchair would fit through all the doors. He had to take a couple off that weren't needed.

'I am not leaving until I know you can manage.' Joe had gone over and over the obsession that he had to get to Sydney to sell Ginger's Place. He could never leave Elizabeth again. He could have easily managed the business from Melbourne, but there was a voice, nagging, clamouring in his mind, saying the time had come to sell.

Elizabeth would have never asked Joe to move back to Melbourne, taking his life away from Ginger's Place, which had meaning as much to him as Lottie's did to her. However, it had been on her mind that she would have to let the café go. She had acted as though it was going to be easy, living in Barry's place on Grey Street. She tried to hide her disappointment from Joe, but Elizabeth knew it was going to be unbearable. How could she do this to Joe, being lumbered with a cripple? She really was one now. Elizabeth made a vow to herself that she wasn't going to be a burden to Joe.

Months passed. Joe had everything ready for Elizabeth's home-coming, not that they were calling it home, as it was regarded as temporary.

'Let's pretend it is a holiday. I'll wheel you down to the beach every day.'

'Thanks Joe. You are my saviour once again.'

The girls from Lottie's made sure that the kitchen was fully stocked and one of them came in every day, checking that Elizabeth had everything she wanted. Joe didn't want to leave Elizabeth alone at night though. Until he could find a cottage that they both could live in together, he stayed over at the café. Before Joe could go back to Sydney, he had to be satisfied that Elizabeth was safe and able to get around, in and out of bed and to the bathroom. It had become Joe's purpose in life now he only had Bill and Elizabeth that meant anything to him, that's where his care would lie.

'I will have to go to Little River before I go back to Sydney, I must see Dad. He always tells me he is fine. I can't be so close without checking.'

'It will give me a chance to learn to live without you, Joe. I don't want you to think you have to be responsible for me. When you get back to Sydney you might change your mind about selling.'

Joe knew he wasn't going to. There was someone on his shoulder telling him it was time.

Bill was doing well, apart from his age. Pixie and Jack were looking after him as if they were a family. Joe had let his father down year after year. Pixie had Nancy's vegetable garden just as it once was. Joe watched her standing at the sink gazing out the window at the growing plants, turning into next week's dinner.

He realised that when someone leaves, they have left a space for another. 'No-one will want my space,' he said to himself. Elizabeth's accident had a profound effect on Joe. The injustice of humanity, the cruelty endured by the innocent was intolerable. He thought of Goldmann, how he had lived his life and almost got away with murder. He'd hurt so many in his greed for power over others. Why do people like him think they have the right to abuse? Taking what they want, and getting away with a lavish lifestyle as if it is a gift due to them for being placed on earth.

Joe held Bill in his arms for longer than his usual goodbye, knowing it could be the last time he would see his father. His space would be empty soon. 'Bye son. Will you come again?'

'Yes, I will be coming back to Victoria to live when I sell up in Sydney.'

'To the farm? Are you coming back to the farm, as I wished you had done years ago?'

'No, sorry dad, I have Elizabeth to look after now.' Joe had never talked about Elizabeth much. He could tell Bill didn't know who he was referring to.

'Is that your wife? I have never met her. Bring her here one day. Is she pretty?'

'Yes, she is the prettiest girl I have ever seen.' Joe smiled to himself, thinking, *She really is.* Joe was thankful that Bill never asked about the girls, forgetting that Joe had children.

'Pixie and Jack will look after you well.'

'Yes, I know they will. They are good people and capable farmers too.' Bill seemed happier than Joe had ever seen his old dad.

It was amazing how well they had pulled the farm together. He had expected to see a loss when he looked at the bookkeeping that Pixie handled. It was a pleasant surprise to see a profit.

There was another job to do when he got to his solicitor. Once Bill was gone the farm was to go to Jack and Pixie. In Joe's mind they deserved it, and there was no-one else to take the old place on. There would be a covering letter of thanks for looking after Bill Pike who never did anyone wrong. Joe was starting to think that was all he had left: empathy. The money that would be gained for Ginger's Place and other investments would be enormous. He had always thought it would all go to the twins one day. That was now out of the question. There was no way Joe was going to pass on his wealth to the children that had no appreciation of their heritage. This may seem spiteful on his behalf. However now he had seen their disrespect, showing that they wouldn't appreciate anything from him. Joe had so much money he didn't know what to do with it. He thought of Goldmann, again wondering why anyone would destroy others in the pursuit of wealth. He did not understand the need to have more than you could use for a comfortable life.

The disappointments of life had taken the spirit and soul out of Joe's being, leaving an empty shell once again. He wondered where the zest for life had gone. As he lay on Ginger's bed staring at the ceiling, waiting for her to send a message that he could hang on to, Joe wondered if the courage had been zapped out of him as a kid with polio. He was a wimp. There was no doubt in his mind. Joe called out to Ginger in a last effort to get her to speak to him.

'Are you happy for me to sell your house Ginger, my beautiful old girl?'

Joe heard nothing.

The next day someone called Joe from the bottom of the stairs. There was a bloke down there wanting to see him. To his surprise, one of Sydney's top real estate agents was holding out his hand, asking him if the hotel was for sale. Ginger had answered.

It seemed the agent had a client wanting a boutique hotel. It was all too easy. Now he needed an answer where to offload the money. It would be mulled over for some time. Joe's heart broke the day he closed the door on Ginger's apartment. A new chapter was about to begin, dedicating his life to looking after Elizabeth.

Chapter 29

The nightmare of Grey Street.
Elizabeth and Joe

ELIZABETH WAS MANAGING IN her new unwanted situation well, as mechanically as possible. Thoughts of the extended disability were dismissed as soon as they entered her mind. It was easy to escape from reality when in her bedroom that Joe had done so well, recreating her flat above the café. She never opened the curtains that exposed Grey Street. This kept her in her isolated cocoon.

Luckily Sally had to pass the unit on her way home, so dropped the takings off each night and picked up the banking on her way back to work in the morning. Elizabeth increased the girls' wages as they all had extra work loads. She made Sally the official manager. The pair had almost grown with the café, working side by side at Lottie's for so long. The only difference was one being the boss the other being an employee. They were almost working on equal terms.

Sally had lived in St. Kilda all her life too and had only worked at Lottie's from the time of leaving school. Looking after a sick mother had curtailed her life. Sally was a lot younger and wasn't around when Free Rita was sitting in a booth waiting, although Elizabeth was sure she had heard rumours. Despite everything, they were friends. 'The boss' as the girls called Elizabeth, had an inbuilt way of positive thinking, or appearing that way to the outside world, which they admired greatly.

The biggest problem the staff faced each day was that they didn't know the recipe for Otto's pumpkin soup. Customers were asking for Elizabeth and the popular dish. Was it time to pass on the recipe and the café as well? These thoughts weighed heavily on Elizabeth's mind. She did her best to hide her fear of the unknown and the uncertainty of her future. She was concerned that she would drag Joe down with her into a pit of misery. They had their usual phone calls, so both knew every move that was made while they were separated.

Joe had never told Elizabeth about his time in America. He never wanted her to know the shame he'd brought upon himself with his drunken binge. However, he did want her to know about his girls and how they had treated him. 'When the time is right,' he would say to himself.

And Elizabeth didn't want Joe to know how hard it was for her living in this unsavoury building. Why hadn't Barry bought elsewhere? He didn't think his daughter would ever have to live in Grey Street, nor did he know the memories that the street invoked. He thought that she would sell. It was the only thing he had to give his child.

'Just until Joe gets back,' Elizabeth would say to herself every day. And that kept her going. A Will had to be arranged with a solicitor, something that had never been done. The accident was a prompt that couldn't be ignored. Elizabeth's money and the Grey Street unit would be divided between Jonas, Emma and her two boys. Lottie's along with the free hold would go to Sally, on the proviso that the décor would be kept in Lottie's memory.

Joe was being seen as an entrepreneur and successful businessman because of the transformation of an old boarding house into a classy hotel, and the added visionary coffee bar. Joe had never seen that in himself, although he knew he had respect around the place. The business world wasn't one he felt at ease with. It was a façade, another hiding place to escape to when nothing else worked for him.

Saying goodbye to Sydney was harder than he'd thought. On the last day he wandered the streets, encountering his memories with Ginger. He spent an hour or so sitting in the pub, staring at the stage, picturing the applause, the cheers. How he loved that time when the microphone was in his hand like a friend, feeling a strength surge into his heart.

He remembered the time growing up with the different band members, the music and the singing. He was always waiting for his big break. The music. Where had the music gone? That was the one thing, apart from Ginger, that he never wanted to lose. *Blossom and the girls had taken their share,* were the thoughts running through Joe's mind. There is no music without a soul and Joe felt he had lost his long ago. He thought Elizabeth was bringing that soul back little by little. Joe couldn't leave the Jag. He hoped it would get him back to Melbourne.

The trip was slow. There were so many memories along the highway that had taken him away in the first place, so full of hope and ambition. A call had come through from Pixie before he left, saying that Bill was in hospital having tests to assess his condition. Pixie told Joe to be prepared for the worst. He went straight to Little River, leaving getting to Elizabeth longer than he had hoped.

He just made it to see Bill for a day before he passed away. Their chats in between Bill dosing off, were rewarding for them both. Joe was able to say, 'I love you Dad,' and Bill was able to say he was proud of his boy. Not that Joe knew why, he'd never seen himself as a good son. He wished he could be as blind as Bill to his offspring's' mistakes. Then he may be able to forgive the girls.

He was relieved when the funeral was over and farewells to Bill and Nancy's friends were done. He gave Pixie and Jack the good news that they weren't out of a job as they would be working for themselves from now on. The look on their faces when Joe told them the farm was theirs was enough reward for Joe. He couldn't have asked for more. Pixie handed Joe a folder full of papers Bill had asked her to pass on if he didn't get back to the farm. He thought he would look at what they were all about when he got to Elizabeth. He hugged the grateful couple before turning to leave the boy that he once was, behind.

Driving away from his childhood home added to Joe's fragile state. The life he had known was vanishing as if it had belonged to someone else. It was a life without courage, without purpose, trying to escape from himself. Bill and Nancy had so much confidence in their boy's ability to reach a great height with his music, and he nearly had, but just lacked the courage to push himself to the limit. He wondered if he had a brain of his own or just had to be led to achieve his protentional. Joe knew he wasn't the tin man, because he had a heart that was breaking for a talented life wasted, most likely because he lacked courage and wondered about the state of his brain.

ELIZABETH COULDN'T WAIT UNTIL Joe arrived. It was a Sunday morning, a quiet time on Grey Street. This was the one day that Elizabeth opened the front curtains. She watched as the car pulled up and parked by the curb. For the first time since the accident, she wished she could run to greet the best friend anyone could have. Joe had his own key. He fumbled to open the door, stepped in and rushed to hold her, his childhood friend. Seeing Joe's strained face, she knew he was physically and mentally exhausted. Her heart went out to the boy hidden in the man's body.

'Will the car be right parked on the street? I might have to find a parking lot to house it until we can buy a place with a garage.'

'Others leave cars out. I hope it will be safe.' Elizabeth had her doubts. It was Grey Street.

'I will worry about it tomorrow.'

'I am sorry you lost your dad. I only have a vague memory of him, a gentle man like you, Joe. Funny, until Barry came into my life, I didn't appreciate the connection really.'

'I feel I wasted most of the time I had with him. My eyes were so full of stars and dreams. I was just eaten up with my own selfishness. Is that what we all do?'

Elizabeth laughed. 'Well, if we have a chance.' They were laughing again.

'The car will be safer behind the café. That can be its home for a while.'

He picked up the folder Pixie had given him. Elizabeth watched Joe's hands fumble with the old yellow papers. He started to flick through the pages. 'I'm not sure why I need all this old stuff. Pixie said dad wanted me to have it.'

'There must be something in there he wanted you to see.' Elizabeth was curious.

Joe could see they were Birth and Death Certificates and some letters that looked like love letters. Most of the names he didn't recognise. Just as he was about to put the papers away thinking he would check them another day when not so tired, his eyes settled on the name William John Pike and the date a few years before his birth, and then another Charles James Pike a couple of years later.

'What's wrong, Joe? You look like you have seen a ghost.'

'I think I just have.' Elizabeth could see Joe had tears in his eyes.

'Joe, tell me.'

'I have just found out that Mum had two sons before me, both stillborn. Oh, that dear woman, and I was so cruel to her. Oh Elizabeth, I put them through all that anger when I lost the cows.'

Joe cried like a baby saying he hated himself over and over. Elizabeth didn't know how to comfort her friend. She knew Joe never wanted to cry in front of a girl.

'I am so sorry, Joe. Don't punish yourself. You didn't know about your parents' heartbreak. They wouldn't want you to take any blame.' She managed to put her arms around him, pulling his head onto her chest, just as a mother would do.

Joe slept on the couch. He was too tired and stressed. Getting to the flat seemed too hard after his trip and the funeral, and now knowing he had dead siblings. In the morning, the car was gone. The last thread of Ginger had left Joe. He had the feeling that she had got him to Elizabeth, and that was where he was to spend the rest of his time. A strange peace came over Joe as if she had waved him goodbye with the acknowledgement of approval.

Elizabeth found it hard to understand why he wasn't more upset about the car until Joe explained the understanding he saw in Ginger's ways. She was envious of the relationship that he had shared with another. It was a strange feeling for her. Ginger's departure settled Joe and the pair started to make plans. They would scan the real estate for a suitable place that would be comfortable for them both. Elizabeth had special requirements. Joe didn't care much as he had spent most of his time in Ginger's small apartment, apart from his time in the suburbs looking after his kids.

'Joe, you never filled me in about your time in America. We seem to have forgotten about it. I've started to wonder why you haven't shared the meeting with Tibby and Hope.'

They were having a down time from their house search and Joe had taken Elizabeth into Lottie's, to everyone's surprise. Some of the customers had tears in their eyes as they greeted her. The staff rushed around, getting them seated with coffee and cake. Joe thought he had to say something to take her mind off the fact that being here to work wasn't an option now with the wheelchair. So, Joe went ahead with his sad tale of rejection. Elizabeth felt for him, knowing what being swept aside like rubbish was all about.

'What did we do Joe, to be treated in ways that wouldn't enter our minds to do to others?'

'I was cruel to Bill and Nancy over the cows.'

'You were a child that had just been through a horrific illness. I'm sure they took that into consideration and excused you.'

'I have never excused myself. My guilt is miles long.'

Elizabeth didn't know how to comfort Joe. She just held his hand. The house hunting was going well. Joe wanted to pay for the whole deal, with his overflowing bank account. He could afford to buy a mansion along the beach front. Elizabeth requested an ocean view, which was hard to find without stairs. Some nights Joe slept on the couch at Grey Street and some nights at the flat at Lottie's, doing odd jobs for the girls before coming back to Elizabeth. They had manoeuvred their way into a routine that worked for both the friends.

Out of the blue one day, after they had a trying day with the real estate agent, as Joe was helping this beautiful girl into her bed, Elizabeth asked Joe if he was sorry he wasn't in a romantic relationship.

'What made you think of that, for goodness's sake, you funny thing?'

'Oh, I don't know. You are a man, and I wouldn't want you to think that I was in the way.'

Joe laughed. 'Oh, my sweet girl. The love I have for you is stronger than a lustful affair. No thank you, my feelings for you go deeper and more enduring than any passion-filled needs.' Joe had never given romance with Elizabeth a thought, not that he didn't see all her womanly attributes, of which there were many.

'Thank you. That is how I feel too, and always have. I didn't want you to think you had to devote your life totally to me.'

'Well, that's settled, a plutonic relationship is for us, and a very comfortable one at that.'

'Joe if you ever get taken in by a shapely dish that crosses your path, I will understand.'

'Okay, I will too.' They both laughed. They were back on track, enjoying each other as if they were back in the ward with Doctor Daisy and SOS.

'Maybe we will never grow up.'

'That is a good thing. Who would want to be an adult anyway?' They laughed their way through their sadness. Finally, a home was found that gave Elizabeth her ocean view with a balcony that she could easily access for the times of day that were special to her. When the breeze was in the right direction the music from the merry-go-round would drift around Elizabeth, a gentle reminder of Otto.

The reflections that intrigued her, dancing in the sky and bouncing off the ocean kept her amused. Filling in her day with other chores, she was managing well. Everything she did was to cover up the difficulty of having to cope with the confinement of the paralysis. She wished she had never complained about her leg brace. It would be a blessing to have it back and be without the wheelchair. The home Joe had made for her was amazing. He always thought of her comfort.

'Funny Joe, when I went to the Goldmann's their wealth was so impressive. Now we have it I wonder why it is so important. We couldn't ask for more. I can't think of another thing we could need, although I do appreciate the style that surrounds us. There are so many more important, meaningful wonders to be had that money can't buy. Soul food, that's what we have.' Joe agreed, saying he felt his soul coming to life as he put a record on the turntable that belted out one of the latest hits.

'When are you going to start writing again? There must be another "True Love" in there somewhere.'

'I might try just for you, sweet thing.'

Joe was spending his days between their home and Lottie's. He wheeled Elizabeth down to her favourite place. Together they sat, watching the waves roll in and out, giving and taking away the tiny grains of sand that walkers could feel between their toes, that Elizabeth was deprived of.

'Can I climb on your mermaid's back and ride to the horizon with you, sweet girl?'

'Any time, my handsome prince.' They laughed away their sadness again and again.

Joe did the heavy work around the house. He had plenty of training, looking after the girls in what he regarded as his past life. It amazed him, the amount of independence Elizabeth had, and was able to achieve, not been able to get out of the chair without a great struggle. It was hard for Joe to feel sorry for himself when he watched her do the smallest task with great effort. So, it would be for a time.

Joe scribbled, took notes, gazed at the stars from the balcony at night after he had tucked Elizabeth into bed. He listened to the silence. Elizabeth was encouraging, telling Joe his songs were nearly there. She did not really understand how you create an original work that satisfied the artist within. The rhythm and beat eluded him. There was no melody left. Life had sapped it away. Joe wanted to believe the words would become a hit and bring him back to his peak, but he knew he was missing the mark.

'I have lost it, sweet girl. I think death must come in many ways. I'm dying without the music, well that part of me. Why can't I write you a song like I did for Ginger?'

'You have to write it for yourself. It's your nourishment, not mine. As much as I want it for you Joe, I am a little selfish too.'

'You are giving me inspiration. I just can't get the words to come together. I think I will have a rest for a week, or so.'

Elizabeth had noticed that Joe was looking tired lately. She worried looking after her was getting too much for him.

'Joe, I can manage here. Would you like to go away to have some time to yourself?'

'Thank you for thinking of me. I am doing just fine or are you trying to get me out of your sight, so sick of me, are you?' Joe said with a smile on his face, putting his arms around her.

'Oh Joe, what would I do without you? I want you to be as happy as is possible, and you are looking tired.'

'It's old age. It is just that you are younger than me, you sweet thing.' They both laughed away another day with humour.

They lived together like an old married couple, as most people thought they were.

Joe had heard Elizabeth coughing night after night. He asked her to go to see the doctor. She always maintained she felt okay, 'I just need to move around more, or I will get a higher pillow,' she would say and change the subject. Her breathing was becoming more laboured. Joe knew she was having trouble getting her breath.

'I am going to have to take charge. You need help, you sweet thing. I will call a taxi and get you to the hospital.'

'Joe, I'm scared. It is like the kids when they couldn't breathe and had to go on a respirator, and then they went away.' Elizabeth's voice was thin and childlike.

'I won't let that happen to you, my sweet baby girl.' Joe tried to sound reassuring.

Later in the day when all the tests were over, the doctor spoke to Joe. The damage had slowly taken a toll on Elizabeth's muscular system, lungs and heart. The deterioration was extreme, all a by-product of infantile poliomyelitis that had worked away for so many years to finally do the destruction that it had set out to do to the small child. Neither wanted the other to know how depleted they felt and made out it was just another hurdle to climb over. And so, it was to be for a short time.

Elizabeth sent the recipe for Otto's pumpkin soup to Sally. She rang Jonas and Emma, wanting to know that they were happy and well. She told her siblings they had given the gift of themselves, bringing meaning into her life in times when she had the need to belong. Her job was done. The only thing left was to save Joe from the worry of her illness.

There was a heaviness in the air as if there was a message of a new pathway that was to be considered and choices to be made.

'Do you feel it, Joe, this strange atmosphere?'

'I do. It is mystical, an out-of-this-world feeling.'

'This is reminding me of a séance that I experienced with Lottie one night.'

Elizabeth had never explained how the idea of Werner's kidnapping had come about. Joe sat and listened intently to the story of the night Otto reappeared.

'Someone is sending us a message. I don't know how to interpret the meaning, do you Joe?'

'No, dear girl, we will have to wait and see where it sends us.'

Secretly Joe thought it was Ginger trying to tell him something that he couldn't comprehend, and Elizabeth thought it was Robert, sending the message she had been waiting for.

The next week Joe went to a solicitor. He had decided where the fortune he had amassed was to go. Elizabeth Kasper's name would live on forever.

Chapter 30

Kasper and Pike Forever
Elizabeth and Joe

JOE AND ELIZABETH WERE locked behind a gate with an unattainable key that had eluded both in their quest for a life free from pain.

Joe watched Elizabeth deteriorate as the months passed. Some days it was hard for her to get out of bed. He became her nurse, not that he minded doing anything to make this sweet girl comfortable. Elizabeth tried to help herself. The workload that was being placed on Joe was becoming extreme in Elizabeth's mind. At times she offered to spend some time in hospital, but Joe wouldn't hear of that.

'Are you wishing you stayed in Sydney Joe, getting stuck with this disaster, a wreck of a human that is becoming useless?' Elizabeth tried to laugh but couldn't get her breath.

'Are you mad, and miss the best part of my life seeing your face every day? You are like a sunbeam lighting my way.' Joe put his arms around Elizabeth to reassure her that she was not a burden to him. He found it hard to watch her suffering and history repeating itself. It was 1946 again. Joe struggled most days getting Elizabeth to the beach in the chair. She was getting frailer and weaker every day, but her face always lit up, watching the waves and hearing the call of the gulls flying overhead into the drifting clouds. Elizabeth was spending more and more time in bed, giving Joe more working space at the café.

Sally didn't know that when Elizabeth was gone it would be hers, so Joe was determined to keep it in a pristine condition for the time she inherited Lottie's. He did tell Sally that Elizabeth was deteriorating and to be prepared for her not to be back in to see her any time soon. Sally sheepishly asked what was going to happen to Lottie's when Elizabeth was gone. Everyone had accepted that was going to be fact. Joe felt he had to tell her that Elizabeth had willed Lottie's to her on the proviso that she kept it as it was in Lottie's memory. Sally burst into tears and ran to the kitchen to hide from the wondering eyes of the busy café. Joe told Sally that it was what Elizabeth wanted. She was proud of having a loyal friend and employee for so many years.

Sally wanted to see Elizabeth and thank her for her generosity. Joe said he would see what he could do. Maybe he would bring her in soon, and left it at that, knowing that Elizabeth wouldn't want Sally or the other girls who had supported her for so long to see her in her present state.

'Are you sure you are up to going to the beach today, Sweet Girl?' Joe could see Elizabeth wasn't looking right. Her eyes weren't bright, and her normal rosy cheeks were grey and drawn.

'Yes, Joe, I am up for an adventure.' She smiled her infectious smile. So, what choice did Joe have? She could get him to do whatever she wanted. They sat on the pier for some time in silence, enjoying all the familiar surroundings that Joe had learnt to love as much as Elizabeth. The day wasn't particularly a beach day so there weren't many around, giving the two a feeling of owner ship of their special place. Occasionally the sun popped out from behind the clouds, giving Elizabeth's grey face a slight glow.

'Joe, could you lift me out of my latest ball and chain and take me down on to the sand, so I can feel connected to the earth?'

As Joe lifted Elizabeth out of her chair with ease, he realised her body was fading away, but her spirit was as strong as it ever was. He laid her gently on the sand, sitting down beside her. Joe rested her head in his lap. The merry-go-round music drifted across them, almost like a halo.

'In some ways, if we hadn't had polio and been in beds next to each other we would never have met.'

'That's right, and your family would never have known you weren't Werner's daughter if you hadn't had a blood test. And you wouldn't have had to live with Gerda.'

Polio had narrated the script for their life from the day they had entered the hospital.

'Funny, the fact that I got away with it better than you, has added to my guilt.' Joe's mood changed as the sky darkened. 'Would you like to go home? You seemed to be getting tired.'

'No, not yet Joe. I've never laid on the sand; I could never get back on my feet without making a fool of myself.'

'I don't want you to get worn out.'

'It is far too late for that!' Elizabeth tried to laugh again, to no avail.

'You are the boss, whatever you say is my command.' Joe was trying to make light of this adventure.

They were quiet for a time. Joe thought Elizabeth had an agenda today and he would just go with her.

'If you hadn't gone to Sydney, you would never have met Ginger. You were meant to go Joe.'

'That was the lucky part. I should have come back here before I got involved with Blossom.'

'Then you never would have known what being a father was all about, and the love that a parent has for a child, making you understand your parents. And if I hadn't had the joy of being a pretend parent to Maggie, I wouldn't have known the depth a mother can feel for a child.' Elizabeth reflected on her mother then and realised that maybe if she hadn't been so bitter, some of the issues may have been resolved with communication. But, on second thoughts, it all went deeper than bitterness.

'I wouldn't have met Robert if it wasn't for Free Rita.' Funny how that time in her life had no guilt attached to what was seen as an unethical past time. The moral issue had never crossed her mind. Self-preservation was a tangible experience that sustained her and her needs.

'I wouldn't have come back if it hadn't been for that murder that your old boss had someone commit.' They sat and thought about how things had brought them together.

'We would have been different people if we hadn't had that debilitating disease. It changed us, Joe. It took away parts of us. The connections were broken; the cogs that turned and rotated the working parts to make us whole.' Joe wasn't sure what Elizabeth was looking for.

'Do you think we deserved to be punished? Do you think we are evil?'

'No, not you, just me.' Joe stroked Elizabeth's hair that had almost turn to grey. Only a few specks of auburn were left behind as a reminder of her youth. He looked into her normally translucent blue eyes. They were blending into the colour of her grey skin. Depression was depleting Elizabeth of strength and life. Joe couldn't think of a way of helping, knowing it was too late.

Just in reach of Joe's hand, a sparrow fell out of nowhere.

'Oh, Joe, a bird. It's hurt. Help it, Joe please.' Elizabeth pleaded.

Joe picked up the tiny creature and held it in his hands. They both stared at the mystery of the tiny creature, a life in need of help. Joe could see that both its wings were broken. He laid it on Elizabeth's chest.

'Poor little sparrow can't fly. It's broken, just like me.' Tears ran down Elizabeth's grey cheeks. She stroked the head and felt the softness of the feathers. Joe watched as they seemed to communicate.

'Our new friend will never be able to fly again, just as I will never walk, as we were both meant to do. We are a pathetic pair. That's what we are, defeated by existence.'

Elizabeth started to shiver. Joe wrapped his coat around them both, knowing neither Elizabeth nor the tiny sparrow would go on to see another day.

'Do you think our praying did any good, Joe?'

'It kept us together. Even when I was on the other side of the world and the sun was setting at a different time, you came into my mind. You were never a grown woman until the day I came into the café and met my sweet girl all grown up and doing so well. So yes, I don't know who we prayed to, but it kept us together.'

'Who would have thought that when we laid next to each other in the ward all those dark and scary hours that turned into years, that we would be lying together decades later?' Elizabeth was whispering now. The weakness was becoming extreme.

'It was my privilege as it is now. You belong in my heart, a heart that has been battered and bruised by many, but not you. The hate that you've felt for those who let you down as a child never destroyed your true soul.' Joe realised that Elizabeth didn't intend to leave the beach, her favourite place, her lifeline to fantasy that had been a dependable, constant support most of her life. Joe decided there and then that he wasn't going to leave her side.

'Do you think Ginger and Robert are waiting for us behind the horizon, Joe?' Elizabeth was having trouble breathing. Joe could see that the strain on her heart was giving her more pain than usual. His sweet girl was ready to surrender her life to the horizon and what lay behind her fantasies.

'I can go alone now that I have my feathered friend as company. I feel that I am this little bird. We have the same significance. The importance of our worth has gone. It isn't fair that your life is to be cut short because I am unwilling to carry on. You shouldn't be branded with the sorrow of my fate.'

Joe didn't have the words to reply for a time.

Finally, his mind was clear. 'And miss out on that ride to the other side with your mermaid that you have kept hidden, from me?'

The purity of the child in them had been taken away by the dark shadow of evil that hit them in a form of a disease.

'I always wanted to be the best I could because of the work and care Doctor Daisy and SOS gave us. It was like a repayment, but I can't do it anymore.' Joe was overwhelmed with emotion. They had shared so much, along with so little of their time in this realm. He wasn't sure there was another dimension, or that Ginger and Robert would be waiting for them. None of that mattered to him. He just wanted to be with Elizabeth. There was nothing to live for without her.

'I am sure old Cauliflower Face would have been proud of you. I think he loved you as much as you did him.'

'Do you think maybe he couldn't wait for me to grow up?' Her face lit up slightly. The thought of old Daisy loving her made her smile.

'You haven't written your new song, Joe. I feel as though if I hadn't been such a drudge, you would have had more inspiration.'

'And just who would have given me that? You are part of me, my spirit. You are my Sweet Girl. I love you.' Joe wanted to cry and scream at the universe with a rage that was out of his understanding, for what it had designated for Elizabeth.

'You are leaving "True Love" behind. I have no footprint, no mark to say that I was ever here. Even the café was Lottie's and Maggie belonged to Dolly. What was my purpose? Maybe Free Rita was the best deed I ever did for anyone. Maybe that was my problem; always wanting to be someone else like Rita Hayworth and having Robert Taylor in my bed. What the hell. I even wanted to be a mermaid. What a crazy bitch I have been Joe.'

'You are a funny sausage. We all want to live in a wonder world.'

'I have had some good times – Lottie and Robert. My only regret is that I never have been able to see Maggie. The greatest thing is you, though Joe. You have given so much and taken so little in return.'

'Being with you has been my reward. You will never realise your value. Your positivity always amazes me.'

'That positivity has been drained out of me now. I am depleted; an empty shell.'

'I have to tell you that your name will live on forever. The population will applaud you for many years to come. All my money will be going into a trust fund in your name for research into childhood diseases: The Elizabeth Kasper bequest to fund research and help sick children.'

Elizabeth looked down to her chest and looked into the sparrow's eyes that seemed to be crying. They cried for each other.

'Maybe we are not so insignificant after all, little bird. Thank you, Joe Pike. You are the kindest. You are my saviour.'

Joe could feel her life seeping into the sand. The tide was reaching their toes. As the sun vanished. The clouds darkened. Magic was happening. As the moon crept over the horizon, they watched the clouds roll past, floating, like three dimensional sculptures.

'That one looks like a giant angel with her tongue poking out at us.'

'I think she has a wand, casting an evil spell.'

Elizabeth asked, 'Would an angel do that?'

'Someone has done this cruel thing.'

'Or is it a mermaid that could carry us, and we could escape to another land?'

'That one looks like a chook with a dick,' Joe said. They tried to laugh.

'It does not. I don't think a chook has a dick – maybe a rooster. Anyway, I think it is an elephant with a trunk.' They both managed a slight giggle.

'Did we really leave the hospital? Did the in-between time really happen, Joe? Or was it just a bad dream?' Elizabeth's voice was coming from a deep, faraway place.

'Yes, Sweet Girl, all just a bad dream.' Joe closed his eyes.

The tide rose. They climbed on the back of the beautiful mermaid with the jewelled tail, soon reaching the horizon. Bringing the dream to an end.

www.ingramcontent.com/pod-product-compliance
Ingram Content Group UK Ltd.
Pitfield, Milton Keynes, MK11 3LW, UK
UKHW022017250425
5645UKWH00007B/304